THE GIRL WHO CAME HOME

THE GIRL WHO CAME HOME

A Novel of the Titanic

HAZEL GAYNOR

WILLIAM MORROW
An Imprint of HarperCollinsPublishers

THE GIRL WHO CAME HOME. Copyright © 2014 by Hazel Gaynor. All rights reserved. Printed in the United States of America. No part of this book may be used or reproduced in any manner whatsoever without written permission except in the case of brief quotations embodied in critical articles and reviews. For information, address HarperCollins Publishers, 195 Broadway, New York, NY 10007.

HarperCollins books may be purchased for educational, business, or sales promotional use. For information, please e-mail the Special Markets Department at SPsales@harpercollins.com.

FIRST EDITION

Designed by Diahann Sturge

Library of Congress Cataloging-in-Publication Data has been applied for.

ISBN 978-0-06-231686-8

20   OV/LSC   20 19 18

This book is dedicated to the memory of
the Addergoole Fourteen and all those who lost their lives
on *Titanic* on April 15, 1912

Never since the dawn of history was such disaster known
Fifteen hundred human bodies on the waste of waters thrown
Ah! The loss of the *Titanic* is deplored in every clime,
And the story sad recorded even to the end of time.

—FROM A POEM BY MITCHELL O'GRADY,
CONNAUGHT TELEGRAPH, MAY 25, 1912

And as the smart ship grew
In stature, grace, and hue
In shadowy silent distance grew the Iceberg too.

—THOMAS HARDY, FROM "THE CONVERGENCE OF
THE TWAIN" (LINES ON THE LOSS OF *TITANIC*), 1912

PART ONE

Marconigram message sent from Julie [Jules E. Brutalom], New York via Cape Cod, to Miss Dorothy Gibson, on April 16, 1912

CHAPTER 1

Ballysheen, County Mayo, Ireland
April 10, 1912

Maggie Murphy stood alone and unnoticed on the doorstep of the thatched stone cottage that three generations of her family had called home. She twirled one of her rich auburn curls around and around her index finger, the way she always did when she was anxious, and watched as the day she had been dreading dawned in the sky above the distant mountains.

Narrowing her usually wide blue eyes against the glare of the early morning sun, she wrapped her arms around herself for warmth as she quietly observed her friend Peggy Madden. Peggy's laughter was carried on a light breeze as she vigorously scooped up armful after armful of cherry blossoms and, giggling like a schoolgirl, threw them into the air. The pale pink and white petals cascaded down onto the heads of her cousin Jack and his wife, Maura, whom Peggy had caught kissing under one of the trees a few moments earlier.

"Just like your wedding day, Maura," she cried. "There's confetti enough here for all of us to be brides, and then maybe there'll be some kissing for us too."

As the two women laughed, Maggie shivered in the cool morning air and wondered how they could be so carefree when her own heart was so heavy and troubled.

Unseen, she continued to watch her fellow travelers for a few moments longer, Peggy fussing with the new hat she had bought especially for the journey to America (*Peggy Madden will arrive in America as she means to live among the American people: as a lady, with style,* she'd said) and Maura placing a hand protectively over her swollen belly, clearly visible beneath her coat even though her baby wasn't due for another few months yet. Maggie was fascinated by it, by the fact that an actual person was growing in there. She wondered how Maura would fare on their long journey. She'd heard talk of the strain that a crossing of the Atlantic could place upon a person, and for a woman in Maura's condition she was certain that it couldn't be such a good idea. She'd expressed her concerns to her aunt Kathleen a few days previously.

"You certainly don't need to be worrying about Maura Brennan, I can tell ye," Kathleen had replied, brushing Maggie's naïve fears easily aside. "She's crossed that ocean more times than most men ever will, and a baby in her belly won't make one bit of a difference. Anyway, we're sailing on the *Titanic,* the biggest ship in the world. Unsinkable, y'know. No better crib for any of us."

Her aunt's words hadn't really reassured Maggie. Neither had the adverts in the *Western People,* which Peggy had insisted on showing to Maggie and their good friend, Katie Kenny, during the previous weeks.

"Look, girls," she'd enthused, hurling herself down onto the grass between them as they sat by the lakeside, shoving the pages of the local newspaper under their noses. "It's amazing, isn't it? Listen to what it says: 'The queen of the ocean, *Titanic,* the finest steamer afloat, over forty-five thousand tons of steel and triple screws.' Can you believe we're going to be sailing on *that*? They say it stands higher than Nephin Mór and that there's a hand basin in every cabin—even the third-class ones!"

Peggy's enthusiasm about the journey to America and the fancy new ship they were to sail on was hard to ignore. Maggie knew that most of the fourteen who would be leaving their small parish that morning had never been on a train or a boat. Were it not for the fact that this journey didn't come with a return fare, they might have been quite excited at the prospect. As it was, most of them—herself included—knew that this would probably be the last time they would see the sun rise over their homes in Ballysheen. It was a thought that cast a dark cloud over many of their hearts.

For Maggie, the prospect of leaving Ballysheen and traveling across the vast expanse of the Atlantic Ocean toward a new life in Chicago filled her with a sense of sorrow and dread. There was nothing she could do, or say, to alter her circumstances. After the death of her mother—her only surviving parent—that winter, her aunt Kathleen had returned to Ireland as Maggie's guardian, and arrangements were quickly made for Maggie to travel to America that spring with her aunt. Her fate was sealed, despite the ache in her heart and the doubts and worries that raced through her mind.

Not wanting to dampen Peggy's excitement and well aware that her pragmatic aunt Kathleen had no time for the silly notions and unfounded worries of young girls, Maggie hadn't mentioned her doubts or anxieties about the trip to any of her fellow travelers. Not even last night, when Joe Kenny had read the leaves in his sister Katie's teacup and told her she would drown.

"For the love of God, Joseph Kenny, don't be tellin' me stuff like that, you great eejit," Katie had hissed at her brother, hoping that Maggie hadn't overheard. "Especially not in front of Maggie, she's nervous enough as it is." But from her perch on the butter churn in a dark corner of the Kennys' cottage, Maggie *had* heard, and wished she hadn't.

Maggie was very fond of Peggy and Katie. They were like the sisters she had never had, and she took some comfort from the fact that, along with eleven others from the parish, they would be making the journey to America together: Peggy to join her cousin in St. Louis, Missouri, and Katie to join her sister, Frances, in New York.

Peggy Madden, renowned for her sharp sense of humor and flighty notions, was the perfect balance to Maggie's reflective, considered nature. She was also renowned for her good looks, with a pretty, heart-shaped face, long blond hair, and full lips, which the boys seemed to especially like. Maggie was envious of Peggy's hair, which she would leave to hang loose about her shoulders whenever she could. Maggie would often frown in the mirror at her own unruly auburn curls, which barely reached her shoulders, brushing and teasing them to try to make them lie sleek and flat like Peggy's hair. They never did.

Katie Kenny was a blue-eyed, rosy-cheeked girl who was well known in the parish from her job at O'Donoghue's shop and well liked for her caring and kindhearted temperament. Maggie knew how much Katie missed her sister, Frances, who had been in America for the last three years, and knew how much she was looking forward to seeing her.

Although she couldn't share in their optimism, Maggie enjoyed listening to her two friends' romantic notions of America, where they imagined lives of wealth and independence waiting for them. Peggy and Katie aspired to the American way of life, which they saw in the likes of Maura Brennan and Maggie's aunt, Kathleen Dolan; women who seemed to bring back more than just a strange lilt to their accent whenever they returned to visit their relatives in Ballysheen. The self-assurance and poise displayed by Maura, Kathleen, and others who had seen America for themselves was undeniably inspiring to the naïve younger girls of the parish, and they could often be found gawping at the "American ladies," whispering remarks to each other about their fancy hats and shiny brass buttons.

Maggie often wished she could join in with her friends' enthusiastic conversations, share in their excitement, and dream about the prospect of a new life in America, but all she wanted, with all her heart, was to stay in Ballysheen, with Séamus by her side.

The sound of laughter outside caught Maggie's attention again, and she smiled as she watched Peggy adjusting the precious new hat on her head. "As fashionable as you might find in any store in St. Louis," the shopkeeper in Crossmolina had told her. It was olive green, wide-brimmed with a silk ribbon and organza detailing, secured with a fancy peacock-feather pin. The gloves were of a matching olive green: suede day gloves, with three dainty silver-tone buttons at the wrist. Peggy carefully brushed some dust from them as the strengthening breeze caused the slender cherry blossom trees to sway easily.

There were fourteen trees in total, flanking the lane between Maggie's stone cottage and the lake. *Fourteen,* she thought. *One for each of us who will make this journey.* She had loved these trees and their candy-colored blooms since she was a young child, loved watching the fragile petals as they fluttered like snowflakes to the ground. Over the last year, she had developed a particular affection for the sixth tree on the lane, as it was there that she and Séamus met every Wednesday after market. It had been his idea, and the arrangement had suited them well. She thought about him now and wondered whether he might change his mind and come to see her one last time. She almost didn't dare hope and closed her eyes to stop the tears coming.

"Right so, Maggie, the traps are ready. It is time."

Maggie jumped at the sudden sound of her aunt Kathleen's clipped voice behind her, her heart leaping in her chest and her breath catching in her throat. This was it then. It was really going to happen.

"Fetch the others, will you?" Kathleen continued as she busied herself, wrapping the still-warm bread rolls in muslin cloths before placing them in the top of her trunk, where she could easily reach them during the several hours of journeying that lay ahead of them to the port of Queenstown in County Cork. "And tell them to hurry. We still have to collect our tickets from Mr. Durcan in town, and we don't want to be late for the train."

Eager to please her aunt, as always, Maggie walked out of the narrow doorway to inform the others that it was time to leave. Shivering in the cool morning air, which easily penetrated the calico fabric of her dress, she pulled her green woolen shawl tighter around her shoulders as she stepped over the cat, which was curled up on the doormat. She envied its ignorance of the events unfolding around them.

"And never mind the train," her aunt called after her. "I doubt whether that big ship will wait on us either."

Maggie turned.

Aunt Kathleen stood in the doorway, filling the space with

her ample frame. Her hands were placed on her hips, an authoritative stance she often took, even when she was chatting casually with a friend. Her long black skirts skimmed the top of the stone step, the billowing tops of the leg-of-mutton sleeves on her fashionable white blouse touching either side of the doorframe, her thick chestnut hair swept up impeccably around her angular face in the American style. Maggie thought she could almost detect a smile at the edges of Kathleen's thin lips. Her aunt wasn't usually a woman to express emotions, other than a sense of satisfaction for a job well done, so the slight smile was somewhat surprising.

For Kathleen and two other women—Maura Brennan and Ellen Joyce—who were among their party, this was a journey without the uncertainties that preoccupied Maggie's imagination and the sorrow that troubled her heart. For them, this was a journey back to their American homes as much as it was a journey away from their Irish ones: her aunt would be returning to the sister and the Chicago home she loved; Maura and Jack Brennan were heading out to join members of their family in Pennsylvania, where Jack had the prospect of a good job; and Ellen was returning, along with her substantial wedding trousseau, to marry her beloved fiancé. No wonder these women could afford a moment of carefree laughter under the cherry blossom trees or a wry smile on the doorstep of the home they might never see again.

Almost as quickly as the smile had crossed her aunt's lips, it faded, and Maggie watched her turn back into the house, with a swish of her skirts, to fetch the last of their belongings.

Maggie walked hesitantly over to Peggy and the Brennans.

"It's time," she whispered, noting how beautiful the cherry blossoms looked in the early morning light.

Her words caused the others to stop their games, and a more

somber mood fell over them immediately. It was Jack Brennan who spoke.

"Right so, Maggie, we'll be right there."

She nodded at him in reply before stooping to pick up a few petals, admiring their fragile construction and breathing in their sweet scent. She absent-mindedly put them into her coat pocket and went on her way. She walked briskly, her sturdy black boots feeling unusually heavy as they crunched on the shale and stones that formed the rough road through their village.

Maggie felt an eerie stillness about Ballysheen that morning as she walked from house to house, knocking at the doors and quietly telling those inside that it was time. It was as if the village, and all its inhabitants, had taken in a deep breath and was afraid to let it out.

Her duties complete, she started to make her way back up the road, watching a solitary cloud drift across the pale blue sky, casting a shadow over the sheep that grazed in the fields at the foot of the mountain. The men were already at work in the lower fields. She imagined their hands muddied from cutting the turf and sowing the potatoes. Taking in the scene around her, Maggie was struck by the thought that to anyone passing through, this would seem like an ordinary, unremarkable spring day in a small rural village. How wrong they would be.

Walking on, she turned the bend in the lane that would take her back to her own home.

And then she saw him.

CHAPTER 2

Southampton, England
April 10, 1912

Harry Walsh studied his reflection in the mirror above the fireplace, checking one last time for good luck. The crisp white jacket, brown waistcoat, blue serge trousers, black shoes, and White Star Line cap suited him, making him look taller somehow. He had slicked his dark hair, parting it down the center in the fashionable style, and was clean-shaven for the occasion. He was pleased with how he looked and turned to his mother.

"I don't scrub up too badly really when I try, do I?"

Helen Walsh was a short, slight woman with a permanent air of dissatisfaction about her. She fussed around her son now, brushing flecks of dust from his trousers and stray hairs from the shoulders of his jacket. He smiled at her, glad of the attention she paid to him and pleased to see the unmistakable look of pride on her face, pride in the fact that her son was to work as a steward on *Titanic*'s maiden voyage from Southampton to New York.

"Not bad, love, not bad at all . . . for a Walsh," she replied, tugging at his waistcoat to remove a slight pucker and pulling at his cap to straighten it. "Now, you remember to work hard, Harry Daniel Walsh," she chided, "and mind that you look after those third-class passengers just the same as you would any of those wealthy Americans. The poor might not have the hats and the fancy shoes, but they deserve to be treated good 'n' proper, you hear?"

With her family roots set deep within the working-class society of Southampton's docks, Helen Walsh had no time at all for the stuck-up American millionaires and socialites who, it was believed, had chosen to sail on *Titanic* to make business contacts or to give them something to boast about at one of their dinner parties. Nevertheless, her background didn't prevent her from being a proud mother, and she was absolutely delighted that her son was going to be one of the three hundred stewards who would work on this much-talked-about ship, taking great pleasure in telling all her friends and neighbors about it. And although the gossip-loving, spying-on-the-neighbors part of her would have quite liked to know exactly how ostentatious the first-class accommodations were, she was especially pleased that Harry had been assigned to steerage class, to look after people like themselves.

Despite his mother's obvious delight that it would be *Titanic* that he would sail on, it hadn't actually been Harry's intention to work on the ship at all. He'd originally been assigned to work on a smaller liner, the *Celtic*, which should have left Southampton a week ago. As a result of the coal strike, she had been berthed, along with most of the other transatlantic liners. Harry had got word, just a week ago, that he had been reassigned and would now work a round trip on White Star Line's impressive new ship, *Titanic*.

Adjusting his cap one last time, Harry leaned down to give his mother a farewell kiss. Her cheeks were flushed and glistening with perspiration from all her fussing and rushing around.

"Love you, Mum. I'll send word when we dock in New York. And tell Dad I'll bring him back a memento of some sort. If I find my way up to the first-class decks, it might be something half decent this time!"

"Sally!" his mother called up the stairs, her voice breaking with emotion. "Your brother's leaving. Come and say good-bye."

Harry watched his sister make her way slowly down the stairs and smiled as he noticed that her eyes were red and swollen. They'd been through this routine of saying their farewells plenty of times, but on this occasion, with their father so unwell, it had affected them both more than usual.

"You going to miss me after all then, Sis?" he joked as she wrapped her arms around him.

"Might do," she said, barely able to look at him. "A bit."

He turned then and gave his mother a final embrace, both of them happy to linger longer in each other's arms than they usually would.

"I love you, son," she said, rubbing tooth powder off his cheek with her thumb. "We'll be coming down to the docks later, to have a good look at this ship and to wave you off."

"Well, then, I'll wave back," he said, smiling at them both as he slung his small duffel bag over his shoulder and walked out of the narrow terraced house into the bright morning sunlight.

"And happy birthday again, love," his mother called after him. "I'll make you a cake when you get home."

He turned, gave her a thumbs-up, and strolled casually to the dockside, whistling as he walked.

Helen Walsh closed the door softly behind her and let the tears fall freely.

Through all his twenty-three years, Harry Walsh had watched his father head out to work at the docks every day, except Christmas. He had never heard him complain, grumble, or fuss, even when the bitterly cold winds that blew in off the Solent in the winter almost froze his hands solid. Harry had fond memories of scampering down to the pier with his father's forgotten lunch, or walking with him, hand in hand, to watch as yet another newer, bigger steam liner sailed into view. Living by the docks was more than just a choice of home for Harry's family, it was a way of life, and it was no surprise that Harry had loved boats since he was a little boy, no surprise that the ocean had called to him for his vocation.

For the past five years, Jack Walsh had been employed as one of the construction workers building the new White Star Line dock, which would accommodate the huge transatlantic liners. He was proud of his work and liked nothing better than to sit with his son on an evening and tell him all about the impressive new dock they were building. "It spans *sixteen acres*, Harry," he would tell him, "sixteen! And it's been dredged to *forty feet!*" It was a scale on which nobody in the community had worked before, and they could barely begin to imagine the sight of the ships that would sail from there.

Although she had been berthed in the White Star Dock for almost a week now, Harry hadn't seen *Titanic* yet. His father's health had been suffering, so his mother had decided that the family would go to stay with her sister in the Devonshire countryside until his father felt better and the coal strike was over, when there would be the chance of employment for the men again. Harry, his sister, and his mother had arrived back in Southampton the previous evening; his father had stayed on in Devon, feeling too unwell to make the return journey. It bothered Harry that after all these years of work his father wouldn't get to see the biggest liner in the world set sail from his hometown, and he had tried to persuade him to come back to Southampton.

"Stop fretting, son," Jack had said. "You're as bad as your mother. I'll come down to see *Titanic* when she comes back. She's not planning on anchoring in New York for the next forty years, y'know."

As he reached the top of the steady incline of his road, Harry could see in the distance the distinctive black tops of *Titanic*'s four funnels towering into the sky, the red flags of the White Star Line fluttering in the bright sunshine on the impossibly high masts at bow and stern. He smiled and broke into a steady jog, his heart racing with excitement.

After weeks of unemployment and uncertainty in the town, there was a sense of jubilation in the air that morning. As he approached the new, purpose-built dock, Harry caught the sounds of drums and trumpets from one of the many local bands who had been hired to entertain the first-class passengers as they waited to board. The chatter and cries of the crowds who thronged the dockside grew steadily louder as he walked nearer. Horseshoes clattered on the cobbled road beside him as the wheels of the carts bringing more passengers generated a steady rumble that reverberated through his body. The incessant cries of the seagulls were the only familiar sound to him among all that was new. All these noises amalgamated into one exhilarating melody of thrill and anticipation as he turned the final corner.

Nothing could have prepared Harry Walsh for the sight of that ship in Southampton docks. No amount of description or expression could have conveyed what his eyes saw now. The sheer enormity of her was breathtaking. He stopped walking and gazed in silent awe; the black steel bow soaring into the sky, the letters TITANIC emblazoned across the front in white. Her funnels reached so high above the waterline that he almost fell over backward, he had to lean his head so far back to take them in. The gleaming steel hull, the endless lines of portholes, every single iron rivet completely fascinated him. She was, quite simply, the most unimaginable thing he had ever encountered, towering above every other vessel in the dock. Even the other mighty liners *Oceanic* and *New York,* which were berthed, out of action due to the coal strike, seemed to resemble children's toys in *Titanic*'s mighty presence. Harry and all the passengers already massing around the dockside were dwarfed by her, and he felt suddenly insignificant, totally overwhelmed.

"She's a beauty, ain't she?"

Harry turned to the voice behind him.

"Billy Wallace!" he exclaimed, relieved to see his good friend, who would also be working as crew on *Titanic*, slapping him on the back as they shared a comfortable embrace. "She's bloody unbelievable, all right. Bloody *unbelievable*!"

"She certainly is that," Billy agreed, craning his neck to try to take in the height of the ship. "D'you know, some fella told me that you can drive a whole locomotive through one of those funnels and a double-decker tramcar through each of the boilers—and there's twenty-nine of 'em. Imagine that!"

The two friends stood side by side for a moment, mesmerized. Harry caught a whiff of beer and cigarette smoke off his friend.

"You been in The Grapes then?"

"Ah, just for one, y'know. For good luck an' all that. There's half of Southampton in there, and every last man seems to be heading off to work on *Titanic*. As usual, some great fools have been drinkin' since last night—I doubt they even know what day it is, never mind what ship they're supposed to be working on. Eddie Collins for one certainly ain't gonna make this sailing, I can tell you. He's slumped on a table at the back of the snug. Arthur Smith says he ain't moved in two hours."

"Eddie Collins? But he doesn't even drink ale."

"Well, apparently he does now. And quite good at it he is too, by all accounts." They both laughed. "Anyway, we can't stand here gawping at her all day," Billy continued, nudging his friend in the back. "There might be some idiots still propping up the bar, but I don't suspect Captain Smith will be best pleased with anyone who turns up drunk, or late, to report for duty on *his* ship. Come on."

The two friends moved through the swarming crowds, unable to take their eyes off *Titanic* as they pushed and shoved their way toward the crew assembly point. All around them was frantic activity: men hefting heavy mailbags onto their shoulders and walking with them up the temporary gangways, the pale white hulls of *Titanic*'s lifeboats swaying gently high above their heads. Passengers with their hats on their laps and overcoats placed casually over their arms sat about on piles and piles of luggage and crates, sharing a cigar, playing cards, or chatting about the journey ahead. A lone bugler on the pier played a haunting tune as porters joked among themselves while they waited to transfer luggage from the dockside. Signal lamps were inspected by port officials and *Titanic*'s officers, who recorded their notes in important forms attached to clipboards. It was an exhilarating sight to Harry and was somehow perfectly organized in all its apparent madness.

Reaching the crew assembly point, he and Billy joined a line of men, mostly familiar faces, a mixture of young and old, friends and neighbors who nodded to each other or exchanged a friendly embrace. For some, this would be the last time they would sail before retirement; for others, it was the first transatlantic crossing. For all, there was a shared sense of relief to be working again and an unspoken excitement about the prospect of sailing on this, the biggest and most luxurious ocean liner ever built.

At the front of the queue, several of *Titanic*'s officers processed the crew members' details. Harry added his signature to the sign-on list, noting his previous voyage details: *Majestic, 1911, First Saloon Steward*. Second Mate Lightoller passed him his steward's badge as he added Harry's details to the crew agreement.

"To be worn at all times to enable passengers to identify any steward whom they might wish to complain about," Lightoller muttered, without taking his eyes off his paperwork.

Harry studied his badge, admiring its copper base with the raised metal star bearing the number 23. "That's funny," he said as the badge was affixed to his right arm with an elastic fastener, which, he noticed, also displayed the distinctive red swallowtail flag of the White Star Line. "That's my age exactly. Today's my twenty-third birthday."

"Really." Lightoller sighed, still not looking up. "Happy birthday. Next!"

Harry picked up his duffel bag and moved off toward the gangway leading to the third-class decks. He turned to Billy, who had been assigned to first class.

"See you in New York then, mate," he said, aware of the fact that with the ship being so vast, they were unlikely to come across each other once on board.

"Yep. See you there. Of course, you'll be there a bit later than the rest of us, what with you being in steerage an' all."

"Ah, sod off."

The two friends parted, laughing, and Harry unfolded the deck plans he had been given and set off to find his quarters on E Deck.

Like most of the other crew members', Harry's accommodation was in the main working crew passageway, which ran the length of the ship. He knew that this corridor, like the crew corridors on other liners he'd worked on, had the nickname Scotland Road after the street of alehouses in Liverpool, which was well known to sailors and those who worked the docks. Dozens of people—cooks, stewards, waiters, plate washers, pantry men, and storekeepers—milled around this endless passageway now. The ship was teeming with activity. The victualing crew was already hard at work in the galleys preparing lunch and the evening dinner; deckhands were constantly brushing and sweeping the decks to make sure they were immaculate for the boarding passengers. There was a definite industriousness, a steady sense of purpose about every single person aboard the ship.

After several wrong turns and missed staircases, Harry located his dormitory cabin. He dropped his bag on one of only two simple iron bunk beds still available among the rows and rows arranged in the large, sparsely furnished room. He chose the bottom bunk, the top one already being occupied by a bag and an overcoat. Placing his coat on the pillow of his chosen bed, he sat for a moment to say a short, silent prayer, as he always did before he set sail.

As the third- and second-class passengers started to board—
the first-class travelers being permitted the privilege of waiting
a little while longer—the call was raised for the crew to report
to their stations. Harry sprang into action, glad of the chance to
begin the work he had been looking forward to for so long.

Having already negotiated the labyrinth of corridors, passageways, and stairwells on E Deck to get his bearings, he was
efficient at showing his passengers to their quarters. He enjoyed
listening to their gasps of amazement and comments as they
walked through the pleasantly furnished general room toward
their cabins, which, although simple and functional, were of a
standard beyond that which the majority of steerage passengers
had experienced on other liners.

As he returned to the gangways, he overheard several passengers being refused entry to the ship, having lost their tickets
or failed the steerage passenger health inspection. Some were
just too drunk from the hours they had spent in the local alehouses and were returned to the White Star offices to exchange
their tickets for another sailing and given stern instructions
to sober up before they attempted to board the next ship. *How
awful,* Harry thought, *to have planned for this journey and now,
at the foot of the gangway, be unable to come aboard.* He didn't feel
sorry for the drunks, but he did feel sorry for the sickly.

At noon, the blue peter pennant was run up the foremast to
signal Imminent Departure. Ascending the three flights of stairs
to the promenade deck to get a final look as *Titanic* set sail, Harry
got another sense of her size. Forty feet above quay level and
still only halfway up the ship, he leaned over the side. In each
direction, for as far as the eye could see, was a wall of blackened
steel. They were high above the rooftops of the buildings below
them, and the people on the quayside looked miniature.

"You wouldn't want to be afraid of heights, really, would you?"

Harry turned to his right, where a young, fresh-faced boy stood, his knuckles white from grasping the railings so tightly.

Harry laughed. "You certainly would not. It's something else. It really is." He considered the boy. "First time sailing?"

"Yep."

Harry smiled, remembering his first crossing of the Atlantic. "Well, enjoy it."

"I intend to."

"Harry's the name," he added, holding out his hand. "Harry Walsh."

"Will," the boy replied, shaking Harry's hand firmly. "Will Johnson."

With the last of the passengers and supplies on board, at 12:15 P.M. the triple-valve whistles were blown three times, their deep tones echoing off the buildings on the quayside. The mooring ropes were cast off, and the tiny tugboats, which looked like scurrying ants alongside the mass of *Titanic*, spewing black smoke from their funnels, moved into place to push her out to sea.

Harry observed the crowds of onlookers all along the quayside, hanging out of the windows of the dock offices and White Star Line offices, many waving white handkerchiefs and raising their hats as a final farewell to their family and friends who massed around the portside railings of the poop deck. He knew that some didn't expect to return to these shores, a fact which made the scene particularly poignant. He searched and searched the faces in the crowd for his mother and sister but couldn't see them. It struck him that he had never wanted to see their faces more than he did at that moment.

As the band played a fanfare of triumphant music, the engines were fired up, sending a shudder through the lower decks. The three massive propellers sprang to life, churning the water into a whirling, broiling mass. Harry's heart pounded in his chest, the rhythm of its beat seeming to match the pulse of the mighty engines.

Titanic was on her way.

CHAPTER 3

Ballysheen, Ireland
April 10, 1912

It had been a cold, clear February evening when Séamus Doyle first asked Maggie Murphy to dance with him. They were guests at Jack and Maura Brennan's wedding, and she'd stepped outside for a moment to take a breath of fresh air, it being so hot and sweaty inside. She'd been admiring the brilliantly starry, moonless sky when he'd appeared, as if from nowhere, at her side.

"Maggie Murphy," he'd said, extending his calloused hand in invitation, a palpable edge of nervousness to his soft voice, "would you like to dance?"

It was the first wedding Maggie had been to, and although she would attend many others in her lifetime, she would never forget that particular one, because of that remarkable sky and the unexpected invitation from Séamus.

She had just turned sixteen at the time but felt as though she had already loved Séamus for most of her life. He was nineteen, the son of a laborer, the grandson of a laborer, and a laborer himself. His crippling shyness was what most people noticed about him. But not Maggie. She'd noticed his gentle manner, the freckles on his bare arms, his unusually long eyelashes, the way his feet turned inward slightly when he walked, the way he licked his lips when he was nervous, the way he cared, uncomplainingly, for his sick father. She'd noticed all of this from a distance, too shy herself to acknowledge the feelings she had for this inconspicuous young man.

The wedding day had brought with it a sprinkling of snow and a rousing hooley, family and friends traveling from the outlying villages of the parish to join in with the *céilí* and the *craic* late into the night. Maggie's heart had fluttered when she'd noticed Séamus among them. The flush in her cheeks hadn't escaped her mother's attention either. "You look very warm, Maggie. Perhaps you should get some air outside," she'd said, smiling.

Maggie knew Séamus from their school days and from Sunday Mass in the parish church. For as long as she could remember, she'd admired him at Wednesday market and the annual summer fairs. She knew that he always walked the three miles from his home to Ballysheen because his father couldn't afford a donkey and cart. She knew that he sold his sheep at market and sold their wool for the Foxford Woollen Mills. She knew that he played the melodeon well and that he had once ridden a horse faster than anyone else during the races in Michael Philbin's field. She knew all this about him, and had often wondered if he'd noticed her at all.

How her heart had soared as they danced together that evening, her entire body seeming to lift skyward with the whirling music, spiraling high up into the rafters along with the stamping of feet and the clapping of hands in time to the beat of the *bodhrán* as Séamus guided her awkwardly in the dance. She knew then that she never wanted him to leave her side.

It was a year after they'd first danced at the Brennans' wedding that she'd finally found the courage to tell him the news she had been dreading.

"I'm goin' to America, Séamus," she'd said as they sat by the fireside playing cards on a wet, dark January evening. "It's all decided. I'm to go with Aunt Kathleen to Chicago. Peggy Madden, Katie Kenny, and the Brennans are to travel with us—and some others." The crackle and spit from the fire had filled the silence which descended upon the young couple. Séamus hadn't spoken. "We're to go in the spring."

The rain had lashed against the windows. There'd been no other sound. Even the fire had seemed to momentarily hush itself.

"We're to sail on a new liner called *Titanic*. They say it's the biggest, finest, safest ocean liner there's ever been built," she'd added, more to break the unbearable silence than anything else. She'd felt silly then. Why had she told him this? Who cared about the ship or how big it was? That was the sort of stuff that her cousin Pat Brogan and Peggy Madden were interested in, not her. To Maggie, the ship they would sail on was an entirely insignificant fact amid the reality of what the departure meant for her and Séamus.

He'd maintained his silence, throwing another sod of turf onto the fire, which sent a wave of moist, earthy smoke billowing across the room.

"Would you think of coming too?" she'd added hesitantly, already knowing his answer.

He'd looked at her, this young man she adored with the uncomplicated certainty of youth, his cheeks rosy from the warmth of the flames. "Ah, Maggie, you know I can't. Not with Da so sick an' all. Anyway, we haven't a shillin' to our name. I could never be affording *one* of those boat tickets, never mind two, even if he was well enough."

They'd talked before about the prospect of emigrating, it being a common occurrence in the parish. Séamus had a brother in Philadelphia, who sent home as much money as he could afford, but with his mam dead and his da too ill to travel, Séamus knew that a trip to America would not be his for the making anytime soon. Maggie's fate, however, lay entirely in the hands of her aunt Kathleen, who had first made the trip to America herself twenty years ago and was completely enamored with the place. She'd written often to her niece about the possibility of joining her in Chicago, about how America offered much better prospects for young women than Ireland ever could, but one thing or another had always prevented it from happening. This time was different. With nobody to care for Maggie in Ireland, Aunt Kathleen had made up her mind: her niece would go back to Chicago with her in the spring. And no matter how much this arrangement might break Maggie's heart, there was no changing Kathleen Dolan's mind once it was made up.

"What can we do, Séamus?" Maggie's voice had trembled with frustration and despair. "What are we to do with me not able to stay and ye not able to go?" Her eyes had filled with tears, the flames of the fire reflecting in them.

"I don't know Maggie, sure I don't." Séamus had sighed, placing his cards down on the fireside before standing up, seeming so tall in Maggie and Kathleen's small cottage, his head nearly touching the beams. "You'll be able to write me. You're good with your letters and words, and I'll enjoy readin' all about your adventures. You can write those stories you're always talking of. You can write about your journey. What is it your aunt writes in? A journal? You could write one of those."

Maggie knew it was an impossible situation they faced, their destinies shaped not by their own decisions but by nature and economics and politics and things they were too young to even understand.

"And if I do write, you must write back, Séamus Doyle, you must, or what will I know of you in years to come?" She'd stood then, allowing him to wrap his strong arms around her as she leaned her head on his chest, listening to his heartbeat.

"I'll try, Maggie, but I'm not the best with my words, you know that." Gazing into the flames over Maggie's shoulder, he'd desperately wished that their circumstances could be different. "Maybe I can ask Bridie to help," he'd added as an afterthought.

Maggie had pulled back from his embrace and looked at him then, seriously. "Yes, do that. Get Bridie to help with your letters, because I don't know what I'll do if I don't hear a word from you. Promise me you'll do that?"

"I promise."

They'd stood then in their fireside embrace for a few moments longer, until Aunt Kathleen had entered the house and reminded Séamus that it was getting dark out and he should be making his way home.

Over the following days, weeks, and months, Maggie and Séamus hadn't talked again of her impending journey to America, continuing with their usual routines and meeting under the sixth cherry blossom tree on Wednesdays after market. They'd talked of simple things: the sowing of the potatoes, the cutting of the turf, the hurling, the Gaelic League, and the excitement of the local summer fairs. They'd watched the snow fall on the mountaintops, the buds form on the trees, and the lambs frolic in the fields. Maggie would usually enjoy these predictable seasonal events, which marked the passing of the months better than any calendar ever could, but now the rhythms of nature she observed in every melting snowflake, each budding leaf, brought her and thirteen other residents of their small community closer to the day when they would leave Ballysheen, closer to the day when she would leave Séamus.

They'd said their final good-byes after Sunday Mass, the last the would-be travelers would attend in their local church.

"I'll not be comin' to any American wake, Maggie," he'd told her, aware of the traditions and plans to see off the four-teen travelers over the next few nights with music and drinking. "I'll not be mournin' you while you've still so much life to live. So this will be my good-bye." He'd pressed a set of rosary beads and a silver hair comb into her hands and promised that he would write. "And when you come back, Maggie Murphy, I'll be waiting, under our tree."

That was where he stood now, under the sixth cherry blossom tree.

Maggie watched a slow, sad smile spread across his lips as she gasped and raised a hand to her chest at the sight of him. She walked forward in a daze, hardly noticing the traps which she passed or the horses nuzzling into their nose bags and kicking impatiently at the ground.

"You came." Her voice was barely a whisper, her hands trembling as they reached out to take hold of his. "You came."

They stood and looked at each other for a moment, neither one of them able to move, neither one of them knowing what to say.

"Yes, Maggie. I came. But I'm not saying good-bye again. I just wanted to give ye this."

He handed her a small package wrapped in brown paper and tied with a single piece of fraying string.

She turned it over in her hands. "What is it?"

"It's my letters, Maggie." She looked at him, not understanding, tears pricking her eyes. "These are my letters to you in America. I've been writin' them for the last while, y'know, on quiet evenin's and when I had a moment free. I asked Bridie to help me. I wasn't sure how long a letter would take to get to America, so I thought that this way you can read them whenever ye like and won't have to be waiting on any deliveries."

The sudden cry of a cockerel nearby made one of the horses skitter, the metal fastenings on the harness jangling noisily against its sturdy flanks until the jarvey shushed and soothed it.

"But, Séamus, I . . ." Maggie's emotions washed over her now, all of the despair, all of the suppressed worry and uncertainty about the journey ahead suddenly overwhelming her. She allowed her tears to fall freely as she clutched the simple packet of letters in her hands.

"And when you're planning on coming back home, you can write to tell me," Séamus continued, grasping the tops of Maggie's shoulders to impress his words upon her. "I'll wait here for you as usual. Every Wednesday after market. I'll wait until you come back, Maggie Murphy." He paused, righting himself to stand tall and taking in a deep, long breath. "You will come back home one day, won't ye? Come back and be the girl I remember? Be the same Maggie Murphy?"

"I hope so, Séamus, I do. I hope so."

Their last, tender embrace among the falling blossoms was one of many that took place that morning in their small village and in homes across the parish. Promises to keep in touch and sentiments of love were exchanged on almost every doorstep; mothers wept for their departing sons and daughters, sisters held on to sisters, brothers grasped brothers, friends embraced friends, and neighbors held neighbors.

Kathleen Dolan observed these touching scenes as she stood for a moment in the doorway of her home. She watched a spider in the doorframe, wondering how long it had lived among those cracks in the wood, cracks she hadn't noticed until now. She wondered how much of this house, of this parish, she would recall in the future, aware that with Maggie in America with her, there would be little reason to return here again. She wondered whether those who dwelled in this home in years to come would ever know the names Maggie Murphy and Kathleen Dolan; would ever know that they, and twelve others, had departed from this small village on a calm spring morning in search of a better life.

As the last of the luggage was loaded into the traps, the fourteen travelers took their seats. Still clutching the packet of letters, Maggie climbed up to take the last seat in the last trap alongside her aunt. With a final blessing of holy water and a prayer for protection from the priest, the jarveys gave a sharp tug on the reins. The horses and donkeys skittered to attention, the harnesses jolted taut, and fourteen hearts lurched as the traps rumbled slowly forward.

WHITE STAR LINE

ROYAL AND UNITED STATES MAIL STEAMERS.

ISMAY, IMRIE & CO.,

LONDON.

LIVERPOOL.

SOUTHAMPTON.

Agent at PARIS —
NICHOLAS MARTIN, 8, Rue Scribe.

WHITE STAR LINE

JAMES SCOTT & CO. Agents
QUEENSTOWN.

GENOA
NAPLES
BOSTON
NEW YORK
QUEBEC
MONTREAL

OCEANIC STEAM NAVIGATION COMPANY, LIMITED, OF GREAT BRITAIN.

THIRD CLASS (Steerage) PASSENGER'S CONTRACT TICKET.
(NOT TRANSFERABLE.)

CHAPTER 4

Cass County, Illinois
April 15, 1982

Grace Butler gathered her long auburn hair at the nape of her neck and held it loosely to one side as she bent forward to blow out the candles on her birthday cake. The bright flames swayed in mesmerizing unison as a light breeze drifted in through the open kitchen window, the motion reminding her of the late summer cornfields around their small farm. *One last dance before harvesttime,* her father had said to her one August evening, as they sat on the old gate and watched a beautiful sunset turn the ripe cornfield to a dazzling display of liquid gold. *One last dance.*

This unexpectedly beautiful remark had stayed with her ever since. She remembered those words again now as she blew out her birthday candles; remembered *him,* as the small group of friends and family who had gathered in her mother's kitchen sang "Happy Birthday" and clapped with love and admiration for a girl who had returned to this humble family home two years earlier to bury the father she adored.

Until that very dark jolt, life had been satisfyingly predictable for Grace, safe and unremarkable. Hers had been a contented childhood, spent playing in the hayfields with her twin brother, Art, and the kids from the other farms around their home. She had fond memories of lazy summer days spent splashing her bare feet in the cooling streams and running her fingers through the crystal-clear waters of the rivers that flowed around their land, catching small fish in jam jar aquariums, eating honeysuckle flowers, and rubbing nettle stings with the large, flat dock leaves that nature had cleverly planned to always grow nearby.

The rivers that meandered and intertwined across the countryside, lazily in the summer and more violently after the winter rains and snow, were as much a part of Grace's life as they were a part of the landscape. For as long as she could remember, she had felt curiously drawn to the water, entranced by the sight of it, soothed by the sound of it, and intrigued by the dangers and mysteries hidden within it. Grace knew that just below the gentle, inviting surface there were dangerous eddies and deceptive currents, which even a strong swimmer like her would not be able to kick against. She respected the water for this, never underestimating its power and admiring its beauty with a cautious eye.

Her father had once told her that water has a memory; that every rock, every stone, every grain of muddy sediment leaves something of a fingerprint in the water that flows over it. Grace liked this idea, imagining the water of the great lakes and oceans of the world to echo with the memories of the places, people, and events it had passed on its journey.

Grace; her brother, Art; and the other kids were a familiar sight in their neighborhood, at one with the wildlife and nature around them, free to roam at will until the inky blue skies of dusk signaled that it was time for them to trudge home along the dusty pathways forged by the tractors and heavy machinery of harvesttime.

From the carefree life of a farmer's daughter, Grace had settled quickly into the routine of school, excelling academically and socially. During the summer of '75 she'd blossomed into a stunning teenager, her natural beauty and developing female form not going unnoticed by the hormonally charged boys in her class. She'd met her first boyfriend the following spring. Sam Adamson was his name. They'd spent most of the summer hidden away in an old hay barn, engaging in awkward encounters with zippers and buttons while the chickens pecked idly at husks of grain on the dusty floor. By the time the leaves were changing color on the trees that fall, the hay barn roof had fallen in and Grace's first real relationship had fallen apart. She was surprised to realize that she was more concerned about the roof.

With her almost luminous fair skin and rich auburn hair, there was little doubting Grace's Irish heritage. It wasn't spoken of very often in the family, but she knew that her great-nana Maggie (her great-grandmother on her mother's side) had traveled as a teenager from Ireland to America, as indeed had her great-grandfather James, the man Maggie had married soon after settling in Chicago. There were very few photos of Maggie as a young girl, but in the rare ones that did exist, Grace could see the unmistakable likeness between them, particularly since she'd hit her teenage years. It was her dream to travel to Ireland one day to see the country of her origins for herself. She'd been planning the trip with Jimmy when her life suddenly fell apart.

She'd met Jimmy Shepard in her first semester at the Medill School of Journalism at Northwestern. He sat next to her in their first lecture and asked her if he could borrow a pen. She spent the next forty minutes trying to sneak a better look at him out of the corner of her eye, catching just the occasional glimpse of his sandy-colored hair, broad jawline, and long dark eyelashes. In reality, she spent most of the lecture admiring his battered Converse sneakers. By the time the bell rang for the end of class, she hadn't written one word on her notepad and had absolutely no recollection of anything the professor had said. Jimmy returned her pen, along with a piece of paper on which he'd scribbled *Thank you, gorgeous. Can I buy you a cup of coffee?* They'd been inseparable ever since.

The vibrant existence she experienced in her first semester at college couldn't have been farther removed from the tranquil, innocent days of her childhood, but self-assured and poised as always, Grace excelled in her new life. While she loved her old school friends for their uncomplicated lives and their reliability, she grew to love her college friends for their complex lives and their spontaneity. They introduced her to new music, innovative writers, and completely different fashions, and she realized how sheltered her life had been. Jimmy was a revelation to Grace; a city boy, he was self-assured, witty, streetwise, and a far cry from the awkward fumblings of Sam Adamson in the hay barn.

She was a popular girl in her dorm, and her talent for writing had not gone unnoticed. "You have a genuine gift," Professor Andrews told her during the fall semester of her second year. She liked this tall, narrow man with angular features and a crooked smile; he reminded Grace of her grandpa. She coughed as he wiped the blackboard vigorously, sending dust flying around the room. "Yes, you have a real talent, young lady," he continued. "So, tell me, who do you get it from, Mom or Dad?"

Grace thought for a moment. "My dad, I guess." She felt a little embarrassed then, afraid that he might think her dad was a successful writer himself. "But he's just a farmer. He doesn't actually write anything himself."

"Ah, a man of the earth." Professor Andrews perched on the edge of the desk. "They make the best poets, in my estimation; full of senses and emotions and in touch with their surroundings."

Grace had never thought of it like that, but it kind of made sense. She had always attributed her love of reading and writing to her father, who had read to her every night at bedtime, no matter how exhausted he was from a hard day's work. "Just one more chapter, Daddy, *please*," she would plead when it was time to turn out the light, especially when he read from *Little House on the Prairie*, her favorite. She liked to imagine herself as Laura Ingalls and her father as Pa, reliving their adventures in her mind and basking in the warmth of their family's unfaltering love for one another. She adored the book so much that she'd cried inconsolably into her pillow when Laura's sister Mary went blind.

It was her father who had inspired her love of books and stories long before her schoolteachers taught her the mechanics of reading, he who had encouraged her to keep writing her little tales about a family traveling across America in a small wagon and princesses locked in towers by evil witches. It was he, a hardworking, unassuming farmer, who had uttered phrases such as *one last dance before harvesttime*, who had told her about the memory of water, who had inspired her to observe the world around her and describe it as beautifully on a piece of paper as she saw it in reality.

"So, Ms. Butler," Professor Andrews had continued, folding his arms casually over his gray sweater, which, Grace noticed, was wearing thin on the elbows. She wondered whether there was a Mrs. Professor Andrews, who might take him shopping to buy a new one, although for some reason, she got the feeling he still lived with his mother. "You're probably wondering why I asked you to stay back." He'd paused for dramatic effect, as he was prone to do, before continuing. "Well, I was speaking to a colleague of mine at the *Chicago Tribune* earlier this week, and I happened to mention to him that I have a very talented young lady in my class." Grace had felt herself blush a little at his compliment and shuffled her feet awkwardly. "He has agreed to take a feature article from you." He'd stood up then, striding around the large desk to collect his briefcase. "So, what do you think of that? You up for the challenge?"

Grace had been stunned. This was big news. A feature slot with the *Tribune* was the Holy Grail of journalism. She knew people who had been pitching ideas to them for months and hadn't even had a response.

"Wow," she'd gushed, her cheeks flaming scarlet. "Um, wow. Thank you. Thank you very much. That's amazing."

"Yes, it is. So, send them the best two-thousand-word feature you can possibly write, and if Bill likes it, he'll run it this summer. Get this right, Grace, and you will almost certainly be guaranteed an internship with them, if not a job when you graduate."

She'd spent the next week researching ideas in the library, sitting for hours at the battered teak desk in her dorm room, typing up her handwritten notes on the typewriter she'd been given as a Christmas present the previous year, only to tear the pages from the machine, crumple them up, and throw them into the wastebasket. The college dorm rooms were small: just big enough to fit two single beds (her roommate, Ella Jackson, was at home sick with mono), two desks, two dressers with mirrors, and a small window. *Thank God for the window,* Grace remembered thinking as she unpacked her case on the first day of the term. The boxy little room with its stark white walls, flimsy furniture, and cold vinyl flooring felt like a cage to a girl who was used to roaming along hedgerows and swinging on the front porch drinking homemade lemonade.

In the days before the Thanksgiving vacation, she gazed out of that small window for hours at a time, hoping that inspiration would strike her. The Pope's recent visit to the United States? Anti-nuclear demonstrations in New York? The gay rights march in Washington? These were all big news stories that dwarfed Grace's confidence and caused her to doubt her ability to do them justice. She needed to find something more personal, a story ordinary people could relate to, a story that, above all else, she felt compelled to write. Professor Andrews always told his students that "great news journalists write with their heads, great features journalists write with their hearts." She needed to find a story that touched her heart, and she was failing to do so.

It bothered her over Thanksgiving and continued to bug her through the holiday season. Although she enjoyed the time at home with her family, catching up with Art, who was back, briefly, from traveling around India; relishing her mom's home cooking; and savoring the late-night conversations with her dad, she was distracted and couldn't wait to get back to the city and college life. A few weeks into the new year and the start of the spring semester, she still hadn't found her story.

"Why can't I *do* this, Jimmy?" she complained as they lay on her dormitory bed, their legs vertical, resting against the wall. Grace often lay like this, enjoying the sensation of the blood flowing down her veins, pulled by the force of gravity. It made her feel weightless, as if she were floating in water.

Jimmy turned to face her, pushing her hair gently from her forehead. "You will find your story, Gracie," he told her, his smooth, velvety voice captivating her as always. "Don't force it, babe. Stop panicking. Something will come to you, it always does." He leaned toward her and kissed her gently on the cheek to reinforce his certainty. They gazed at each other for a moment, and as her eyes fell across the familiar contours of his face, she wondered what the future held for them, whether their relationship would continue, or whether, like so many college-bred romances she had seen, it would fall apart outside the familiarity and security an academic institution provided.

As she considered this, Macy Johnson, the dorm monitor, knocked on her door to tell Grace that her mother was on the phone. Her father had been involved in a serious accident. All thoughts of her feature, and her future with Jimmy, were forgotten.

Jimmy drove as quickly as he could while Grace sat motionless in the passenger seat of his blue Ford Mustang. She gazed at the light winter fog that shrouded the tops of the higher buildings in downtown Chicago. She noticed odd things, like the last of the recent snowfall still clinging to the curbs like moss, and she remarked on the new digital time and temperature display on one of the buildings. She did anything she could to silence the voice inside her head which spoke her worst fears.

They reached the hospital at 7:32 P.M. Nine minutes too late. Her father had been pronounced dead at 7:23. By the time Grace got to his bedside, a frightening array of tubes and drips hung listlessly from the machines around him. They had failed to stop the internal bleeding; failed to keep him alive. He'd been hit head-on by a truck on a blind bend just outside their farm. The truck was traveling way too fast for the road conditions and had lost control. Her father, sensible and practical as always, had been on his way to get salt to grit the roads because he knew they were dangerous to drive on.

Grace stood in front of her father's lifeless body, stunned into silence. All she could do was entwine her fingers tightly around her mother's careworn hands—her mother, who was only forty-one years old and already a widow. She'd barely had a chance to put away the gifts from the wedding anniversary they had recently celebrated. Mother and daughter didn't speak. Together they wept desperate, relentless tears.

The hours, days, and weeks that followed were a blur, within which Grace suppressed her own grief in the knowledge that her mother's was far greater. Jimmy returned to campus five days after the funeral. She hardly remembered him leaving.

She made the phone call to Professor Andrews exactly two weeks after Macy Johnson had knocked on her dorm door. Sitting on the bottom stair in her family home, tracing the abstract spiderweb carpet pattern with her toes, she dialed the numbers carefully on the old rotary-dial telephone. The circular dial seemed to move in slow motion as it rewound to the start position after each digit; her heart thumped as she listened to the hypnotic whir of the internal mechanism. She hoped Professor Andrews wouldn't pick up. He did.

Twisting the gray telephone cord anxiously around her fingers, she explained quietly what had happened and that as a result she would be dropping out of college to remain at home with her mother for the time being. She went on to explain how her mother suffered from multiple sclerosis and how she was worried about her mother's condition worsening under the stress of her father's death. She spoke for a long time as Professor Andrews listened silently, waiting patiently until Grace had finished before speaking himself. He told her he understood entirely and supported her decision and was extremely sorry for the terrible situation that had forced it upon her. Sensitive to her grief, he hesitantly mentioned the feature.

"I hate to raise this now, Grace, but is this something you think you can still work toward? It really is such an outstanding opportunity for you, and I'm sure Bill would wait awhile, given the circumstances."

"I'm so sorry to let you down, Professor Andrews," Grace replied, speaking softly into the receiver, her words concise and measured, "but please can you pass the opportunity to someone else? I'm just too distracted to write at the moment. For now, I have to put my career to one side and be here for my mom."

Although she would never know it, her professor was so moved by her sense of duty to care for her mother, by the maturity she displayed for a nineteen-year-old girl, that he shed a tear himself when he replaced the receiver.

Two years later, she still hadn't been able to let go of that sense of duty to her mother, and that was why Grace Butler stood there now, celebrating her birthday in the small kitchen of her family home, the same wallpaper with the repeating patterns of barnyard chickens providing the backdrop to her birthday photographs, just as it had done since she was a little girl. The sense of loss—not only of her father but of her own life, her hopes and dreams—suddenly enveloped Grace, and she stepped out of the kitchen onto the back porch, tears streaming down her cheeks.

While the rest of the guests had gathered around Grace to watch her blow out her candles, Maggie, her eighty-seven-year-old great-grandmother, had been sitting quietly on the back porch watching the celebrations from a distance, the faintest whisper of a smile playing across her paper-thin lips. She saw Grace step out of the kitchen, watched the tears tumbling down her face, and called her over.

"Come here," the old lady whispered, patting the seat next to her on the porch swing. "What has you all upset on your big day?"

Grace walked over, the hum of conversation fading slightly as she moved away from the main gathering of guests.

"Oh, I don't know, Maggie. Old age, probably!" Grace always used Maggie's first name, at her great-grandmother's insistence. *Great-Grandmother. Great-Nana. It all makes me sound so old!*, she'd said. *Maggie will do just fine.*

"Just ignore me," Grace continued, dabbing at her tears with a tissue. "I'll be okay in a minute. Here, I brought you a slice of cake. It's your favorite—chocolate sponge with fresh cream and Aunt Martha's homemade raspberry jam."

The back porch was lightly scented by the fragrant camellia bushes that grew in the garden. Grace loved the smell and inhaled deeply as she handed over the birthday cake. The old lady took the plate from her, the involuntary shaking of her hands causing the silver dessert fork to rattle on the avocado green plate. It was part of a wedding anniversary present that had never been out of the box until today. Grace had watched her mother wash and dry each plate, cup, and saucer with great care, especially for the occasion, and it hadn't gone unnoticed by anybody that the simple act of opening that box of dinnerware was as much a symbolic gesture of her mother moving on in her life as it was a practical response to the need for more plates.

"You're a very kind girl," Maggie said, with a slight nod.

"Birthdays always bring out the emotions, don't you think? I should know. I've had my fair share of them!"

Grace noticed that Maggie's distinctive duck-egg blue eyes seemed lost in distant thoughts as small pools of water gathered at the corners. It struck her how fragile Maggie looked recently, particularly since James, Grace's great-grandfather, had died a few years ago. She seemed so frail and diminutive, her skin almost translucent, her tired body unable to function without the assistance of medication and a cane. It was hard to believe that this same woman had started the four generations of the family that was gathered here now; that it was this almost insignificant old lady who, as a girl of only seventeen, had made the difficult journey from Ireland to America in the hope of starting a new and better life.

"Did I ever tell you that it snowed the day you were born?"

Grace laughed through her tears. "You did, Maggie. Just a few times!"

Maggie often told the story: the soft white flakes mingling with the pink cherry blossoms that fell in a blizzard from the trees outside the hospital, dancing and whirling in the brisk breeze and drifting around the cars parked outside. Maggie had a particular fascination with the annual spectacle of the cherry trees bursting into life with their colorful blooms; she loved to watch the flowers fall. "Like the prettiest snowflakes," she would comment, "or a bride's confetti." She said it reminded her. Nobody knew what it reminded her of.

"Now, you wipe away those tears. I've something to talk to you about."

"What is it?" Grace asked. "Do you want another slice of cake?"

Maggie slapped her playfully on the wrist. "No, I do not want another slice of cake. I want to tell you something. Something important." She had Grace's full attention now. "Are you still writing those stories of yours?"

Grace looked down at her feet, almost guilty about her response. "Well, not so much. Not since Dad died, really. Everyone's been too sad, and I've been too busy with Mom to write anything."

"And what about that college you were enjoying so much, and that boyfriend of yours? When are you going back to them?"

Grace was surprised. Maggie had never really spoken to her about any of this before. She didn't think her great-grandmother would even remember Jimmy, it was so long since she'd mentioned him, or since anyone from the family had seen him.

Since her father's accident, Grace and Jimmy had drifted apart. They'd kept in touch for a while, but as the months had passed they had spoken on the phone and exchanged letters less and less frequently. Grace had eventually written to tell him that while she still loved him, she realized that she couldn't expect him to wait for her. It was the hardest letter she had ever written. She thought about Jimmy often, had wanted to get in touch with him so badly, but something had stopped her. Now she simply blocked him out of her mind and tried to forget him.

"I don't know, Maggie. Maybe I'll go back to college and to Jimmy . . . one day."

The old lady studied her intently. "You know, I left my home when I was around your age. I left people I loved and cared about, but I had no choice. I *had* to leave, had to come here to find a better life. Your mom doesn't want you moping around here forever. I think you've done a wonderful thing staying here to care for her, but she can make arrangements, you know—for nurses to come in. And your aunts are around to help out. Maybe you should pick up that notebook of yours and your boyfriend's phone number and go get on with your life."

This was said as much as an order as a hypothetical possibility. Grace knew Maggie was right. She'd been trying to find the right time to talk to her mother about the possibility of returning to college, but the moment never seemed to come.

"Maybe you're right," she said. "I'm not sure I can still write a good story, though; it's been so long. And good stories are very hard to find."

"Well," Maggie continued, "if it's a good story you're looking for, I've one to get you writing again." She paused then, to take a bite from her cake. Grace waited patiently, conscious of the fact that the guests were starting to leave. "Do you know what the date is today, Grace?"

Grace chuckled, nudging her great-grandmother gently on the arm. "It's my birthday. April fifteenth."

"Ah, yes, but do you know what else happened on this day? A long time ago?"

Grace thought for a moment. Had she missed someone's birthday, or a significant anniversary? She couldn't think of anything. "I don't know. What?"

Maggie paused again. She took a deep breath. Something about her expression had changed, her shaking hands stilled, her eyes staring deeply into those of her great-granddaughter.

"Did I ever tell you about *Titanic*, Grace?"

Grace put her glass down on the floor, sensing the significance in Maggie's tone.

"No, Maggie. You didn't. You never speak to anyone about *Titanic*. Why?"

"It sank seventy years ago today, you know."

"Really? What, *actually* today? April fifteenth? So I was born on the anniversary of *Titanic* sinking? Wow! I didn't realize that." She was just about to call over her mother to share this revelation when Maggie put her hand firmly on Grace's arm.

"And you know how I remember the date so well, Grace, don't you?"

Grace stared intently into Maggie's glassy eyes. The very air around them seemed to still. The hairs stood up on the back of Grace's neck. "Yes, Maggie. I know."

"I was there. I was on *Titanic*." Maggie paused. The relief of saying the words out loud after so many years of refusing to talk about it clearly unsettled her.

Grace remembered her mother once telling her and Art about Maggie's *Titanic* connection. That she had sailed to America on *Titanic*, but that she never spoke about it and they were never to ask her about it.

Grace took hold of Maggie's hands as the old lady continued to speak in a near whisper, as if afraid to let the words leave her mouth. "Fourteen of us from our small parish in Ireland boarded that magnificent ship," she continued. "Fourteen of us. I was only seventeen years old. Just a girl." She looked down at the floor then, unable to look her great-granddaughter in the eye. "Over fifteen hundred people died on that ship, you know. And many were just children. Innocent young children. I was one of the lucky ones. I got the last seat on the last lifeboat thanks to a man who helped me. I often wonder what happened to him."

Grace watched Maggie closely, seeing something different in her; a sense of loss, of fear that she hadn't noticed before.

"And what about the other thirteen? What happened to them?" she asked tentatively.

The scent of camellias washed over the porch as the breeze strengthened. Maggie looked at Grace and took a long, deep breath.

Male Berth............
Female Berth............
Married Berth............

ROYAL AND UNITED STATES MAIL STEAMERS.

WHITE STAR LINE

ISMAY, IMRIE & CO.,
1. COCKSPUR STREET, S.W.
68. LEADENHALL STREET, E.C.
LONDON,
30 JAMES STREET
LIVERPOOL
AND
CANUTE ROAD, SOUTHAMPTON

Agent at PARIS:
NICHOLAS MARTIN, 9, Rue Scribe.

WHITE STAR LINE
18 VIA VELLA MONTÉALA
21 PIAZZA DELLA BURSA
44 D'ARGENTREET
3 BROADWAY
62 DALHOUSE STREET
BELL TELEMONE KILLOWEN
110 NOTRE DAME STREET WEST

GENOA
NAPLES
BOSTON
NEW YORK
QUEBEC
MONTREAL

JAMES SCOTT & CO.   Agents
QUEENSTOWN.

OCEANIC STEAM NAVIGATION COMPANY, LIMITED, OF GREAT BRITAIN.
THIRD CLASS (Steerage) PASSENGER'S CONTRACT TICKET.
(NOT TRANSFERABLE.)

CHAPTER 5

Private Journal of Maggie Murphy
Queenstown, Co. Cork
April 10, 1912

At last we are arrived in Queenstown. At times I thought
we would never get here, the journey across the Windy Gap
in the traps seeming to take forever and then the endless
train journey from Castlebar—Lord! I lost count of how
many times we changed trains at this station and that
station—it's a wonder we didn't lose any of our luggage
on the way, we were in and out of so many carriages. We
nearly did lose cousin Pat—he'd fallen asleep what with the
rocking motion and all, and nearly didn't get off at Limerick. Thanks to Maura Brennan's quick counting up and
noticing we were one short, or God only knows where he
would be by now!

Other than that, nothing much happened on the train
journey, except a lot of weeping and sniffling, the girls missing their mammies and all. We didn't talk to each other

much, which was a strange thing as we'd usually never be short of a joke or a story or a song. We was all too busy thinking our private thoughts and watching the fields fly past the windows. I saw a hare dart across one field, startled by the noise of the engine, and a hawk hovering above another. I wonder whether they have hares and hawks in America.

Peggy was the only one to make any sort of a noise on the journey to Claremorris, getting a fit of the giggles at the sight of a fat woman trying to pull something down from the luggage rack. She kept falling backward and forward and sideways with the movement of the train—she looked drunk, so she did! Aunt Kathleen chided Peggy for sniggering and said it was poor manners.

We was starving by the time we reached Cork and were glad of Mrs. Brogan's oatcakes and Aunt Kathleen's soda bread. It's strange to think she baked that bread in our cottage just this morning. I can hardly remember what it looks like, it already seems such an age since I was there.

By the time we boarded the train to Queenstown, most of the weeping had stopped. Katie cheered us with her songs, and Jack Brennan took to playing cards with Michael Kelly—he told me he thought it might stop the young lad's mind from dwelling too much on home. I've watched Pat take his lucky sovereign out of his pocket a few times. His mam gave it to him this morning as a good-luck token, but he dropped it as he climbed into the trap—I saw it and I know some of the others did too, but we all pretended not to notice and he hasn't talked of it. I know what he's after thinking, though, as he turns it over and over in his hands, because it's bad luck to drop a sovereign. We all know that.

Queenstown is a strange town. I've never seen a place like it in my life. There wasn't a spare inch of space around the train station without a person or a cart or a horse or a piece of luggage on it—half of Ireland seems to have come here tonight. The sea air feels damp on my skin, and there's an awful stench of salt or seaweed or something hanging over the place. It makes me feel like I want to be sick. The seagulls make a horrible noise, a sort of shrieking cry, like a bawling baby. It makes the hairs stand up on the back of my neck.

Aunt Kathleen arranged the lodgings for us all, speaking with one of the runners at the station who found this place, the McDonnell Rooming House at the Beach. Aunt Kathleen is familiar with boardinghouses, after running one of her own in Chicago and all, and seems pleased because this one is close to the cathedral for Mass in the morning.

We are split up across three rooms, the two boys and Jack Brennan sharing one; Maura Brennan, Eileen Brennan, Katie, Peggy, and Ellen Joyce in another; and myself, Kathleen, and four of the other girls in this room. I heard Ellen telling Pat that it has cost 7s.6d. each for the night's lodgings. Pat told me that's practically a week's wages and that the owner must be making a fortune. She seems like a nice enough woman, but she breathes heavily when she goes up and down the stairs and an awful smell of sweat comes from her. Thanks be to God we only have to stay for one night.

Poor Peggy is in a dreadful state. I don't know how it happened 'cause not a one of us saw him, but she says that a strange man dressed all in black approached her at Queenstown train station. He appeared from nowhere and tapped her on the shoulder. She says she leaped nearly ten feet into the air, not knowing who the man was at all. She tried to pass him a few pennies from her purse, thinking he must be a Traveller, but he refused them and told her that she was going on a long journey and there would be a terrible disaster, but she would survive. He then disappeared into the crowds. She's a bit shaken up with it all. What with this and Joseph Kenny's tea leaves, I'm almost beside myself with the nerves now. Aunt Kathleen says we're letting our imaginations run away with us and reminded us that we couldn't be sailing on a safer ship.

Séamus has been constantly in my thoughts since we left Ballysheen. I wonder what he says in his letters. I have them in my coat pocket for safekeeping—I haven't opened the packet yet. I think I should wait until we're far out at sea before I read them—I'm half afraid that if he has written too fondly or offered a proposal of marriage, I will have to run off to be with him again. Aunt Kathleen would never forgive me if I did something like that, so I'll wait until we're on the ship. I can be sure I won't be doing any running off to him when there are miles of cold, dark ocean stretching between us.

Aunt Kathleen says that Titanic will be on her way from France by now, and should arrive to Queenstown by midmorning. All going well, we should be sailing by the afternoon. I can't imagine what it will feel like to be on the water—I've never seen a steam liner, other than the pictures Peggy showed me in the newspaper. I wonder what I'll think of this ship after all the talk and the fuss. It is only a ship when all is said and done. I might not think much of it at all.

Anyway, it's getting late now and Aunt Kathleen is fussing about getting a decent sleep for the journey tomorrow, so I've told her I'll be finished in a few minutes. Most of the others are already asleep, tired out from our journey today. It seems to have taken so long to get here, and New York is another week away. How we are going to fare on a boat for seven days I do not know. I hope Séamus will visit me in my dreams tonight.

CHAPTER 6

Queenstown, County Cork, Ireland
April 10, 1912

For the love of God, girl, would you look at the time, it's gone eleven. Put that book down, whatever it is you're scribblin', and get some sleep now. We've an early start in the morning and there's plenty more miles to be covered yet before we reach America."

Although tired from the long day of traveling, Kathleen Dolan was restless herself. She was relieved to have finally started their journey but anxious to be back in her comfortable home in Chicago with her familiar belongings and just her sister and her niece for company. She didn't mind most of the others in their party—with the exception perhaps of Ellen Joyce, whom she found a little superior—but large groups were not things Kathleen usually surrounded herself with. She found them rather unsettling.

It was no surprise to those who knew Kathleen Dolan that it was she who had galvanized the group of travelers to make this journey. She had made no secret of the tantalizing tales of prosperity and opportunity America offered and knew that she had captured the imaginations of the women and men of Ballysheen when she spoke of her American life. Many of them—even if they wouldn't admit it—wished for more than a life of failed harvests and employment in the cotton mills of England, and Kathleen knew exactly what she was doing when she mentioned, quite matter-of-factly, that *Titanic* would sail from Queenstown on the eleventh of April and that anyone who wished to be aboard could obtain their ticket from the local White Star Line shipping agent, Thomas Durcan of Castlebar, at a cost of seven pounds, fifteen shillings. Kathleen Dolan was a formidable force when she set her mind to something.

Her demeanor over the past weeks had been one of prudent efficiency and a resolute impatience to get going. Now she enjoyed the opportunity to lie still, glad of the silence. As she watched her niece settle under her eiderdown and glanced around the room at the sleeping forms of the other young girls, Kathleen was reminded of her own emigration journey as a nineteen-year-old. Far from all the tears and worry she'd witnessed that day, she'd considered it a prodigious adventure.

Painfully aware that she was unremarkable in many respects, ordinary enough to look at with her square jaw, rugged complexion, and deep-set eyes, which gave the impression that she was older than her years, Kathleen knew it was only her determination and resolve to improve her situation in life that made her stand out from the other girls her age. With her eldest sister already settled in America, Kathleen had sat for years in the bedroom she shared with her remaining sister, Nora, both of them consuming every word of the letters Mary wrote about her alluring American life: the employment prospects, the gaily colored clothes, the opportunities to be away from the social constraints of Irish life. Mary's words, transported on the steam liners that would remove another batch of emigrants from Ireland's shores, offered enticing prospects for a farmer's daughter whose domestic duties were drearily predictable, whose clothes were drab, and whose social position had been defined from the moment she was born. From the moment her opportunity arrived with a ticket paid for by her sister in Chicago, Kathleen had reveled in the prospects America held for her. Undaunted by the fact that she was leaving with little money, she had departed Irish shores with very little fuss and even less regret.

Like many before her, she'd settled easily into the rhythms of metropolitan life in Chicago. So many of the neighbors were of Irish descent that she often found it hard to believe she was in America at all, catching the unmistakable Irish brogue in exchanges on the street or in the local grocery store: Offaly, Mayo, Donegal, Kerry; she was certain all the counties would be represented if you listened hard enough.

She'd written often to her only remaining relative in Ireland, her sister Nora—Maggie's mother—and to her good friend Maura Byrne. In her letters, Kathleen described the buildings reaching up into the clouds, the grand homes, carriages, and motorcars of the wealthy, the well-paid opportunities for women in domestic employment, the impressive avenues, and the majestic department store at Randolph Street and Washington Boulevard where you could buy anything and everything. She knew that the recipients of her letters enjoyed hearing about this "new world," so far removed in both distance and experience from their own.

But, no matter how settled in and involved with the American way of life she became, a letter with news from home was always a welcome sight to Kathleen's eyes and caused her heart to beat a little more rapidly than usual. It was such a letter that had prompted her recent return to Ireland, a letter that, she realized as she lay in the uncomfortable boardinghouse bed, had, in many ways, led to the fourteen of them being in Queenstown that night.

The letter had arrived on a crisp fall day, the leaves on the trees that lined the sidewalk outside the Chicago home she shared with her sister Mary glistening in the bright sunshine. It was a modest but perfectly pleasant home on North Ashland Avenue, close to the boardinghouse she'd previously owned on Lincoln Street. Her sister had made a comfortable home, her choice of furnishing befitting two women who were doing well in life.

As she picked up the letter, Kathleen immediately recognized Maggie's familiar handwriting and the distinctive Castlebar postmark. Walking into the front room, she settled herself on the chair at the writing table and carefully opened the envelope, expecting the usual gossip and casual news from home.

October 22, 1911
Ballysheen
Co. Mayo
Eire

My dear Aunt Kathleen,

I write with the sad news that Mammy is very sick with the influenza. She has told me to write to you to ask you to come back to Ireland as soon as you can, as she worries about me should anything happen to her. I am sorry to have to write to you with this news and hope that we will see you in Ballysheen soon.

Good-bye.
Your niece,
Maggie

Kathleen had placed the letter on the table, stood up, smoothed her skirt, and turned to her sister.

"It's from Maggie. Nora has the influenza. I must go to Ireland as soon as I can arrange a ticket. I'll write to Maggie straightaway to tell her I'm coming."

Crossing the Atlantic was almost second nature to Kathleen by the time she'd set sail for Ireland that October, since she had made the journey between her American and Irish homes several times over the years. She was, however, well aware of the fact that her arrival back in Ireland that autumn had not passed without remark. This time she'd returned noticeably different, a successful, astute businesswoman who, although connected to the stones, earth, and rivers of her Irish home, was somehow changed by her extended experience of a new life, by her knowledge that there were better prospects to be found elsewhere. For those who had neither the financial means nor the desire to travel and had stayed behind to continue their lives at the same steady, unremarkable pace, it was unsettling to witness the lightness in Kathleen's step and the glare of her colorful overcoat, and to hear the occasional unfamiliar turn of phrase the returning traveler brought with her.

The hushed whispers and furtive glances as she went about her business didn't bother Kathleen, although the rumors that she had remained in Ballysheen after the death of her sister in order to look for a husband did. It was a subject that came up time and time again, and was one of few things in Kathleen's life that bothered her. It had started before she'd even left Chicago.

"You know, it might not be any harm to consider looking for a suitable husband while you're back in Ireland, Kathleen," Mary had mentioned, tentatively, as she'd helped her sister pack the last of her belongings. "You've a good dowry now from the sale of the boardinghouse, and the prospects you can offer a future husband are much improved. You should think on it."

It wasn't the first time that Mary had raised the issue of a husband with her sister, whose apparent indifference to the matter was something she found completely incomprehensible. Unlike her friend Maura, and her sisters, Kathleen had never really considered marriage, her successful boardinghouse business occupying most of her time and her thoughts. It was an issue that refused to go away, though, as someone or other would make a remark or throw a suggestive glance in her direction whenever there was talk of engagements or weddings. Having read the excitement in the letters from Maura Byrne about her engagement to Jack Brennan, Kathleen had found her thoughts turning to the matter, although never for too long. Because she was a fiercely private woman, the thought of discussing the issue of marriage with anyone else, even her own sister, left Kathleen feeling distinctly uncomfortable. As far as she was concerned, whether she had her mind set on finding a husband in Ireland or not was nobody's business but her own.

"May God have mercy on me, Maura Brennan," she'd said to her friend one morning after overhearing some of the women gossiping about her in the street, "I am certainly not waiting around in Ballysheen in some desperate attempt to find a man who will spend all my hard-earned money on silly notions of running a shoe factory or making buttons. I'm here to make arrangements for my niece—and anyone else who cares to join us—to come back with me to America."

Kathleen chose to ignore the Ballysheen gossips for the remainder of her time in Ireland. Whatever the truth was about her having remained in Ireland since returning last autumn, Kathleen would board *Titanic* in the morning along with her niece and twelve others from the parish and without a husband. Marriage could wait. For now, she was more concerned about getting a good night's sleep.

CHAPTER 7

RMS Titanic
April 10, 1912

The journey from Southampton to Queenstown, *Titanic*'s final embarkation stop before heading out into the vast reaches of the Atlantic, passed smoothly enough—with the exception of the *New York* pulling loose from her moorings and nearly causing a collision with *Titanic* before she had even sailed out of Southampton harbor. This caused a few heart-stopping moments among the passengers and crew, who saw it all from their vantage points on the decks. For the ship's financiers and those in positions of authority and influence within the White Star Line, it was a near disaster.

Returning to his dormitory to have a quick wash before the life jacket inspection and preparations for dinner service, Harry stopped just short of the Scotland Road passageway as he saw two men deep in conversation at the top of the D Deck staircase. He recognized them as Mr. Ismay of the White Star Line and Thomas Andrews, the ship's designer. Harry leaned against the wall of the corridor, which ran at right angles to the staircase, making sure he was well out of their sight. He listened carefully. They were discussing the incident with the *New York* and sharing a much-needed smoke out of sight and earshot of their first-class passengers.

"Bloody hell, Bruce, that was a bit too close for comfort. There can't have been four feet between them before that tug pushed her aft."

Andrews rubbed his hand anxiously through his hair and loosened his tie as Harry observed from his vantage point. He seemed to Harry to be a nervy man, although no wonder, Harry thought, when the ship he'd spent the last few years designing had almost been grounded within minutes of raising its anchor.

"My God, man, imagine the shame if we'd had a bloody collision in Southampton harbor," Mr. Ismay replied, taking a long drag from his cigarette. "We wouldn't have had much of a maiden voyage to celebrate then, would we, never mind breaking speed records for crossing the Atlantic."

Andrews nodded in agreement. "We'd have been financially ruined, never mind the field day the press would have had. Things like this just can't be allowed to happen. Not on *this* ship. Not on *this* voyage."

"Well, let's just consider it a very fortunate escape from an untimely and embarrassing disaster then," Mr. Ismay whispered, lowering his voice as two officers walked past them, "and let's get on with the business of making sure this ship lives up to its billing for the rest of the journey. We're already behind schedule for our stop in Cherbourg. I'm going up to the bridge to encourage Captain Smith to increase the speed."

The two men separated then, Andrews heading up the companionway corridor, Ismay taking the elevator to the boat deck.

Harry already felt strangely at home on *Titanic*. He was impressed with the facilities provided for the third-class passengers, which were far superior to any he had encountered before.

He was perfectly happy to work here and settled into his duties easily, despite the second- and first-class stewards' taunts to the third-class stewards that if they weren't careful down there among the rats and the nit-infested, clap-riddled steerage folk, they'd be arriving in New York with a lot more than their duffel bags.

He was minding his own business and setting out the cutlery for dinner when a familiar voice behind him made him jump.

"Well, Lucky Harry strikes again."

Lucky Harry was a nickname he'd been given by some of the other lads he knew in Southampton due to the endless amounts of good fortune he had whenever they played a game of cards. He recognized the voice right away.

"Billy? What the hell are you doin' down here? You nearly gave me a heart attack." He carried on laying out his place settings. "I thought you were too posh now to be slummin' it down 'ere with us *steerage* lot. You'd better get back upstairs before you catch something!"

Billy laughed. "Yeah, I am too posh. But I need you to come and help me upstairs. We've stewards laid up and are short of hands to help out with evenin' dinner. The officers are panicking that the dinner service will be late, and they don't want people to start complainin' before we've even got to Ireland. I suggested a few names to the officers to come and help, and you're one of 'em."

Harry thought his friend was pulling his leg, being partial to a practical joke as he was. "Ah, bugger off, Billy. You're 'avin me on. Get lost, will ya, I've a proper job to do."

"I'm not kiddin'. Honestly. They want you to come up now. I've a first-class uniform all ready for you."

After a little more cajoling, Harry was convinced and left

what he was doing to go with Billy up the staircase to D Deck, where the first-class dining saloon was. He quite liked the idea of the all-white uniform worn by the first-class stewards.

"Oh, and I forgot to tell ya," Billy added as they ran up the stairs two at a time, "there's some fancy woman fussin' about 'er dog upstairs. She needs someone to take it for a walk and I thought you might be able to help 'er out."

Harry stopped. "So, that's what you really got me up here for? I can't believe I fell for it."

Billy slapped his friend on the back. "Ah, stop moanin', will ya. I thought you might like a snoop around up here, and the ladies aren't bad-lookin' either, y'know. Thought you might like to check out some new girlfriend material, seeing as how you've tried just about every lass in Southampton and scared her off with your rubbish chat-up lines and your interfering mother."

Harry laughed, despite his annoyance that Billy had tricked him. He actually did quite fancy having a look around the first-class decks, and if it meant taking someone's dog for a walk to do it, then what the hell?

Vivienne Walker-Brown reclined on a deck chair, enjoying the warmth of the late afternoon sun on her petite face and the feel of the gentle sea breeze in her smooth, dark hair. She was glad she had tied it up loosely, having noticed how quickly the dampness and salt in the air could wreak havoc on a hairstyle. Edmund, her Pekingese dog, sat quietly under the chair, enjoying the same warmth on his face and the same sea breeze in his dark fur. Robert, her fiancé, had gone belowdecks to fetch her fur stole, her neck being a little too chilly and threatening to give her a nasty cold. He returned quickly and handed her the garment.

"Now, darling, you can sit here as long as you like without worrying about catching a chill," he announced, ignoring the dog, which had curled its lip slightly at him. Robert Isaacs didn't care for the animal at all. He would have quite liked to give it a sharp kick with the toe of his shoe but resisted and sat down in the seat next to Vivienne's. "Anyway, it will be time for dinner soon. I think the bugler calls at seven P.M. sharp."

Vivienne wrapped the stole around her neck, snuggling into the instant warmth it provided. "Well, I have to wait for our dog walker to arrive first," she said curtly, "bugler or not. They've gone to see if it might be possible to hire a boy from the steerage crew. I doubt they'll miss one steward at dinner. They probably have to make the meals for themselves down there anyway!" She laughed at her own joke. "Ah, this must be him now," she exclaimed, relieved to see the first-class steward she had spoken to about her predicament walking toward her with another young man. He introduced him as Harry Walsh, a reliable crew member who would attend to the needs of her dog and anything else she might require assistance with.

"Wonderful," she enthused, standing up to shake the man's hand. "Edmund needs his daily constitutional, you know, just the same as we do. Don't you, sweetheart?" The dog raised its head and patted its tail enthusiastically on the deck. "And since my aide is suffering with the seasickness, we had to find an alternative arrangement, didn't we, Edmund? Yes we did, didn't we?"

Robert winced at the ridiculous affectations Vivienne added whenever she addressed the dog, as if it were a small child who might one day talk back to her. The raised eyebrows between the two stewards didn't go unnoticed by him.

"Well, I'll leave you to it then," the first-class steward said, turning to depart. "I must go and start preparing for evening dinner service. It wouldn't do to keep the first-class passengers waiting now, would it! Good day to you."

Vivienne laughed at the joke. "Oh, yes. Very good." She turned to the other steward. "Right then, Mr. . . ."

"Walsh," Harry prompted, already taking a dislike to the woman and her dog. "Harry Walsh."

"Yes, indeed. Well, Walsh, Edmund would be very happy if you could take him twice around the ship . . . Of course, strictly speaking, he should be walked on the poop deck, along with the kennel dogs," she continued in a whisper, passing the dog's lead to Harry, "but I don't think we need to worry ourselves with minor details such as that, do we? I wouldn't want him catching anything." She shuddered in mock alarm. "The exercise is good for his legs, you know. I would take him myself but we shall be called to dinner soon and I have some business to attend to with my ladies. Come along then, Robert, I shall die of thirst if I don't have a gin and tonic before dinner."

Robert gave Harry a simpering half smile before following his fiancée inside to the reception area at the bottom of the Grand Staircase, where predinner drinks were being served.

For his own part, Harry was quite pleased to have the opportunity to stroll around the first-class decks and get a proper look at the luxury that had been boasted about by the ship's designers. He also knew his mother would be very keen to hear all about how the other half lived on board, so he paid attention as he walked along, the small dog trotting beside him.

It was everything he had imagined it would be, and more. From the boat deck, standing between the first and second funnels, he could look right down through the massive wrought-iron-and-glass-domed skylight onto the spectacle of the Grand

Staircase, which swept in graceful arcs to the lounge and beyond, all the way down to E Deck. He watched the passengers descending the staircase, dressed in their finest dinner outfits. Others stopped at the bottom of the first tier of steps, greeting one another before congregating in comfortable-looking chairs at round mahogany tables, where they were served drinks before dinner.

On the promenade deck a similar scene of opulence was repeated. Harry gazed into the ostentatious gentlemen-only smoking room, admiring its sumptuous leather chairs and heavy wooden paneling. Farther along the deck, he caught sight of the Palm Court, with its delicate wicker chairs and dainty vases of flowers. He glanced into the reading and writing room as he strolled past, the huge bow window affording him a good look at the interior, painted in elegant white, luxurious curtains draped around the windows, and a fire blazing in the center of the room. This room alone was bigger than the entire downstairs of his house.

As he strolled, he passed a bellboy walking a miniature dog. It had never occurred to Harry that people might take their pet dogs on a trip across the Atlantic, but as he was starting to realize, there was very little about this ship and its occupants that didn't surprise him.

Taking a second circuit of the decks, as instructed, he passed the rows of lifeboats that hung, covered in their white tarpaulins, suspended on ropes from the huge steel davits. They were a strange, awkward, bulky sight amid all the luxury and elegance. Harry was almost surprised that they hadn't been made from a dark mahogany and embossed with ornate carvings to be more in keeping with the opulence of their surroundings.

Walking down onto the port side, he almost forgot he was

on a ship, almost forgot entirely about the silly little dog trotting along behind him, so caught up was he in the elegant atmosphere of the place. The delicate sound of a piano drifted
across the starboard side of the ship, and the gentle melodies
of a string quartet came from the port side. Nothing had been
overlooked; the passengers were even entertained and soothed
as they walked their dogs or strolled with parasols or sat about
with their aperitifs and their cigarette holders.

Harry was glad Billy had given him the chance to see all this.
Even though he'd been impressed with the standard of accommodation given to the steerage passengers, the furnishings of
the general room and the third-class dining saloon now seemed
unnecessarily sparse when compared to this grandeur. Never
in his life had Harry seen such a stark demarcation of class in
one place, and for all of its jaw-dropping elegance, it turned his
stomach.

His mother was right; he would take extra-special care of his
steerage passengers now and do everything he could to make
their journey as pleasant as possible. The first-class toffs and
their silly little dogs could get well and truly stuffed.

WHITE STAR LINE

ROYAL AND UNITED STATES MAIL STEAMERS.

ISMAY, IMRIE & CO.

WHITE STAR LINE

OCEANIC STEAM NAVIGATION COMPANY, LIMITED, OF GREAT BRITAIN.
THIRD CLASS (Steerage) PASSENGER'S CONTRACT TICKET.

CHAPTER 8

Private Journal of Maggie Murphy
RMS *Titanic, April 11, 1912*
Day 1 at sea

We are finally sailing! I don't think there are enough words to describe this amazing ship or how it feels to be floating on top of the ocean (a fact I don't like to think about too often)—but I will try!

First, I'll explain how we came to be here.

Our day started very early this morning, Aunt Kathleen rousing us all with a brusque shake of the shoulders or a hard rap on the door. I'm used to her no-nonsense ways—some of the others aren't, and I don't think they took to the rude awakening too well.

When we were all up and dressed, we attended Mass in St. Colman's Cathedral. After Peggy's tale of the odd stranger, I paid more attention than usual to the prayers. The priest offered a special blessing to those in the congregation who would be departing Irish shores that day. There were many, many more than our fourteen; in fact, almost the entire congregation seemed to be heading to America.

It was then time to assemble at the White Star Line wharf at the Deepwater Quay, where we had to wait for a tender boat to take us out to Titanic, which was anchored some miles offshore at Roches Point. I asked Jack Brennan why we had to take one boat to get to another, and a friendly gentleman standing nearby explained that Queenstown harbor isn't wide enough, deep enough, or equipped with the right facilities to manage such an enormous ship as Titanic. I told him I thought the harbor looked very big. He laughed and said it still wasn't big enough. He wished me a pleasant journey and went to join a pretty lady who wore a hat twice the size of Peggy's. I saw Peggy admiring the hat and adjusting her own. I think she might care for that silly hat of hers more than she cares for her own brothers back home!

We stood for a while among the other passengers outside the offices of James Scott & Company, shipping agents. I enjoyed listening to the conversations, hearing accents from other parts of Ireland that I haven't heard before and watching people arrive from the train station or by cart and gather, with the rest of us, on the wharf side. Some were dressed like us, others in finer clothing and with grander luggage. I thought it funny that we would all sail on the same ship, no matter how battered our trunks or how scuffed our boots.

Queenstown harbor was a much nicer sight in the bright morning sunshine than it had been the previous night. The colorful houses lining the seafront looked pretty, and we *could see the cathedral we had just prayed in standing out on the skyline. Although we were all still a bit jittery and anxious now to get going, there was a much happier mood about us. Dear God, nothing could be worse than that terrible maudlin feeling that had hung about us all a day earlier. Katie said that she feels so far away from home now that it's almost impossible to be sad about it. I think I know what she means.*

The two tenders, Ireland and America, were moored alongside the wharf. They were nice-looking boats themselves. We stood together, the fourteen of us, some talking, some thinking of home, and some, like me, watching the piles and piles of mailbags being loaded onto the boats, the red flags of the White Star Line and the colorful bunting fluttering in the breeze. It must have been quite a spectacle for the newspaper reporters and the crowds who had gathered to see people off.

It was a bit of a struggle to get us all and our luggage aboard the tender America, but once on board we huddled around the front of the boat, I think it is called the bow. It felt a bit odd swaying from side to side as the boat rocked in the water. We had to wait for a while as a late-running train from Cork had just arrived carrying more passengers. I thought how lucky they were not to have missed the tenders, or Titanic itself for that matter! Ellen Joyce went a bit green while we stood there—I think she was struggling not to get sick.

As we waited for the delayed passengers, a young photographer from one of the local papers climbed from the other tender, Ireland, onto ours, saying it would give a better viewpoint for his pictures. I thought him a bit reckless jumping from one boat to the other; I hope his pictures are worth the risk of falling overboard!

All the passengers seemed to be in good spirits. We talked among ourselves and to strangers, sharing stories of the journeys we'd already made and talking about where we were headed to in America. I spoke to a friendly, nervy-looking girl who told me she was also from Mayo. We didn't know of each other or our families. She was traveling alone to join her five brothers who were already in America. I said she should look out for me on board the ship and to come and chat or play cards if she was feeling lonely.

"All one hundred and thirteen third-class aboard, sir," I heard someone call.

With Ireland in front, the two tender boats left the wharf then, chugging back along the waterfront of Queenstown, passing the White Star Wharf again. We each blessed ourselves with the sign of the cross as we sailed past the cathedral, and a tall man standing just near to me began to play "A Nation Once Again" on his uilleann pipes. He played well, and the gathered passengers sang along and clapped when he finished. He smiled at me and then played "Erin's Lament," a sadder tune that made some people cry. I didn't look at any of our group, afraid that I would take to weeping again if I did.

As we moved farther away from the wharf, the boat became quieter. The men shuffled their feet, and the women cuddled their children against them or stared into the distance. Everyone had their own private thoughts at that moment; mine were of Séamus and the time we had danced *at Maura and Jack Brennan's wedding. I wondered if he was thinking of me at all.*

The boats then turned a bend in the channel, and that was when we saw her.

All that could be heard were gasps. The piper stopped his playing altogether.

Not one person spoke, stunned into silence by the towering mass of this ship that was anchored in the waters before us. I have never seen, and doubt that I will ever see again, a sight so astonishing.

Some of our group, who have traveled on steam liners before, were less impressed than the rest of us, who have rarely seen a rowboat on Lough Conn, but I even heard Aunt Kathleen comment on how large and magnificent the ship appeared.

As our now tiny tender pulled alongside the wall of steel, a door opened in the side of the ship and a gangplank was lowered. At the top of the gangplank were the ticket inspectors and the doctors who carried out the health inspections. Not one of us was able to stop ourselves from craning our necks to take in the height of the decks and the masts soaring high, high into the clouds above. I didn't want to look down, didn't want to see the swell of the ocean under my feet.

There was a delay in the inspection line, and I heard another passenger tell her friend that a girl up ahead had a rash and was being refused entry. Then I saw who the person was; it was the Mayo girl I had spoken to on the wharf, the girl who was going to join her brothers. As she walked back down the gangplank, sobbing, I heard a crew member explain to her that she would have to travel on another ship when her rash was healed. "The Celtic *sails tomorrow, miss, and the* Oceanic *next week. A few days won't make much of a difference." I wanted to call to her but didn't even know her name. My heart was so sorry for her, and I hope she can board the* Celtic *tomorrow.*

We waited more anxiously then for our own inspections, wondering what would happen if one of us was turned away. As we waited, I saw a man hiding among the mailbags to be taken back to Queenstown—a stoker or a boiler man, judging by his dress and the muck on his face. I'd noticed him walking off Titanic *and covering himself with the gray mailbags. I saw him and I'm certain that he saw me. He had the fear of God in his eyes—like a man who was running away from something. Maybe he is in trouble. When I watched the tender chug back to the quayside, I wondered what the man was running from and hoped that it was for good reason he didn't want to sail to New York.*

The doctors eventually examined our eyes and our hair and checked our faces and hands. All fourteen of us passed with a clean bill of health, and finally, one by one, we stepped onto the deck of the ship which would take us to America.

The passengers who had already boarded in England and France watched us from the decks above and from benches and seating areas scattered around the deck we stood on. We were the new arrivals. I felt as though we had arrived late to a grand party. These people had already been aboard for a day and looked comfortable in their surroundings. An old lady smiled at me as we followed a steward who was to show us to our cabins. I smiled back and swapped my trunk into my right hand, the left growing tired of the weight. The steward noticed.

"Let me take that for you, miss," he said, taking the trunk from me. "You've probably carried it far enough already."

I smiled, relieved to no longer have it banging against my shins, which were black and blue by now from heaving it across half of Ireland. The steward had a kind face, and I noticed the crew member badge on his arm. Number 23, whatever that meant.

Our cabins are quite fine. Ours is number 115. There are four beds; two bunk beds. Me and Peggy have the two top bunks, and Aunt Kathleen and Katie have the two bottom ones. They all have proper mattresses and are as comfortable as any bed I have ever slept in. There is a hand wash basin in the cabin itself with two White Star Line hand towels hanging from silver hooks on either side. There is even a bar of White Star Line soap for us to use! When we were settled, the steward, Harry is his name, showed us where the life jackets were kept and took us up to see one of the sixteen lifeboats. Pat said the lifeboat was almost as big as the tender we had just left and how could anyone imagine that a ship could be built that was big enough to hold sixteen of them? Pat is like a child walking around this ship; he has the poor steward's ear half bent off by asking so many questions about it!

We set sail at 1:30 P.M. according to Ellen's gleaming gold watch, which she takes out to tell the time at every possible opportunity. The thrust of the engines sent a shudder through my bones and a steady vibration through the wooden benches we were sitting on in the general room. Realizing we were setting sail, everyone rushed back out to the deck, eager to watch, to remember the moment when we departed Ireland's shores.

We stood for a long while at the white railings at the stern of the ship, silently watching the swell of the ocean, each crashing wave taking us farther away from everyone we loved and everything we knew.

The man with the uilleann pipes stood next to me for a good while, but neither of us spoke. "She's a mighty fine land," he said eventually, "you should be very proud to have known her, wherever life might take you."

I turned to him. "Yes," I said. "Yes, I am. Very proud indeed." I remember feeling for the precious packet of letters in my coat pocket, still bound by their packaging and string. Grasping them and my rosary beads, I said a silent prayer.

Titanic followed the coastline of Ireland for the rest of the afternoon, past the Old Head of Kinsale and on, following the cliffs and the mountains. We returned to our cabins now and again, coming back up to the deck occasionally to check whether land was still in sight. The sun was just beginning to dip in the sky as Titanic passed the final lighthouse. Aunt Kathleen told me it is known as "Ireland's Teardrop" on account of it being the last sight of Ireland for those emigrating to America. I told her I thought that was a terrible, sad name. It is the right name, all the same, because I could not stop the tears then as Titanic turned to head out across the ocean, and the last part of Ireland faded into the sea mist and was obscured from view.

PART TWO

Received April

NO_____ CK_____   TIME RECEIVED_____

TO

Jules E. Brutalom 31 East 27th St Nyk: Safe picked
up by Carpathia don't worry. Dorothy.

Marconigram message sent from Miss Dorothy Gibson,
Carpathia, to Julie [Jules E. Brutalom] on April
18, 1912

CHAPTER 9

Cass County, Illinois
April 21, 1982

In the dimly lit dusty attic in her great-grandmother's house, Grace rummaged among cardboard boxes and plastic bags, moving things to one side only to discover yet more boxes hidden behind the first layer. Nothing was labeled; there was no sense of organization. In fact, there was a distinct sense of disorganization. She leaned back on her heels, sighed, and placed her hands on her hips, glancing from one end of the attic to the other. It stretched across the length of the house and was littered with unwanted junk accumulated over the course of a lifetime.

She'd already been looking for over an hour, and still the small black case she was searching for would not reveal itself. *This is impossible,* she thought, jumping at the sensation of a cobweb brushing against her arm. *Maybe, after all these years, this case doesn't want to be found.*

Since the night of her birthday party, Grace had been unable to think about anything other than Maggie and *Titanic.* Since Maggie had opened up to her about the events of that night, Grace found it incredible that her great-grandmother had sailed on that iconic ship and had survived such an awful tragedy. So many people—historians, writers, documentary makers—had wondered what life must have been like on board and what it was like to have experienced the terror that occurred four days into the voyage.

Grace remembered doing a school project about the disaster when she was nine years old. She remembered the faces of the strange, ghostly-looking people in the black-and-white photographs of old newspaper articles. She remembered the childish pictures she had drawn of the disaster: a big black ship with one of the funnels broken and a small hole in one side. She wasn't good at drawing people, so there weren't any in her picture. Perhaps that had been when her mother had mentioned to her that her great-nana was on *Titanic*. She recalled how she had been so insistent that Grace must never ask Maggie about it. Nobody had spoken of it since.

When Maggie had told her the entire, incredible story, had explained her unbearable sadness and her inability to accept what had happened, Grace had begun to understand why she'd wanted to completely eradicate something so traumatic from her life.

"Why would God have spared me," Maggie had said, "an insignificant young girl from Ireland, when so many others drowned?"

If it was never spoken about, she'd explained, perhaps she would be able to distance herself from *Titanic* and simply see it—as thousands of people all over the world did—as an event that was fascinating in its telling and tragic in its reality. Maybe then she would be able to forget that she was on board; that she was one of the many hundreds of people involved.

"Are you sure it's a *black* case I'm looking for?" Grace shouted down the small hole in the attic floor that she had clambered through earlier that morning. "I can't seem to find it anywhere." As much as she wanted to find the case, it was getting hot and claustrophobic in the attic and Grace was thirsty.

She could hear Maggie pottering about in the kitchen underneath, teaspoons clattering on teacups, the cookie tin being opened. She imagined Maggie placing one of her paper doilies carefully onto a china plate, arranging the biscuits (which she insisted on calling them out of loyalty to her Irish roots) in a perfect overlapping circle. It was a "thing" of Maggie's, her "biscuit" display, an almost unreasonable amount of attention being paid to a seemingly trivial activity. But Maggie took pride in many things in life, and providing her guests with a nice pot of tea and a plate of uniformly arranged biscuits on a china plate was one of them.

"Yes, dear," she shouted back up, the projection of her voice causing her to cough slightly. "A small black case. About the size of a pillow. It's probably near the back. Underneath a load of your great-grandfather's old junk."

You don't say.

Just as she was about to give up and go down the stepladder for a tea break, Grace caught the slightest glimpse of a solid black corner jutting out between two fallen boxes. She clambered over to it, the ache in her stooped back and the pain in her knees suddenly forgotten. Her heart raced as she pushed the heavy boxes to one side and, grabbing the edge, pulled the small black case out onto the bare boards. It was about the size of a pillow.

The hairs stood up on the back of her neck. She could hear the blood rushing through her ears, her heart hammering in her chest. *Yes,* she thought, *yes. This is it!* She swept her fingers across the top of the case, sending a shower of dust motes whirling into the air around her, blurring her vision temporarily and making her cough.

As the dust settled, she saw what she had been searching for. A luggage label bearing the name *Maggie Murphy* and the address *North Ashland Avenue, Chicago*.

"I have it, Maggie!" she called, coughing again in the dust. "I've found it!" Her voice was shrill with excitement. Her great-grandmother didn't respond. "I'm coming down; you can pour the tea."

Maggie placed the case carefully on her lap. She sat for a moment, closing her eyes, lost in the distant memories of her life. The small clock on the mantelpiece struck eleven, a bird sang from the old blackberry bush in the garden, a fly buzzed annoyingly in the hallway, and dust danced in the shaft of sunlight streaming in through the window. Nothing else moved for those few quiet moments. Grace hardly dared breathe.

"I shouldn't have it, really," Maggie said softly, rubbing her hand across the top of the case. "It's ridiculous now when I think about it, the ship sinking and me and Peggy going back for her hat. We didn't realize how bad it was, though, you see, Grace; we didn't think she would go down. It was only when we got back to the cabin that I took my coat and suitcase. I don't even remember holding this little case. But I must have. All that time, it must have been in my hand." She sat silently again then, as she prepared herself to face her past.

"Do you remember what's in it, Maggie?" Grace asked.

Her great-grandmother looked at her, a softness, a sadness in her eyes. "I do, Grace. I do. Even after all these years."

Grace watched quietly as Maggie fiddled with the rusted fastenings, her frail hands shaking more than usual, the latches grating and groaning but refusing to open. Those few moments felt like hours to Grace; the small black case like a barrier, a dam against which a deluge of memories had strained for decades and that now threatened to engulf her great-grandmother as soon as it released its secrets and revealed its history.

"Are you absolutely sure you want to do this?" Grace asked tentatively, afraid that opening the case might have a bigger impact on their lives than either of them had anticipated.

Maggie looked at her. "No, I'm not sure at all. But we're here now, aren't we? And I don't know about you, but I'm certainly not going to put this case back up in that stuffy old attic without seeing what's inside."

Finally the fastenings clicked open. Gently, Maggie lifted the lid, emitting a tiny, barely audible gasp as her eyes settled on the contents.

It was a moment Grace would never forget, watching this dignified old lady whom she loved so much, as she stared into a small case she'd last seen when only a girl. A lifetime of memories flooded Maggie's lined face; a lifetime of forgetting was washed away. It was a moment of silent reflection; a moment laced with poignancy.

Maggie lifted her head, resting it against the back of the chair, a sense of release washing over her, the dreadful burden of carrying this tragedy with her for all these years seeming to lift from her small shoulders.

Grace sat quietly in the chair opposite, rubbing her fingers over the rough, plum-colored upholstery, digging her nails into the edges of the intricate pattern, just as she had done since she could first remember coming to this house as a small child. She almost felt uncomfortable now, as if she were intruding on a very private moment. As she watched Maggie, the magnitude of her story hit Grace fully for the first time. *She had been on* Titanic. She had watched that great ship sink into an icy sea. She had heard the screams and terror of a thousand voices and had lost everything except for the contents of that small, insignificant case and the clothes on her back. It struck Grace that this was no longer about a story to reignite her journalism career; this was real life, and she was watching it happen in front of her very eyes.

From the case, Maggie began to lift out the items, caressing and studying each one as if it were the most precious of treasures. A simple steel hair comb, a handled mirror, an emerald-colored brooch, a pair of black cotton gloves, a Bible, a set of rosary beads and a bottle of holy water, a green third-class health inspection certificate, a menu card, a small book, and a bundle of what looked like newspaper clippings. Memories flashed across Maggie's mind, each item provoking a remembered conversation, a place, or a person.

Maggie held her *Titanic* boarding ticket for a good while, rubbing gently at the fragile paper with her fingers. She closed her eyes and was immediately transported back to the clattering hooves of the horses as they rode into the streets of Castlebar. She remembered walking into Mr. Durcan's office on Main Street to collect their tickets. She recalled Tom Durcan as a stout, middle-aged man with a whiskery mustache and small, shifty eyes. He'd smiled at her and winked as he handed the tickets to her aunt. "She's a beauty," he'd whispered to her. "Forty ton of potatoes on board, they say, and no less than forty thousand eggs. Ye certainly won't be starvin', that's for sure."

Her eyes had widened at the sheer thought of that many eggs, and she'd said something about looking forward to being among the first to sail on the ship before her aunt had bustled her out of the office saying if they stood around chattering all morning, *Titanic* would sail without them and then they wouldn't be eating a one of those eggs, let alone forty thousand. She remembered herself and Peggy admiring their tickets with the impressive picture of *Titanic* on the front; remembered how her heart had sunk to know that she was looking at the ticket that would take her away from Séamus. Peggy had been excited to note that their tickets were sequential, hers being 330923 and Maggie's 330924. How inconsequential that ticket number had turned out to be.

"Not much really, is it, to start a new life," Maggie said now, turning the items over in her hands. "Not much at all. Of course, the rest of my things were in my aunt's larger case, and we know where that is now. We kept the trunks under the bunk beds, but I kept my personal possessions in here, you know, for safekeeping. I kept this case at the bottom of my bed with my coat. There were some letters that I kept in my coat pocket. It's a shame I didn't keep them in here, I suppose."

Grace moved over to her and knelt at Maggie's side, placing a hand on hers. "Do you mind if I look?"

"Of course not. It's of no use to me now, is it?"

Grace studied everything carefully, asking Maggie about the story behind each item and unwrapping the bundle of newspaper clippings. It was an archivist's dream.

"Oh, my goodness, Maggie, this is amazing. These are actual newspapers from the time. Look, the *New York Herald*, April sixteenth, 1912." Grace read the headline. THE TITANIC SINKS WITH 1800 ON BOARD. ONLY 675, MOSTLY WOMEN AND CHILDREN, SAVED.

They sat for a while then, poring over the fragile, yellowed newspapers.

"It was the nurses at St. Vincent's Hospital in New York," Maggie explained. "They'd kept all the newspapers to follow the story. Of course, the papers got it all wrong at first, you know, reporting that *Titanic* was sailing back to Belfast for repairs. Look." She pointed to another headline, reading it out loud: " '*Titanic*'s passengers all rescued.' And look at this one from the *Washington Times*: 'Liner *Titanic* kept afloat by watertight compartments. Being towed into Halifax, N.S.' They didn't know we were all drowning, you see." She paused for a moment as they studied some more of the incredible newspaper headlines. "And look, here I am being quoted by the reporters who came to talk to us in the hospital."

Grace studied the page where her great-grandmother's words were quoted. "Wow, Maggie. This is amazing!"

"One of the nurses gave most of these to me when I left the hospital," Maggie continued. "She said I might want to keep them. She said that *Titanic* would still be talked about in a hundred years' time. I thought she was joking."

She paused then as she handed a small black notebook to Grace. "I used to fancy myself a bit of a writer too, you know."

"What is it?" Grace asked, turning the book over in her hands and flicking through the pages.

"It's my journal. I started to write it the night we got to Queenstown. A friend gave me the idea. I thought I might like to show it to my aunt Mary when we arrived in Chicago; thought I might sit with my children one day and tell them all about the fantastic ship I had sailed to America on. I was writing an entry when we hit the iceberg. You can even see the shudder in my handwriting. Look."

Maggie pointed to a page about halfway through the book: *there'll be quite a party planned for our arrival at the docks in New York I should think. The other three are already fast asleep. I should probably turn out the light soon and get some slee—*

There was indeed a definite jerk in the handwriting. The rest of the page was blank.

"Maggie, this is incredible. I just can't take it all in. How do you feel seeing all these things again now?"

Maggie sat and thought for a moment.

"D'you know something? I thought I would feel sadness. But I don't. I think I finished with all my sadness a long time ago. Now? Now, I guess I feel comforted by seeing these things. It's just a shame about the letters. I'd have liked to see them again."

Grace stood up then to stretch her legs and walked over to the window. She liked to watch the birds that always flocked to the feeders and nesting boxes dotted around Maggie's garden. "What were the letters, by the way?"

"Ah, now that's a different matter altogether. That does make me feel a little sad."

"Why? What were they?"

Maggie laughed to herself. "They were from my boyfriend. I left him in Ireland. He wasn't so good with his words, but he gave me a packet of letters the morning I left our village. I remember him saying it would mean I didn't have to wait on any deliveries, that I could read a letter from him whenever I wanted to. He told me he'd written fourteen letters, one for each month we'd courted. I'd only read four of them. I thought I should wait until I reached America to read the rest, thinking that I might read one a month, as if he'd actually just sent it to me. That way I could be reminded of him whenever I was missing him the most." She paused then, remembering him: his gentle manner, his soft eyes, his beautiful red hair. "We used to meet under a cherry blossom tree after market on a Wednesday morning. It was a nice arrangement." She smiled to herself.

"So what happened to the letters?"

"I lost them. They were in my coat pocket, you see, and I have no idea what happened to it. I had it on when I got into the lifeboat and it was gone when I left the hospital. I vaguely remember giving it to a child, to try to keep her warm, and that a well-to-do lady who was on the lifeboat with me gave me her overcoat because I was shivering so much with the cold. She was a Ziegfeld star—a singer, I think—Vera or Violet or something; I can't remember her name now. Anyway, it was all so confusing, you know, trying to track people down, trying to find out if they had survived or gone down with the ship. I'm sure nobody paid much attention to a simple black coat. I've often wondered what those other letters said. It would be nice to know."

Grace waited for a moment before asking, "And did you ever write to him again? Your boyfriend? You know, afterward?"

"Yes, I did. Once or twice. He only wrote back once, though." A gentle smile crossed Maggie's lips as she remembered him, but Grace sensed that she didn't to want to dwell on this.

"And did you never go back to Ireland?"

"No, I didn't." Maggie spoke quietly, as though this were the hardest thing to say. "I never wanted to set foot on a ship again after that terrible night. And I felt so guilty, you know. Why had I survived when so many others, even tiny little babies, had died? I knew I could never go back home, knowing the sadness there would be there and knowing that I escaped with my life while I had watched so many others die." She paused for a moment, collecting her thoughts. "I was sailing to America to start a new life, and in a funny way, that was the only way I could carry on after *Titanic*, with a new life. The girl who had left Ireland was gone to the bottom of the ocean with the rest of them. I had to start over. Start again. Of course, the family knew about *Titanic*, but I never wanted to talk about it. I just wanted to forget."

The two sat then for a good while longer, Maggie leafing absentmindedly through the newspaper clippings and touching her belongings, Grace reading through the journal. There was no need for either of them to talk. Eventually, the clock on the mantelpiece chimed noon, the first chime startling them both and causing them to laugh.

Grace got up and walked into the kitchen. "Are you ready for another cup of tea yet? I think we could both do with one."

Maggie looked up and smiled. "Yes, dear. That would be lovely. And, Grace . . ."

"Yeah?" Grace popped her head back around the doorframe.

"Have you called that newspaper editor of yours yet?"

"Not yet."

"Well, you should, y'know. I think he might just be interested in my little story. Do you?"

She winked at her great-granddaughter and started to put everything back into her small case. She imagined, for a moment, a small packet of letters, wrapped in brown paper and tied up with a fraying piece of string, and wondered where they had gone that night. She thought about the man who had written them.

"What day of the week is it, Grace?"

"Wednesday," Grace shouted back over the sound of the kettle boiling. "Why?"

Maggie smiled to herself. "No reason. I just wondered."

CHAPTER 10

New York
April 11, 1912

Frances Kenny placed her empty teacup carefully on the saucer and glanced at the clock on the mantelpiece, the rhythmic *tick, tick, tick* a comforting constant in her perfectly ordered, peaceful home. If she had the hours of time difference correct, Katie would be sailing by now. Frances wondered how her young sister was feeling, having never been on an ocean liner before.

She looked into her teacup, a cursory glance over the scattered leaves, showing, she noted with relief, nothing remarkable. Reading the tea leaves was a tradition in their family. She remembered her grandmother pointing out the vague patterns and images to her. It had entranced Frances as an impressionable young child, although she was never quite sure whether her granny was pulling her leg or could actually foresee the things she claimed to see in the leaves. As she had grown up and witnessed various predictions come true, Frances had started to take reading the tea leaves more seriously, and she took pride in reading them herself now. She had yet to predict anything successfully and often wished she had paid more attention to her granny's mutterings.

She stood up to look in the large mirror over the fireplace while she fiddled with the tiny buttons on the high collar of her blouse. She found the tightness around her throat mildly uncomfortable, leaving the very last buttons until it was time to go. She considered her reflection in the mirror; she looked a little tired, older than her thirty-four years. She wondered how she would look to Katie and how Katie would look to her now, twenty-four years old and no doubt with an enviable lust for life and an even more enviable healthy complexion, both of which came from a life spent outdoors.

Carrying her breakfast things into the small kitchen of her one-bedroom East Side apartment, Frances filled the sink to rinse them. As she swirled the soapy water around with the dishcloth, washing her teacup, saucer, bowl, plate, and spoon methodically, it occurred to her that Katie might not have boarded the ship at all. She'd sent money home to Ireland once before for Katie's passage, but, by all accounts, their parents had decided to spend the money on a cow rather than on the intended ticket to America. The regular discussions about Katie coming to America to join her sister had lessened in the intervening months. It was only recently, when several others from Ballysheen, including her good friends Peggy and Maggie, had begun to purchase their tickets, that Katie's interest had surfaced again.

The two sisters had exchanged letters regularly over the years, Frances enjoying hearing the news from home and Katie enjoying Frances's descriptions of her life in America. *Tell me about the motorcars,* she would ask, in her own letters, *and the buildings that reach into the sky. And is it really true that the theaters on Broadway can seat thousands of people at a time?*

The latest letter from Katie had arrived just a few months ago, stating that she would like to be able to travel over with the others from Ballysheen, it seeming like a good opportunity to be among friends rather than make the long journey all on her own. Of course, Frances had sent the money immediately, including with it a note to Katie and their mother assuring them both that she would meet Katie at the docks in New York. *I am, after all, quite keen to see this "Titanic" for myself,* she'd written. As a postscript, and fearing that they might spend the money on another cow instead, she'd emphasized that Katie should buy the ticket from the local shipping agent in Castlebar as soon as possible.

Assuming Katie *was* on board with the Ballysheen group, Frances imagined that she would be quite excited. With so many familiar faces from home around her, she was sure that any doubts and anxieties about the journey, or about leaving behind the three younger brothers whom Katie adored, would be soon forgotten. For her own part, Frances was very much looking forward to seeing her beloved sister again. It had been more than three years since she had seen her last, before she had made the trip across the Atlantic herself. Traveling on that occasion with her friend Maura Byrne, she had made a quiet, discreet departure from Ballysheen. Nobody even knew the name of the ship they were to sail on; it had never occurred to anyone to ask. How different Katie's experience would have been, leaving amid such a fuss and flurry as so many homes waved off a loved one to sail on the most celebrated ship ever built, a ship whose name *everyone* knew.

Frances pictured her sister now, sure that she would make the most of every minute on board. Unlike her own reserved, practical self, Katie was a confident, impulsive girl with all kinds of fanciful notions running around her head; a trip on the world's largest and most luxurious ocean liner with some of the world's most successful businessmen would no doubt have her planning her own wedding to a rich socialite before she had even disembarked!

Frances glanced at the calendar hanging on the wall. It was only three days until Katie would celebrate her twenty-fourth birthday. She always enjoyed a party, and a birthday aboard *Titanic* would be the perfect excuse for singing and merrymaking. Yes, Katie would enjoy America, Frances thought as she put on her coat and her hat; in fact, America would enjoy Katie.

She left her apartment block and, crossing the road, walked the short distance to the Ninth Avenue Elevated line at South Ferry. Although the elevated line took longer, she preferred not to take the subway system, being slightly claustrophobic. The idea of speeding along in a small underground train made her feel dizzy, so she preferred to travel aboveground by the El for her day of work as a domestic at the Walker-Browns' residence.

As she took her familiar journey north that morning, along Greenwich Street and Battery Place to Gansevoort Street in lower Manhattan and on to Ninth Avenue in midtown and finally on to Columbus Avenue and the leafy suburbs of the Upper West Side, it occurred to Frances that she might take a trip to Macy's one evening after work that week. She thought it would be nice to pick up something special for Katie for her birthday, a hatpin maybe, or a nice pair of gloves, she wasn't really sure. *Perhaps I'll ask Mrs. Walker-Brown, see what she would suggest,* she thought. Mrs. Walker-Brown was very au fait with matters of style and taste, and with her daughter, Vivienne, being a well-known singer in the Ziegfeld shows, she always seemed to be aware of the latest fashions. By a strange turn of coincidence, Vivienne Walker-Brown was also sailing on *Titanic,* returning with her fiancé from a European vacation.

Seated in her favorite position by the window, Frances watched the hustle and bustle of a normal New York workday taking place on the streets below, listening to the noise of the tramcars, to the crashing hooves of the horses as they pulled carts laden with crates of fruit and vegetables, to the honking of the horns of motorcars, and to the young newspaper vendors shouting the morning's headlines from their stands. She remembered how strange and loud and unpleasant this had seemed to her when she had first arrived in the city, such a contrast to the peaceful hush of their quiet country village. Now these were pleasing sounds to her ears; they were noises which suggested excitement, industry, and prosperity.

Frances smiled to herself as she took this all in, acknowledging how far she had come in a few short years and wondering what sounds Katie was hearing at that moment; what sights she and Vivienne Walker-Brown and the hundreds of other passengers would be seeing. With the Walker-Brown girl traveling on a first-class ticket and Katie traveling in third class—assuming her ticket had not been exchanged for another cow—Frances suspected that the views the two girls had from *Titanic* would be very different, defined not by the eye but by their social ranking.

Arriving at her destination, Frances stepped onto the sidewalk, just as she had done yesterday and as she had been doing for the last three years, and walked down the tree-lined avenue to the Walker-Brown residence. She admired the smartly dressed ladies who passed her by and gazed wistfully at the elegant couples strolling casually along with their arms linked, laughing at something one or the other of them had said.

Frances hadn't married, had never been asked, and hers had sometimes felt like a lonely existence among the thousands of people who inhabited this city. But in just a few more days all that would change. In just a few more days, her darling sister would be with her, and from that point in their lives, any journeys they had to make, they would make together. To Frances Kenny, that was all that mattered. That fact alone gave her far more comfort than any of the fancy furs and soft silks draped about the bodies of the Upper West Side ladies ever could.

Turning left at the side of the imposing residence of her employer, she walked down the stone steps of the domestics' entrance. As she did, it occurred to Frances that although people like the Walker-Browns and those who occupied the other lavish houses on this street might live lives of opulence and wealth, with her beloved sister arriving on these shores in just six or seven days, she was the fortunate owner of riches far greater than any their money could buy.

CHAPTER 11

Ballysheen, Ireland
April 11, 1912

Dusk was settling over the rugged landscape, casting long shadows and shrouding the mountains in a blanket of mute darkness as Molly d'Arcy and eight other women walked slowly toward the Holy Well on the edge of the village. They were a somber group, making their short pilgrimage to pray for the safe passage of the fourteen who had left their homes just a day ago. To these eight women—some of them mothers, some of them sisters, and some of them grandmothers of the departed—it already seemed as though their loved ones had been gone for many months, rather than a few short hours.

There was something of a tentative silence hanging over the women who, on any other day, could be heard exchanging friendly banter as they went about their daily chores in the village or laughing at a shared joke and snippet of juicy gossip as they enjoyed a drop of porter in the alehouses. Theirs was not normally a quiet existence, but at that moment it was very much so. Only the haunting sound of a barn owl's screech broke the silence around them. Approaching the well, they attended to their familiar rituals and said their own private prayers before kneeling on the hard, stony ground and, taking their rosary beads in their hands, began, as one, to recite their Hail Marys.

To a distant observer such as Séamus Doyle, who watched now from the window of his father's small farmhouse, this was a particularly moving sight, serene in its setting and mesmerizing in its solemnity. How touched Maggie and the others in the group would be, he thought, to know how deeply their departure was felt in this small community; how heartened they would be to see this declaration of absolute faith being made in their honor. But they could not know, would not see.

Like those of most people in the parish, Séamus's thoughts had returned often to the fourteen people who had left the previous morning, but most particularly to his beloved Maggie.

After giving her the packet of letters he had written and saying a final farewell, he had stood silently to watch the travelers depart. He'd thought them an oddly colorful group considering the solemnity of the occasion, with the bright woolen blankets draped about their shoulders and knees to keep them warm against the chilly April morning and the vivid green of Peggy's new hat bobbing along. He'd watched the traps as they made their way like a funeral procession down the village, the wheels sounding like distant rolls of thunder as they rumbled along the stone road.

He was familiar with the route they were taking, having traveled it himself on a few occasions to help the men buy grain or new farm tools and supplies from the town of Castlebar. They would pass out of Ballysheen, through the small, familiar towns of Knockfarnaght, Tobernaveen, Levally, Bofeenaun, Curraghmore, and Cuilmullagh and on to the top of the Windy Gap. The terrain was rough up there, and he imagined the traps jostling their passengers around like rag dolls as the wheels struggled over bumps and rolled in and out of the many potholes.

They would then follow the winding road down to the Burren and Sion Hill before clattering into the town of Castlebar itself. Séamus knew that some of the women would also have made this journey before to sell their eggs, but he didn't recall Maggie ever having gone. To her, it would be unfamiliar territory; beyond the train station at Castlebar, it would be unfamiliar territory to them all.

He wondered what thoughts were crossing Maggie's mind as the group trundled past the familiar sights of the local schoolhouse, the water pump, the broken fence, the hopscotch squares etched with chalk onto the flagstones outside O'Donoghue's shop, the gorse bushes with their bright, fragrant yellow flowers, the stone walls she had sat idly on, swinging her legs, and the fields where she had taken lunch up to the men at harvesttime. He wondered whether she would notice, with particular interest, the smell of ale as they passed O'Carroll's bar or the smell of the turf fires burning in the homes of her family and friends, homes that she had spent almost as much time in as her own. He wondered what it must feel like to see all of this and wonder whether you might ever see it again. He wondered whether he might ever see Maggie again.

Theirs had been an unexpected, simple romance of snatched embraces and brief kisses on the banks of the lake whenever they could escape from their chores. They'd looked for opportunities for their hands to touch as they reached water from the well and for their paths to collide when one or the other of them ran an errand. Séamus was pleased to have suggested the arrangement of meeting every Wednesday after market under the sixth cherry blossom tree, it being slightly set back from the others and offering a little privacy as it was near neither house nor store. If either one of them wasn't there, the other would know that some circumstance had kept them away. More often than not, they both made the agreed-on rendezvous and would spend at least a short while together, strolling casually down to the lake in the summertime to catch fish, or seeking comfort by the fire in Maggie's cottage in the winter, before it was time for him to walk the three miles home. It was a happy arrangement that suited them both. And then Maggie's mam had died, her aunt Kathleen had arrived from Chicago, and Maggie had told him that she was to return, with Kathleen, to America that spring. Now he knew nothing of what the future held for them.

A s he watched the women pray by the Holy Well, Séamus wondered whether Maggie had opened his packet of letters. He'd written one for each of the fourteen months they had been courting and to represent each of the fourteen cherry blossom trees she loved so much that lined the road from her cottage into the village. He had ended each letter with fourteen simple words—*I will wait for you under our tree until the day you come back*—and was quite pleased with the symmetry of it all. And then he had written one final letter, for the day she had departed.

He wondered whether she was thinking of him at that moment and, if so, what scene she was observing as her thoughts traveled back over the miles already between them. He hadn't really understood the notion of love before he met Maggie, mainly considering it a foolish thing for fellas who'd taken too much of the *poitín* and didn't fully possess their own minds. But he didn't drink, and something had certainly affected his mind when he walked up to her and asked her to dance at Jack and Maura Brennan's wedding. From that moment, he understood a little more about the notion of love, and over the months since that night, as he'd grown fonder and fonder of Maggie, he'd come to understand what it truly meant to be in love.

Séamus wasn't the type of man to dwell on misfortune, so the fact that Maggie's plans to travel to America had come about so soon after their courtship had started and during a time when his father was so sick was, to him, just as life was meant to be. It wasn't worth agonizing over or wishing for things to be different or declaring that life was cruel in its playing out; that was just how it was, and how it would always be. So Séamus did the only thing he could do: he disregarded what was done and looked instead to the future. *I will wait for you under our tree,* he'd said to her, *until the day you come back.* And although he meant it, something deep within his heart told him she would not return to this land.

As the sun dipped behind the top of Nephin Mór, the women finished their prayers and started to make their way back along the dusty track to the village. Séamus watched them pass before going to check on his da, who was resting in a chair next to the fire. Kneeling quietly beside him, Séamus took up his Bible and said a prayer of his own: for his da's health; for Maggie; for those she was traveling with; and for all the mothers and fathers, brothers and sisters, cousins and neighbors in Ballysheen, who, like him, sat beside their fires, praying that their loved ones would one day come home.

CHAPTER 12

RMS Titanic
April 11, 1912

Harry Walsh was known for being lucky. He could turn a final card and win an entire hand when the deck seemed to be completely stacked against him. His friends had lost count of the times he'd correctly called a toss of heads or tails and, as a result, had skipped his turn to go to the bar or pay for a round of ales. Lucky Harry, Billy had called him one evening when he'd won twelve tosses of the coin in a row. It was a nickname that had stuck ever since.

The only aspect of Harry's life in which he wasn't lucky was love, and it wasn't for want of trying. There had been plenty of girls brought home to dinner and tea or taken to a dance at the town hall or for a stroll along the quayside, but despite his good manners, pleasant face, well-scrubbed fingernails, and polished shoes, none of them seemed especially keen on him. They always lost interest after a couple of dates, spending more time talking to his mates than to him, until they eventually went to a dance with one of them instead, like Nancy Parker, who was now engaged to Dave Ward, or Barbara Lacy, who was married to Brian Addison and had three kids. Harry sometimes wondered whether any of his mates would be married at all if it wasn't for him providing their wives.

And whenever he did meet a girl who seemed genuinely keen on him, it seemed that Harry's mother wasn't especially keen on her. There had been many times when a girlfriend had left the house after Sunday dinner, complaining that she was sure his mother didn't like her. He would deny the fact, but he knew that they were absolutely right. His mother knew just how to add a certain tone to her voice when offering another slice of apple pie which told a girl, quite clearly, that this would be the last time she sat at Helen Walsh's kitchen table and ate her apple pie.

He wasn't all that bothered about it, really. In recent years Harry had watched his friends settle down and raise families, and the more he saw this happen, the more he realized that he wasn't quite ready for all of that just yet. He was enjoying his life too much for settling down and had a few more oceans he wanted to cross before he left a wife at home to worry about him coming back. Anyway, he felt instinctively that he would know when he met the right girl, a girl who would be good enough for him—and his interfering mother—and who would get along with his mates without running off with one of them; a girl, perhaps, like the pretty Irish one who had just boarded at Queenstown.

Amid the hundreds of people boarding the ship at this, the last embarkation stop, she caught his attention straightaway. She and her friends were hard to ignore with the charming lilt of their Irish accent, their infectious giggles, and the mass of luggage they had brought with them, which bashed against their legs, and his, as he negotiated the narrow corridors to show them to cabin number 115 on E Deck.

He listened carefully to their excitable conversation and

gasps of wonder as he walked them deep into the lower section of the ship. In the time it took him to escort them to their cabin, he learned that the girls were part of a group of fourteen friends and family who were traveling together from a small town in the west of Ireland to join members of their families in America and start a new life. He didn't quite understand why he found them so captivating, but he felt oddly moved by them and their story, by the notion that these young girls, and the people traveling with them, had left their homes and the land of their birth to take their chances in a distant and unfamiliar land.

With the words of his own mother ringing in his ears, Harry realized that, unlike the socialites and the honeymooners and the returning European travelers and the theater stars with silly little dogs who had already boarded the ship in joyous and jovial mood at Southampton and Cherbourg, the many steerage passengers who were boarding at Queenstown had a strange air of remorse about them, a distinct sadness that was lifted only fleetingly by the chatter of these young girls.

He couldn't help but smile as he listened to their irrepressible excitement at the spectacle of the ship, their gasps of amazement echoing the feelings he'd had himself just twenty-four hours earlier. "Jesus, Mary, and Joseph, girls, would you look," the pretty one had said as they walked through the general room. "This room alone is bigger than the whole of Ballysheen!"

Titanic seemed to do that to people, inspire them, astound them, draw them together, and connect them in a shared sense of awe at the magnitude and splendor of this spectacle that had been derived from riveted steel plates. Because, after all, that was all she really was, sheets of metal held together with rivets. And yet she was also so much more than that. *Titanic* was a ship that would change lives, transporting her passengers toward a life of opportunity and prosperity. At least, that was what they hoped. Harry knew that for some, the crossing of the Atlantic would result in nothing more than the exchange of one life of poverty for another.

Harry hung around the Irish girls' cabin a little longer than usual to make sure they were happy with their accommodations (which, judging by their remarks about hand basins and towels and bars of White Star Line soap, they clearly were); then the pretty girl turned to thank him for his help, smiling warmly at him. It was a smile he gladly returned until he noticed the rather stiff-looking woman glaring at him. She seemed to be minding the group of girls, and Harry assumed she was the mother of one of them, most probably the girl he was smiling at, judging by the disapproving scowl on her face. He could almost hear the words of his friend Billy in his head: *Bloody hell, that's a face to melt steel if ever I saw one*. Harry stopped smiling then, wished them a pleasant journey, and returned to the gangway to collect more passengers.

Queenstown was a busy embarkation stop for the third-class stewards, with the majority of passengers who were boarding there traveling on third-class tickets. As was customary, the stop meant a life jacket inspection. Harry was quite familiar with this practice, now common among the large transatlantic liners to ensure that all crew understood how to assist passengers with the cork-filled jackets. He stood in line with a group of other stewards and crew, joking about how like the ladies with their corsets they must look trussed up in their life jackets.

As they were being inspected by a junior officer, the head purser, Mr. McElroy, approached them. He introduced the man with him as Father Browne, a Jesuit priest from Cork.

"Father Browne has been recording life on board the ship

with his camera since we left Southampton," Mr. McElroy explained. "He will be disembarking in a few moments but wondered whether he might take your photograph beforehand."

"Quite a spectacle you are with your life preservers on," the priest commented, smiling at the group. "Perhaps a picture taken by a priest will bless them with good fortune and ensure they will not have occasion to be worn again. What do you say?"

Spirits were high among the group, and they laughed, charmed by the soft Irish brogue and the distinguished manner of the man. They obliged, posing happily for his picture. He thanked them and moved on with Mr. McElroy to photograph the captain and some of the officers before getting off the ship.

The stewards returned then to the business of showing the remaining passengers to their cabins. Amid all the noise and disorganization and wrong turns down long corridors as he guided the next group of wide-eyed passengers to their accommodations, Harry couldn't get the Irish girl out of his thoughts, her impish face imprinted firmly on his mind. *Maybe Lady Luck is smiling down on me on this mighty ship,* he thought. He'd already had an unexpected, albeit temporary, transfer to the first-class decks thanks to his mate Billy; they'd just had the life jackets blessed by a priest; and a lovely Irish lass had landed in his midst without his mother being anywhere nearby to frighten her off. Also, there wasn't much chance of a girl running off on him on a ship in the middle of the Atlantic Ocean, no matter how big it was. He hoped he would have the chance to find out more about her over the coming days and realized that he didn't even know her name, an oversight he decided to remedy at the earliest opportunity.

As he continued in his work, whistling an Irish tune he'd heard a piper play on the deck, Harry recalled one of the posters for *Titanic* that had been put up around the town ahead of this maiden voyage. "The Ship of Dreams" was its mighty claim. Harry Walsh was beginning to wonder whether this might not be such a bold statement after all, and smiled as he purposefully walked the longer way back to the crew quarters, a route that would take him past cabin 115.

CHAPTER 13

Cass County, Illinois
April 24, 1982

Grace sat in the swing on the back porch of her mother's house, enjoying the rocking sensation and the light breeze that danced around her bare feet. It was a warm day, full of blossoms on the trees and bees buzzing among the early-blooming azalea bushes. The first buds of wisteria were forming around the trellis that framed the doorway. Grace had always loved the wisteria, with its fragrant, cascading bunches of purple flowers; the pale, gnarled branches and stunning green foliage reminded her of the California grapevines she had seen on a family vacation. Her father had explained all about the harvesting process and the pressing of the grapes to make wine. It had seemed so magical to her and something that her father had described so poetically. Ever since, the wisteria had reminded her of that vacation and in turn, of her father.

It was two years since the accident, two years since she'd left her college life and a promising future as a journalist, two years since she'd begun to drift away from Jimmy. Her life felt so different now; *she* felt so different now from the girl who had raced home that January day, but had still arrived to the hospital nine minutes too late. She'd been thinking recently about what Maggie had said at her birthday party, about going back to college and getting in touch with Jimmy again. She hadn't read the last letters he'd sent to her, storing the unopened envelopes in a shoe box under her bed and storing Jimmy in a place in her heart from where she hoped that, one day, she would be able to move on, as she had told him to do.

Grace's reaction to her father's sudden death had been to shut herself off completely from college life and focus on helping her mom. She hadn't allowed herself to entertain any thoughts of returning to her journalism studies, or to Jimmy. Since everyone was so wrapped up in the loss of her father, nobody had really stopped to think about her. She hadn't really expected them to. But listening to Maggie's *Titanic* story had made Grace start to wonder. Here was a woman who'd had no choice in the direction of her life, no choice but to leave the home and the land and the man she loved and start over. Fate had intervened in the most dreadful way imaginable, leaving Maggie as a girl, not yet turned eighteen, lost and alone in a strange country, with just a small case of trinkets and mementos in her possession. Maggie had suffered real loss in so many ways, and Grace felt that she might have been a little foolish, a little hasty in locking herself away from the life she had been so enjoying and the man she had been enjoying it with.

Her mom was much better recently, in terms of both her grief and her illness, which had been eased by new medication. Things such as opening the wedding anniversary dinner set were small but definite signs that she was starting to move on. Grace's brother, Art, was due to come home that summer from the archaeological dig he had been working on in Egypt, and he'd promised to spend most of his time with his mom and sister. Yes, there was a definite wind of change circling around the Butler household.

As she swung and watched their marmalade cat chase a bee buzzing idly among the flowers, Grace swept her hair back behind her ears and tucked her feet up under her. For the first time in as long as she could remember, she allowed herself to wonder whether it might be time to go back to her own life, whether it might be okay to move on. She decided to broach the subject with her mother over dinner and then closed her eyes, letting the gentle rocking of the swing soothe her into a restful doze.

You look well today, Mom. Really pretty," Grace remarked as she set a jug of iced tea down on the dinner table. "Your new hairstyle is lovely. The color really suits you."

It had been a while since Grace had been genuinely able to say that. Her mom hadn't paid much attention to her appearance in a long time. She looked more like herself that evening, more like how Grace remembered she *used* to look.

"Thank you," her mother replied, touching her hair. "It is kinda lovely, isn't it?" She'd been into town for the day with a friend and had decided to have her hair curled and colored at an upmarket salon. "Cost a fortune, though. I really shouldn't have." Her smile showed that she actually wasn't too worried.

"Mom, I've been thinking," Grace began, sipping her iced tea nervously.

"Thinking what, honey?" Her mother put down her fork to give her daughter her full attention.

"Well, you know, I've been thinking about maybe going back to college—picking up my journalism studies again."

Her mother smiled. She didn't seem at all surprised. "Good. I am *very* glad to hear it. So, what's brought all this on?"

Grace had told her mother about Maggie confiding in her about *Titanic*. She had told her details of the event and the aftermath that Grace's mom—and even Grace's grandmother—hadn't heard before. Although she was surprised that Maggie had spoken of *Titanic* again, after so many years of silence, Grace's mother was secretly delighted that it was Grace to whom Maggie had entrusted her story. Maggie had said she was happy for Grace to share her story now. She'd said it felt as if it had taken her a lifetime to talk about it properly and she didn't think she was up to the task of saying it all over again. As far as Maggie was concerned, Grace could go off and tell the entire world, just as long as *she* didn't have to do any more of the telling herself.

"I think that listening to Maggie's story has reminded me that you can never—and *should* never—take life for granted," Grace explained. "I think I need to start moving on with my life again, and was thinking that with Art coming back for the summer and you seeming to be a bit happier these days and with Aunt Martha moving closer and your new medication helping with your attacks . . . " Grace trailed off, hoping that she hadn't misread the signs.

Her mom laughed. "Do you know, Grace, that I was only twenty years old when I had you and Art? All a bit of a surprise to your father and me. We'd only been married a few months and then, wham, you two came charging into our lives." She smiled at the memories and pushed the corn around on her

plate. "You definitely cannot take life for granted. If your father's death has taught me anything, it is that." She paused for
a moment as Grace rested her hand on her mother's arm. "So,
what about Jimmy? Have you given any thought to him?"

Grace knew that her mom had always been very fond of
Jimmy, and although she'd understandably been too distracted
by her own grief to really notice Grace's reasons for not seeing
Jimmy anymore, Grace suspected that her mother had often
wondered about him.

"I'm not sure, Mom. Sometimes I think about him, but he's
probably forgotten all about me by now. He'll be graduating
this summer anyway. He's probably moving on somewhere to
take a job."

"My goodness, Grace, there's an awful lot of *probably*s in all
of that. You should *probably* get in touch with him and find out
whether any of your *probably*s are actually realities. I'm sure
he'd love to hear from you. We all went through a very tough
time, and you were so, so selfless to stay here with me. I don't
know if I can ever thank you enough for that. You and Jimmy
are certainly not the first couple to drift apart after a tragedy—
and I doubt you'll be the last. I, for one, would be delighted to
see the two of you back together."

Her mother's words reminded Grace of Maggie, of how
she'd blocked all sorts of people and memories out of her life
after *Titanic*.

"If there's meant to be a future for the two of you, I'm sure
he will still be waiting for you—even though you told him
not to. And if not, then at least you'll know the truth rather
than spending the rest of your life in a world of *probably*s and
*what-if*s."

They continued eating their dinner in silence as a light rain began to fall outside.

"So, why don't you call that professor friend of yours? See if you can go back for the fall semester, pick up where you left off, and find out if that feature opening might be resurrected? You've some story to go to them with now!"

Grace had been thinking about this for the past week. After she'd struggled to find an original angle for a feature when Professor Andrews had first told her about the opportunity with the *Chicago Tribune*, one had now landed right in her hands.

"Yeah. Maybe. I'm not sure I want to write Maggie's story, though, Mom. I'm afraid I won't be able to do justice to her and to the memory of all those people. I'm not sure I'm ready to tackle a story as big as *Titanic*."

"Nonsense," her mother replied, looking at her seriously. "Now you look here, Grace Butler. All your father ever dreamed of for you and Art was to do something you loved in life. He didn't care about fancy qualifications or fancy clothes or cars, just that you were both happy and fulfilled. He was so excited about your dreams for a career as a journalist, and he would be so proud to see his daughter's name in print. You're a great writer, Grace. If you want my opinion, which I realize as my daughter you probably don't, you should take this opportunity that has fallen into your lap and use it to write Maggie's story. Nobody will ever be able to bring those poor people back, but we can certainly remember them through your wonderful words." Her mother paused for a moment, refilling both their glasses before adding, "You would make her incredibly proud, you know."

Grace was quiet. She hadn't heard her mother talk so forcefully or passionately about anything for years—another sign, perhaps, that it really was okay for her to move on.

"So?"

Grace smiled at her and wiped away a tear. "Yes, Mom. You're right. I will. I'll call Professor Andrews tomorrow, and I'll think about contacting Jimmy, I really will." She placed her hand on her mother's and squeezed it. "Thanks, Mom. For everything."

"No, Grace. It should be me who is thanking you. I know you've made a huge sacrifice being here with me these last few years, and I want you to know how much I love you and appreciate what you've done for me. You deserve some time to yourself now."

Gathering the dishes from the table, she walked over to her daughter and gave her a tender kiss on the top of her head. Grace remembered her doing this when she was a small child. It was a comforting, reassuring gesture.

"Oh, and there's something else," her mom added. "I want to turn your bedroom into a guest room—it's about time those awful posters came down and that dreadful wallpaper was taken off, don't you think?"

The rain continued to fall softly outside, bringing a refreshing scent of camellia through the open door. A plane flew overhead. The cat ran inside, shaking itself to remove the raindrops from its fur. The timer on the oven rang to signal that the apple crumble for dessert was ready. *Everything's good here,* Grace thought, *everything's as it should be.*

For the rest of the evening, Grace sat in her bedroom surrounded by Maggie's journal and the bundle of old newspaper clippings, listening to the rain falling on the decking outside. She looked around her room. Her mom was right. Her bedroom hadn't changed much in recent years; the posters of her teenage pop idols were still on the back of the door where she'd stuck them as an impressionable high schooler. She still had the same faded pink-and-white-checked comforter cover she'd loved as a kid. It was kind of reassuring to have these familiar things from her childhood around her, and neither she nor her mom had been in a rush to change things, both of them subconsciously wanting to leave things as they were before her dad died. Her mom's suggestion that she start reorganizing and decorating must be a sign that she had really turned a corner.

With a notebook by her side, Grace pored over every detail of the press reports from Maggie's small black case. THE TITANIC SANK AT 2:20 THIS MORNING. NO LIVES WERE LOST, stated the headline of one newspaper, and another said, CARPATHIA REFUSES TO GIVE ANY DETAILS OF TITANIC'S LOSS AND AS FRUITLESS HOURS GO BY, SUSPENSE GROWS MORE MADDENING. She wondered how the Irish travelers' relatives must have felt, waiting for news of the disaster, reading these mistaken headlines and having hope, only to see them replaced in the following hours and days by the terrible truth. 1,302 ARE DROWNED OR MISSING IN TITANIC DISASTER, LATEST REPORT, and the final details: TITANIC'S DEATH LIST, 1,601; ONLY 739 LIVES ARE SAVED. Other pages reported strange details; one paper claimed, AS VESSEL PLUNGES TO HER FATE, BAND PLAYS "NEARER MY GOD TO THEE," and another bore the shocking headline FOREIGNERS WHO REFUSED TO OBEY ORDERS ARE SHOT DOWN.

Grace then unrolled a couple of smaller newspaper clippings, one of which was dated April 20, 1912, from the *Connaught Telegraph*.

20TH APRIL 1912

CONNAUGHT TELEGRAPH

Immediately the news reached Castlebar, one of the local agents for the White Star Line, Mr. Thomas Durcan, wired to the head office in Liverpool and received the following reply: Liverpool. 4.30 p.m. Tuesday. "Referring to your telegram re. *Titanic*, deeply regret to say that latest word received is steamer foundered; about 675 souls, mostly women and children saved." The presumption is that all the passengers booked by Mr. Durcan have been lost, still there is a hope that some of the females may have been rescued. In the list of survivors published on Thursday the name of Miss Maggie Murphy appeared.

race continued reading late into the night, poring over the newspaper clippings and the scrawled pages of Maggie's journal. She was so completely immersed in Maggie's *Titanic* world she barely noticed day turn to dusk and eventually to the darkness of evening, absorbing every last detail as Maggie described life on board the ship: the linen tablecloths in the dining room; the friendly manner of the crew; the steward she referred to as Lucky Harry, who seemed to have befriended Maggie and some of the other girls in their group; the sounds of the *uilleann* pipes and fiddles played in the general room after dinner; the sparkle of the diamonds Maggie saw on the fingers of some of the first-class ladies. She read each page of the journal, lost in the thoughts of a seventeen-year-old girl, through whose eyes she saw this most famous of ships in an entirely new light.

April 11, 1912
Day 1 at sea

. . . the third-class quarters are very nice. We have real mattresses on the beds and there is a reasonable amount of space—at least there is for the four of us sharing our cabin, number 115. The steward told us that there is a family of nine sleeping in the cabin next to ours and that it is exactly the same size. I asked him how they could fit everyone in. He told me there are two in each bed and the baby sleeps in a suitcase on the floor. I can hardly believe how cramped that must be and feel a bit guilty that we have this space just for the four of us. Peggy says she reckons you'd be able to fit one of our cabins into the first-class rooms four times over and still have space for a set dance. It is an unbelievably big boat—we've been wandering around for hours now and I don't think we've even seen one whole side of it.

. . . Peggy keeps talking about wanting to see the first-class quarters. Katie told us that she heard someone saying there are eight giant crystal chandeliers in the first-class dining room. I think my eyes would pop right out of their sockets if I saw such a sight!

. . . I think about Séamus a lot and hope his da is getting better. I took the packet of letters from my coat pocket today and read the first one. It was so nicely written and the words were so kind it set me to crying. He says he has written one letter for each of the fourteen months of our courtship together in Ballysheen—the first letter is called

"February," and he has written about his memories of the first night we danced at the Brennans' wedding. He says he thought me lovelier than all of the stars that shone in the sky that night. I wish he was here with me now. I don't think I'll ever be able to explain to him what this ship is like—maybe he will sail on it himself one day if he can ever come to America to join me.

April 12, 1912
Day 2 at sea

. . . Peggy is complaining that the vibrations from the engines kept her awake last night. I think it's quite a nice noise—a sort of humming sound like a big swarm of bees have set up a hive in the boiler room. Katie says Peggy should stop thinking about that English steward we met yesterday—she thinks it's more likely him which is keeping Peggy awake at night and not the engines at all!

. . . I was lost earlier today! I'd been for some fresh air on the bridge deck (insisting I'd be grand on my own for a few minutes, even though Aunt Kathleen frowned and said she really didn't agree, but what harm would a few minutes be) and couldn't find my way back to our cabin. I think I went down the wrong stairwell and ended up on D Deck instead of E Deck. Luckily there are always plenty of crew members around and I asked someone where I was. He walked me personally back to E Deck and all the way down the crew passageway, which he told me is called Scotland Road, to

the place where our cabin is. I was glad to be back but didn't say a word of it to Aunt Kathleen. She tutted when I finally returned and said that time must work differently at sea because that was the longest "few minutes" she'd ever known. I gave myself quite a fright being separated from everyone like that. I think I'll ask someone to come with me for fresh air next time.

. . . The meals on board are very nice. We are already used to the call from the bugler, who signals that we can make our way to the dining saloon, where we sit at tables covered with white linen tablecloths! Today we had smoked herrings for breakfast, brawn for lunch, and corned beef and cabbage for dinner. I think I'll be needing some new clothes in America if I keep eating at this rate. To think that there's a whole army of crewmen peeling our forty tons of spuds and carrots and boiling our forty thousand eggs while we sit on our backsides! Tea and biscuits are served in the afternoon. Katie says they have the biscuits laid out in such neat rows on the plates it would nearly stop you taking one so as not to break up the pattern.

. . . We are all in good spirits, even though it feels like we are a very long way from home now. We're always talk-ing of the people we've left behind, though—one of us will remember something somebody said or a time they made us laugh, and we try to get the time of day right in our heads so as to imagine what they are doing while we steam farther away from them across the ocean.

April 13, 1912
Day 3 at sea

. . . The general recreation room is for steerage passengers to use for reading or playing cards or a bit of dancing. It's a big room with a piano for us to play whenever we like. Some French fella plays most of the time; he's very good. He likes to play some of the ragtime music I've heard a little. I think John O'Dea back home would have mighty craic *with that piano; it would put the small yoke he plays in O'Connell's pub to shame! The man with the* uilleann *pipes plays a fair bit too. He's very good and gets a good old singsong going among us Irish—there's plenty of us; I'd say we take up at least half of the steerage if not more.*

. . . Today Peggy and me played with some of the young ones. One woman has seven children with her and is traveling all alone, God love her. I think she might be Italian or something, none of us can understand a word she says, but she's nice and her kids are sweet little things. I played with the baby a lot. He likes to drop things and watch you pick them up again.

Maura Brennan was talking with a family from a place called Wiltshire in England. The mam and da are taking their five little ones to join relatives in Philadelphia. The youngest is just two years old, and the eldest is turned sixteen. She's a nice girl, Elsie is her name. She told me about her home and it sounds a bit like ours with the fields and the lake.

. . . Ellen Joyce has found another woman who is to be married when they arrive in America so they are all talk about wedding gowns and veils and admire each other's rings all the time. There are four other newlywed couples in our section of the ship who are headed out on honeymoon, and Maura has been talking with another woman who'll be having a baby soon. It's quite the social gathering altogether! Peggy and Katie have taken to fanciful talk again about what they'll do when they are in America and what the fancy homes they'll live in will look like.

. . . There are some sad stories of people who are unhappy to be leaving loved ones behind, or who are traveling to visit a sick or dying family member. I heard someone say there are over two thousand people on board this ship, so I would imagine in all of that there are plenty of sad hearts as well as many happy ones.

. . . The English steward Harry (Lucky Harry is his nickname) is very sweet on Peggy. He talks to her at any opportunity and makes up all sorts of excuses to knock on the cabin door, or to fuss over her at dinner. He admired her hat yesterday, and she was practically married to him then! He's a nice fella and is great craic altogether with the stories he tells us about how Titanic set sail from Southampton with bands playing and people standing on the quay to cheer and wave as she slipped her moorings. He swears he saw five grand pianos and a motorcar being loaded onto her before she left Southampton—but I think he's pulling our legs about that.

He says that the stewards on the upper decks wish they were assigned to third class—they have a pain in their arses with all the fussing and complaining of the first-class passengers. Some of them can be awful rude apparently and demand that their rooms are cleaned several times a day and grumble about the wrong sort of linen on their beds! He told us that one of the stewards says he wouldn't be surprised if they asked him to wipe their arses for them next! Peggy told Harry all about the tea leaves and the strange man at Queenstown. He told her not to be worrying because he had personally seen a priest blessing the life jackets so we couldn't be anywhere safer!

. . . It's nice to walk on the deck in the sunshine and breathe in the fresh sea air, although it is chilly up so high and with the ship going along at such a rate of knots there's a fierce cold breeze blowing all the time. Pat fancies himself a bit of a crew member, giving us daily reports of speed and iceberg warnings. These are posted every day outside the dining room, and we let him tell us the latest news because he enjoys it, although if the truth be told, we're not a bit interested! Peggy, Katie, and I have found a place on the bridge deck where we can catch a glimpse of the first-class ladies as they promenade. Peggy says that silk dresses and elegant hats are far more interesting than Pat's dull talk of "rate of knots" and icebergs.

. . . Lucky Harry is friendly with the radio operators who work for the Marconi Wireless Telegraph Company in the radio room on the ship. He told us that the first-class passengers can pay to send messages from the ship to loved

ones back in England or France or in America! Apparently some singer has been sending messages to her mother in New York telling her how much she and her fiancé are looking forward to setting a date for their wedding when they are back home, and then she sends other messages to her sister telling her about a handsome millionaire she's got friendly with and that she has "confused feelings"! Peggy says that only someone who works in the theater would be able to lead such a strange life and that she doesn't understand what's to be confused about when there's a handsome millionaire involved! She's so wicked sometimes, but she makes us all laugh and her silly chatter stops my mind from wandering back to Ballysheen too often. I'd love to be able to send a message to Séamus. I don't even know how the messages work, though, because he doesn't have a wireless in his house. I'll ask Harry about it all.

Grace scribbled frantically in her notebook as she read Maggie's words, the detail and ideas rushing at her faster than she could capture them on the page, anxious to get them written down before they slipped away again. Then she reworked the notes into legible, ordered paragraphs, mindful of the journalistic mantra of story first, detail later as she mapped Maggie's revelations into words that flowed as easily as the water she had sailed over.

The rain was still falling and the early light of dawn was spreading from the east when she eventually turned out her light and slipped into a peaceful sleep, with visions of Maggie, Peggy, Harry, and *Titanic* drifting through her dreams.

PART THREE

WIRELESS

Received April

NO_____ CK_____   .   TIME RECEIVED_____

TO

Saks New York: Leila safe and well cared for edgar missing.

Marconigram message sent from Leila Meyer, *Carpathia*, to Saks & Company, New York, on April 17, 1912. Edgar Meyer was married to Leila Saks of Saks & Company. He was lost when *Titanic* went down.

CHAPTER 15

RMS Titanic
April 13, 1912

Harry watched the Irish girls closely as they made their way from the dining saloon, Peggy's laughter clearly audible from the other side of the room. She really was a stunning girl, with those bewitching green eyes that could warm any man's heart and that smile that could melt it completely. His own heart skipped a beat as she and her friends made their way over to him and wished him a good night.

"Good night, ladies," he replied, his cheeks flushing. "Enjoy your dancing down there."

"Ah, sure, don't we always," Peggy replied. "And you make sure those gates are good and locked tonight, Lucky Harry," she called over her shoulder as the three girls reached the top of the stairwell that would take them down to their cabin. "We don't want any o' those first-class folk comin' down to be botherin' us with their shiny jewels and fine shoes, givin' us some posh disease with a fancy name now, d'ye hear?"

The girls giggled. They were in a fine mood after another hearty meal and were looking forward to the postdinner singing and dancing deep in the bowels of the ship.

Harry drew the gate across the top of the stairwell, as was the regulation at night. "But what if some of those rich American bachelors want to come down, Miss Madden?" he called back. "What should I do then?"

Peggy turned at the bottom of the stairwell, placing her hand on her hip, an expression of mock consideration on her face. "Well, then, tell 'em that they should ask for a Miss Peggy Madden on arrival in New York, where she would be delighted to consider their offers of marriage. Now, please excuse us. We've to show these borin' folk from England how to sing a decent song."

Returning to his own dormitory, Harry lay on his narrow bunk bed, his hands behind his head. He had been on his feet since 6:00 A.M. It was now nearly 11:00 P.M., and he was exhausted.

His thoughts turned to home, wondering whether his father was feeling well enough yet to return from Devon and how his mother and sister were coping without them both. He imagined his mother sitting quietly in the living room, reading a newspaper or darning his father's socks, getting up every few minutes to adjust the tablecloth or straighten a cushion or poke the fire. His mother was a restless woman, and without her two men to fuss over she would be finding small, insignificant ways to occupy her time. Harry knew that she was always anxious when he was at sea. No matter how many times he sailed, she was fretful until he walked through the front door again, safely back in the family home. He imagined she would have been to church to pray for his safe voyage.

For all her annoying mannerisms, Harry was very fond of his mother. She'd had a huge impact on his life, always there for him, always supporting him, always waiting for him to come home. She often teased him about getting married and getting out from under her feet to set up a nice place with his wife. "I'm sick and tired of picking up after you and washing your filthy socks, Harry Walsh," she would chide, but he knew she didn't mean it. He'd just laugh at her and say that she would most likely be washing his socks for the rest of her life because no woman would ever be good enough to marry her precious son.

"Quite probably," she'd reply. "But maybe if you sail far enough on those ships of yours, the world might just reveal a woman good enough for you, Harry Daniel Walsh."

As he lay on his bed now, the sound of *Titanic*'s twenty-nine massive engines droning in the background, sending the now-familiar vibrations through his spine, Harry wondered if he might have found her after all, a woman who was good enough for him and his mother. At least he'd found out her name now, Peggy Madden, and he knew that she was going to stay with her sister in St. Louis, Missouri. He also knew that she'd bought her new hat and gloves especially for the journey and that she liked it when he admired them. He had three, maybe four more days to get to know her a little better, to impress her and possibly pluck up the courage to ask her to take a stroll with him on deck between his shifts; either that or he'd have to be making a trip to St. Louis, Missouri, himself, wherever that might be.

He remembered then that it was their friend Katie's birthday the following day and wondered if he might be able to sneak the girls up the crew ladder for a bit of a lark. In addition to the stewards' stairway, which extended from E Deck right up to an opening beside the third funnel casing on the boat deck, the iron ladders gave the crew quick access between decks. While their purpose was intended to be purely functional, Harry and some of the other third-class stewards had taken to climbing the ladders to spy on the fancy ladies taking luncheon in the Parisian-style café or walking their tiny dogs on the promenade deck before afternoon tea. They'd watched the men reclining in comfortable chairs, smoking cigars and discussing matters of important business. He'd even seen Captain Smith and Mr. Ismay strolling casually along the promenade deck together, deep in conversation. How proud they must have been walking among their passengers, seeming like gods or kings in their command of such a vessel.

Apart from the limited view he'd snatched from his precarious perch on the ladder, Harry had, of course, seen some of the luxury of the first-class accommodations up close. He'd taken great delight in regaling the Irish girls with his tales of the elegant reading and writing room, the painted glass windows of the smoking room, the cascading sweep of the Grand Staircase, and the Turkish baths, heated swimming pool, gym, and barbers (those last he hadn't seen himself but had heard talk of). It never ceased to amaze him to think that some people traveling on this ship would experience more luxury and a better standard of living in the seven or so days it would take to reach America than all the people down in steerage would experience in a lifetime. How Peggy and her friends would gawp if they could see it for themselves, he thought, laughing, and decided to bring them up for a quick look the next day.

The morning of Sunday, April 14, started early for Harry as usual, with the breakfast to prepare and seven hundred hungry passengers to feed. He paid particular attention to his Irish girls, as he had done for the last three mornings.

"Now, ladies," he whispered conspiratorially as he served

them their herring, "I take it you'll be attending Mass this morning after breakfast, and then how would you like to see how the first-class passengers live? Bet you'd like to gawp at the ladies and flutter your eyelashes at the eligible bachelors, eh?"

"The nerve of 'im," Peggy replied as she shook out her napkin. "We will of course be goin' to Mass, because we are good, God-fearin' girls and wish to take part in the praying an' all, isn't that right?" They all giggled. "And yes, we might like to have a quick look at first class, but it'll be them posh folk who are gawpin' at us with our fancy clothes and me with me fine hat and proper ladies' gloves!"

Kathleen Dolan had been observing the girls' friendliness with the steward over the last few days, mindful of stories she'd heard about crew taking advantage of young girls who were lonely and vulnerable on the transatlantic liners. They were in especially high spirits that morning with it being Katie Kenny's birthday, and Kathleen was growing distinctly uncomfortable with how flippant they were becoming.

"Peggy Madden," she hissed in a stern voice, leaning across the table purposefully. "I do not think it is very proper for a young lady to be so friendly with a steward. You'd do well to be doin' a little less talkin' and a bit more eatin'." The girls looked down at their plates and started to eat quietly. "And mind you pay attention at the service this mornin' too; it wouldn't do any one of you any harm to be doin' a lot more prayin' either."

Her seriousness caused the girls to giggle, but they continued to eat their breakfast without any more talking, kicking one another under the solid wood table, trying desperately to avoid looking at one another for fear of starting another fit of the giggles.

Not wanting to get them into any more trouble, Harry went

about his work without saying another word to the girls, but as they were leaving the dining room, he drew Maggie to one side, making sure that her aunt was well out of sight and earshot.

He was fond of the girl Maggie. He'd learned that she was the youngest in the Irish party and felt a little protective of her. She reminded him of his sister, with her giggles and her auburn curls. But she also had an air of constant sadness about her, and he wondered why she seemed so uncertain about this journey when the other girls—although they spoke fondly about their families back home—were clearly excited about the prospect of settling in America.

"Listen, I know of a ladder on C deck that goes right up to the upper decks," he whispered to her, taking her arm and pulling her gently to one side of the door so the other passengers could get past them. "If you want to have a look later with your friends, meet me near the crew quarters on Scotland Road after the religious service." He smiled at her and winked.

"Right so," she replied, winking back. "Oh, and I wanted to ask you somethin'," she added, lowering her voice and coloring a little in the cheeks.

"Yeah? What is it? I don't think I'm going to be able to get you upgraded to a first-class stateroom, y'know!"

Maggie laughed. "No, it's nothin' like that. It's just that my cousin Pat tells me you're quite friendly with the Marconi radio operators. I was after wonderin' if you'd be able to help me send a message. Y'know, to home, like?"

"Yeah, I know them all right," he replied. "Is it a message to your mam?"

Maggie shuffled her feet. "Um, no, it ain't for me mam. I'm not sure what sort of service those telegram fellas are offerin', but I doubt they're up for sendin' messages to heaven now, are they?"

Harry looked at his own feet now, annoyed with himself for being so stupid. "Oh, bloody hell, miss. I'm sorry. I didn't mean to upset you."

"It's all right. Ye weren't to know. Anyway, would it be all right, d'ye think? To send somethin'? Even if it's not for me dead ma?" She smiled shyly up at him.

"Yeah, I'm sure I can get something sorted out for you. Write it all down on a piece of paper and keep it short. Pass it to me later. I'll see what I can do."

Maggie smiled warmly, delighted at the prospect of sending a note back home, and thanked him several times before scurrying off to catch up with her friends. She passed her cousin Pat, who had stopped to check the ship's log again.

"What's the report today then, Pat?" she teased, finding his fascination with the speed of the ship and the conditions of the sea quite amusing for a boy who had never been near the ocean in all his life.

"It's a calm sea, twenty-two knots, and icebergs ahead," he replied.

"And is that good or bad?" she asked. "The knots and the calmness an' all?"

"Well, it's mainly good." He laughed at his young cousin's naïveté. "We're almost going full speed. Some are sayin' we might be in New York a whole day ahead of schedule, and that would be the fastest crossin' of the Atlantic there's ever been! The ships have to watch out for the icebergs, though," he added. "One of the crewmen told me that some of them can be so big you could probably spot them from Ireland on a clear day." He whistled at the thought. "Anyway, come on, we've got to get on our Sunday best for Mass."

They both laughed then, knowing full well that they were already wearing their Sunday best, it being the same as they had worn the day before and the day before that.

CHAPTER 16

RMS Titanic
April 14, 1912

A s they gathered for Father Byles's Catholic Mass, which was to be held in the third-class lounge, Kathleen Dolan reminded the younger members of the Ballysheen group to have proper manners about them during the service and not to be staring at the other passengers, some of whom, she said, might be better dressed than they were, even though they were all traveling on third-class tickets. She was a woman of immense pride and stood staunchly by her heritage and her people, proud of who she was and where she had come from and not the least bit inclined to apologize for the class of ticket she was traveling on or for the simple, rural clothing she noticed among the others in her group.

During her years living in Chicago, Kathleen had encountered all classes of society. She'd rubbed shoulders with the desperately poor when she'd helped at a charity soup kitchen and had, equally, come across the upper classes in society. She still wasn't sure which group was the more pitiful. As far as she could gather, the very rich might appear from the outside to have lives of luxury and indulgent happiness, but more often than not, there was a litany of family trouble, business trouble, or other sorts of trouble bubbling away underneath the glossy, coiffed exteriors, the sort of trouble that, in her estimation, tends to come about when people have too much money to spend and too much time on their hands to find ways in which to spend it.

As the priest led the assembled passengers in familiar prayer, first in English and then in French, Kathleen's thoughts turned to those they had left back in Ireland. She was well aware that many of the mothers and fathers left behind felt it was her influence that had encouraged their sons and daughters to make this journey. They were partly correct, and she made no apology for the fact.

Aside from caring for her dying sister, her time back in Ballysheen that winter had given Kathleen Dolan the perfect opportunity to spread her message about a better life overseas. She'd already told Maggie that they would travel to America together in the spring, and as the months since her return passed by, her influence and conviction began to have an impact on a number of families. Discussions took place behind closed doors, finances were considered, and letters to relatives already overseas were written, expressing intentions to travel. By the time the last of the snow had melted from the thatched roofs of their homes, many in Ballysheen were seriously considering a passage to America.

Kathleen was no fool and was well aware that among some of the parishioners she was not a popular woman, having offended them with her "American ways" and her insistence that there was a better life waiting for them and their children in the New World. She knew that they considered her to have airs and ways above her station, and thought that with all her talk of a better life in America she was in some way insulting their own lives in Ireland. But this didn't trouble her too much; she knew that the people who had made this journey, who stood next to her now in the humble yet pleasant surroundings of the third-class lounge, would never look back; would always be grateful that they'd listened to her advice and had the courage to leave the familiar and try the new.

As she sang the familiar words of the hymns, Kathleen glanced around the congregation. In front of her she saw people she already recognized as fellow passengers from steerage, people she'd shared a conversation or a game of cards with over the last few days. There were all manner of people, others from towns and counties in Ireland, families from Finland and Russia, and young men and women from all over England and America. The social aspect to this journey had surprised her. She would normally keep very much to her own company on a transatlantic crossing, but there seemed to be an entirely different atmosphere about *Titanic*, and she was almost enjoying the evenings after dinner when the passengers would congregate in the general room.

To her left stood Maggie, now almost as tall as herself and developing into a fine young woman. It was hard to believe that she'd been just nine years old when Kathleen had first arrived back in Ballysheen with her cases and her fashionable skirts. It had been a short visit on that occasion, but despite the brevity of the meeting and her rather stern nature, Maggie and Kathleen had formed a pleasant bond and, over the intervening years, had mutually enjoyed their exchange of letters. Kathleen had always intended for Maggie to go to America, and had discussed the matter with her sister Nora on several occasions. Looking at

Maggie now, Kathleen wished that her niece's journey had come about under less traumatic circumstances than the death of the mother she had loved very much.

Looking down the row to her left and her right, Kathleen observed the other Ballysheen men and women. They were indeed a large group, and she was certain that every one of them felt comforted and reassured to have so many familiar faces around them. She considered them now, knowing the personal motivations of each for making this journey; all of them with their own reasons for leaving Ireland, all of them with relatives in America eagerly awaiting their arrival, and all of them with relatives back home in Ireland who were, no doubt, still mourning their departure.

Next to Maggie stood Maura and Jack Brennan, hoping to start a new business and a new life. With his father dead since January and Jack having inherited the family smallholding, Maura had encouraged him to sell. It was with the money raised from the sale of that land that Jack Brennan could pay for passage to America for himself, his wife, and his sister and still have enough left over to invest in a business in Chicago. Jack's devoted sister, Eileen, stood with them. The family had agreed that she would travel with her brother and sister-in-law and would settle with them in America.

Then there was Ellen Joyce, a proud, confident woman who had returned to Ballysheen from Chicago to visit her sick mother and to announce her engagement. Kathleen also suspected she had relished the opportunity to show off her diamond solitaire engagement ring and her new gold watch, a gift from the man she was to marry in several months' time. She'd spent her last few days in Ballysheen packing a trousseau of wedding gifts she'd received and other items she'd purchased for her bottom drawer. Her sister was to stay at home to care for their mother. Ellen was traveling with the Brennans, who knew her and her family well, their homes being just across the field from each other.

Next in the row stood Katie Kenny. Kathleen was very fond of the Kenny girl and knew how excited she was about seeing her sister, Frances, in New York. She had stuck to her promise of keeping everyone's spirits up with her songs and had half the steerage passengers singing along to their favorite Irish ballads.

Then there was Michael Kelly, a slight young fella whose mother was very unhappy about his decision to join his two brothers in New York. He'd boasted of the new pocket his sister had sewn on the inside of his jacket to keep his money and ticket in. "It's a fine pocket with neat stitching, isn't it, Miss Dolan?" he'd announced to her.

Alongside Michael stood the painfully shy Mary Dunphy, the daughter of a friend of Kathleen's, and beside Mary was Kathleen's boisterous nephew, Pat, with his shock of red hair. Mary and Pat were both going to stay with Pat's sister in Philadelphia. After the incident with the dropped lucky sovereign, Kathleen had advised him to keep it in his sock for the duration of the journey.

At the far end of the line, Kathleen could just see the faces of some of the younger girls among the group: Bridget Moloney, Maria Cusack, Margaret O'Connor, and Peggy Madden, who was still wearing her new hat. They were each heading to family in Chicago, New York, and St. Louis.

It occurred to Kathleen as she looked down the row that theirs were just fourteen stories among nearly two thousand aboard this ship. Following Father Byles in his final prayer, she closed her eyes and prayed to God for all of their good health and good fortunes, wherever they had come from, wherever they were going, and whatever their reasons for making this long and remarkable journey. As soon as the service was over, most of the Ballysheen group returned to their cabins or to the general recreation areas of the ship. Kathleen, however, took a short stroll on deck, wrapping her shawl tightly around her shoulders as the icy breeze nipped at her cheeks. She looked to the horizon. It would not be many more days before New York would be in her sight.

Captain Smith finished his religious service for the first-class passengers, leading the congregation in the hymn "Eternal Father, Strong to Save" before he and his officers returned to the bridge. From there he gave the orders for the 11:00 A.M. lifeboat drill to be canceled, for the boilers to be stoked, and for the speed to be increased to full steam ahead. He gazed out over the vast expanse of the Atlantic Ocean, proud in the knowledge that they would dock in New York in just two days' time. Then he retired to his cabin, requesting that a pot of coffee with sugar and cream be brought to him and that any further ice warnings be brought to his immediate attention.

WHITE STAR LINE

ROYAL AND UNITED STATES MAIL STEAMERS.

OCEANIC STEAM NAVIGATION COMPANY, LIMITED, OF GREAT BRITAIN.
THIRD CLASS (Steerage) PASSENGER'S CONTRACT TICKET.
(NOT TRANSFERABLE.)

CHAPTER 17

RMS Titanic
April 14, 1912

Dearest *Séamus, all is well. Titanic is a fine ship. I hope your da is well. Don't wait for me, come to America as soon as you can. Maggie.*

Maggie put her pencil down on the bedcovers and read over her words once again before reading them out to Katie, who was sitting at the other end of the bed playing solitaire with a pack of cards, her legs curled under her like a cat.

"So, what do you think?"

Katie thought for a moment as she moved the jack of hearts onto the queen. "I think it's grand, Maggie. Stop worryin' about it and just give it to Harry, will you, or we'll be in New York and you'll never have it sent at all."

Maggie knew her friend was right but still wasn't sure she'd written exactly what she wanted to. Having finally plucked up the courage to ask Harry about sending a message, she hadn't been at all sure what she wanted to say. It seemed trivial almost to say so few words when there were so many more she wanted to write down, but Harry had told her to keep it short. "The first-class passengers send these messages for a bit of a lark," he'd told her. "They're amused by the technology, and the chance to communicate with their friends and family while they're on board a ship is too big a boast to miss out on. Some of 'em send two or three messages a day at twelve shillings and six-pence a time and think nothing of it, telling people what they've eaten for lunch or gossiping about a conversation they've over-heard. It pays well for the Marconi boys—and makes the day a bit more interesting for them; otherwise it's just relaying boring messages to the captain from other ships about sightings of ice and wind direction."

Maggie read over her words again. She'd already written eight different messages before asking for Katie's advice. "For the love of God, Maggie." Katie had laughed, reading over her friend's first few attempts. "Sure, why would he be carin' about what you were eatin' for dinner last night? Just tell him you miss him and you love him. That's all ye need to write."

Maggie didn't even understand how it was possible to send a message by radio from a ship in the middle of the Atlantic Ocean to a small town in Ireland, but she somehow felt that since it *was* possible, the words of the message should be care-fully considered and should really mean something to the sender and the recipient.

As Maggie considered a tenth attempt, Peggy came bound-ing into the cabin. She'd been out on the deck for a stroll after Mass, and her cheeks were flushed red from the breeze, her hair whipped into straggly rat's tails by the moist air.

"Maggie Murphy!" she cried in mock anger, throwing her-self down onto the bed between her two friends, bringing the distinctive scent of fresh sea air into the room. "If you are still feckin' around with that note, I'll murder you with my own hands, I swear I will. Come on, we're to meet Lucky Harry for our personal tour, and I'm sure he'll not be hangin' around for us *cailíní* all mornin'."

Although Harry had said their trip to the upper decks would be a birthday treat for Katie, they all knew that it was really for Peggy's benefit, the young lad obviously having fallen for her quick wit and country-girl looks. Maggie carefully folded the piece of paper with her short message to Séamus and tucked it into her skirt pocket just as Aunt Kathleen walked into the cabin. The three girls sat perfectly still and stared at her.

"Well, if ever I saw a sight of girls who were up to no good, I'm seein' it now in front of my very eyes," she said, putting her coat neatly on her bed. "What are you up to, the three o' ye?"

The girls glanced anxiously at one another, Maggie feeling the note in her pocket as if it were stolen diamonds. Peggy was the one to speak up.

"Nothin' much, Kathleen, there's nothin' much for us to be doin' on this ship after a few days. We were just goin' to check on the ship's log and go for a stroll on the decks or maybe join some of the others for a game of cards." Kathleen seemed placated, but just to make sure, Peggy continued. "Miss Dolan, how many more days is it now until we get to New York? We couldn't remember whether it was two or three."

Kathleen looked at them all, apparently convinced by Peggy's tale, feeling momentarily sympathetic for these young girls, stuck in the confines of a ship when they were so used to running in fields and busying themselves with chores.

"Only two more days, girls, and then ye will have the whole of America to explore. Go on now, be off with you, but mind you're not causin' any trouble."

Grabbing her coat and making sure the packet of letters from Séamus was still in the pocket, Maggie walked casually out of the cabin with Peggy and Katie. As soon as the door closed behind them and they felt sure they were out of Kathleen's earshot, they ran, giggling, along the labyrinth of passageways and corridors, across stairwells, and past elevators toward the stewards' cabins on Scotland Road where Harry had agreed to meet them.

Far from being as boring as Peggy had portrayed to Kathleen, their days on *Titanic* were some of the most extraordinary the girls had ever experienced. There were endless amounts of new people to meet, hot meals served to them three times a day, warm running water to wash themselves in, and a new life in America to look forward to. If Maggie hadn't felt such an ache in her heart for Séamus back in Ireland, she was sure that she would have the same carefree attitude and lust for life as she saw in Peggy and Katie. For now, she felt as if she was going through the motions; occasionally she'd forget herself and join in with the *craic* and the daily surprises of life aboard this remarkable ship, but then something would remind her of what she had left behind, like the bottle of holy water she felt in her coat pocket now. She'd forgotten that she had put it there after one of her neighbors gave it to her on the night of the American wake.

Maggie had been at those sorts of gatherings before, to drink tea and eat treacle cake and send off a cousin or a neighbor or a family friend and wish them well on the journey ahead. This time it had been different. This time there were so many of them leaving together, a mixture of young and old from five different villages in the parish; this time, she was one of the departing travelers.

As was usual with the American wakes, the evening had been an odd combination of celebration and despair, excitement and dread, haunting ballads and rousing song. For every tear there was raucous laughter, for every lament and prayer a tale of courage and hope. Maggie had observed the backslapping, the raising of the glasses of porter and *poitín*, the dancing of the jigs and the reels to the strains of the fiddle, up and down, up and down the flagstone floor of the Brennans' cottage into the small hours of the morning. She'd sat on an upturned crate in a cool corner of the room and wondered if anyone knew of the feelings of sadness and trepidation stirring in her heart.

It was a neighbor, Bridget Kelly, who had pressed the bottle of holy water and a batch of oatmeal cakes into her hands. "For good fortune and sustenance on the journey ahead," she'd said, tears streaming down her rosy cheeks.

Maggie had thanked her and clutched the items to her as if her very life depended on them.

That final night's combination of mirth and mourning was the culmination of weeks of exchanged visits, shared advice and intimacies, discussions about what clothing might be suitable for the journey, private farewells, and moments of quiet personal reflection. Maggie had seen enough tearful embraces on the doorsteps of their village to last her a lifetime.

"I hope I never witness such a sight again," she'd said to Peggy, "wake, burial, or otherwise."

Not even a week had passed since she'd put that bottle of holy water into her coat pocket and walked home across the fields with her aunt Kathleen. It already seemed like a lifetime ago.

Approaching the crew quarters now, the girls spotted Harry leaning against the wall, waiting for them. They stopped running and slowed to a walk as they neared him. He certainly looked handsome in his steward's uniform. His face was pleasant, clean-shaven and friendly looking. Maggie wasn't surprised that Peggy was sweet on him. It never surprised her when fellas were sweet on Peggy.

"Right, ladies. Now you must keep very quiet and try not to gasp too much," he teased, leading them up the steward's stairway in the direction of C deck, from which they would climb the ladder. "You can be thrown off a ship, you know, for gawping at the first-class ladies without permission!"

Maggie and Katie looked anxiously at each other, not entirely sure they wanted to take the risk.

"Ah, Harry, would you stop," Peggy whispered, sensing the others' hesitation and digging him in the ribs with her elbow. "You'll have their hearts crossways, God love 'em."

He laughed and motioned to the narrow steel ladder that led upward to B and A decks, several feet above them.

"He's only messin' with ye," Peggy continued, facing her two friends and smiling at Harry, pleased to be in on his joke. "Don't mind him at all. Right, Maggie, you go up first; Katie, you next; and I'll go last."

Climbing up carefully, they emerged at the back of the first-class promenade deck, poking their heads up before hoisting themselves onto the deck and scurrying behind one of the collapsible lifeboats, which kept them well hidden from view. They settled down into a crouch, their long skirts tucked up under their knees, their chins resting on their hands, which grasped the edge of the lifeboat for balance.

"That's the gentlemen-only smoking room," Harry whispered, pointing to a room across the deck. The girls craned their necks to catch a glimpse of the handsome gentlemen who were sitting about in crimson leather chairs, smoking cigars as they read their newspapers or wandered around the room, chatting with friends and admiring the artwork on the walls or the painted glass panels in the windows, which shone brilliantly in the sunlight streaming through them.

"And that's the Palm Court," Harry continued, enjoying his role of tour guide while keeping a good lookout for officers or senior stewards, who would not be at all pleased to see the group of them lurking in their hiding place. "See, there are palm trees and plants climbing the trellises. I bet you didn't reckon on there being proper plants growing on a ship!"

The girls were not at all interested in the flora; instead they gazed wide-eyed at the elegant ladies who sat in the wicker chairs and poured tea from dazzling silver pots into delicate china cups, the stunning cobalt blue and gold of the exclusive *Titanic* china glinting in the sunlight. Small white vases of elegant pink roses and white daisies sat on each table; silver sugar tongs rested on dainty saucers next to succulent slices of fruitcake, the sight of which almost made the girls drool.

They watched in silent awe as three young ladies, about the same age as themselves, chatted and laughed at one of the tables nearest to them, their Oriental-style silk dresses draped elegantly over their slim hourglass figures, ending just below the ankle to show a hint of their exquisite shoes. At another table, a group of older ladies—possibly their mothers, Maggie thought—were equally elegant in their more reserved lace blouses with stylish narrow sleeves and full-length skirts. All the ladies, young and old, wore huge hats decorated with all manner of accessories: lace, feathers, satin, ribbons, and stuffed birds. Maggie noticed a small boy behind them playing with a spinning top.

The three friends were stunned into silence by the splendor and grace of it all. It was as if they were watching their own private silent movie, unable to hear the conversations but able to admire the rich plums and teals, the soft pastel peaches and pinks, the virginal white, every conceivable manner of fabric, color, and style which seemed to be sitting in that room.

"See that girl there with the cigarette holder and the long white gloves?" Harry whispered, pointing out the particularly elegant lady sitting nearest to them. "She's a famous singer in the Broadway shows. Vivienne Walker-Brown." The girls had never heard of the woman, but she oozed such style and sophistication that all three of them wanted to trade their lives for hers immediately. "And that's her stupid little dog, Edmund, sitting under her chair," he continued. "It goes everywhere with her. I took it for a walk the other day, I'll have you know. Ugly little thing. I was half tempted to throw it overboard!"

At that, Peggy snorted a laugh so loud that it almost gave away their hiding place. If it hadn't been for the violinists entertaining the ladies, Maggie was sure they would have been heard.

"Peggy Madden! Shush!" Maggie scolded as they clambered quickly back down the ladder before anyone could arrest them or throw *them* overboard.

By the time they were all safely down, all four were laughing, partly with nerves and partly at the thought of Harry throwing a famous Broadway singer's dog overboard.

"Well, that's all very nice an' all," Peggy announced as she finally composed herself, wiping tears of laughter from her cheeks, "but I bet they can barely breathe trussed up into their corsets like stuffed turkeys. You wouldn't catch me sitting up there for all the fancy teacups in china." At the foot of the ladder, she turned to face Harry. "Well, young man, that was a very interesting excursion," she announced in a mock upper-class accent that had them all in a fit of the giggles again. "Thank you very much," she continued. "I . . . *we* look forward to seeing you at dinner, don't we, girls?"

The flush in her cheeks and the sparkle in her eyes were visible to them all as she turned to walk down the passageway to their cabin.

Maggie hung back, grabbing for the paper from her pocket.

"I wrote my note," she said, passing the folded page to Harry, feeling awkward at handing over her private words to a relative stranger, few words though they were. "You promise not to read it now, will ye, just give it to your friend, so?"

"Of course I won't read it. That's your words written down, and it's none of my business what you're saying or who you're sayin' it to. The Marconi boys will have to read it, though, y'know, in order to send it. You did know that?"

He looked at Maggie, feeling for her embarrassment.

"You great eejit, Harry, of course I know *that*," she replied, cuffing him on the shoulder. "And thanks for it. For helping me, like. Are you sure they won't be needin' the money, 'cause I don't have that many shillings with me."

"They'll do it as a favor to a friend," Harry replied. "Now don't be worrying about it. I said I'd help you and I will. I'll take it up to them straightaway. Now, get lost all of you, I've your lunch to get ready!"

The girls walked back to their cabin, chattering nonstop about what they had just seen.

"Imagine, girls," Peggy whispered. "If we work hard and marry well, we might sail back to Ireland on *Titanic* one day and sit among those ladies on that veranda. What about it, eh? Wouldn't that be a fine thing?"

"It would, Peggy," Katie replied wistfully. "It certainly

would for sure. But for now, a full belly, clean hands, and a game of rummy on the deck of one of the finest ships ever to sail the Atlantic ain't too bad for three *cailíní* from Ballysheen, is it?"

Laughing, they dashed past the *uilleann* piper, who was walking back to his cabin.

"Mornin', ladies," he announced, raising his cap to them. "And fine form ye all seem to be in today."

"It's my birthday," Katie shouted as they ran past him, "and what better place to be celebrating it, eh, Mr. Daly?"

He smiled; their good humor was infectious. "No better place indeed, miss," he replied. "No better place at all."

WHITE STAR LINE

ROYAL AND UNITED STATES MAIL STEAMERS.

ISMAY, IMRIE & CO.

COCKSPUR STREET, S.W.
LEADENHALL STREET, E.C.
LONDON,
JAMES STREET
LIVERPOOL
AND
CANUTE ROAD, SOUTHAMPTON

Agent at PARIS—
NICHOLAS MARTIN, 9, Rue Scribe.

WHITE STAR LINE

GENOA
NAPLES
BOSTON
NEW YORK
QUEBEC
MONTREAL

JAMES SCOTT & CO. Agents
QUEENSTOWN.

OCEANIC STEAM NAVIGATION COMPANY, LIMITED, OF GREAT BRITAIN.

THIRD CLASS (Steerage) PASSENGER'S CONTRACT TICKET.
(NOT TRANSFERABLE.)

CHAPTER 18

For a few rare moments, Maggie found herself alone in the cabin. She was enjoying life on board the ship more than she thought she would, but sometimes it overwhelmed her. There was so much noise all the time, from the baby bawling where it lay in its suitcase in the cabin next door to the constant drone of the engines and the endless fall of footsteps rushing along the corridor outside their cabin, crew and passengers coming and going at all hours of the day and night. They were noises Maggie wasn't used to, and she found it exhausting at times, yearning for the pitch blackness and total quiet of her familiar cottage bedroom.

When her aunt, Peggy, and Katie were occupied elsewhere on the ship, as they were now, Maggie often took the chance to return to the cabin for some peace and quiet. She used the time to write in her journal or to read one of the letters from the packet Séamus had given to her. She had read three of the letters so far, one for each day she'd been on *Titanic*. In his letters, Séamus had written about the times they had spent together, the first three letters covering the months from the start of their courtship in

February last year through to that April. Maggie was surprised by the tenderness of his writing; at how vividly he recalled the details of their time together during those months.

She took the packet from her coat pocket now, carefully untying the piece of string which held the bundle together. She took out the piece of paper at the front, marked *May 1911*, and unfolded it. The noises outside the cabin walls faded into the background, and a silence enveloped her as she began to read.

May 1911

Dear Maggie,

It is May now and the spring is here. The cherry blossom trees are still in full bloom. They are a mighty spectacle all right—I'd barely noticed them before, but now I can see them for all their loveliness, as you do.

I stood and watched you for a while today. You didn't know I was there, but I hid myself behind the barrels which were being loaded off the wagon outside O'Carroll's. I watched you under the cherry blossom tree as the drayman hoisted the barrels onto the ground and rolled them past me into the hatch of the cellar. I'm sure he thought I was in trouble and hiding from someone, not watching my lovely cailín.

You looked mighty pretty so you did with your curls all blowing in the wind and the petals falling about you. You were sitting on the grass with your back leaned against the

tree, and you closed your eyes. I wondered if you were thinking of me.

Then Peggy Madden came up and she gave you a fright
and you were after almost leaping off the ground! She said
something to make you laugh before she went on her way,
swinging her basket from her arm, the fellas all gawping at
her as they do.

I thought to myself, "They can gawp away, I've a girl
lovelier and prettier than any other in the whole of Ballysheen—in the whole of Ireland," and I was so pleased that
you were waiting for me under that tree and not just taking a
rest or waiting for some other fella.

When you saw me walking over to you, you smiled, like
you always do, getting those dimples in your cheeks. We went
strolling then, down to the lake, and threw stones and you
picked some flowers for me to take back to Da. When we
walked back, you put your arm in mine and leaned your head
on my shoulder and told me that this had been your favorite
day and that you wished all days could be like this; warm
and happy and the blossoms blowing in the breeze. I thought
I would burst I was so happy at that moment, and if I could
make that day happen for you again and again, Maggie
Murphy, I truly would.

Yours,
Séamus

As with the previous three letters, he had ended with the words *I will wait for you under our tree until the day you come back*.

Maggie held the letter for a few moments longer, letting the tears roll down her cheeks. Then she folded it carefully, placed it back among the other letters, and returned the packet to her coat pocket. She would read another letter tomorrow.

She turned to write in her journal then.

Private Journal of Maggie Murphy
April 14, 1912
Day 4 at sea

I can hardly believe that this is already our fourth day at sea. I sometimes feel like we will never be off this ship or away from the gray ocean—the lush fields of home seem far distant now. I've been wondering what my legs will feel like when they're back on dry land. They say that sailors sway in their sleep for a while after returning from sea. What a strange feeling that will be!

There was to be a lifeboat drill at eleven o'clock today, but it was canceled. Jack Brennan says it must be because of the cold—"probably too cold for the rich folk to be up on deck," he said. Aunt Kathleen has asked a steward for extra blankets for the beds tonight after we were waking up cold last night. Harry told me that most of the spare blankets are being used by the first-class ladies to keep their knees warm while they sit on the decks in the sunshine. I suppose we will just have to make do with what we have.

After Mass this morning, Harry took us up a special crew ladder to the upper deck. He's so bold—he could have got himself into a right bother of trouble if anyone had caught us, but what a sight we saw from our hiding place behind a lifeboat: the ladies taking tea and the gentlemen smoking their cigars. I think it took Peggy every bit of control in her body not to run straight up to one of them and ask them to marry her then and there. They really do live among such luxury up there, I wouldn't wonder if some of them never want to leave the ship at all.

I watched a little boy for a while who was playing with a spinning top. He was dressed all nicely in a cap and jacket and short trousers with long black stockings to keep his legs warm. A white teddy bear was on a deck chair near to him—I think it must have belonged to him. A few men stood about the deck and watched him—he made quite a sight being so engrossed in his little game, but I didn't see his parents anywhere nearby, only a lady who seemed to be his nanny, but she was occupied with some friends. I should think his parents were too busy taking their tea and talking with their rich friends to pay much attention to his little games. I felt sorry for him and would have liked to play with him myself for a while. He had a nice little face.

I have given Harry my message to Séamus. He says he'll make sure it gets sent today. He reckons on it reaching Séamus within a week—imagine what he'll think, a message from a ship in the middle of the Atlantic Ocean! It'll be the talk of Ballysheen without a doubt.

Hearing the unmistakable voices of Peggy and Katie chatting enthusiastically as they came toward the cabin, Maggie put her pen down and closed the book. Her few moments of solitude were over.

CHAPTER 19

New York
April 14, 1912

I t had been a hard day's work for Frances Kenny, and her plans to head to Macy's to buy a birthday gift for her Katie now seemed thoroughly unappealing.

Her employer, Emily Walker-Brown, was in full flow preparing for the homecoming of her daughter, Vivienne, and Vivienne's fiancé, Robert, after their vacation in southern Italy, where they had spent the past two months. Robert was a film financier Vivienne had met through her theater contacts, and after the run of her latest show had ended in January, he had proposed over tea in the Waldorf. They'd taken themselves off then to enjoy a little winter sunshine on the Continent, the Italian Riviera seeming to be the perfect spot for a young, well-connected American couple.

As Frances was well aware, having overheard many a conversation in the Walker-Brown household, Vivienne was greatly interested in anything European, finding the ladies so elegant and the countries so interesting. "New York may boast the highest buildings and the finest jewelry store and department store in the world," she'd heard Vivienne proclaim over tea one afternoon, "but that is nothing compared to the beautiful cobbled streets of a medieval Italian town or the frescoes in the Sistine Chapel. So much more culture. So much more elegance than this stinking hellhole."

Vivienne was a well-traveled, well-connected young lady who had educated herself in European culture and prided herself on the fact. She found most of New York's other society ladies dully misinformed and tired easily of their endless talk of millinery and couture. These things interested Vivienne as passing diversions, but they didn't engage her for long. When the chance of a winter in Italy came along, she'd grasped it with both hands and had literally dragged her new fiancé to the docks to board their steam liner. That they were unmarried and traveling unchaperoned had produced quite the society scandal—a fact that caused Vivienne great amusement and caused her mother to suffer from a terrible migraine for an entire week.

According to Mrs. Walker-Brown, whose conversations Frances also frequently overheard as she went about her business in the house, the theater bosses had contacted Vivienne by telegram, stating that they required her back in America to star in a new revue as soon as possible. Forced to cut her holiday short, Vivienne had been preparing to be quite furious about it all until the opportunity arose for her and Robert to travel back to New York on the White Star Line's new ship, *Titanic*, and on her maiden voyage too. This opportunity to mingle among America's richest and most influential businessmen and social elites was not to be missed.

Robert had booked their first-class tickets immediately; they would travel from Cherbourg along with the Astors and the Guggenheims, who had also been vacationing on the Continent. They had sent a telegram immediately informing Mrs.

Walker-Brown of their plans to return home and boasting of their having secured tickets for *Titanic*.

"Imagine it," Mrs. Walker-Brown had declared as she recounted the story to one of her luncheon friends. "They will be the first to ever sail on *Titanic*, and amid such luxury! They say her bedrooms are finer than the Waldorf-Astoria's and that she has the best of modern conveniences, a heated bathing pool, and six-course dinners every evening. The ladies are even permitted exclusive use of the gymnasium for several hours a day. I fear Vivienne may have good cause to visit the gymnasium if she is dining so well for seven days at sea!"

Anyone who was anyone in New York society was talking about *Titanic* that week. With so many influential businessmen and so much wealth aboard, people felt distinctly envious if they were not a part of it and distinctly delighted if they were.

For herself, Mrs. Walker-Brown was enjoying the chance to boast of her daughter's involvement in *Titanic*'s maiden voyage, making reference to it at every possible opportunity: while lunching with the ladies, while having her hair styled, and while informing her domestics of their duties for the day. Frances Kenny had heard so much about *Titanic* through Vivienne's many telegrams to her mother that she sometimes felt she was onboard the ship herself. She had ventured to tell Mrs. Walker-Brown that, as far as she was aware, her own sister, Katie, was also traveling on the ship, along with thirteen others from her hometown in Ireland.

"Oh, that's nice, isn't it," her employer had responded, barely acknowledging the fact. Frances suspected Mrs. Walker-Brown felt that there was little comparison to be made between the luxury with which her daughter would be surrounded during her journey on *Titanic* and the distinct lack of luxury surrounding her sister's own *Titanic* experience.

Frances knew that Emily Walker-Brown was extremely proud of her daughter's achievements and hoped that she and Robert would settle on a date for their wedding soon after returning to America. Vivienne was Emily's only daughter, and Emily was so thrilled about the impending wedding that she'd already settled on the hat she would wear as the mother of the bride. She'd shown it to Frances in the pages of *Harper's Bazaar* magazine. The hat was being worn by the First Lady, Helen Herron Taft, while she planted a cherry blossom tree in Washington.

"Isn't it wonderful?" Mrs. Walker-Brown had enthused in a rare moment of personal communication with her employee. "I don't think I've ever seen a hat quite as exquisite, and all those blossoms falling around her feet remind me of confetti. As soon as I saw that picture I knew that it was this very hat I would wear at Vivienne and Robert's wedding."

True to her word, she had tracked down the designer and ordered the exact same hat. It was waiting for her to pick it up in Bloomingdale's. All she needed now was the occasion to wear it, and it was her intention that before the summer was out, a wedding date would be fixed, and before the year was out, the hat would finally be introduced to her head.

Mrs. Walker-Brown had kept her domestics busy all that week, and with Vivienne having sent a telegram message to inform her mother that they now expected to dock in New York in just two days' time, the house was a hive of activity.

Being a widow, Emily Walker-Brown placed more emphasis than some other mothers might on her daughter's presence in the family home. She busied herself now, planning for welcome home parties and bridge evenings with the ladies and dinners with influential business executives and their wives and other socialites of New York's elite families. Having been socially dormant over the winter months, she felt a renewed vigor, which ensured that after a day's work, her home was left gleaming and her employees were left exhausted.

Before she finished up for the day, and sensing that her employer was in a more jovial mood than usual, Frances decided to ask Mrs. Walker-Brown's opinion about a suitable birthday gift for Katie.

"I'm thinking it would be nice to buy her something small from Macy's," she explained. "This being her first time in New York, and it being the largest department store in the world. But I was wondering, since you have such impeccable taste yourself, what you might suggest as a nice gift for her."

Clearly flattered, Emily Walker-Brown suggested gloves. "No lady should be without a decent pair, and Macy's has a wonderful selection of the finest styles. You are aware, of course, that Isidor and Ida Straus are traveling on *Titanic* also." Frances looked blankly at her, having no idea who Isidor and Ida Straus were. "The owner of Macy's department store and his wife!" Emily Walker-Brown continued condescendingly. "So, I think, considering that your sister will have celebrated her birthday aboard the very same ship that the owner of the store is sailing on himself, a gift from Macy's would be entirely appropriate. Entirely appropriate indeed. Yes, I should settle on gloves."

Frances resisted the temptation to inform her employer that she was sure Katie couldn't care less whether the owner of Macy's was sailing on *Titanic* or not, and thanked her for her advice before requesting permission to leave for the day. It was given.

Despite her exhaustion, Frances set out in the direction of 151 West Thirty-Fourth Street. A short while later, she emerged from the store, delighted with her purchase of a pair of white cotton gloves, elegantly presented in the traditional Macy's packaging, a white box with a red star in the center of the lid.

RMS Titanic
April 14, 1912

Katie Kenny looked at her dinner plate, admiring the White Star Line emblem on her otherwise plain white dish: a red swallowtail flag with a white star in the center. The same by-now-familiar detailing appeared on her coffee mug and soup bowl. It was little things like this—the logo of the ship's owners stamped onto every knife, fork, and spoon; the woven blankets on their beds, red with white detailing and the distinctive White Star Line star and lettering—that continually surprised and delighted her. It was a level of attention to the absolute last detail that she had not encountered before and certainly had not expected on a steerage ticket.

As Peggy started up another chorus of "Happy Birthday," encouraging half the passengers to join in (having done the same at breakfast and lunch), Katie smiled, delighted at the fuss and attention she was getting. She'd already had a good gawp at the first-class passengers and some of their fancy rooms, and Harry had brought a tray of cakes to the cabin a little earlier, the like of which Katie had never seen before, exquisite little tarts and buns and delicate slices of Madeira cake.

"They were for some fancy woman's afternoon tea," he'd explained, clearly delighted with himself. "They were sent back to the galley because the lady isn't partial to these particular types of cakes."

His exaggerated upper-class accent had sent the girls into a fit of the giggles as they scarfed all the cakes in a hurry and then felt sick.

And yet for all the day's amusement, and the plans for dancing and singing that evening, Katie wished that her family was there to celebrate with her. She thought of them back in Ireland, her mam and da and her brothers, and wondered how it must have felt for them to watch the travelers leave a few mornings ago—such a sight they must have been clattering out of Ballysheen. She thought of her sister, Frances, waiting for her in New York, and wondered how she would look after all these years of city living. She had heard that it could turn your face pale, what with sitting indoors a lot of the time and the fumes from the motorcars making you cough.

If she knew her sister at all, Katie imagined that she would be happily occupying herself getting ready for her arrival. She would have the house spotless from top to bottom and would no doubt have taken to getting extra pillows and bedding for her comfort after this strenuous journey stuck on board a stuffy ship with barely a board to sleep on. *How she'll laugh,* Katie thought, *when I tell her of the luxury we have known, of the knives with the White Star Line flag on the handles, the electric lighting and fresh running water in our cabins.* Katie's stomach flipped slightly at the thought of seeing her sister in just a few days.

Her thoughts were interrupted by Peggy, who was fussing at her to hurry up and eat her dinner.

"For the love of God, Katie Kenny, would you ever stop daydreamin' and eat that bloody corned beef and cabbage. We've a party to be havin', and we can't start it until you're there, what with it being for your birthday an' all."

Katie laughed. She was so fond of her friends Peggy and Maggie and so glad of their company. It had made the journey so much easier traveling all together.

"Right so, I'm hurryin'. Oh, and will we be expectin' the pleasure of young Lucky Harry for the hooley tonight?" she asked, winking at Peggy, fully aware of the affection she had formed for the steward.

"Might be," Peggy replied coquettishly, "Might not. I might have other men asking me out tonight for all you know. I saw that rich millionaire one lookin' at me upstairs!"

The girls laughed then as they finished their meals and rushed off to wash before starting their evening's merriment.

"D'you know what, girls?" Katie added as they neared their cabin. "I think this is my favorite birthday ever. When I'm an old lady, I'll tell my grandchildren how I spent my birthday on the grandest ship afloat, right in the middle of the Atlantic Ocean. They'll never believe me, sure they won't!"

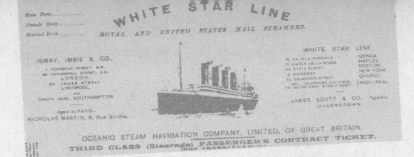

CHAPTER 20

Private Journal of Maggie Murphy
April 14, 1912
Day 4 at sea
2:30 P.M.

    Katie is having a fine birthday altogether what with Peggy singing endless rounds of "Happy Birthday" and Harry bringing posh cakes and showing us the first-class decks, and now we're just back from another huge lunch. Lord, my stomach aches. I think Mr. Durcan was right about the forty ton of spuds being on board—I feel as if ate half of those for lunch alone.

    It's a clear, bright day, so we've all come up on deck to walk off some of the food and get some wind in our hair. I'm sitting on a chair looking at nothing but endless ocean as far as my eyes can see. Peggy and Katie are leaning over the white iron railings around the side of the ship. They like to look over the edge and try to catch the spray on their faces. I daren't at all. It makes me feel dizzy being so high up and it's such a long way down and with the waves crashing and booming against the ship it's enough to scare the life out of you just looking. I don't even want to think how far down that ocean goes—it sends a shiver down my spine.

Katie was fretting for a while earlier when she thought she'd lost the piece of string she'd used to take the measurement for little Ailís O'Donoghue's finger. She's promised to send a ring back from America to Ailís and was careful to measure her finger with the string before we left home, so she could be sure of the correct size. The string turned up under her mattress of all places. Peggy had her on that a rat must've taken it and was planning to use it to make its nest in her bed. Peggy is so wicked sometimes.

I've been thinking on Séamus while I'm sitting here. I just remembered a day when we sat by the shore of the lake and threw stones together. He got one to bounce twelve times, the most he'd ever managed, he said. I wonder what he's doing now as I sit here. I wonder if he'll remember me this time next week, next month, next year. Our lives are going to be so different now, but I hope I don't get too interested in fancy skirts and hats while I'm in America, as all the girls seem to do. I don't think Séamus has much of a care for girls who fuss about skirts and hats and the like. I'd not like to go home and be all prissy and snobby about a life working in the fields. Traveling can do that to people, make them all talk of new and foreign things and make them forget where they come from in the first place. I hope I never forget Ballysheen.

I'm going back inside now. It's really getting cold and my fingers can barely hold the pen.

11:30 P.M.

Well, we are just back to the cabin from the best night of dancing and singing for Katie's birthday. Lord, it was mighty craic *altogether! I almost thought my sides were going to burst with the laughing. Some of them are still there, still singing and making music.*

Katie was in fine voice, singing her favorite songs, getting half the steerage passengers up on their feet and stomping out the beat. Even Ellen Joyce stopped talking about her wedding for a few hours and joined in with the singing, and Maura Brennan surprised us all by standing on a table and giving us a rendition of "Moonlight in Mayo"—and her being with a baby an' all! I thought Aunt Kathleen was almost going to die with the shame of us.

I walked out onto the deck for a few minutes to cool down from the heat and sweat of so many bodies dancing. It's such a cold night tonight, so I didn't stay out for long. It's a night to make your eyes stream with the chill, but there isn't a hint of a breeze. You'd almost be fooled into thinking the boat has stopped, the air is so still. The sea is so calm it almost looks like we're afloat on a piece of blackened glass. Other than for the millions of lights from the boat which light up the sea for a mile around, you'd hardly know we were here at all. She must be quite a sight to see from a distance.

I sat and watched the stars for a while—they seem to be out in their thousands tonight. It reminded me of the night of the Brennans' wedding—the night Séamus first asked me to dance. It was exactly the same moonless sky I gazed at that night. I felt for the letters in my pocket as I thought about him, and in the other pocket I found cherry blossom petals, of all things! I'd forgotten that I'd picked them up on the morning we left Ballysheen. They're withered and brown at the edges now and sorry-looking—I almost wish I hadn't put my hand in my pocket, hadn't remembered them.

We passed Harry as we returned to our cabins. He was retiring for the night himself, having already set the tables out ready for breakfast tomorrow morning. I cannot even think about food, my belly is still so full from all I've eaten today.

Of course Pat had to stop and check the ship's log outside the dining room one last time before going to his cabin. He told us it said, "Calm sea, twenty-two knots. Icebergs ahead."

"Pretty much the same as for the last three days then," Peggy said, and we all fell about the place laughing!

I hope Katie has enjoyed her birthday—she must be sad not to be celebrating with her ma and da and brothers as usual. They'll be thinking of her and missing her, especially today no doubt—and her sister, Frances, who is waiting for her to arrive in New York. How excited she must be to see the sister she hasn't set eyes on in three years! What with so many waiting to catch the first glimpse of their loved ones, there'll be quite a party planned for our arrival at the docks in New York, I should think.

The other three are already fast asleep. I should probably turn out the light soon and get some slee

The sudden jolt and the continuous shudder that followed rocked Maggie's bed. She sat bolt upright, wondering what on earth it was. The strange noise, as if a piece of calico was being torn, was followed by a sound she could liken only to that of one of the steam trains they had traveled on from Castlebar. She looked around the cabin. Her aunt Kathleen was sound asleep in the bed below her, and Peggy and Katie were also both fast asleep, the shaking and noises not having woken them.

After a few minutes, the shaking stopped and so did the noise. All the noise. Maggie sat in complete silence, her light flickering off for a few seconds before coming back on again. She realized that the familiar background drone of the engines had ceased.

"We must be stopped," she said aloud to herself. She couldn't think why this should be, though, and came to the conclusion that they must do this every night, shipping rules or something. As she was usually asleep by that time, she wouldn't have noticed it before.

To reassure herself, she got out of the bed and tiptoed silently across the floor, not wanting to wake the others. Opening the cabin door slightly, she peered out into the corridor. Nobody was about, nothing seemed amiss. Reassured, she crept back into her bed, placed her journal in her small black case, and turned out her light. She shivered for a while in her thin nightdress, wishing they had been able to get those extra blankets after all.

CHAPTER 21

Harry Walsh was a man of his word. He'd told Maggie he would deliver her note to Phillips and Bride in the Marconi room, and that's what he'd intended to do until he became distracted by an incident in the dining room at lunchtime when one of the passengers started to choke on a piece of bacon. There had been all manner of fuss and panic until Harry had given the man a hefty thump between the shoulder blades, at which point the offending piece of bacon had propelled itself across the dining room. Harry had been asked to write up an incident report for the officers, and when that was complete he'd called in on the man himself to check on his health.

"I had a lucky escape, young lad, thanks to you," the man had said with a chuckle when Harry asked how he was feeling. "It wouldn't have been very pleasant for the other passengers if I'd died right in the middle of lunch, would it? Imagine the headlines the papers would have had in the morning—'Man chokes to death on *Titanic*. Safety inspection under way'—now that would have taken the shine off the ship's triumphant arrival in New York, wouldn't it?'"

Harry had laughed at the man's sarcasm. "Yes, sir, I suppose it would! Not quite the headlines Captain Smith and Mr. Ismay are after! Well, I'm glad to see that you're fully recovered. Enjoy the rest of the trip."

As a result of this unexpected interlude in Harry's normal routine, all thoughts about Maggie's note were forgotten until he was just about to make his way to bed that night. Having laid out the tables for the following morning's breakfast—the final task before saloon stewards were permitted to retire for the evening—Harry felt in his pocket for the keys to his dormitory. That was when he discovered the piece of paper with Maggie's note on it.

"Oh, bugger it," he said aloud, stopping in his tracks.

"What's up, Harry?" asked one of the other stewards, who was also just finishing up, having laid the starboard side of the room while Harry had attended to the port. "Have you just realized you've put a spoon facing the wrong way or something?"

The other third-class saloon stewards liked to tease Harry about his insistence that everything be perfect before he would leave for the night.

"No, no, not a spoon." Harry was distracted, wondering what to do.

"What's that? A love letter from that Irish lass? You want to be aiming a bit higher, mate," the steward continued, pointing toward the ceiling. "That's where the lasses are who you want to be flirting with, not these nit-riddled steerage types."

"Aw, bugger off, will ya. You don't know what you're talkin' about."

The other steward laughed and went on ahead to the crew quarters.

Harry turned and walked back down the corridor toward the elevator. He'd promised Maggie he would get her message sent out that day, and being a man of his word, he was going to do exactly that.

The elevator carried him up to the portside boat deck, where he ran along the corridor past the officers' quarters to the wireless radio room.

"Phillips! Phillips!" he hissed, barely setting foot inside the room.

Jack Phillips, one of the two radio operators, turned in his seat and took the headset from his ears, his dark hair ruffled as if he had been running his hands through it, his cheeks flushed with concentration, his eyes looking tired.

"Bloody hell, Harry, what are you doing creeping around up here at this time of night?"

Harry handed him the small piece of paper. "Send us this, would you? Favor for a steerage girl with no cash."

Phillips glanced at the folded piece of paper. "Dunno, mate. I'm working Cape Race. We're backed up with messages from yesterday when the bloody wireless went down. I need to get them sent out before we lose the frequency. I'm making a bloody fortune!" He smiled and turned back in his seat. Harry could hear the crackle and whine of messages in Phillips's headset. "And," he continued, "there's ice warnings coming in from all over the place. Here's one that came in earlier. Haven't even had chance to take it up to the bridge yet."

Harry read the message over Phillips's shoulder.

WIRELESS

Received

NO_____ CK_____   TIME RECEIVED_____

From Mesaba to Titanic: Ice report in latitude 42°N
to 41°25'N, longitude 49°W to 50°30'W. Saw much
heavy pack ice and great number large icebergs.
Also field ice. Weather good, clear.

He waited patiently while Phillips finished sending another
message.

"Jesus Christ!" Phillips suddenly threw his headset down
onto the desk. "Bleedin' idiot!"

"What?" Harry asked. "What is it?"

"It's the bloody *Californian*. Nearly sent me deaf." Phillips
rubbed his ears.

"What did they say?" Harry asked.

"That they're stopped and surrounded by ice." Phillips replaced his headset and tapped out a reply.

"What did *you* say?"

"I told him to shut up—that I'm busy working Cape Race."

Waiting a moment for Phillips to calm down, Harry broached
the subject of Maggie's message again. "Oh, go on, mate, just
send us this one will you?" Harry cajoled, passing the piece
of paper to Phillips. "Just this one. I swear there won't be any
more. I think it's to her fella back home, and I promised her."

Phillips sighed and unfolded the paper. "All right then, just this one, though. Now sod off, will you, and let me get on with my work."

He put his headset back on, pushing the ice warning for Captain Smith to one side of the desk.

"Thanks, mate," Harry whispered, backing out of the room. "I owe you one."

Phillips ignored him, concentrating on his work.

Relieved to have Maggie's message on its way, Harry headed back down the corridor. A couple of second mate officers, strolling casually toward him, nodded as they passed. He admired their dark blue uniforms and decided at that moment that the next time he sailed on this ship, or any as magnificent, he would be wearing that uniform. His steward's uniform looked well on him, and seemed to attract the attention of giggly Irish girls, but an officer's uniform would look very well indeed. His mother had always told him dark blue brought out the color in his eyes.

A short while after Harry left the radio room, Phillips unfolded the piece of paper Harry Walsh had given him. Exhausted from the night's work, he started to tap out the words.

WIRELESS

Received

NO_____ CK_____   TIME RECEIVED_____

```
From Maggie Murphy Titanic to Séamus Doyle
Ballysheen Co Mayo Ireland: Dearest Séamus all is
well Titanic is a fine ship I hope your da is well.
Don't wait for me
```

A sudden jolt caused his finger to slip.

Phillips waited for a moment, sensing an unfamiliar vibration beneath his feet. He didn't like the feel of it. Not one bit.

The junior wireless officer, Harold Bride, emerged from the sleeping quarters at the back of the room, rubbing his eyes against the glare of the lights. "What the bloody hell was that?" he asked.

"Dunno, mate. It felt like an earthquake. Can you get earthquakes in the Atlantic?"

"Don't be such an idiot," Bride said. "That wasn't an earthquake. It feels like the engines have stopped."

"Does, doesn't it." Phillips looked at Bride. Neither of them spoke for a moment. "Go on up to the bridge and see what you can find out, will you? I want to get the last of these messages sent before I go to bed."

Bride left the room. Phillips continued with his work.

The shudder was barely noticeable, but it sent a dull vibration through Harry's shoes all the way up to the cap on the top of his head. Standing at one end of the long Scotland Road passageway, he grabbed on to the iron grille of the elevator door to steady himself. "What the hell was that?" he said aloud, although there was nobody else there.

He stood for a moment, the vibration continuing all the way through the metal, up his hands and arms into his shoulders. It made the hairs stand up on the back of his neck. Then it stopped and he heard a different sound, one he was familiar with. The engines had been put into reverse, and that could only mean that they were stopping the ship.

He considered going down to the boiler rooms to ask the

stokers what was going on but thought he might get more sense out of Phillips. The stokers could be curt at the best of times, and if they were busy putting the dampers down, they'd be less than pleased to see him.

He started to make his way back up the stairwells to the boat deck. As he turned to walk down the officers' corridor toward the radio room, he heard banging on doors and shouts of "All hands on deck!"

Leaning his head around the wall, he caught a glimpse of the two officers he'd walked past earlier. They were standing outside another officer's cabin, talking earnestly, their expressions serious. Straining to hear over the pounding of feet overhead and the shouts from the other officers, Harry caught snippets of their conversation.

" . . . hard-a-starboard . . . iceberg . . . reversed the engines . . . taking in water . . ."

Taking in water?

Hardly able to comprehend what he was hearing, Harry continued on along the corridor, unnoticed among the anxious faces, hushed conversations, and orders. He pushed open the Marconi room door. Phillips was huddled over the radio equipment.

"Oi! Phillips!" he whispered.

Phillips turned around. "For crying out loud, Walsh, what now?"

Harry could see from the look on Phillips's face that something was happening.

"I felt the shudder. The engines have stopped. What's happening?"

Just then Bride entered the room, ashen faced. "We hit an

iceberg," he said, his voice a low whisper. "There's damage to the starboard side below the waterline. She's taking in water. We're to radio for help. Captain Smith's orders."

"Radio for help?" Phillips looked stunned. "It isn't bad, is it? Surely they can close the watertight compartments?"

The three men stared at each other then, the crackle from the receivers the only sound in the small room. The look of fear on the radio operators' faces told Harry everything he needed to know. He nodded and walked slowly from the room, closing the door quietly behind him.

Almost in a daze, he wandered out onto the deck. Already there was a crowd of passengers there, first class, Harry presumed, judging by their formal dinner wear. They were mostly gathered around the starboard side of the ship, some leaning over the railings, others staring at the gigantic mass of ice which towered a little way in the distance behind the ship. It was a truly terrifying thing to behold.

Harry had never seen a real iceberg before. He'd seen them in picture books and encyclopedias as a child, marveling at the gigantic blocks of ice that glistened like turquoise jewels against the brilliant blue seas of the Arctic and Antarctic. He remembered being fascinated by them as a child, wondering how ice could possibly turn blue and questioning his father endlessly about how cold they would feel to touch and how they were made and whether it was true that the iceberg you can see is only a part of the entire thing. He remembered his father laughing at his inquisitive nature. "There's a saying, son: 'the tip of the iceberg,' that means you're only just seeing the beginning of something. If you saw an iceberg that was a hundred feet tall, there would be six or seven hundred feet more under the sea." Harry had thought his father was joking.

Staring now at this ice giant—which bore no resemblance to those in his childhood picture books—Harry wondered what his father would say. Far from being a glittering jewel, this iceberg was a chilling sight, looming dark and ominous from the black sea below, the mass of the thing almost unfathomable.

Harry shivered and drew his thin jacket around his shoulders, wrapping his arms around himself to try to retain some warmth in his body.

He heard children laughing and turned. Just behind him, huge lumps of ice, which had been knocked off the berg, lay on the deck. A group of young boys pushed them back and forth, watching them slip and slither across the polished wooden planks, their breaths of laughter caught in a fine mist before dispersing into the freezing night air. It was a bizarre sight, a surreal moment that Harry seemed unable to tear his eyes away from.

"Must be a hundred feet tall, that." His thoughts were disturbed by a gentleman in full formal dinner dress who had appeared at his side, gazing at the spectacle of the iceberg. "I hear the ship glanced off the side of it," the man continued. "No significant damage, though. Just as well we are aboard the mighty *Titanic*, hey! That berg could have easily sunk a smaller ship."

He laughed to himself then and pulled a white handkerchief from his breast pocket to wipe his spectacles, which had misted up in the cold.

"But I hear that she is taking on water, sir." Harry was hesitant, not wishing to cause a panic but unable to leave this man without telling him the truth of the matter.

"Really? Ah well, a bit of water won't bother a ship like this. They'll pump it out, lad, and we'll be on our way. Mark my words." He coughed slightly against the cold. "Well, I don't know about you, young man, but I think I'd rather finish my brandy than stand out here freezing to death. Good evening to you." He tipped his hat then and went inside.

"Good evening to you, sir."

Harry stood for a few moments longer, observing the normality going on around him. The looks on Bride's and Phillips's faces had told him everything. *Titanic* wasn't just taking on water, she was sinking and they were radioing for help.

As he watched, more and more finely dressed passengers appeared on deck, interested to see the iceberg for themselves. He recognized the theater singer whose dog he had walked that first day aboard.

"We were playing bridge," he heard her say to a colleague, "and then all this commotion occurred on deck, so we came out to see what all the fuss was about. I see now it is only a bit of ice. I've seen bigger lumps in my gin and tonic! Come along, ladies, let's go back in. It's freezing out here."

Harry remembered seeing her earlier that day, when he and the Irish girls had crept up the ladder and spied on the upper deck. It suddenly occurred to him that while these passengers were joking about the ice and returning to the warming blaze of the fires to finish their nightcaps, Peggy and Maggie and Katie and all the other passengers down in steerage would have no clue about what was happening. It was also their cabins that would be closest to the damage.

As he turned to make his way back down to E Deck to alert them, Harry passed a crew member who was starting to uncover the tarpaulin from one of the lifeboats.

"Excuse me, sir?"

"What is it, boy?" the man snapped, working the ropes as

quickly as he could, frozen as they were with the cold and his numbed fingers unable to grasp the fastenings.

"How long before she goes down?"

The crewman stopped then and looked at him, shocked by the directness of his question. It was a look of absolute fear that chilled Harry to his core.

"Two hours they say, lad." He continued to fiddle with the lifeboat ties. "The nearest boat won't be here for four," he added, unable to look Harry in the eyes.

There was nothing else to say.

Harry turned and ran as quickly as he could, his heart pounding in his chest, his mind racing, his mother's words ringing in his ears, "And mind that you look after those third-class passengers just the same as you would any of those wealthy Americans."

He had to get to Peggy and the Irish girls. He had to get them to the lifeboats.

PART FOUR

Captain Smith S.S. Titanic: Anxiously awaiting
information and probably disposition passengers.
Franklin.

Marconigram message sent from Mr. Franklin, White
Star Line, to Captain Smith, *Titanic*, on April 15,
1912

CHAPTER 22

RMS Titanic
April 14, 1912

Peggy. Peggy. Pssst, are ye awake?"

Silence.

"Katie. Katie Kenny. Aunt Kathleen?"

Silence.

Maggie sat up in her bed, stooping her head and shoulders so as not to hit the low ceiling. The electric lights had gone out. The darkness in the cabin was so intense she couldn't see her own hand as she waved it now in front of her face. She could hear her blood pumping through her ears.

"Pssssst, wake up," she hissed into the black silence, raising her voice a little now. "Is anyone awake?"

Her heart was pounding. She had never felt more alone in all her life. Too terrified to try to climb down from her bed in such darkness, she sat still, unable to ignore the sense of panic rising in her, the cold and adrenaline causing her to shiver in her thin nightdress.

The lights flickered momentarily on and off again.

She could hear running overhead.

The baby started bawling in its suitcase in the cabin next door.

She sat stone still, her ears straining to catch any noise from the corridor outside the cabin: occasional shouts, thumping on doors, footsteps pounding. Her thoughts returned to Joseph Kenny's tea leaves, Pat's dropped sovereign, and the strange man who had spoken to Peggy at Queenstown. Something was wrong. She was sure of it.

The bang on the cabin door made her jump, knocking her head on the ceiling.

"Peggy! Maggie! You in there? It's me. Harry."

There was an urgency to Harry's voice, an edge that Maggie didn't like.

"What the feck was that?" The bang on the door had woken Peggy.

"Peggy, thanks be to God . . ."

Another bang on the door.

"Girls, you in there?"

"Harry, yes, yes," Maggie was shouting now. "We're here."

"Jesus, Mary, and Joseph, Maggie Murphy, what the devil has you shoutin' in the middle of the night? What time is it? Who turned off the lights?"

Kathleen was awake now, followed shortly by Katie, who rubbed her eyes sleepily as the lights flickered and, much to Maggie's relief, stayed on.

"Oh, thank the Lord," Maggie exclaimed. "I'm coming," she shouted to Harry, climbing as quickly as she could down the steps at the side of the bunk bed. Walking the few steps to the door, she flung it open to reveal Harry standing in the corridor, trying to catch his breath.

Maggie shook, whether with the cold or anxiety she wasn't

sure. She squinted against the glare of the brightly lit corridor.

"Harry. What is it? What's wrong? Why have we stopped?" She was shocked by the look of dread and anxiety on his usually smiling, relaxed face.

By now the three other women in the room were sitting up in their beds, their blankets wrapped around them against the cold, leaning out to hear what Maggie was saying.

"Stopped?" Kathleen exclaimed. "We've stopped?"

Maggie turned to her aunt. "Yes. Did ye not feel the shuddering? The lights have been off. I was callin', but none of ye would wake." She turned back to Harry then, looking at him seriously, intensely, as another steward ran along the corridor behind him. "Harry?"

"You need to go up," he announced slowly, trying to regulate his breathing and lowering his voice, not wanting to cause a panic. "There's a problem with the ship and you need to go up now. Y'know. To the lifeboats."

Maggie couldn't believe what she was hearing. "Lifeboats?" She said this louder than she'd intended to, loud enough for the others in the cabin to hear. "I thought they'd maybe run out of coal for the boilers or hit a whale, but . . . lifeboats? What's after happenin'?"

"What's that you're sayin' about lifeboats?" Peggy had joined Maggie and Harry at the door.

Harry looked at the two girls, wondering how much to tell them. Wondering what the words he was about to say would mean for their plans for a life in America; what they would mean for their lives, period. It was as if everything had suddenly changed for all of them, for everyone on this ship.

"They've hit an iceberg." He closed his eyes briefly, unable to look directly at these two girls whom he'd shared such fun with in the few brief days they'd known each other. He felt as if this were somehow all his fault.

"An iceberg?"

"Yes, Peggy. And it's done plenty of damage, by all accounts. The ship's taking on water."

He continued to tell them everything in a rush, suddenly relieved to be able to share his knowledge. "You've got to go to the upper decks straightaway—and put on your life jackets. It isn't safe to stay here, girls. Honestly, you have to believe me. I heard the officers themselves saying. There's ice all over the decks up there, and you should see the iceberg, it's as big as a mountain and—"

"You can still see the iceberg?"

"Peggy, be quiet now." Kathleen was up and had heard every word Harry said. "How bad is it?" she asked, pushing her way in front of the girls to talk to him directly, her blanket wrapped around her out of modesty before the young man. "How bad is the damage? Will the ship go down?"

"Go *down*?" Peggy was horrified by what she was hearing. "But this ship's unsinkable. I read it in the adverts in the papers."

Ignoring Peggy, Harry responded to Kathleen's questions as he knew she needed him to, with stark, honest facts. "It's the starboard side, miss. Too many of the watertight compartments are damaged. I heard someone say two hours."

Kathleen listened and nodded calmly. "Thank you. For coming to alert us. It was very good of you, sure it was."

Putting her shoes onto her bare feet and grabbing her coat, Kathleen turned then to the three girls. "I must go and tell the others. Wait for me here. I won't be long." There was a certainty to her aunt's voice that Maggie had heard many times in her life, most recently on the morning just four days ago when they'd left Ballysheen. *It is time,* she'd said, the words sending a shiver down Maggie's spine with their finality and purpose. It was the same finality and purpose she heard in her aunt's voice now. "Gather your things together and be ready to head up on deck as soon as I get back."

She turned then, and Maggie watched her stride purposefully along the corridor. It struck her how much less imposing Aunt Kathleen looked in just her nightdress and coat. No swishing, fashionable skirts. No carefully styled hair. Her aunt looked, for the first time in Maggie's life, like the middle-aged woman she was. The vulnerability frightened her.

"Girls, listen." Harry stepped into the cabin, pushing the door almost closed behind him. The three girls huddled around him, all previous thoughts of flirting and playfulness gone from their minds. "This is *really* serious. The ship *is* going to sink, and the nearest boat is too far away to reach us in time." The girls stood in shocked silence. "As soon as she comes back," he added, nodding in the direction Kathleen had gone, "make sure you go up to the decks. And put your life jackets on. Do you understand?"

"Yes, Harry." Maggie spoke in barely a whisper. "We understand. Will ye be goin' to tell the others, so? There's a family of nine in the cabin next to us and they've a small baby." He nodded. "It sleeps in a suitcase," she added, a fact that had troubled her every night, especially since she'd seen the opulence of the first-class decks.

Harry turned to walk out, pausing for a moment as if wanting to say something else. He looked at Peggy. She returned his gaze. There was an unspoken understanding between them, even though neither one said a word.

With Kathleen gone and the sounds of Harry pounding on

the door of the cabin next to theirs, and then the next and the
next, the three girls quickly put on their life jackets and then sat
together on Katie's bed, trying to take in what they had heard,
the unspoken recollections of predictions in the tea leaves and of
strangers in railway stations hanging ominously in the air between them.

Peggy spoke first. "Well, let's be gettin' our things ready
then, girls. Kathleen will be back soon with the others and then
we'll all be wantin' to go up them stairs to the decks."

"They'll have opened the gates, won't they?" Katie's question was left unanswered. None of them knew. "Well, maybe we
should say a prayer first," she suggested. "Y'know, for all our
safety like."

They looked at each other and nodded in agreement. Maggie
grabbed the rosary beads that Séamus had given her as a parting
gift, and together the three girls sat on Katie's bed, the White
Star Line blankets they had admired so much when they first
saw them wrapped around their shoulders for warmth. They recited their Hail Marys with more sincerity than they had ever
recited them before.

Their prayers complete, they sat in silence, holding each
other's hands, afraid to let go.

Harry ran from cabin to cabin, pounding on the doors until
they were opened and telling the occupants that they needed
to put on their life jackets and make their way to the upper decks
immediately. Other crewmen and stewards were doing the same.

Many of the occupants didn't speak English and couldn't understand what Harry was saying, throwing their hands upward
in frustration. Those he did manage to rouse barely took him
seriously, assuming it was the drill that had been canceled ear-

lier that day. They said that they would put on their life jackets, before closing the door and returning to their beds. Others didn't even respond to the banging on the door, too stupefied from a night of drinking in the bar to hear Harry or any of the commotion that was now building in the corridors.

After rushing around the cabins for forty minutes or more, getting occasionally lost among the endless maze of corridors and companionways, Harry noticed a definite list in the ship, having to walk up an incline as he made his way along Scotland Road and using the walls on either side of him for balance. He was relieved to bump into his friend Billy.

"Christ, mate. Have you heard? We're bloody sinking."

"Y'don't say. She's almost totally underwater in the first five compartments. Christ only knows what's gone on in the boiler rooms. They've closed the watertight doors—with the stokers still inside, I reckon. There's men down there trying to keep the generators going so at least we'll have some light to watch ourselves drown by."

"Christ, Billy, don't. It's terrifyin'. Did y'see the size of that iceberg?"

"Yeah. I went up. There's fellas up there drinking their brandy being serenaded by the violinists. You'd think it was a special bleedin' iceberg cruise or somethin'. There's a whole gang of Irish in the dining room. Have you seen them? Some are already at the booze and others are sittin' around prayin' with those beads they have—fat lot of use they'll do 'em at the bottom of the ocean. Captain Smith's ordered the lifeboats to be swung out."

Something within Harry sensed that he needed to go to the dining room. "Right, keep banging on the doors and waking people up. I'm going to the dining room to shift everyone up the stairs." He started to make his way back along the corridor. "Oi! Billy," he called back to his friend. "I'll see you up there. Right?"

Billy turned and gave him a thumbs-up with his trademark cocky grin. "Not if I see you first, Walsh!"

Before going to the dining room, Harry returned to cabin 115, where he found the three girls still waiting patiently for Kathleen to come back.

"Harry," Peggy gasped when she saw him. "We can feel the ship leanin'. We don't know where Kathleen is."

"You've got to go, girls," he urged. "There's a lot of Irish gatherin' in the dining room. She's probably gone there to find everyone in your group. You should go there. Now. It's not safe to hang around here. The corridors are getting busy with people movin' their cases, and the stairs are getting blocked. Go on, go and wait for her in the dining room. You can come back for your cases when you find her. I've got to go and keep helping others."

He left them alone again.

"Right then," Peggy announced, standing up and grabbing her coat. "You heard what he said. Let's go."

Maggie was anxious. "But she said to wait here."

"I don't care what she said, Maggie. She might have got held up somewhere, or caught in a crowd. Y'heard what Harry said about the corridors getting blocked, and I don't know about you, but I don't like the way this ship's leanin'. There'll be water creepin' in here soon, and I'm certainly not plannin' on hangin' around just so as I can say I touched a bit o' the Atlantic Ocean. Come on, we'll find your aunt Kathleen. I know we will."

Kathleen could see the look of panic on her friend Maura Brennan's face and noticed how she instinctively placed her hand on her swollen belly.

"We've got to gather our things, Maura," she explained to her again, "and make our way to the upper decks. I'm tellin' everyone to meet in the dining room first, so we know everyone's accounted for. Y'know, like we did on the train journey down."

"Should we dress?"

"There's no time. Just coats and shoes—and hats. It might be chilly up there."

"It will all be all right, Kathleen, won't it? They'll be sendin' a boat to rescue us?"

"I'm sure they'll be doin' their best, Maura, yes. Now don't be standin' here chattin'. Get to the dining room. I'm going to wake the others."

From cabin to cabin, Kathleen moved quickly and calmly, passing on the information about the iceberg and the need to get up on deck. As ever, she was purposeful and pragmatic, reminding the others in her group to take their cases and to put on their life jackets.

As the minutes passed, she could feel the panic spreading throughout the ship. Raised voices, orders being shouted, people crying, others calming them, children being soothed as they tried to understand why they had been taken from their beds in the middle of the night. The corridors were becoming crowded with people trying to carry their luggage, cases of all shapes and sizes and entire trunks being pushed along. Bodies were pressed against the walls to let others pass. Kathleen realized things were becoming chaotic. It made her nervous.

Having passed on the instructions to the Ballysheen group and sure that they were moving to the dining room, Kathleen returned to her own cabin to collect the girls, holding on to the walls as she walked down the noticeable slope.

Her feet felt the water first, the shock of the icy cold causing her to jump.

"Oh, good Lord above," she cried out, realizing that the cabins at the front of the ship were already being flooded. Splashing through the ankle-deep water, she shouted ahead, an urgency to her voice. "Girls, come along now! We must hurry!"

Pushing open the door to the cabin, she stopped dead. It was empty. The girls had gone. Just Peggy's hat and Maggie's small black case remained on their beds.

CHAPTER 23

It was a strange scene that met the three girls as they arrived at the dining room, with people sitting about next to their luggage as if they were waiting for a train. The room, which was usually full of neatly ordered rows of tables with relaxed chatter and the clink of cutlery on china filling the space between them, was now filled with tension and praying and anxious conversation.

Maggie watched as men paced the floor, rubbing their stubbled chins in thought. What should they do? How could they help their wives and children get out of this awful situation? Some were bent down on their haunches, asking others what *they* had been told, trying to glean whether they knew any more than they did before returning to their own families to relay the latest information and rumors. The only certainty was that nobody really knew what was happening. Some had been told there was nothing to worry about, while others had been told the ship was sinking. What they all seemed to agree on was that they should wait there for further instructions from the crewmen or officers. Their social status meant they were familiar with awaiting instructions, so that was what they did now.

Among the men, women sat in groups reciting Hail Marys; mothers wrapped blankets around their small, confused children, soothing them, trying to dispel their fears, although Maggie could tell by the look in their eyes that their own fears were as real as those of their children. Those who could not understand or speak English sat in huddled, private groups, unsure of what to do or whom to ask. Someone was playing the piano; others were taking advantage of the confusion and taking a drink from the bar. It struck Maggie that the tables were all laid out neatly for the morning breakfast service, the crisp white linen tablecloths and the neatly arranged place settings at odds with the confusion and disorder around her. She had admired all of these small details over the last few days—now it seemed ridiculous that a ship that was sinking with thousands of people on board still looked so neat and tidy.

It was Maura Brennan who saw them first.

"Maggie! Girls! Over here," she called, standing up on a table so they could see where the voice was coming from.

"Oh, thanks be to God, girls, look. It's Mrs. Brennan and the others."

They pushed their way through the gathered groups of passengers, stepping over cases and trunks that lay scattered on the floor, weaving in and out of people who blocked their path. Maggie passed the young English girl, Elsie. She was sitting with her family, cradling her baby brother in her arms. The two girls looked at each other and smiled a desperate smile. Maggie saw the *uilleann* piper talking rapidly with a group of other men. How familiar these faces had become in the few days they had shared the space on this magnificent ship. She wondered what would become of them all.

"Where's Aunt Kathleen?" Maggie inquired, immediately scanning the familiar faces of the Ballysheen group, but not seeing her aunt's among them.

"She's been waking everyone, Maggie. Just like your aunt, organizing us all, walking up and down those corridors until every one of us was woken and dressed with our coats and shoes. She told us all to wait in here—that she'd join us."

Maggie glanced around again. "But she's not here, Mrs. Brennan! I don't see her."

"Well, she must have gone back to fetch ye girls. She'll be here soon. Don't be worryin', child."

"We shouldn't have gone without her. She'll be wonderin' where we've got to. Maybe she's waitin' for us in the cabin. Should I go back?"

"Good Lord, girl. You will certainly *not* go back. The ship is sinking. If we need to go anywhere, it's up to the decks."

"Ah, Maggie. My hat! I forgot my hat." Peggy was already turning to walk back for it.

"Wait! Peggy, wait!" Maggie cried. "I'll come with you."

And with that, before anyone could stop them, the two girls started to push their way back through the crowds, out into the corridor, running when they could and excusing themselves to push past people when they couldn't.

As they approached their cabin, they saw the water creeping ominously along the corridor.

"Oh, Peggy, look. It's already goin' down!"

Without thinking for a moment Peggy strode through the water, pulling Maggie with her, the cold making them both gasp and shriek, the bottoms of their coats dragging through the water.

"Yes, Maggie. It is goin' down. And I'm not plannin' on lettin' my lovely new hat go down with it."

Entering the cabin, they quickly realized Kathleen wasn't there. Maggie felt frightened for her and hoped that she would be among the others by the time they got back to the dining room.

Reaching up to her top bunk bed, Peggy grabbed her hat and the gloves that she always kept inside it. Turning to clamber back down, hardly able to bear the thought of putting her legs back into the freezing water, she noticed Maggie's small black case sitting at the foot of the opposite bunk bed.

"Are ye plannin' on leavin' that here, or d'ye want to take it with you?" she said, pointing up at the case.

"I forgot about it completely," Maggie replied as she stood on the edge of Kathleen's bed and reached up, feeling around until she grabbed hold of the case.

Stepping hesitantly back down into the water, she instinctively reached into her coat pocket, the reassuring bulk telling her that the packet of letters was still there. Then they left the narrow room that had become their home for a few brief days, splashing back up the corridor.

"We had some fun in there, didn't we?" Maggie whispered, her teeth already chattering with the cold. She thought about how they'd giggled after Harry had smiled at Peggy and the chats they'd had late into the night about what it would be like to live in America. She thought of the look Aunt Kathleen had given them when she'd caught them deciding what Maggie would write in her telegram message to Séamus. They'd gone up the ladder to the upper decks then to spy on the rich and famous.

She briefly wondered what was happening up there now; their after-dinner drinks and restful slumber had been rudely interrupted, no doubt, by the noise being made as the crewmen got the lifeboats uncovered.

"We did, didn't we?" Peggy stopped, turning to face her friend. "Maggie, I can hardly believe the ship is sinkin'. I'd think I was dreamin' if I wasn't so scared out of my mind. We will be all right, y'know. That fella in Queenstown said I would survive—and I'm not survivin' without you, y'know."

The two shared an uneasy smile and grasped each other's hands.

"Come on, Peggy. I don't like the look of that water at all. We need to get up to the lifeboats."

Shivering from the icy chill of the water that seeped out of their shoes, their feet squelching inside, the bottoms of their coats and nightdresses soaked and clinging around their knees, the two girls splashed back to the dining room as quickly as they could.

In the few minutes they had been gone, it had been transformed into a scene of total panic and confusion. There seemed to be twice as many people in the room as there had been before, and the girls made their way back to the area where they'd left the others. They were still there, but there was no sign of Kathleen.

Harry struggled as he pushed his way through the crowd that had gathered on the staircase to the upper decks. It was almost impossible to get up with the cases and life jackets impeding everyone's movements. It was becoming a desperate situation, and he knew that time was running out. It was almost an hour now since they had struck the iceberg. He knew that there could be only an hour left for them to get off the ship.

He was trying to escort a group of about twenty-five passengers up from the steerage accommodations, but it was virtually impossible. As he finally emerged onto the deck, the noise and the icy chill of the night air hit him with surprising force. It was a scene very different from the one he had left an hour ago, when a strange calm had clung to the ship. Now there was anything but calm, as a frantic attempt to get people into the lifeboats was well under way, crewmen shouting orders to one another across the intermittent hiss of steam rushing to escape from the funnels—a deafening, shrieking noise that made Harry place his hands over his ears.

Relieved to have got the group of passengers safely up on deck, he moved them toward the portside aft, where he knew the lifeboats would be lowered first. Officers were shouting instructions as passengers hesitated, unsure about climbing into the wooden lifeboats that were being slowly lowered over the side of the ship to begin the terrifying seventy-foot descent to the freezing ocean below.

"I'll not get in, John, I'll not," he heard one woman protesting to a man who was coaxing her into the lifeboat. "I'll not leave without you."

"I'll be in the next boat," he assured her. "When all the women and children are safely in, then they'll let the men go. Now, get in. You're holding up the others and we don't want to cause a fuss."

The woman relented finally, climbing reluctantly into the lifeboat, where she sat among forty or so other women and young children. At that, it was lowered away. It occurred to Harry that there seemed to be room for many more in the lifeboat, but he assumed the crewmen knew what they were doing. Perhaps the lifeboats could take only so much weight?

Having guided his own group of twenty-five or so toward the front of a small crowd waiting to get into the next lifeboat, Harry retraced his footsteps to get back to the dining room to collect more. He was especially keen to see Peggy and the others, assuming that they were all still down there, waiting for instructions as to what to do next.

Returning to the stairwell, he realized there was little point trying to make his way back down. It was, by now, a seething mass of bodies and luggage. Stewards and crewmen were standing at the top of the stairs, blocking anyone from stepping onto the deck. It was clearly going to be impossible to get back down that way. Harry looked around him, from left to right. It was the same scene everywhere he looked.

"Oi! Mate," he called across to one of the stewards whom he recognized from the dormitory and who seemed to be in charge of the mass of steerage passengers trying to get up from the lower decks. "What's goin' on? Why are you not lettin' 'em up?"

"Officer's orders, mate. They're creating a panic, all rushing to the lifeboats and tryin' to jump into them as they're being lowered over the side. I've already seen one woman fall overboard. They've gone crazy. And they've all brought their bloody luggage. Look at 'em. Cases, trunks, the lot. You'd think they were trying to rebook themselves onto a pleasure cruise, not get off a sinkin' bloody ship."

"But you can't keep them penned in the stairwells. How's anyone else gonna get up?"

The two men looked at each other and the steward shrugged. "Damned if I know, mate. Damned if I know. I'm just followin' orders. That's all." There was a sense of resignation in his voice that Harry didn't like.

It was then that he heard a dog barking. Turning toward the sound, he caught sight of the first-class woman whose dog he had walked on the upper decks a few days ago. She was standing in a white silk evening gown, her fur stole around her neck, a fur hat on her head, and her coat draped elegantly over her shoulders. The dog was in her arms, barking at all the noise and commotion. Her fiancé was trying to persuade her to put on her life jacket.

"Oh, stop fussing so, will you, Robert, for goodness' sake," she chided. "I am perfectly sure that the officer meant for the life jackets to be worn only when people are in the lifeboats. There is absolutely no good reason for putting the damned thing on when we're still standing around on the deck. It will just get in the way. They're such ugly-looking things anyway. I refuse to wear it any sooner than is absolutely necessary."

"Oh, on the contrary, darling," Robert replied, trying to lift the life jacket over her head. "They're the very latest thing this season. Everyone is wearing them now! Look around."

"Oh, Robert," she chastised, a look of disgust on her porcelain face. "Don't be so utterly ridiculous. And could you please ask Anna to hurry up with a blanket for Edmund. The poor mite is trembling with the cold. Look at him!"

Harry watched the exchange in disbelief. She seemed to be in no hurry whatsoever to get into a lifeboat, and was she *really* worried about how she looked at that particular moment? The ship was sinking, for God's sake. People were already dying in their efforts to save themselves, and all Vivienne Walker-Brown was worried about was how she looked and whether her precious little dog was all right.

Harry recalled how he had taken a dislike to the woman from

the minute he'd first seen her. She now appeared to him the epit-
ome of selfishness, and he wondered how the Irish girls could
have been so impressed by her when he'd sneaked them up the
ladder to spy on her and the other first-class idiots.

The ladder!

Why hadn't he thought of it before?

Taking a moment to get his bearings, he ran around to the
other side of the ship, past the gentlemen's smoking room and
the Palm Court, toward the crew ladder he had brought the girls
up that morning. In his hurry, he barely acknowledged the fact
that many of the first-class passengers were standing around in
their life jackets, chatting pleasantly, finishing their drinks and
smoking their cigars while the musicians played soothing music
in the background. The iceberg still loomed ominously in the
distance, and people were still crowding around to look at the
chunks of ice that had been knocked off it onto the deck.

Clambering down the ladder, which was empty, Harry ran
the length of Scotland Road, negotiating his way along the now
familiar labyrinth of corridors to the third-class dining room,
encouraging the people he passed to wait there. "I'm coming
back!" he shouted to them. "Wait here. The stairwells are
blocked. I know a way up. Wait here."

By now the dining room was completely chaotic. He pushed
his way through the crowd, heading toward the piano, where he
had last seen Peggy and the Irish group.

They weren't there.

He looked frantically around the room until he saw a distinctive green hat. Peggy! Relieved, he ran toward the group,
urging them to come with him. He grabbed Maggie by the
shoulders.

"Maggie, listen. You're not going to be able to get up on deck using the stairs. D'you understand? They're all blocked with people and they're not letting anyone up at the moment."

She looked at him, a wild terror in her eyes.

"D'you remember the ladder, Maggie? The one I took you up this morning?"

"Yes."

"Go there now. It's the only way up. Take your group and I'll meet you up there. D'you remember the way?"

Peggy was listening. "I do," she said. "I remember. I'll take them."

"I'm going to fetch some others to come up with us," Harry continued. "I'll see you on the deck. Wait at the top of the ladder. I know where there's a lifeboat."

Maggie grabbed his arm. "Harry, can you take the family sittin' over there?" She pointed in the direction of Elsie, the young English girl, and her family. "They've a small baby."

"I will. Now go, all of you. And hurry. There isn't much time." Seeing them start to reach for their cases and luggage, Harry spoke again. "You'll have to leave the luggage. There's no room for it and it's making it difficult for people to move, getting in the way an' all."

Maggie watched as Harry moved over to the English family and spoke quietly to the father.

Among her own group there was consternation as they started discussing whether they should leave their cases behind as Harry had instructed.

"Well, let's do as the man says," Maura Brennan announced in a clipped tone, assuming the role of group leader in Kathleen's absence. "There's nothin' in these cases we can't replace. If it's my life or my possessions, I know which I'd rather be keepin'. Now come on, all of ye. Let's at least give ourselves a chance."

Reluctantly they moved away from the pile of trunks, Ellen Joyce crying more than most at the thought of leaving all her wedding gifts behind. Katie put her arm around her as they walked out of the room.

"You still have your ring, Ellen, and your beautiful gold watch. Your fella wouldn't want you to be fussin' about linen and lace when we're in such trouble, y'know."

Maggie didn't even notice that she was still clutching her small black case as she and Peggy led the rest of the Ballysheen group out of the dining room and along the corridor to the crew ladder.

As Harry had said, the ladder was not blocked by other passengers. Just a few crewmen and stewards were making their way up it. Maggie gripped the cold iron rungs. Their route to the boat deck, and to safety, was clear.

Kathleen was hemmed in on the stairwell. She couldn't move up onto the decks because the officers wouldn't let them and she couldn't move back down because of the surging mass of people behind her.

She'd started up the stairwell to help a little boy who'd become separated from his mammy. She'd come across him in the corridor on the way back to the dining room after she realized that the three girls had gone from their cabin. "Mammy! Mammy!" was all he would say, whimpering and cowering in a corner. There wasn't a bone in Kathleen Dolan's body which could leave him there. When she'd urged him to tell her where he'd last seen his mammy, his tiny finger eventually pointed toward the chaotic stairwell. Taking his hand, Kathleen had rushed with him to the stairs. His mother was near the top, calling for him, frantically searching the blur of faces behind her. Kathleen had carried him up to her and was now stuck.

She was sure she could make out the voice of the steward Harry, asking the officer at the top of the stairwell what was going on. If she hadn't been a proud woman, she might have considered calling out to ask him to tell the others that she would see them on deck, but she still had her dignity, despite the desperate situation, and screeching someone's name like a fishwife was not in Kathleen Dolan's nature. So she stood among the many others and waited patiently until it was their turn to ascend and get into the boats.

It was at that moment that Kathleen heard a gunshot. For the first time in her life she was terrified. For the first time since Harry had woken them to tell them what had happened, she truly wondered whether she would ever see her niece or the others again.

CHAPTER 24

Cass County, Illinois
May 1, 1982

Grace loved the wildness of the wind, the way it whispered through the barley fields and sent ripples rushing along the rivers and lakes, and the clouds hurtling across the sky. To a girl who had spent her childhood outdoors, the wind brought a feeling of reckless freedom, reminding her that she was alive, feeding her soul with a new energy.

It was two weeks since her birthday party and a welcome, blustery Saturday afternoon as she drove the short distance from Maggie's home to the nearby town. Maggie sat in the passenger seat, commenting, as she always did, on the irresponsible speed of the other drivers, tutting loudly as they overtook other cars. Grace didn't notice. She was thinking. For the first time in years, she was *really* thinking, about her past and about her future. She was excited, purposeful, hopeful.

As she had done every Saturday afternoon since she dropped out of college, Grace was taking Maggie out for afternoon tea. It was a happy arrangement they'd fallen into by chance, stopping at a small café on the way back from a trip to the cemetery where Grace's great-grandfather was buried. Maggie had suddenly announced that she would like a cup of "good, strong tea" and the Cherry Tree Café, pleasantly situated along the river, with an enticing pale pink door, had taken her fancy. The café, as it turned out, served the best apple pie in town, and their Saturday afternoon ritual was born.

The Cherry Tree Café was a quaint, intimate place, simple in its cottage kitchen design but clean and well looked after. The owner was a very friendly, terrifically overweight woman named Beth, whose raucous laughter could often be heard coming from the kitchen. She always insisted that Maggie be taken especially good care of. She said that Maggie reminded her of her own grandma and that it was nice to see the old lady walking through the door every week. Maggie, of course, loved all the fuss and attention and particularly liked the white linen tablecloths with the little vases of pink and white daisies that always stood on the tables. She said it looked elegant and re-fined, like a little café she had once seen a very long time ago.

After parking in their usual space just outside the entrance, Grace helped Maggie out of the car, the two of them giggling as the wind whipped around their hair and tugged at their coats. They entered the café in a breeze that blew all the menus over on the tables and found their favorite spot near the window. Grace helped Maggie to take off her coat and then settled herself into the comfortable Shaker-style chair. The waitress brought over two slices of apple pie and a pot of tea for two, their usual order.

"Well, Grace, would you look at that." Maggie chuckled. "There's tea for two and I haven't even gotten my ass into my seat!"

Grace laughed. "So, Maggie," she said, sinking her fork into the soft apple pie. "I've been dying to ask you something."

Maggie considered her great-granddaughter from behind her

china teacup, the short burst of fresh air having given a lovely radiance to her usually pale cheeks. "Yes, dear? What is it?"

"Well, I've been wondering why you decided to tell me all about *Titanic* and everything now. Y'know, after all these years. Did you really never talk to Mom or Grandma about it, or anyone else in the family?"

Maggie sighed, staring into Grace's warm chestnut eyes. They had looked so dull in recent months but seemed to have got a little of their spark back recently, a fact that pleased her.

"Well, Grace, it's as simple as this: it seemed to me that you needed a story and I knew that I had one of the best to tell you. I think it was also watching you on your birthday. Birthdays can do that to old folk like me, y'know—turn you all nostalgic, make you realize you've been lucky to see another year pass. I guess I started thinking on the fact that I might not be around for very much longer and that perhaps my *Titanic* story would be lost with me." She took a sip of her tea and broke into her own slice of pie. "People in the family knew I'd sailed on *Titanic*, but they also knew I didn't want to talk about it. So nobody did. I decided to tell you the whole story 'cause I figured it was too important to be forgotten about entirely."

"But you must have talked to Great-Granddad James about it?"

"Oh, yes, dear. Of course. Your great-granddad knew all about it." She paused, as she often did when she spoke about her husband, momentarily lost in her private thoughts of a man she had clearly adored and missed terribly. "But, y'know, Grace," she continued, "that night when *Titanic* went down was so terrible that some survivors, like me, just wanted to stop talking about it."

She took another bite of apple pie, taking her time to savor it and commenting on how delicious it was before continuing. "And I suppose people move on, history moves on, and there will, sadly, always be something more terrible waiting around the corner. Do you know, almost sixty thousand American soldiers died in Vietnam?" She paused to brush a crumb from her mouth.

"But people have always been fascinated by *Titanic*," Grace remarked, motioning to the waitress that they'd like more milk. "I knew all about it, and it always comes up in history lessons at school."

"Ah, yes, dear. I know that. But for those of us who survived, it was too painful a memory. To people like me, *Titanic* wasn't about impressive bedrooms and huge boilers to make her go faster than any liner before her. To me, *Titanic* was about real people, real lives, real hopes for the future. That was what I saw disappearing into the ocean." She paused for a moment to gather her thoughts. "I certainly never wanted to talk about it again after talking to all those press people in New York and telling my aunt Mary everything when I eventually got to Chicago. I had to tell her, you see, had to go over the whole thing. Terrible thoughts go through your head, you know—thoughts about them poor souls at the bottom of the ocean and . . ."

Grace saw the tears glistening in Maggie's eyes and took hold of her hand. "Don't, Maggie. Don't think about it. It's too upsetting for you."

"I refused to talk about it after the first anniversary had passed," Maggie continued, "and *Titanic* just wasn't mentioned in the family. Your great-grandfather and I only ever talked about it on the anniversary, when we would light a candle and say prayers for those who had been lost, but as far as anyone else was concerned, it was a part of my past that they knew I didn't want to revisit. Since your great-grandfather died I haven't spoken about *Titanic* at all, and with me not getting any younger and watching you blowing out your birthday candles, it struck me that in years to come my great-great-grandchildren would know nothing about their great-great-grandma's involvement in the whole terrible event. And perhaps they should."

Grace poured more tea into both their cups. Neither of them noticed the breeze that filled the room as other customers came in. They both sipped their tea in comfortable silence.

"And which great-great-grandchildren might these be anyway?" Grace asked, smiling and hoping to lighten the mood a little. "You and Nana and Mom might have all had kids before you were in your twenties, but I'm certainly not planning on having any babies until I'm at least forty!"

"Exactly!" Maggie replied. "And there's not much chance of me being around for that, is there? So I figured I would tell you now, while I still have my senses straight and you wouldn't be whisking me off to that 'institution' they all talk about, thinking I'd turned crazy in my old age." She winked at Grace and reached for her other hand. "As my aunt Kathleen used to say, 'Time is a great storyteller.' I guess she was right."

They paused for a moment as the waitress came over to check that everything was all right. It seemed to Grace to be a strange conversation to be having here in this inconspicuous little café. What would the people around them think if they knew Maggie's background?

"*Titanic* had a very big impact on my life, Grace, but I sometimes think that even if it hadn't sunk, the fact that I was leaving my home and so many people I loved would have changed me forever anyway. As it turned out, I got lucky. I got off that boat and carried on with my life. I married a wonderful man and we spent many very happy years together. We had three wonderful kids, plenty of grandkids, and even a couple of great-grandkids. I really can't complain now, can I?"

Grace absentmindedly prodded at the few remaining crumbs on her plate. "You've lived a very happy life, Maggie, haven't you? Despite *Titanic*."

"Not exactly." Maggie looked at Grace, her hands shaking slightly as she brought her teacup to her mouth. "I've lived a very happy life *because* of *Titanic*. Life is fragile, Grace—it is no more than a petal of cherry blossom: thriving and in full bloom one minute and blown to the ground by a sudden gust of wind the next. We shouldn't take our life for granted, and we should do whatever we can to make ourselves happy." She paused then for a moment, remembering something privately, a small smile playing at the corners of her mouth. "Are *you* happy, Grace? Really happy?"

Grace stirred her tea slowly, using the opportunity to think a little before responding. She loved the way Maggie was always able to tell how she was feeling—she'd missed this from her father and was glad to have her great-grandmother there to take his place.

"I guess not. Not really. But," she continued, squeezing Maggie's hand, "I will be. I *will* be happy. Your whole *Titanic* revelation, and especially the way you wrote in your journal about your love for Séamus, has really made me think over the last couple of weeks. I want to feel love like that, Maggie—and I did once. With Jimmy. So I've decided to try and get in touch with him again. God only knows whether he'll want to hear from me. I doubt it, but I can only try. And," she continued, feeling that she needed to say all these things now, before she changed her mind, "I'm going to send the article I've written about your

Titanic story to my college professor. I want to see whether he thinks it might be good enough to approach the editor at the *Tribune* again. I don't really rate my chances all that highly, but, well . . ."

"I guess you can only try," Maggie interjected.

"Yeah." Grace smiled. "Exactly."

Maggie said nothing for a while, finishing every last mouthful of her apple pie and draining the last drop of tea.

"Well, I'm very glad to hear that, Grace. It might seem right now that you'll never be able to get your life back on track after everything you've gone through, but it will happen. Lord knows, it took me plenty of years to feel like I'd *really* gotten off that ship—I sometimes feel that I'm still on it, even now. As my own mammy used to say, God rest her soul, 'On an unknown path, every foot is slow.' Take your time, Grace. Take one step at a time."

Grace stood up and walked around the small circular table. She threw her arms around this dear old lady, who was always so wise and so certain, hugging her frail body gently.

"Thank you, Maggie. Thank you—for everything. For confiding your story in me and for making me realize that it's never too late."

"I didn't make you realize any such thing. You realized it yourself—you just needed an old woman with a bit of a story to help you on your way."

Maggie picked up her empty teacup, staring into it as she turned it around in her hands. "You know, I think it's a shame they use tea bags nowadays," she remarked. "I quite liked the notion of reading the tea leaves—although I didn't always like what they predicted. *Piseóga,* we called them, superstitions, like reading the tea leaves, putting eggs among the new hay, respecting the fairy forts and hearing the banshee—and of course you know all about those silly little leprechauns." She chuckled to herself. "Perhaps we could get some proper tea leaves in the store before we go home and I'll teach you how to read them—a bit of an Irish tradition for you to pass on to those kids you're gonna have one day."

Grace laughed. "Well, I'll get you the tea leaves, Maggie, but I can't promise anything on the kids, I'm afraid."

CHAPTER 25

Grace was well aware of the fact that Maggie's story had given her the perfect way to resurrect her neglected journalism studies. Stories like this probably came around once in a lifetime, and the fact that a *Titanic* survivor had been discovered would, Grace had no doubt, be pounced upon by the media. This could be more than a break into an apprenticeship with a notoriously difficult features editor; it could really put Grace Butler's name on the map.

But aside from the indisputable strength of the story, Grace sensed that there was more to this for both her and Maggie. The more she read about her great-grandmother's love for Séamus and the more Maggie told her about the packet of letters she had lost the night *Titanic* sank and about the steward who'd helped her, and about Peggy and Katie and her aunt Kathleen—in fact, all those she had traveled with—the more Grace wanted to know about what had become of them all, the letters included.

Grace didn't know much about Maggie's life—it had never really occurred to her to ask. In a way, she supposed she had taken her for granted, just a frail old lady whom everyone fussed over at Thanksgiving dinners and other family gatherings. She was simply Great-Nana Maggie. Who she had been before that Grace didn't know—and now she wanted to. So she continued to read the newspaper clippings, some of which were dated some months after *Titanic* sank, and she continued to read Maggie's journal, which she had started writing again from the hospital she was taken to in New York after being rescued. For three days and nights, Grace immersed herself totally in Maggie's life, editing and perfecting the article on her electronic typewriter until she was finally happy with it. Only then did she breathe a sigh of relief, which felt like two years' worth of sighs, and went to skim stones on the lake, feeling a lightness about her that she hadn't felt for a considerable time.

Through the process of unraveling Maggie's past life, Grace thought more and more about the shoe box under her own bed. It contained the unopened letters Jimmy had written to her after she'd stopped writing to him. Ever since, she had tried to ignore the nagging urge to crawl under the bed, take the rubber band off the shoe box, and tear open the envelopes to see what Jimmy had wanted to say to her. She had also tried to ignore the urge to call him. It wasn't that she didn't love him anymore. She did. Completely.

Although she had tried to forget about Jimmy, had stopped herself from rushing to the phone to hear the sound of his voice, stopped herself from reading his letters, addressed to her in his distinctive handwriting, Grace had never stopped thinking about him, or loving him. She had forced herself to let him go, to give him the freedom to enjoy his college years while she focused on caring for her mother and letting the wounds of grief for her father heal. She'd been stopping herself from loving Jimmy Shepard for two years, and she was exhausted.

Since Maggie had taken her aside at her birthday party and confided in her about *Titanic,* Grace had started to feel different about her own life. With every new revelation about Maggie's life in Ireland and through the words she had written in her journal, Grace felt an increasing sense of purpose, of focus and renewal. She sat on her bed now, the dusty shoe box in her hands, and imagined how Maggie must have felt as she sat in that trap on the long journey from Ballysheen to the train station, being taken farther and farther away from her home and the man she loved; how she must have felt sitting on the narrow bunk bed of the cabin she shared with her aunt and her two friends, clutching the packet of letters from Séamus, carefully unwrapping them one day at a time as she sailed away from him.

Maggie had told Grace that she had read only four of the letters. The contents of the others were never known, because they were lost on the night of the sinking. Maggie had said that she would have liked to know what was in the rest of the letters, even though she realized that it really didn't matter now. *I have a chance to know,* Grace thought as she looked at the shoe box that contained the letters from Jimmy. *I have a chance to find out.*

Her hands shaking, she removed the rubber band from the box, sending a shower of dust into the air. She lifted the lid and looked at the four envelopes. The postmarks were from January to June 1980. After that, there were no more. After that, Jimmy had understood that Grace was not going to respond; that she had meant it when she'd written him to say that he wasn't to wait for her, that he was to get on with his own life while she tried to patch together what was left of hers.

As the spring rain fell soft and steady outside her window, Grace remembered something her father had said to her once. "Never leave yourself open to regret, Grace. We can only make a decision when we know the choices we are faced with. If we shy away, turn our backs and hide, we will simply never know. And that is when you end up old and wondering and regretting. Live a life of hope. Don't live a life of regret."

Those words swam around her mind now, and she knew that he was right. Whatever had made Maggie break her silence after all these years, there had been a reason, and if even part of that reason had been for Grace to realize that she had so much to be grateful for in her own life, had so much to look forward to, she knew now that she had to act on that reason. Her hands carefully opened the first envelope. She took a deep breath and began to read.

By nightfall, Grace had placed four typed pages of paper into a manila envelope. The title at the top said *The Girl Who Came Home: A Life Beyond Titanic*. She addressed the envelope: *Private and Confidential, Professor Peter Andrews, Medill School of Journalism, Fisk Hall, Evanston, IL*. Within the packet, she placed a smaller envelope, marked *Jimmy Shepard, fourth-year student of journalism, c/o Professor Andrews, Private and Confidential. Please deliver if possible or return to sender*. Inside the envelope was a single piece of paper with the handwritten words *I am so, so sorry. Please can I buy you a cup of coffee? G.*

A week later, Professor Andrews sat back in his chair, placed the typed pages onto his desk, and put his hands behind his head.

"Unbelievable!" he said aloud, a smile spreading across his

narrow face. "Absolutely unbelievable." He excitedly rummaged around in his top drawer looking for a phone number, muttering to himself. "I knew you had it in you, Miss Butler! I knew it, I knew it!"

Finding the business card he was looking for, he stood up with the folded sheets of neatly typed paper in his hand and dialed the number for Bill O'Shea's office. After a few rings, it was answered.

"Bill, how are you? Peter Andrews here." He paused, waiting for Bill's response, chuckling intermittently as they exchanged pleasantries. "I've got something here that I think you might like," he continued. "A student of mine has finally got around to writing a feature article for a slot you offered to her two years ago." Again he waited for his colleague's response. "Yes, that's the one. Grace Butler. Yes, that's right, her father died very suddenly. Well, it turns out Miss Butler is the great-granddaughter of a *Titanic* survivor!"

At this he paused again, preempting the reaction he knew he was going to get. He could sense the excitement at the other end of the phone, knew that Bill O'Shea would realize he was onto a scoop.

"I know, I know," he continued, "and it's one heck of a story—written beautifully as well. I'll get Sandra to make a few copies and send it over to you."

Replacing the receiver, he picked up the smaller envelope that had come with the typed pages. *Jimmy Shepard, fourth-year student of journalism . . . Private and Confidential. Please deliver if possible or return to sender.*

He smiled and walked out of his office to his secretary, asking her to make three copies of the article and have them couriered to Bill O'Shea at the *Tribune* right away and to deliver the other envelope, in person, to a Mr. Shepard, who was a senior. He instructed her to say that it was an important message from Professor Andrews.

Although very tempted, he considered it best not to call Grace at home—not yet. He was a wise man, preferring to wait for the responses from the two men to whom he had just forwarded the documents. His sense was that Bill O'Shea's would be more than favorable. As for the Shepard boy, he had no idea, but he hoped that Grace got the response she was hoping for.

The following day, Peter Andrews heard from Bill O'Shea that the article submitted by Grace Butler, "The Girl Who Came Home," would be published in two weeks. Since Bill didn't have any contact details for Miss Butler, he asked if the professor could be so kind as to contact her and ask her to call Bill's office with a brief author bio that they could run with the piece. Bill suspected that once the story went out, there would be quite a bit of interest in Grace Butler and her great-grandmother.

Professor Andrews also received a visit from Jimmy Shepard that day. Jimmy thanked him for forwarding the envelope and assured him that he would attend to the very important matter without delay.

WHITE STAR LINE

ROYAL AND UNITED STATES MAIL STEAMERS.

ISMAY, IMRIE & CO.,

WHITE STAR LINE

OCEANIC STEAM NAVIGATION COMPANY, LIMITED, OF GREAT BRITAIN.

THIRD CLASS (Steerage) PASSENGER'S CONTRACT TICKET.

CHAPTER 26

RMS Titanic
April 15, 1912

I t was the stars Maggie saw first as she clambered up on deck. The millions and millions of twinkling stars, illuminating the sky like the magical lands of her childhood imagination, the very same stars she used to look at in Ballysheen, captivated by their beauty and unfathomable distance.

The vast empty space of the sky above her now seemed to make this ship, which she had gasped at in wonder and awe just a few days ago, feel very small and extremely fragile. At that moment, as the noise and confusion on the deck engulfed her, she longed, more than anything in her life, to be back in her humble stone cottage warming her fingers over the glow of the fire as Séamus sat by her side.

She looked around wildly, standing on her tiptoes to peer over the heads of the masses of people swarming around her. Where was Aunt Kathleen? She *had* to be here.

"Aunt Kathleen!" Maggie shouted as loudly as she could. "Aunt Kathleen! It's me! Maggie. I'm over here. Aunt Kathleen! Where are you?"

She'd never felt so far away from home, so lost and terrified.

"Maggie! Maggie, over here." But it was Harry's voice, not Kathleen's, that called her name. "We have to go up again," he shouted, trying to make himself heard above the noise of the panicked passengers and the continual hiss of steam from the funnels high above them. "There's a few boats left on the upper deck."

Maggie stood in a daze, unable to comprehend what she was seeing. All around her, people were running, some carrying deck chairs, some holding wooden crates or empty trunks, others clutching life rings—everyone desperately searching for something they might be able to hold on to in the water—something that might mean the difference between life and death.

Masses of bodies crowded around the next lifeboats to be lowered. Men were being prevented from getting in while women and children clambered in reluctantly, almost as frightened about the prospect of drifting endlessly through the freezing black night as they were about staying on the sinking ship. Maggie watched with heart-wrenching helplessness as several women climbed back out of their lifeboats, unable, in the final moment, to leave without their husbands, fathers, and brothers. She had never witnessed such a terrifying sight and stood frozen in fear.

Men called to women, encouraging them to take to the lifeboats without them. "Be brave; no matter what happens, be brave and keep your hands in your pockets, it is very cold weather," she heard one man say to a woman Maggie presumed was his wife. Another woman was lifted, kicking and screaming, into a boat. "Go, Lottie!" a man called after her. "For God's sake, be brave and go!"

Maggie watched in horror as another woman, who clearly refused to leave her husband, lifted her young daughter and baby into a boat, entrusting them to the care of their nurse before collapsing on her knees on the deck, clinging to her husband's ankles as the boat was lowered over the side. Maggie could barely move as she watched these scenes of grief unfolding in every direction she looked, each more distressing than the last.

There were already several lifeboats rowing away from the ship, the tiny dots of white from the life jackets worn by the occupants reflecting back off the lights from the ship, which still lit up the water all around them. Other boats were being lowered down the side of the ship, the crewmen shouting instructions to each other to make sure they were lowered evenly while the women inside screamed and sobbed. She saw one woman clamber out just as the boat was being lowered over the edge, and watched her run back to a man on the deck, who embraced her as they both wept desperate tears.

"There are no more boats on this deck," Harry shouted. "Follow me."

He took the group toward another ladder, which led up to the boat deck, the highest point on the ship. This ladder was already teeming with bodies, people of all ages and classes trying desperately to get up to the remaining boats as they felt the forward compartments of the ship sink farther and farther under the water. Large, burly men pushed past Maggie in an attempt to secure their own escape, or to help women and children who were with them get a foothold on the ladder. Maggie recognized Father Byles, the priest who had celebrated Mass the previous morning. He was reciting prayers to a group huddled at his feet, their heads bowed. She scanned the group for a moment, wondering if Aunt Kathleen might be among them. She wasn't.

It was a frantic scene that frightened Maggie to her core. She knew that Harry, Maura and Jack Brennan, Eileen Brennan, and

Michael Kelly were ahead of her. Behind her were Peggy, Katie, and the rest of the girls, with Pat Brogan insisting he follow the last of them up. Struggling with all her might against the surge of bodies behind her, she eventually got a foothold on the ladder and started to climb.

"Oh, Jesus! My hat! My hat."

Maggie knew immediately it was Peggy's voice and, craning her neck around, saw her friend scrabbling about on the deck for her hat, which had been knocked off her head. In the confusion, others climbed up ahead of her, forcing Katie and the others back.

"Peggy!" Maggie cried. "Peggy, leave it! We have to go! Katie! Katie!"

"Peggy! Leave it. You've got to get up the ladder!" Harry's voice joined Maggie's, but his words, like hers, were lost amid the panic and confusion as Peggy was lost among the crowd.

Maggie looked at Harry; the wild, desperate gaze in his eyes seeming to speak her own terrible thought: that they would not see Peggy again.

Pushed along by the crowd behind her, Maggie had no choice but to keep climbing, emerging onto the boat deck terrified, shivering uncontrollably with the cold, and separated from everyone from her group other than the four who stood with her. The emergency rockets being fired into the sky sent a bright red light across the ship, which was now audibly creaking and groaning under the strain of the water flooding the lower compartments.

Maura Brennan stared wildly at the unfamiliar faces emerging from the ladder behind them. "Maggie, where are the others? They were right behind us."

"They got pushed back. I don't know. I don't know where

they are." Maggie's fear developed into gasping tears then, the enormity of what was happening suddenly hitting her. "I don't know where they are, and I don't know where Aunt Kathleen is either."

Grabbing her arm, Harry pulled Maggie and the others he had managed to bring up the ladder toward a lifeboat. "It's women and children first," he told them. "The men will follow."

Maura Brennan grasped Harry's arm. "What in God's name d'ye mean, women and children first? Can we not all go together?"

"Officer's orders, miss. Women and children first."

A terrible silence fell over the group then. Maggie looked at all their faces as an officer manning the boat started shouting at them urgently.

"Everyone in, miss. Come on, everyone in, right now. There's room for a few more."

Seeing that Maura was pregnant, he ushered her toward the boat, pushing Eileen and Maggie with her. A surge of passengers behind them caused them all to be pushed forward, their legs crushed momentarily against the hard edge of the lifeboat. Some men tried to clamber aboard. A shot rang out. Maggie turned to see the officer waving his gun in the air.

"Get back, men. Get back and wait your turn."

Amid the confusion, Maura Brennan stood perfectly still, a determined composure and certainty about her. "I'll not go," she whispered. Maggie stared at Maura, who stood at the edge of the boat. "I'll not go without Jack. I will never go without Jack."

Next to her, Eileen started to sob desperate tears. "I'll not go either, Jack. I'll not leave my brother standing here. I'll not leave you to drown."

As the women hesitated, their seats were gladly taken by others.

The officer pushed Maggie forward. "Miss, one seat left. I would take it now if I were you, before it's too late."

Maggie hesitated, looking wildly from one face to the other, at Michael Kelly's face streaked with tears.

"Let the boy in," she said to the officer, pushing Michael forward. "Let him go in this boat. He has a mammy at home."

"Women and children first, miss. He can go in the next boat."

"But I can't go alone," she cried, clutching at Maura's thin coat. "I can't leave you all here. And what about the baby?" she added, conscious of the life growing within Maura's belly.

"We'll take the next boat, Maggie," Maura replied calmly, taking Maggie's hand and gently prizing it from her coat sleeve. "When all the women and children are accounted for, they'll let the men take their turn. Peggy and Katie and the others will have made their way up by then, and we'll all come together. If I know your aunt Kathleen, she'll have been helping others get into the boats and will be on one herself by now, probably rowing the blessed thing herself."

Harry moved forward. "Maggie, you *have* to get in. They're starting to lower the boat." He stared earnestly into her tear-filled eyes. "Remember who's waiting for you back home," he added, reminded of the message she'd been so keen to send.

Maggie relented then, no energy left in her body to protest. She allowed Harry to lift her gently into the boat.

"You—steward twenty-three." Harry turned to the officer who was addressing him. "Man this lifeboat, and when you get on the water, row away from the ship as quickly as you can or she'll take you down with her. Do you understand?"

"Yes, sir, I understand. You'll bring the others in the next boat, will you?"

Harry looked into the officer's eyes, where he saw fear the like of which he had never seen before and hoped he would never see again.

"This is the last boat," the officer replied, lowering his voice. "There are no more."

Climbing into the boat, Harry heard the orders for the lifeboat to be lowered over the side and closed his eyes to the tragedy unfolding on the decks above them.

Maggie's heart felt as if it had broken in two as she stared up at the faces of Maura, Jack, Eileen, and Michael where they stood together, watching her, Eileen and Michael weeping desperate tears, Maura clutching her rosary, all four of them holding hands as they leaned over the railings. There was simply nothing anyone could say. Maggie watched them, isolated among the chaos and despair, until their faces finally disappeared from view.

Maggie gripped the edge of the lifeboat, which jerked violently as it was lowered roughly down into the black ocean. As she stared numbly at the scene around her, something stirred within Maggie, an incredible will to survive, a desire to live a long and happy life.

"I will not die here," she whispered, her teeth chattering with the cold that had penetrated every inch of her body. "Not here. Not now. I'm coming home, Séamus," she repeated over and over again. "I'm coming home. I'm coming home. I'm coming home."

Searching the frantic, panic-stricken faces on the decks they passed, and among the boats that were already lowered, Maggie prayed that she would see her friends or her aunt. But she saw nobody she recognized.

"Séamus," she sobbed into her hands. "Séamus, Séamus, Séamus—I should never have left you."

An elderly lady placed her arm around Maggie's shoulders, assuming that, like all the other women in the boat, she was sobbing for a man she had left behind on *Titanic*.

"You have to be strong now, my love. You have to believe you will see him again. If not in this life, then the next."

Maggie stared up at the unfamiliar, wrinkled face, barely able to see through her tears.

"But I love him," she cried, clutching the woman's frozen hands and gasping though her sobs. "I love him and I want to go home."

CHAPTER 27

Ballysheen, Ireland
April 15, 1912

aggie! Maggie! It's all right. I'm coming."

Séamus woke in a cold sweat, unsure whether it was his own voice he'd heard calling Maggie's name or someone else's. She was drowning, calling out desperately for him to help her as she slid under the water. "*Séamus! Help me!*" she kept shouting. "*Help me!*"

He sat up in the bed, grabbing for his pocket watch to check the time. Lighting the candle by his bed, he looked at the glass face. It was just past 2:00 A.M.

The dream had shaken him. Knowing that he wouldn't fall asleep again, he got up to check on his father. He'd taken a bad turn in the last few days and the doctor had told Séamus to be prepared for the worst. Séamus stood for a moment, watching the frail old man's outline until he caught the definite signs of the blanket moving slowly up and down with each labored breath. He walked over to the dresser then and cut himself a slice of bread.

"*Séamus! Help me! Help me!*"

The words kept replaying in his mind. He could see Maggie

as clearly as if she were standing in front of him now: her small heart-shaped face, her lustrous curls falling naturally around her face, her wonderfully soft blue eyes and her small mouth, which formed into a perfect Cupid's bow.

Trying to put the images of the dream out of his mind, Séamus turned to wondering whether she'd read his letters. He'd been unsure what to say when he first sat with the blank sheet of paper in front of him, but when his aunt Bridget suggested that he write about what he remembered most from each month of his relationship with Maggie, the words had flowed freely, openly. There was so much he wanted to remember about his time with Maggie that he hadn't struggled to fill the pages. But as he'd reached the final letter, the month they were in now, it had become harder to express his feelings about her going away. He knew she desperately wanted him to go with them, but it was impossible with his da so sick.

He'd pondered for many nights, wondering what to say to her in that final letter, until it had suddenly become very clear. How would she feel, he wondered, when she read those final words? Would she be pleased, or angry maybe that he'd made it impossibly difficult for her? Would she write to him from America with an answer? Would she write to him at all? He wandered back to his bed, closed his eyes, and tried to push the disturbing dream from his mind. He just wanted to be with her, wanted to protect her.

For an hour he lay in the darkness, unable to shake his troubled thoughts. Eventually he got up, dressed, and did what he always did when his mind was troubled; he went outside, to nature.

The pitch black that fell across the landscape at night was always dramatic but something Séamus found exhilarating, especially with the mass of Nephin Mór looming over everything—its brooding silhouette just visible against the dark sky. A light rain had fallen, bringing the distinctive smell of the wet, peaty earth from the ground around him. There wasn't a sound as he walked, with a small lantern to light his way, down the narrow track that led from his father's cottage to the Holy Well. He hadn't intended to go there but felt somehow drawn to prayer. He knelt, crossed himself, and prayed for Maggie, and for all those she was traveling with.

He sat then in silence, staring up at the stars, imagining those same stars illuminating the sky above the vast Atlantic Ocean, where Maggie would be sleeping now. He closed his eyes and thought about her, willing her, wherever she was, to hear his voice. "I'm coming," he said out loud into the silent night air. "I'm coming, Maggie."

As Séamus prayed alone in the all-consuming darkness, his father took a last, rasping breath and the covers on the bed were still.

New York
April 15, 1912

Frances Kenny was glad of the early-morning spring sunshine as she made her way to the Walker-Browns' residence for her final day of work before Katie was due to arrive. The first soft rays of sunlight brought a small degree of warmth against the distinct chill that still hovered above the New York skyscrapers.

As she walked down Fifth Avenue, Frances passed businessmen in their smart suits and ties, catching snippets of their conversations about important matters of industry and finance. She passed other domestics, like herself, setting out to spend the day cleaning the houses of those businessmen, and others like them, knowing that it would be many exhausting hours before they returned to start cleaning their own homes. Walking farther away from the elegant avenue, she overheard the construction workers, shouting above the noise of their machinery, talking in a hundred different accents as they continued with the seemingly endless task of building more and more offices for the businessmen to occupy, going higher and higher into the clouds above. The profound diversity and cruel contradictions of this city never ceased to both amaze and appall Frances Kenny.

She passed a few coins to a tramp sitting on the steps of a church, telling him that he was not to buy ale. "Get yourself a cup of soup or some hot tea from the Army," she said, speaking to him quietly yet firmly. "They will look after you."

"God bless you, miss," he replied, his accent unmistakably Irish.

It saddened her to think that his story had followed the same path as so many other Irish she had encountered since arriving on these shores herself: traveling to America in search of a better future and yet finding their lives had been worsened by their crossing of the Atlantic Ocean. She sighed and directed her thoughts to the work ahead of her, ticking things off the list in her head as she walked: things she needed to do in final preparation for Katie's arrival the next day. Her anticipation at seeing her sister had been heightened by the excitement in the Walker-Brown household the previous day, when a telegram from Vivienne and Robert had been delivered.

"Oh, look! It's from the Marconi company. It must be from Vivienne," Emily Walker-Brown had shrieked, bustling through the large entrance hall, the two small Pekingese dogs she kept yapping at the hem of yet another new skirt.

Frances was used to these showy displays from her employer. She knew that she was required to continue with her dusting as if she couldn't hear the conversation between Emily and her sister, who had called in for tea, but that really much of what was said was purely for her benefit.

"Listen, Bea," Emily said, visibly puffed up with self-importance as she settled herself on the edge of the chaise longue next to the large, ornate fireplace. "She says, 'Dearest Mother. Had the most wonderful dinner with Captain Smith—quite the occasion altogether. Mr. Astor dined with us along with his new young wife. Robert is well and Edmund is enjoying the sea air. Will arrive Tuesday! Fondest affections. Vivienne.' So they will arrive a day early," she continued, standing up and clapping her hands. "They will arrive tomorrow! Goodness me, and there is still so much to do!"

Frances chanced a half smile in the direction of the two women, the excitement in the room impossible to ignore.

"Isn't that terrific news?" Emily enthused, almost acknowledging Frances's presence. "And how wonderful to have dined with Captain Smith himself! I believe he is to retire after his arrival in New York. Twenty-six years at sea—no wonder he is ready to retire, after all that rocking from side to side. It's a wonder the man can walk in a straight line at all!" The two sisters laughed heartily at Emily's joke. "I presume the dinner was in honor of the many years' service he has given to the White Star Line," she continued. "I suspect it nearly killed that dreadful Bruce Ismay to bestow such an honor upon him."

The sisters set to gossiping then about the many millionaires and influential businessmen traveling on *Titanic*, the most interesting topic of conversation seeming to be Mr. Astor and the scandal of his recent divorce and the disgrace of his hasty marriage to a young girl, only nineteen years of age. "And him nearly fifty years old. Goodness me, he's old enough to be her father."

Frances busied herself, her mind racing at the prospect of her sister arriving tomorrow—a whole day earlier than expected.

As she finished work for the day, she plucked up the courage to speak to Mrs. Walker-Brown about her hours the following day. "I was wondering whether it might be acceptable for me to start work an hour earlier tomorrow so as I can leave a little earlier than usual," she explained as politely as possible. "I couldn't help hearing you mention earlier that *Titanic* is expected to arrive a day early—and I would love to be at the terminal when my sister arrives."

Distracted by her own excitement at the prospect of Vivienne and Robert's arrival and the setting of a date for their wedding, Emily Walker-Brown gave her consent. "Oh, yes. Of course. I do keep forgetting that you have someone on the ship also! With all Vivienne's talk of the grandeur of the first-class accommodations, it's easy to forget that there are others traveling in the lower portions of the ship. That will suit me anyway as I will be asking the chauffeur to drive me to the docks so I can welcome Vivienne and Robert myself. They say that there will be quite some party to welcome *Titanic*—I shouldn't wonder that half of New York will turn out for a look at her!"

Frances left then to make her way home. It was later than usual, since she had stayed on awhile longer to attend to a few extra chores and make sure that her employer had absolutely no reason to keep her late the following day, as she was apt to do whenever she had visitors arriving.

Her thoughts preoccupied with making plans for Katie's first few days in New York, Frances did not immediately register the crowd clustered around the newspaper stand at the corner on Fifth Avenue. Moving into the gathering, she overheard fragments of conversation.

"An iceberg apparently. Early reports said she was limping back to Belfast for repairs."

"Well, I heard she sank like a stone. They didn't stand a chance."

Bewildered and sickened with panic, Frances continued to move through the crowd. It was then that she saw the newspaper, bearing the day's headline in oversize black typeface.

NEW LINER TITANIC HITS AN ICEBERG; SINKING BY THE BOW AT MIDNIGHT; WOMEN PUT OFF IN LIFEBOATS; LAST WIRELESS AT 12:27 A.M. BLURRED

She simply couldn't comprehend it. She gazed frantically around the crowd, not sure what she was looking for. Seeing a smartly dressed gentleman standing to her right, she approached him, grabbing at his arm in her panic.

"Excuse me, sir, is it true? Do you know what has happened?"

He turned to her, a look of concern and shock on his face.

"I'm very sorry, miss. I don't know. I really don't know. They are reporting that she hit an iceberg in the night and went down in a matter of hours."

"Went down?" Frances gasped, her head spinning, her knees feeling as though they would buckle under her at any moment. "But everyone's all right. Aren't they? My sister is traveling on *Titanic*." Frances was now desperate to get confirmation about what had happened to the passengers. "The women were all rescued, weren't they? It says so here," she added, pointing at the headline.

"So it seems," the gentleman replied. "We need to await further news. My wife and young daughter are aboard. I am praying for good news myself. I'm going straight to the White Star Line offices on Broadway. Maybe an official there can confirm the facts."

Without hesitation, Frances knew that was what she would do. She started to run and didn't stop until she saw a large crowd already gathered outside the offices, a palpable air of tension and confusion surrounding them. Men and women rushed up and down the stone steps with urgency. Passersby turned their heads to observe the commotion, some stopping those already converged outside the building to inquire about what was happening. Police officers on foot and on horseback moved among the crowd, which spilled off the sidewalk into the street, trying to restore calm and order. Motorcars and horse-drawn carts stopped in the middle of the road as the occupants conversed with the officers or with the uniformed White Star Line officials who had braved the crowds to relay information.

Frances's gaze fell on a group of women dressed in the finest clothing and wearing the most impressive hats. They stood alongside humble, conservatively attired domestics like herself, who in turn stood next to smartly dressed gentlemen in bowler hats and ties, themselves standing alongside dockworkers with the grime of a day's hard labor still evident across their hands, faces, and clothing. All of society, it seemed, was gathered there, all divisions of rank and social class forgotten.

Walking through the gathered crowd, she overheard someone saying, "My cousin works for the White Star Line, and he reliably informs me that Captain Smith personally ensured that all the women and children were safely removed in the lifeboats before any men were permitted to board, himself included." Over the shoulder of another man, she caught the headline of another newspaper that read ALL SAVED FROM TITANIC AFTER COLLISION.

Frances stopped at the foot of the stone steps. She had never felt so helpless, so confused, so frightened.

Hours passed. Still, nobody seemed able to confirm exactly what had happened. Rumors raced among the waiting crowds. White Star Line officials were pressed for information, but their answers were vague and unhelpful. They did nothing to reassure the anxious crowd. Frances settled herself on the stone steps and prayed.

It was many hours later when a woman sat down on the step beside her. A young child settled in the woman's lap, and she held an infant in her arms. Tears streamed down her face, words of desperate prayer tumbling from her lips. She gazed up and caught Frances's eye.

"They say it's gone," she wailed. "They're all gone. My husband and my brother, gone, miss. What will I do? Whatever will I do? How will I survive with them gone?"

Unsure of what to say to comfort her, Frances moved forward and bent down to the woman. Placing her hand on her shoulder, she simply said, "Courage and faith. We must all try to find courage and faith until we know for certain."

Unable to process what she was seeing and hearing, Frances turned then to the other people gathered nearest to her, all talking frantically—to each other and to anyone who looked to be at all official—trying desperately to get some reassurance that the passengers were all right. It was simply incomprehensible that anything had happened to *Titanic*, let alone that she had sunk. Frances couldn't begin to imagine what must have happened or how terrifying the experience must have been. Her poor sister—her poor little sister. She tried to take some small comfort from the fact that at least she had some of the more mature women with her, like Kathleen Dolan and Maura Brennan. They were strong, confident women, and at least they would mind Katie and tell her what to do.

Without much thought and barely able to stay upright with the shock coursing through her body, Frances resolved to wait outside the offices for further news. She pulled her coat around herself and bent her head in silent prayer as the sun began to set behind the towering office blocks, casting a dark shadow across them all.

It was late in the evening when the wires started to come through, confirming everyone's worst fears.

From the Marconi radio station on top of the nearby department store, messages were picked up from the steamship *Carpathia* confirming that *Titanic* had gone down and that there had been a significant loss of life. Survivors were aboard the *Carpathia*, which was expected to arrive in New York on Thursday night. The survivors' names were being transmitted from the steamship and would be displayed in the window of the White Star Line offices as soon as possible.

As news of the scale of the disaster became known, an eerie silence fell across the mass of anxious relatives and friends gathered on the street outside the White Star Line offices, all the way across to Wanamaker's Department Store. As people filed into the office, praying that the names of their loved ones would be among those listed as having survived, the first tears started to fall. Frances watched as men and women emerged from the revolving doors, ashen faced and weeping, falling into the arms of others as they relayed the terrible news that the names they had been hoping to see were not there.

"Will you go and look for me, miss?"

Frances turned to the young woman who still sat beside her.

"I can't bear to go and look. Will you please check the list for me?" She bounced the baby up and down in her arms as she spoke, trying to soothe its crying.

"Yes, of course," Frances replied, although she could barely stand the thought of scanning the list for Katie's name, let alone anyone else's. "Yes, I'll look for you."

The young woman gave her the names and Frances stood then, smoothing her skirt before walking up the steps, patiently waiting her turn to start scanning the list.

For nearly thirty minutes she stood there, reading each name twice over before moving on to the next. When she had read the entire list once, she read it again, her throat tightening, making it hard to breathe. The names seemed to shift and blur in front of her. All around her, people gasped with delight and relief at seeing a name they knew, or fell to their knees in grief when they did not.

She recognized only one name on the list: Vivienne Walker-Brown. She envied the relief her employer would feel when she learned that her daughter was safe. She scanned the list again and again, desperately reading the Kenny names. There were several: Arthur, Eileen, Elizabeth, and others, but the name Katie was not among them; neither were any of the other names Frances might have recognized from the Ballysheen group. And neither were the names the young woman outside had given her.

With all hope lost, Frances returned to the stone steps and sat down. The young woman looked into her eyes, her two children nestled inside her coat, sleeping and unaware of the different path their lives were about to take. Frances looked at the woman, took her hands in hers, and shook her head.

"No," she whispered as her own tears began to fall. "No."

Castlebar, Ireland
April 16, 1912

Thomas Durcan stood in the middle of the unremarkable office he owned on the main street of Castlebar, unable to believe his eyes as he read the message informing him that *Titanic* had foundered in the Atlantic with great loss of life.

Rumors had been rife among the people in the town since late the previous evening.

"Is it true, Mr. Durcan, about *Titanic*?" people had asked, stopping him in the street. "But they said she was unsinkable. They must have their facts wrong."

He barely knew what to believe himself.

"Ah, yes, probably limping back to Belfast as we speak for some swift repairs!" he'd replied, although he was no more convinced by this remark than were the people to whom he made it.

Feeling a distinct sense of responsibility for the dozen or so passengers he personally had booked on the ship, Durcan set about receiving confirmation for himself. He recalled the young girl Maggie, with her aunt, Kathleen Dolan, of Ballysheen, and how they'd exchanged a joke about the thousands of eggs there would be aboard the ship. It simply didn't bear thought that any harm had befallen those poor people who were just trying to better their lot in life.

He wired the head office of the White Star Line in Liverpool and anxiously awaited a response. Eventually it came through.

WIRELESS

Received

NO_____ · _____ CK_____   TIME RECEIVED_____

Liverpool. 4:30 P.M. Tuesday: Referring to your telegram re. Titanic, deeply regret to say that latest word received is steamer foundered; about 675 souls, mostly women and children saved.

Thomas Durcan knew that *Titanic* was capable of carrying more than two thousand passengers. Such a loss of life was unimaginable. He sank to his knees and wept.

WHITE STAR LINE

ROYAL AND UNITED STATES MAIL STEAMERS.

WHITE STAR LINE

ISMAY, IMRIE & CO.

OCEANIC STEAM NAVIGATION COMPANY, LIMITED, OF GREAT BRITAIN.
THIRD CLASS (Steerage) PASSENGER'S CONTRACT TICKET.
(NOT TRANSFERABLE.)

CHAPTER 28

Atlantic Ocean
April 15, 1912

Taking hold of one of the long oars, Harry pulled against the might of the ocean with all his strength. He knew enough about boats to know that if *Titanic* went down, she would create a massive whirlpool, which would suck anything close enough down with it, and he had understood fully what the officer meant when he'd told him to row away from the ship.

"Grab hold," he shouted to the women in the boat. "Grab hold and pull. We need to get farther away."

Slowly, with the help of several of the stunned and freezing passengers, lifeboat 16 moved farther and farther from the ship, the distress flares still being sent up into the clear black sky adding a marvelous red aura to the millions of stars shining down upon the dreadful events unfolding on the ocean below.

Amid the panic and terror, it occurred to Harry that this must be the most tragic fireworks display ever seen, and his thoughts turned fleetingly to crisp November nights when, as a young boy, he had watched the few rockets his father could afford shooting up into the dark sky and exploding into a dazzling display of color. His sister always cried with fright at the bangs and cracks, but he loved it. He thought the display was beautiful.

He thought of his family then, his mother sitting alone in the front room, his father—coughing relentlessly—and his kind, gentle sister. He longed to be in his comfortable home and couldn't bear to think about how worried everyone in Southampton would be when they heard about the catastrophe. There were so many boiler men, stokers, and crew from the city, already dead, he was certain, locked in the bowels of the ship when the watertight doors were closed. He knew many of them and knew there would be many mothers and sisters left without their sons and brothers now.

He rowed and rowed, lost in silent thoughts of his own family, of Peggy—who had made his heart skip a beat when she smiled at him—and the others in the Irish group, of Bride and Phillips in the Marconi room, of Billy and everyone else he had worked with and had such a lark with along Scotland Road. He wondered what had become of them all.

With rising feelings of panic, dread, and anger surging through his body, producing a strength he didn't know he was capable of, Harry rowed and rowed with the strength of ten men, determined not to die in the suction from the ship, determined not to die now that they had got so close to safety.

In the lifeboat, the minutes passed slowly. Time seemed suspended.

The iceberg loomed like a ghost from the jet-black water, reaching up almost as high as *Titanic*'s funnels. Maggie had never seen an iceberg before. She gazed at it now dully, barely registering the continual slapping noise of the water against the edges of its great gray bulk.

Gazing mechanically around the lifeboat at her fellow passengers, she recognized the Irish man with the *uilleann* pipes and wondered for a moment how he had managed to get into the boat before noticing another man, huddled at the back of the boat under a woman's coat. She thought of Michael Kelly, who had been refused a seat, and noticed then the space to her right and left, ample room for a young boy to sit. In fact, as she looked about the boat she saw space for all fourteen of the Ballysheen group to have had seats. It was a thought that angered her, until her attention was caught by the shrill cry of a baby. The bawling was coming from an old sack, the baby swaddled inside.

"She was too small," the mother said, noting Maggie's gaze. "They had to lift her down to me in the sack. My husband is still out there," she sobbed, rocking the infant in her arms, shushing and soothing it and letting her tears fall.

Maggie saw other mothers clasping their children to them to try to give them some extra warmth; older women staring blankly into the distance; and several ladies, still dressed in their finest silk evening gowns, their fur stoles and fancy hats offering meager protection against the icy air.

She thought she recognized a dignified-looking lady with a fur coat around her shoulders. She was clutching a small dog, soothing its frightened whimpers as if it were a child. Despite her almost catatonic state, Maggie was struck by how completely unjust it was that babies and children were drowning in the sea while a small dog was here, sailing to safety. It was just one of the many injustices she would feel about the whole tragedy at that moment and for many, many years to come. She shook uncontrollably with the cold and fear and pulled the emergency blanket tighter around her shoulders, knowing that in a few more moments she would have to pass it to someone else to get a short burst of protection against the bitter night air.

All around them other lifeboats moved slowly away from *Titanic*'s bulk. The sound of the oars slapping against the water and the moaning and sobbing from the occupants seeming to fill the spaces between them all, the mist of their frozen breaths rising up, up into the blank nothingness above.

Straight ahead, *Titanic* sank lower and lower, the thousands of electric lights casting a dazzling glow onto the still, calm ocean, adding a brilliant illumination to the tragic scene of people thrashing desperately in the freezing water. Unable to comprehend what she was seeing, Maggie closed her eyes.

With her eyes shut and her body numbed with the cold, her ears took on a heightened awareness. Amid the perfect melody from the violinists who were still playing on the upper decks, she heard, with chilling clarity, the terrifying orchestra of a thousand people dying, heard their haunting shouts and screams. She could bear it no longer and placed her hands over her ears and buried her head deep into her lap. She shivered uncontrollably, but she didn't shed any tears. Her body and mind were shocked beyond the ability to weep.

Fifty minutes had passed since she'd left the ship.

It felt like a lifetime.

They were farther away from *Titanic* now. Her bow was slipping deeper and deeper into the water, until only the foremast was visible.

Maggie opened her eyes and watched as the stern of the ship

soared higher and higher above the water, the massive propellers looming out of the blackness. Despite their distance, the reality of the horror was still audible to her frozen ears.

Listening to the human screams and the crunching and grind-
ing of metal, Maggie retreated into herself. The faces of those
she had encountered on this journey flashed across her mind:
the boiler man hiding among the mailbags at Queenstown, the
girl with the rash who was so brokenhearted to be turned away
at the health inspection line. Maggie had thought it a shame at
the time that these people wouldn't share the experience of sailing across the Atlantic on this breathtaking ship. Now it seemed
that God had had a mind for those people and had spared them,
as he had spared her.

Unable to find a way to respond to what was happening,
Maggie wondered about the lady traveling on her own with
the seven children, about Elsie and her family traveling from
Wiltshire, about the honeymooning couples they had met, the
little boy she had watched playing with the spinning top, the
Marconi boy Harry had asked to send her message, the ladies
she had watched taking afternoon tea in their fine silk dresses.
She saw every one of their faces in her mind now and wondered
what their fates were, wondered whether they were out here on
the sea with her or screaming in terror on the sinking ship. She
could not even begin to think about those she had traveled with,
her aunt and cousin, the friends she regarded as brothers and
sisters. She tried desperately to block their panic-stricken faces
from her numbed mind as she rocked back and forth, cradling
her shivering knees.

"Good Lord," one woman gasped as a dreadful rumbling
roar came from the ship, which appeared to snap in two, the
bow disappearing into the ocean as the majestic funnels ripped

from their fixtures, crashing onto the decks and all who stood on them. "May God have mercy on their souls."

Another woman led the group in prayer while the scraping and crunching of steel filled the air around them. Maggie peered through the icy air as the brilliant lights of *Titanic* finally flickered and went out.

Despite the enveloping blackness, the remaining bulk of *Titanic* was just visible as an eerie silhouette against the starlit sky. For a few brief moments the stern reared up, perfectly perpendicular, before plunging, with a peculiar gracefulness, into the icy waters.

"She's gone," somebody gasped. "God bless us and save us all. She's gone."

Maggie felt strangely calm. It was as if she were in someone else's dream, almost unable to believe that this was actually happening to her, unable to believe that she had just seen *Titanic* disappear into the sea.

The bitter cold of the Atlantic night seeped through her body, her uncontrollable shaking her only conscious sensation.

The night engulfed them. Time seemed endless.

With the lights from *Titanic* gone, they were plunged into total darkness. For a while, the frantic thrashing of a thousand people in the water and their desperate cries for help continued, but eventually they faded and stopped.

Silence.

Drifting in and out of consciousness, Maggie saw blurred images of icebergs around her, was vaguely aware of the ominous creaking coming from them. She had waking dreams that the ice was alive, silently, menacingly creeping toward their tiny lifeboat, ready to consume it and all who sat in it. She screamed in terror. A man placed his arm around her.

Images flashed across her salt-filled eyes: other lifeboats bobbing around in the water, frozen bodies, blue faces.

Sensations came and went.

She took off her coat to give to a young child whose lips were blue from the cold. The mother wept with thanks.

"I have two coats," she heard a well-spoken American lady say. "Give the girl this one. It will give her some warmth at least." She had a sensation then of a heavy, dry coat being placed around her. She heard a dog bark next to her and the same lady shushing it. "Be quiet, Edmund. We can give the girl a coat, can't we?"

She tried to say thank you, but no words would come from her mouth.

She heard people talking about paper to burn for light so the rescue ships would be able to see them; heard them searching in their pockets, looking for letters or other scraps of paper. For some reason Maggie thought she had some letters in her coat pocket, but her hands couldn't feel them. She assumed she must have dreamed it.

Babies crying, mothers comforting them, women comforting the mothers and wives who wailed for their sons and husbands who had been left behind.

The pale light of dawn streaking across the sky.

The sensation of a small case, clasped in her hand.

She closed her eyes.

Time stood still. There was nothing.

"I'm so cold," someone said.

The sound of prayers and sobbing.

It was hard to breathe.

Another voice. "A ship."

She was being lifted then, pulled. Her frozen hands tried to grasp a rope. A ladder? Was she back on *Titanic*? Was it a dream?

Her body wouldn't move. She had no idea where she was. Where was Aunt Kathleen? Where was everyone?

"She had this small case with her," someone said. "Irish, I think."

A bitter taste in her mouth. Hot coffee? Then brandy. Coughing. Spluttering.

She tried to open her eyes, but they were too sore from the salt and the cold.

She tried to speak. "I can't see. Am I blind?" The words came out as an indecipherable mumble.

"It's all right now, miss," someone replied. "You're on *Carpathia*. It came to rescue us. You're going to be okay. You're safe now."

A blanket was wrapped around her. She let the tears fall.

For the next two days, Maggie barely noticed the sunset or sunrise, barely acknowledged the faint shafts of early morning light that reflected off a piece of metal through the window in front of her, sending light dancing across the deck. She stared dimly ahead, the sun almost irrelevant to her, unable to warm her, unable to illuminate the shadows of thirteen people that clouded her broken heart.

"Where am I?" she asked a woman lying next to her.

"The library," she replied. "There wasn't room for us all in the cabins, and those of us who were last to be rescued were placed in makeshift dorms, like this one."

"What ship are we on?" Maggie inquired, still confused.

"The *Carpathia*. They came to rescue us. Remember?"

She didn't.

"Are you alone, miss? Was there anyone traveling with you?"

"The others are all gone," she whispered. "All of them."

RMS Carpathia
April 17, 1912

It wasn't until late in the afternoon of the second day on *Carpathia* that Maggie found enough strength to sit on the deck. She was still shaking under her blankets, and a kind man with blue eyes, who said he was the doctor, told her that she wasn't cold anymore but the shock of what she had been through had her nerves bouncing all over the place. She was unable to cry any more tears. All she could feel was fear and a desolate loneliness.

On the doctor's advice, she tried to think of comforting thoughts, thoughts of home. She thought of Séamus, picturing his soft eyes, hearing his gentle voice, feeling his warm embrace. She recalled their first tender kiss on the shore of the lake and how her stomach had felt it was doing cartwheels with the joy she'd felt.

She reflected on the journey she had taken from Ballysheen. She was almost able to hear the rumble of the traps as they'd set off, before a sort of stillness had fallen over them as the rutted tracks gave way to the softer sandy road at the edge of the village. She remembered how she'd watched the three traps ahead of the one she shared with her aunt and how she had wondered what thoughts were passing through all their minds as they moved slowly across the landscape that had framed their whole lives.

She recalled how she had watched Peggy, in the trap ahead, speaking some words of comfort to Katie, who was twisting a sodden handkerchief around and around her fingers. She remembered that they had stopped once for a driver to remove a stone that had become lodged in a horse's hoof. She remembered how she had tried so hard to blink back her tears as they passed the familiar sights, afraid that her aunt would be annoyed with her for showing such sadness at leaving.

She'd watched the homes of her friends and neighbors pass by, imagining the black iron pots hanging on the cranes over the fires, the bread already baking. She'd wanted to remember it all: the dances, the wakes, a shared joke with a neighbor, every heady scent of the gorse and heather, every tree, every stone wall, every field. She remembered how she had hoped that if she stared intently enough, listened hard enough, and really concentrated on those sights and sounds and smells, she would impress the memories into her brain, ready to recall at will in the years to come, as the vast ocean and the passing of time attempted to erode them.

It was these small, intimate details she thought of now as she sat, shaking and alone, although whether she remembered this in her dreams or in waking moments she wasn't quite sure.

"We arrive in New York tomorrow evening," she heard someone close by say. "And not a moment too soon. This ice is wreaking havoc with the minds of the poor unfortunates. They must be terrified it's going to happen all over again."

"Well, I commend the bravery of Captain Rostron," the man's colleague replied. "There aren't many men who would have acted as swiftly and calmly as he did, and then set a course directly through the ice fields to get us back as quickly as possible. Nerves of steel he must have—or a sixth sense."

"Excuse me, sir," she whispered.

The man heard her and turned. "Yes, miss?"

"What day is it today?"

"It is Wednesday, miss. April seventeenth."

"Wednesday," she repeated. "Thank you."

She closed her eyes then and slept, dreaming of cherry blossom trees and Séamus, waiting for her.

PART FIVE

Received April

NO_____ CK_____   TIME RECEIVED_____

TO

W.W. Bradfield, Marconi Telegraph Company: Still
no names of crew survivors received is Carpathia in
touch with any station please spare no expense to
obtain information tension on relatives awaiting
news very acute harrowing scenes amongst crowd
awaiting information.

Marconigram message sent from Philip Curry, manager
of the White Star Line offices in Southampton, to
W.W. Bradfield, Marconi Telegraph Company, London,
on April 18, 1912

WHITE STAR LINE

ROYAL AND UNITED STATES MAIL STEAMERS.

Male Berth............
Female Berth...........
Married Berth..........

ISMAY, IMRIE & CO.,

1 COCKSPUR STREET S.W.
30. LEADENHALL STREET, E.C.
LONDON.
30 JAMES STREET
LIVERPOOL.
and
CANUTE ROAD SOUTHAMPTON.

Agent at PARIS—
NICHOLAS MARTIN, 9, Rue Scribe.

WHITE STAR LINE

19. VIA ALLA BORSETTA
31. PIAZZA DELLA BORSA
24. STATE STREET,
9. BROADWAY
53 DALHOUSIE STREET
BELL TELEPHONE BUILDINGS
16. NOTRE DAME STREET WEST.

GENOA
NAPLES
BOSTON.
NEW YORK
QUEBEC.
MONTREAL.

JAMES SCOTT & CO. Agents
QUEENSTOWN

OCEANIC STEAM NAVIGATION COMPANY, LIMITED, OF GREAT BRITAIN.
THIRD CLASS (Steerage) PASSENGER'S CONTRACT TICKET.
(NOT TRANSFERABLE.)

CHAPTER 29

Cass County, Illinois
May 25, 1982

"Grace, there's a man on the phone says he'd like to talk to you."

"Oh, Mom, can you do me a favor and tell him I'm out?" Grace shouted from her bedroom. "It'll just be another reporter looking to get their pound of flesh out of Maggie."

The interest in Grace's article about Maggie's *Titanic* story had been amazing. Since she'd received the phone call from Professor Andrews to tell her that Bill O'Shea had fallen in love with her article, life had become crazy. When the piece finally appeared in print, Grace's and Maggie's names were all over town. Grace was being hailed as the young girl who'd scooped the biggest story of the year and was already being touted as one to watch for the sensitive and heartfelt way she had handled the story. Maggie was a local hero.

With the success of the article and the revelation that a *Titanic* survivor was living among them, other local newspapers and journalists wanted a piece of the action, and the phone hadn't stopped ringing. Everyone wanted to cover the story in their own newspapers and magazines, wanted photos of Maggie, photos of Grace, photos of the family together. There had even been a piece in a local paper about Grace and how her studies had been put on hold when her father died. It was all becoming a bit intrusive, and Grace was hesitant to talk to anyone else—wary of their intentions.

"He says it's very important," her mother shouted back up the stairs. "He says he's honestly not a reporter and that you will definitely be interested in what he has to say."

Not believing a word of it, Grace put down the admissions form she was completing—necessary, if tedious, paperwork for getting herself reenrolled in the journalism program—and walked casually downstairs. Sighing and rolling her eyes, she took the receiver from her mother, who mouthed "He seems very nice" before wandering back into the kitchen to finish washing the breakfast dishes.

"Hello. This is Grace Butler," she announced without interest into the receiver. "How can I help you?"

"Miss Butler. Oh, um, hello. Thank you so much for taking my call." The voice on the end of the line was a man's voice, well spoken, if slightly nervous. "Um, Miss Butler, I'm afraid this is all going to sound a little strange, but I would appreciate it if you would hear me out."

Grace warmed a little to the pleasant, polite voice and sat down on the bottom step, tracing the pattern on the carpet with her bare toes as she admired the neon-pink nail polish she'd applied earlier that morning. "Okay," she said, distracted. "I'm listening."

"My name is Edward Lockey. I read your article in the paper last week. It's a remarkable story and beautifully written, might I add. Your great-grandmother is an incredibly brave woman."

Grace was used to hearing this from the dozens of reporters who had called over the last week. She gave her usual response. "Yes, thank you. She is an amazing lady indeed."

"Well, it turns out to be quite a coincidence that I read your article. I don't usually read the *Tribune* you see, I'm more of a *Sun Times* man, but I was with my sister last week and she always gets the *Tribune* and . . . oh well, look, that doesn't really matter now. Basically, Miss Butler, I think I may have something that will be of interest to your great-grandmother. You see, an uncle of mine was also on *Titanic*."

Grace sat up then, her attention caught. "Really? Oh my gosh!"

"Yes. He was a third-class saloon steward on the ship," he continued. "He sailed from Southampton in England." Grace felt the hairs on the back of her neck stand up as goose bumps formed all over her arms. "He sadly passed away a few years ago, but when he died, a few of his personal possessions were given to me. I'd never really paid much attention to them before, but then I read your article and something clicked."

Completely captivated now by this quietly spoken man and his connection to *Titanic*, Grace wanted to know more. "What?" she asked. "What clicked?"

"Well, you see—and I am aware that I may be completely mistaken here—but my uncle had in his possession a lady's coat and a packet of letters. The name Maggie is handwritten on the front of the packet of letters, and there's a note scribbled on them, which I presume was written by my uncle. I have it here in front of me. Would you like me to read it to you?"

"Yes, yes please." Grace was now on the very edge of the step.

"Okay, let me just find my reading glasses. Ah yes, now, here we are. It says, 'Possessions of a Miss Maggie Murphy who traveled from Ireland on *Titanic* with her aunt and two young women—Peggy and Katie. Items found in lifeboat on *Carpathia*.'" Mr. Lockey paused for a moment. "I have to assume, Miss Butler, that these items belong to your great-grandmother."

Grace couldn't believe it. Maggie's letters! The letters from Séamus. After all these years. "That's amazing!" she gasped.

"Yes, isn't it?" Mr. Lockey continued. "And from what I hear from members of my own family, my uncle was very eager to see these items reunited with their owner. He seemed to think that Maggie had given her coat to a little girl who was in their lifeboat and that the coat was then left in the boat when the *Carpathia* took the survivors on board. He had come across it when he, and some other crew, were unloading *Titanic*'s lifeboats onto the White Star Line wharf when *Carpathia* arrived in New York. He had tried to find Maggie on the *Carpathia* and in the New York hospitals, but with all the confusion and with survivor names being misreported and misspelled, he never found her. So he kept the coat and the letters in the vague hope that one day he, or they, would find her again." He paused for a moment to take a breath. "I am hoping that, after all these years, they possibly have."

Grace couldn't speak for a moment.

"Miss Butler? Are you still there?"

"Oh, yes, yes, I'm sorry. I'm here. I just can't believe it! I can't believe you have Maggie's letters. Are they all still there?"

"Well, miss, I'm not sure, but the packet certainly seems to have been kept in very good condition. My uncle was very particular about them and insisted that nobody read them—those were his specific instructions in his will. He apparently told members of the family that he believed they were love letters from a boyfriend Maggie had left behind in Ireland and that only if Maggie was found should they be read."

Grace was stunned, her heart racing at what this would mean to Maggie. Her letters finally returned to her. It momentarily crossed her mind that it might all be a bit too much for her great-grandmother. She often seemed reluctant to talk about Séamus, as if thinking about him upset her.

"This is just incredible, Mr. . . ."

"Lockey. Edward Lockey."

"This may be a silly question, Mr. Lockey——"

"Please, call me Edward," he interrupted, laughing.

"Sorry, Edward. Was your uncle's name Harry by any chance?"

Now it was his turn to be surprised. "Yes! Harry *was* his name! How did you know that?"

"Maggie kept a journal on *Titanic*," Grace explained. "She mentions a Harry often, or Lucky Harry, as she and the girls she shared a cabin with seem to have called him. She told me a steward named Harry helped her get to the lifeboat. It must be him."

They spoke for a few moments more about the incredible coincidences: Edward reading Grace's article, and him being related to the man who had helped Maggie get off *Titanic*, and that he had what they believed to be Maggie's lost coat and letters. It was simply amazing.

"I think it would be useful to meet," Edward Lockey continued. "I'd prefer to hand over the items to you in person if that isn't too much of an imposition. I certainly wouldn't want to rely on the postal service to get them back to Maggie—it would be terrible if they were to be lost after all this time."

Grace agreed, and they made arrangements to meet the following week at a coffee shop they both knew in downtown Chicago. She thought it best not to say anything to Maggie just yet—in case the man turned out to be a crackpot. The letters clearly wouldn't change anything for Maggie now, whatever they said, but Grace hoped that they might bring her some sort of closure, allow her to lay to rest some of the ghosts that had haunted her since that night.

She put down the phone and walked into the kitchen.

"So?" her mother inquired from inside the pantry, which she was rearranging. "Was it another reporter?"

Grace sat down at the kitchen table, absentmindedly taking a banana from the fruit bowl. "No, he really wasn't a reporter. It's unbelievable, Mom. He says he's the nephew of someone else who survived *Titanic*, and we think it's someone who Maggie knew."

Her mother appeared then, wiping her hands on the front of her trousers. "Really?"

"Yeah! Really! And he seems genuine. And you'll never guess what."

"What?"

"He thinks he has Maggie's coat and the packet of letters. You know, the ones she says she left on the *Carpathia*. The letters from Séamus."

The two women sat at the table then, as they often did when they had something important to discuss, and Grace filled her mother in on all the details that Edward Lockey had passed on to her. They agreed there was a chance that this was a hoax, but deep in their hearts, they both hoped that he was genuine.

May 30, 1982

On the morning that Grace had agreed to meet Edward Lockey, she received a letter. In her hurry to make the agreed-upon rendezvous time, she almost walked past the pile of mail her mother had placed on the small console table on the front porch, assuming that it would just be bills for her mom as usual. But something made her stop and pick them up. She recognized his handwriting immediately.

"Jimmy," she whispered.

Trembling with excitement and dread, she tore open the envelope. Her heart fell at the sight of a single piece of notepaper folded in half. *Good news comes in large packages* she remembered her father saying when she had first applied to college and was waiting to hear whether she had been accepted. *If it's bad news, it'll be short and sweet.* This was definitely short and sweet. Hesitating, afraid of what she would see written on the page, she unfolded the single piece of paper.

Hey, stranger. Read the article—amazing! I knew you'd find a story eventually. How about that cup of coffee?

He didn't need to sign it.

Despite there being only a few words written on the page, they were the best words she could have hoped for. She read them over and over and over again. It was an olive branch. It was more than an olive branch. He wanted to meet her for coffee. He'd read her article. He was still there, still waiting, still interested—maybe. A million thoughts and emotions swirled around Grace's mind.

Since opening the box of letters she'd kept under her bed, she'd held out some hope of a reunion. *I guess this is just too hard for you,* he'd written in his final letter. *I'm not sure I really understand, Grace, but I am trying to, I really am. So I'm going to leave you now, to heal in peace. I'm not going to write to you again, Grace, because it's too painful when I don't hear back. Take your time and mourn your father as you need to. I don't know how long that's gonna take—possibly forever? But maybe, someday when you've gotten over this and feel a little better, maybe you could write me? Maybe I could buy you a cup of coffee and we could start over? Think about it. You know where I am. I will be waiting. Always, J xx*

After reading the letter, she'd written to Jimmy's old home address and sent the note for his attention in care of Professor Andrews along with the manuscript for her article. She'd left her phone number but, not having heard anything, had assumed he had given up and moved on with his life—as she had told him to. This small note that she now held in her hand told her otherwise.

Recognizing the number he'd added to the bottom of the note as a Chicago exchange, she wondered whether she should call right away. She remembered the words Maggie had said to her in the café. *Life is fragile, Grace—it is no more than a petal of cherry blossom.* Her mind was made up.

She paused, just for a moment, to check her appearance in the hall mirror. Her cheeks were flushed; her eyes sparkled. She looked like the girl who used to stare back at her from the mirror, a girl whose lust for life and whose vibrancy oozed through her every pore. The girl looking back was a girl she hadn't seen for a long time. She adjusted her hair and dialed the number quickly, before she could change her mind.

The phone rang and rang at the other end. Her heart raced,

her mouth was as dry as sandpaper. "Pick up, pick up, pick up," she muttered under her breath.

"Hello?"

Her heart did a somersault at the sound of his voice. She had to fight back the tears as she responded.

"Jimmy," she whispered, her voice shaking. "It's me. It's Grace."

WHITE STAR LINE

ROYAL AND UNITED STATES MAIL STEAMERS.

WHITE STAR LINE

ISMAY, IMRIE & CO.

LONDON,

LIVERPOOL

SOUTHAMPTON

Agent at PARIS:—
NICHOLAS MARTIN, 9, Rue Scribe.

GENOA
NAPLES
BOSTON
NEW YORK
QUEBEC
MONTREAL

JAMES SCOTT & CO. Agents
QUEENSTOWN.

OCEANIC STEAM NAVIGATION COMPANY, LIMITED, OF GREAT BRITAIN.

THIRD CLASS (Steerage) PASSENGER'S CONTRACT TICKET.
(NOT TRANSFERABLE.)

CHAPTER 30

New York
April 18, 1912

Frances Kenny handed her yellow ticket to the inspectors at the top of West Street. Satisfied that she was a relative awaiting the arrival of *Carpathia,* which was expected at around midnight, the inspectors gave her permission to access the fenced-off area, and she made her way to join the hundreds of others already gathered at the docks.

The flags in New York harbor, all lowered to half-mast, flapped and snapped in the wind gusting over the exposed harbor, rattling the flagpoles, blowing out the ladies' skirts, and lifting umbrellas from rain-soaked hands. It was just past three o'clock in the afternoon, but the darkening sky cast a hue of nightfall over the entire city.

Frances knew she had many hours to wait before the expected arrival of the rescue ship, but she didn't care. She didn't feel the wind or the pouring rain. She didn't worry about catching a chill. "I'd rather stand in a blizzard than spend any more time alone in this house," she'd told her neighbor who had stopped in earlier that day to ask whether there was any further news of

Katie. "I'm walking in and out of the guest room like a caged tiger," she'd explained. "I've spent weeks preparing for my sister's arrival and now I don't know whether the bed will ever be slept in. I stand and stare at those pillows and wonder whether they'll always remain as smoothed and plumped as I have made them with all my fussing and ironing. I would give anything to have Katie's beautiful head to rest upon them and mess them all up again."

She hadn't been to work that day, or for the several days since news of the *Titanic* disaster. Her heart was so full of despair it was hard to summon up the energy to wash and dress in the morning, let alone travel across the city and wash Mrs. Walker-Brown's endless floors. As it transpired, one of the other employees at the Walker-Brown residence had called to Frances's home to pass on the message from Mrs. Walker-Brown that Frances's services wouldn't be required for the time being. Mrs. Walker-Brown had apparently taken to her bed with grief for her daughter, who despite being listed as one of the survivors, appeared to be returning on the rescue ship without her fiancé. Mrs. Walker-Brown was unable to bear the thought of her daughter having suffered such horror and could not imagine what terrible conditions she was traveling in on the rescue ship. She was distraught to learn that Robert had, most probably, perished when the ship went down and was inconsolable, refusing to eat and not wishing to see anyone until her daughter was safely returned to the family home.

According to the young kitchen maid who had visited Frances, Vivienne Walker-Brown's pet dog, Edmund, was also listed among the survivors. She assumed the officials had thought Edmund Walker-Brown to be the lady's son, and not just a dog.

Frances had seethed with anger when she heard this, unable to comprehend how a dog could be permitted to survive when so many had lost their lives.

Now, as she walked along the wharf, oblivious to the steadily falling rain, she wandered past the yellow taxicabs and the sleek black limousines that cast their lights onto the rain-soaked pavement, reflecting the sights of the dock buildings and freight cranes at her feet. She could barely register the absurdity of the situation that would permit some survivors to walk off *Carpathia* into immediate luxury, while others would undoubtedly arrive without a cent or a pair of shoes to their name.

Alongside Pier 54—the Cunard pier—the lines of ambulances waiting to ferry the shaken and injured survivors to the hospital reinforced the severity of the situation and the scale of the tragedy. It struck Frances for the first time that even arriving safely in New York would not be the end of the ordeal for these poor people, many of whom would still be far from their final destination.

As she walked, she caught fragments of conversation that shocked and scared her all over again.

"Not enough lifeboats by far, they're reporting. There wasn't a chance for half of the passengers. It's a disgrace. Probably saving room for some more of those fancy first-class staterooms."

"It's my fiancé I'm waiting for. We're to be married next month. I didn't see his name on the list, but I had a dream that he survived. He has to have survived."

"Mammy and Da and me four little brothers were sailing. Only Mammy survived," a young girl sobbed. "It was their first time coming over. We was all planning a life here together."

It was unbearable to hear.

Frances walked past large groups of Salvation Army and Sheltering Society volunteers, dressed in their uniforms, ready to provide assistance wherever possible, serving hot coffee and sandwiches to the waiting relatives and to the dozens of dock-workers who had arrived of their own will, eager to help in whatever way they could.

A dozen or so black-robed Sisters of Charity gathered in quiet prayer, awaiting the rescue ship's arrival. They stood alongside representatives from the Pennsylvania Railroad, who were ready to provide assistance and tickets to those trying to travel on to Philadelphia or points farther west. It was a rescue and humanitarian operation the scale of which Frances had never seen before. It moved and encouraged her immensely.

"You're doing a wonderful job," she remarked to a Salvation Army volunteer who offered her a cup of hot coffee. "It is much appreciated."

"You're welcome, miss," the young volunteer replied. "It's all so terribly sad, we're just glad to be able to help in some way, no matter how small. There's thousands gathered in Battery Park. Just waiting to see those poor folks safely home."

Frances walked on as the storm clouds gathered ominously overhead and the first crackles of lightning lit up the sky.

The atmosphere among the waiting crowds was one of numbed sobriety and tension, anxiety and grief lining the faces of those she passed, dark shadows and red-rimmed eyes bearing witness to the suffering these people had already endured as, like her, they had scoured and scoured the lists of survivors only to discover that the names they were looking for were not present.

Observing the steadily growing mass of people and waiting volunteers now gathering along the wharf did little to calm

Frances's fears or reassure her troubled mind. Would Katie be on *Carpathia,* or would her worst fears be realized when all the survivors had disembarked?

She'd telephoned the White Star offices every day since news of the disaster broke.

"What have you heard?" she asked when her call was answered.

"Nothing new, miss," came the somber reply from the anonymous person at the other end of the line.

Frances very quickly realized that "Nothing new" meant that the first reports of survivors hadn't changed and that the names of many of the travelers from Ballysheen, who had been reported as lost, were accurate and had not changed. But although Frances had not found the name Katie Kenny—or others from the Ballysheen group—on any of the issued survivor lists, her heart would not allow her to give up hope. She had seen a Kate Kennedy listed and a Katherine Denny and had prayed every day that one of those was her sister, the name having been misprinted or mistakenly taken down in all the confusion.

Except for the lists of survivor names, there'd been a frustrating silence from *Carpathia* over the last few days; the anticipated details of the events that had unfolded on *Titanic* had not been forthcoming, and rumors among the press were rife that the surviving Marconi radio operator, Harold Bride, had been told to keep quiet until *Carpathia* docked, at which point his story would be sold for a large sum of money. Looking around at the harrowing scenes of grief and despair, Frances found it impossible to conceive that anyone could hope to prosper from such unimaginable tragedy.

As the hours passed, Frances and the hundreds of other anxious relatives and friends of *Titanic*'s passengers huddled against the strong wind and lashing rain and watched the gathering nightfall. Many, who knew their loved ones were safely aboard *Carpathia,* waited quietly. Others, like Frances, were left to pray that there had been a mistake and that the person they so longed to see would emerge from the liner when she docked.

It is as if the entire city is stricken with grief, Frances read in the newspaper she had picked up at the stand, looking for the latest reports. *Rich and poor are united under one great wave of sorrow and sympathy. God has indeed spoken.*

Turning her rosary beads over and over in her hands, Frances sat under the large letter *K*, corresponding to the surname of the survivor she was so hoping to greet. She said a silent prayer, closing her eyes against the rain and the impossible situation she found herself in.

Time passed slowly.

I t was just before nine o'clock when a shiver seemed to cross the waiting crowd as the first sightings of *Carpathia* steaming up the Hudson River were relayed from the tugboats that had gone out to meet her. Everyone stood up then, desperate to see the ship itself, as if, until that moment, this could all be imagined. Men, women, and children stood on tiptoes, craning their necks, peering into the gloom as if watching a theater show, waiting for that moment when the magician delivers the prestige.

The unmistakable single funnel of a steam liner emerged from the murky mist. Just a few lights were visible from the upper cabins and the masthead. Otherwise, all was darkness around the great mass of the ship.

Frances watched *Carpathia* glide, as if in slow motion, toward the White Star Line Pier, 59, where she rested to unload the lifeboats belonging to *Titanic.* It was a somber moment, the S.S.

Titanic sign on the white lifeboats the first sighting for all gathered there of the much-lauded ship, a simple, humble calling card of the greatest ocean liner ever to set sail.

For many, the suspense and grief of the last few days was too great, and they collapsed into convulsions of tears at the sight of the rescue ship. For Frances, it was a moment she wished she could suspend in time, not sure whether she finally wanted to learn if the face she was waiting so desperately to see would come walking ashore or if her sister had lain at the bottom of the ocean for the last four days and would never be seen again.

An eerie hush fell over the waiting crowds as the huge steamer approached the Cunard Pier, just the muffled tears of the women audible above the wind and splashes of rain on umbrellas and the corrugated iron containers on the wharf side.

The dozens of doctors and nurses, the volunteers from the Women's Relief Committee and all the officials from the city, the government, and White Star Line walked purposefully now among the crowd, the tension evident on their faces as they prepared to carry out their duties.

Later in her life, Frances would find herself saying that the scenes she witnessed as the survivors were gradually brought ashore were too terrible to define. What her eyes and ears tried to comprehend during those moments was indescribable. Not in the farthest reaches of her imagination could she have believed such outpourings of emotion were possible in a public place. For every poignant reunion, it would seem that there was also a heartbreaking moment of finality at the realization that relatives or friends had not walked toward the waiting crowd.

Husbands clutched wives who had returned without their children; children clung to grandparents, their parents lost at sea; sisters greeted sisters and wept for their lost brothers; brothers greeted sisters and cried for their lost mothers and fathers. There wasn't a person who didn't shed a tear for himself or for someone else.

As Frances waited, she watched these scenes play out, involved and yet strangely detached. It was through tear-filled eyes that she observed a finely dressed young lady emerge from the gangplank, a small dog under her arm and barely a hair out of place. Frances would not have recognized her as Vivienne Walker-Brown had she not heard the shriek across the crowd.

"Vivienne! Darling! My darling Vivienne," Emily Walker-Brown cried hysterically as she pushed toward the gangplank.

Frances watched, unnoticed, as the mother and daughter shared an emotional embrace, Emily weeping for the loss of her future son-in-law. But Vivienne Walker-Brown did not cry. Frances overheard her reassuring her mother that Robert did the honorable thing and ensured that the women and children took the seats in the lifeboats, as instructed, "unlike that dreadful Ismay fellow," she added at the top of her voice. "Shameful behavior, saving himself without a care for the poor souls left to perish in the icy sea."

Frances watched then as the family walked toward a waiting taxicab. Vivienne and her dog would be back within the comfort of their Park Avenue home in thirty minutes. The steerage passengers hadn't even started to emerge from *Carpathia*.

For hours, Frances watched and waited as the remainder of the first- and second-class survivors made their way unsteadily along the gangplank and into the waiting crowds; the gathered press pack, corralled behind the fencing on West Street, shouted questions to the bewildered passengers, trying desperately to get a scoop for the first editions of the morning papers.

It was nearly midnight when the steerage passengers began

to disembark. It struck Frances how much they resembled the emigrants she had seen in pictures of the famine ships a generation ago. Most were wearing only their nightclothes, some had just blankets around their shoulders for warmth, and many walked without shoes. Numbly she watched the faces, staring as some survivors were taken straight to the waiting ambulances.

She stood quietly, patiently, hopefully, barely noticing the crowds dispersing around her.

"Please come, Katie my love," she whispered. "Please be there."

It was only when the crew of *Carpathia* started to appear on the gangplank that her hopes began to fade.

"Excuse me, miss."

She turned. A White Star Line official stood by her side.

"They're all off. It's just *Carpathia* crew now, miss."

She looked desperately into the man's eyes. "No," she whispered. "No. They can't all be off. I'm waiting for my sister. Katie Kenny is her name. From Ballysheen, Ireland."

"I'm very sorry, miss. All the survivors are ashore now." He tipped his hat then and disappeared into the rain.

Frances stood alone, drenched to the skin, staring at the looming, empty bulk of *Carpathia*. The remaining people around her on the wharf dissolved into the darkness that engulfed her.

"No. No. Not Katie," she gasped. "Not my darling Katie. Please, no."

She sank to her knees and wept with every part of her soul. Not even the relentless rain could compete with the flood of tears that fell in New York that night.

CHAPTER 31

Private Journal of Maggie Murphy
St. Vincent's Hospital, New York
April 20, 1912

I feel numb. Cold. Frightened. I cannot stop the tears falling. They tell me I am in a hospital somewhere in New York. I barely know how I got here. I barely know my own name. My hands are misshapen—swollen and purple from the cold and frostbite. My God, it was so cold on that lifeboat.

I can barely hold the pen but the nurse says it is good for me to try and write; that it will help to get my circulation going again. I don't know what to write, don't know what to say. Part of me wishes I had died too.

I want to go home.

April 21, 1912

We must have been at sea for some days on the Carpathia *because the girl lying in the bed next to me says it is Sunday and it was a Sunday when I last wrote in this journal on* Titanic. *How can a whole week have passed?*

Sometimes when I wake from my sleep I forget where I am and what has happened. For a few minutes I feel quite peaceful. Then I see the bare hospital walls and the rows and rows of beds and I remember.

I recognize some of the people in the beds near to me. It seems like a dream that we shared a song or danced a jig together on that mighty ship that is now at the bottom of the ocean. I have searched the faces again and again, desperately hoping that I'll see Aunt Kathleen or Peggy or Katie or anyone from our group—but I know it's hopeless to think that they somehow survived. I wonder what happened to Harry, the steward. He was in the lifeboat with me, but I didn't see him again. Everything was so confusing on the Carpathia. *I only added my name to the survivor list the day before we arrived in New York.*

I'm frightened. I don't like being alone here.

I do not know what will happen to me at all. I don't even know if Aunt Mary in Chicago will know about the disaster—or anyone in Ireland. It is so terrible. So many people here have lost everyone and everything. I can barely imagine how I can live again. I sometimes wish I had gone down with the others. Why would God save me when thousands died—some of them rich millionaires? I saw babies in that water frozen blue with the cold. I think their faces will haunt my dreams for the rest of my life.

I am too tired to write any more.
I want to go home.

April 21, 1912—evening

My small black case has been left on my bed. I don't even remember taking it with me into the lifeboat. But I do not have my coat. I think I gave it to a child in the lifeboat. A well-dressed lady with a dog on her lap gave me her coat. I seem to remember that she was wearing two coats—an everyday one and a fur one, she said. She handed me the everyday coat to keep me warm, and that was what I arrived here in. I still have it but I don't know what became of my own coat, and there were some letters in the pocket, I'm sure of it. Letters from Séamus. Poor Séamus. What must he be thinking hearing about the ship being sunk and all and me in no fit state to contact him to tell him I'm alive. I wish I had his letters—they would comfort me. Now I'll never know what those letters said. I know I shouldn't feel sad about a few letters what with all those poor people dead, but I do.

I want to go home.

April 22, 1912

The Salvation Army women came today. They gave us all parcels of clean clothes and some money to continue our journeys. There's all sorts of relief efforts and money being raised for the survivors—thousands of dollars. A kind lady called Elizabeth told me that my aunt Mary had been in contact and it has been arranged that she will meet me off the Pennsylvania train at Union Station in Chicago in two days. I am writing those names down so as not to forget.

When I was changing my dress to put on a clean one from the donated clothes, I found twenty-five dollars in bills pinned to my old one. I hadn't noticed it before, but then I vaguely remembered a man talking to me when I was first brought to the hospital from the Carpathia. He had a whiskery beard and plump fingers, and his breath smelt of tobacco. He spoke a lot of words to me, but I was too shocked to take it all in. I remember he asked me to sign a paper that he handed to me. I thought it was a train ticket to Chicago I was signing for, but the nurses now tell me that it was a "waiver for damages." I'm not really sure what that means, but it seems that the White Star Line people wanted to make sure I didn't come back and try to get money from them for the suffering I've experienced and for all my losses. They seem to think twenty-five dollars is compensation enough for my troubles. I remember the man had to hold my arm to help me write my own name because my hands were too numb to hold the pen properly. I am too sad and alone right now to be angry with them.

The newspapermen are crawling all over the hospital. They want to talk to us about what really happened the night Titanic sank. I have said a few words to them about how I got to the lifeboats, but I really do not want to go through all the terrible moments again. I cannot get the faces of those poor people out of my head, standing against the railings, praying for their lives, and those terrifying sounds of the crunching, grating, screeching metal and the desperate screams of a thousand people. It will haunt my dreams forever, I am sure of it.

I want to go home.

There are some terrible tales being told about what happened to people when Titanic sank. We sit about and say a few words to each other now and again—normally talking about someone else's experience rather than our own. I think we all just want to lock away our own memories and try to forget.

One of the nurses who tends to me most of the time has told me about a young Finnish girl who doesn't speak a word of English. She sits in the bed across the room from mine and looks to be in a constant daze. Her brother, her uncle, and the man she was to marry were all lost in the disaster. She is to sail back to Finland on Wednesday. I cannot imagine the fears she must have about sailing again. I wish I could help her in some way.

The nurse also told me about the small Swedish woman at the end of the ward who refuses to leave her two little children. Her husband, their father, was lost. The children have the fairest hair I have ever seen, and the mother dotes on them day and night, so she does, stroking the little dresses that came in for them from the Women's Relief Committee. Apparently she told the nurse that when she started to climb down the rope to the lifeboat, which was already being lowered, she realized she could only carry the youngest child and hold the rope at the same time. Her three-year-old daughter clung, terrified, to her skirt all the way down that rope, the black Atlantic sea heaving beneath them. Thank the Lord the little girl held on good and tight *and they all three made it safely to the boat, although the father was lost.*

There is another woman here who has just married her sweetheart in the hospital. They were separated on the deck of Titanic, *and she thought him lost until they discovered each other in different wards. She had been clinging to an upturned lifeboat for eight hours. The nurse tells me it's important to try and be grateful for stories like this, despite our own terrible losses. I know she is right, but the faces of my friends and family still disturb my dreams at night.*

April 23, 1912

Some of my words have been printed in the morning newspaper. My nurse showed it to me. She has given me a bundle of newspapers that she says I should take with me when I leave. She says that I should keep them somewhere safe because Titanic *will be talked about in a hundred years' time and people will be interested in seeing them. I cannot see why anyone would want to remember this terrible event, but I have folded the pages that mention* Titanic *and put them into my case anyway, along with the few other possessions I have somehow managed to keep with me through all of this: the silver hair comb and rosary beads that Séamus gave me on the morning we left Ballysheen, my* Titanic *ticket, my health inspection certificate, a bottle of holy water, and a few other items. Some people might want to talk about* Titanic *for the next hundred years— after I leave this hospital and get to Chicago, I never want to talk about it again.*

I will leave the hospital tomorrow. I have no idea what life has in store for me, but I know that I can never cross the ocean again. I will never step foot on a ship as long as I live, which means that I will have to try and forget about Ireland and those who we left behind. How could I ever look into the eyes of those poor mothers and fathers and sisters and brothers—knowing that I got off the ship when their loved ones did not and perished in the freezing seas? I can never see their faces—I can never explain what happened that night.

Peggy is alive! I cannot believe it. She is ALIVE!

She walked right into the ward where my bed is and woke me from my sleep. "Is it really you, Maggie Murphy?" she said. We took to crying and hugging each other—I am beyond words. I thought it was a ghost at my bedside for a few moments; I dared hardly believe it was really and truly her—alive and well and with her beautiful golden hair falling about her shoulders as usual. We sat and stared at each other for an age—laughing and crying—neither of us knowing what to say or do with ourselves.

We caused such a commotion with all our shrieking and crying that the nurses came running—they thought someone was dying. We brought tears to their eyes when we told them we'd been sailing on Titanic *together and thought each other dead along with everyone else we loved and cared for.*

When we finally calmed down a little and the nurses had brought us both a cup of hot, sweet tea, Peggy told me that after we were separated on the ladder, she'd seen Katie and Maria and Pat heading up toward the back of the ship to escape from the water. She told me one of the great funnels broke loose from its fixings then and smashed into everything underneath—she doesn't even want to imagine that it was that funnel that killed them all, but she didn't see anyone from the Ballysheen group again and ran, with a group of crewmen, to the starboard side of the ship and somehow managed to jump from the deck to a lifeboat that was being lowered some fifteen feet down. She said she was never more terrified in her life, but she knew that leap was her last chance to survive. Then, when the lifeboat reached the water, it was capsized by people who were already thrown overboard, trying desperately to clamber aboard.

She wept when she described the fear of being in that icy water and the people all thrashing around her. Her face went under the water a dozen times, she told me, what with people trying to climb over her to reach the boat. But brave Peggy managed to somehow swim to an upturned collapsible lifeboat, which she clung to in her sodden clothes right through the night. She was rescued along with twelve others from that upturned boat—one of the Marconi radio boys was with her. Bride, she said his name was. Harold Bride. I remember Harry the steward telling me that was the name of one of the boys he knew. Maybe it was him who sent my telegram to Séamus. I am glad to know that he survived.

Peggy had suffered terribly from being in that icy water for all that time and was unconscious when they pulled her onto Carpathia. *She has only just recovered her strength and her senses enough to come looking for me. Imagine, Peggy being on* Carpathia *with me and in the same hospital as me for all that time and we never found each other until now.*

When she had told me her frightening story, I told her all about how I got into the lifeboat and how Harry was charged with rowing it to safety. I wept as I explained that Maura and Eileen were unable to leave Jack Brennan and that the young lad, Michael Kelly, wasn't allowed to climb aboard, what with it being women and children first. We held each other and wept for everyone and prayed to God for sparing us and vowed to live a long and happy life as thanks for being given this chance. Peggy is to travel on to St. Louis to meet her sister. We have exchanged addresses and promised that we will keep in contact.

April 24, 1912

I dreamed last night that the steward, Harry, was looking for me and Peggy. He was asking for us but the nurse told him we had already been discharged. He seemed to have something important that belonged to me and wanted to return it. I tried to shout out, "I am still here," but no words would come and then I woke up and Harry was not there.

Peggy left early this morning. We shared a pitiful, teary farewell and promised to keep in touch. I feel frightened now that she has gone—I feel alone again and wish she was traveling on with me to Chicago.

I am on a train with the few pathetic possessions I own and wearing donated clothes that hang off me and make me look like an unloved rag doll. How Aunt Kathleen would flush with embarrassment if she were here to see me now.

When it was time to leave the hospital, I cried. The nurses have looked after me so well. I told one of them I might like to be a nurse myself when I have properly recovered from all this. She said that nurses have to be incredibly brave and special people—so I would make a very good one. She hugged me tightly, and I never wanted that hug to end. It reminded me of how Mammy used to hug me when I was a little girl.

Before I left the hospital, I walked around to the beds of the other survivors who are still there—there are not many now, most having recovered well enough to move on or return home. I will never forget those people—their sad, empty faces and weak smiles of a vague hope for the future. We shared an understanding as we held hands and looked into each other's eyes.

So I am finally leaving New York, the city I had heard so much about and thought I would see for the first time from the bow of Titanic as we sailed gracefully into the dock. I'd imagined we would be greeted by all the well-wishers and ragtime bands and fluttering flags. Who could have ever known that we would arrive on a different ship altogether? I never even saw the Statue of Liberty and doubt I ever will. This place will always hold dark memories for me now. I think I am best to leave those memories among the echoing corridors and starched bedsheets of the hospital.

I still feel very unsteady on my feet and am sure my hands will never function right again. The nurses told me that I am still suffering from shock and exposure and that it could take months for me to recover fully.

I am huddled into a seat on the train, hoping that nobody will pay me any attention at all, although I can feel them looking at me and whispering and guessing my story.

Sometimes I catch their eyes and they look sympathetically at me, trying to show me with their tilted heads, furrowed eyebrows, and bland smiles that they understand, that they know of the suffering I have endured. I stare back. They can never know of the suffering I have endured.

It is odd to think that I had never been on a train until just over a week ago—I thought I felt an aching sadness in my heart then as we puffed out of Claremorris station. How could I ever have known that there was a far greater sadness awaiting me?

I am grateful for the borrowed coat and the donated clothes, but how I wish I had my own coat and the packet of letters. How I would love to read them now as I sit here all alone. How I would love to see Séamus's writing and touch the paper his hands have touched.

I wondered today about my message to Séamus and whether it was ever sent by that Marconi boy—whether it ever reached him. I hope so. He must be worried to death if he has heard any of the news about Titanic. *My message might lift his spirits, and maybe, after hearing of what has happened, and knowing that I am all alone, he might be able to come to America himself soon.*

I find it all too upsetting to think about. I will stop writing now and try to sleep until I reach my destination. I can barely stand the thought of seeing Aunt Mary; she will be so sad about her dear sister, and I wish I could be arriving here with her as we had planned.

It is almost impossible to rest with the rocking and thumping of the train carriages and with people needing to inspect my ticket and step past me to get on or off at a station. I'm so exhausted I barely said thank you to the lady from the Catholic Women's League who gave me two hundred dollars and a few more donated clothes. She's moving through the train making sure that all the Titanic survivors are being met by relatives at the other end. I hadn't even noticed there were any other Titanic survivors on the train. I have hardly looked up from my feet, I am so sad and so ashamed to be traveling like this.

Dear God almighty, how did it ever come to this? How did that bright spring morning when we left Ballysheen turn into this—a train journey with not a soul I know for company and with all those I traveled with, bar one, dead and lost forever in the sea?

I wish I had never left my home, wish I had never left Séamus. At this moment I wish I had never been rescued. I think it is easier for those who perished and will never have to face their future alone—like I do. I wish I was back under the cherry blossom tree watching the petals fall around me. I doubt I will ever know such happiness again as I knew in those months I spent with Séamus in Ballysheen. I think my heart is actually broken and may never be mended again.

CHAPTER 32

Ballysheen, Ireland
April 17, 1912

The day Séamus Doyle buried his father, nature unleashed an almighty storm across County Mayo and blew down all but two of the cherry blossom trees that lined the road through Ballysheen. It was an awful sight to behold, their thin trunks cracked and split by the force of the wind.

"Snapped like matchsticks," an old woman muttered as Séamus surveyed the scene of devastation. "And yet would ye look at those two, standing strong as iron, as if there was never a breath of wind at all."

He was relieved to see that the sixth blossom tree was one of the two still standing—he knew it because the initials *MM SD* for himself and Maggie were still there, scratched into the bark by his own whittling knife.

The howling wind and lashing rain fell across the parish relentlessly that day, echoing the despair and solemnity of the occasion. The priest stood at the graveside and tried to make sure his prayers for Séamus's father could be heard over the din of the weather. Later in his life, Séamus would speak about that raging storm, the worst in the history of the parish, and how he had felt his day couldn't possibly get any worse, until he'd received a telegram from the RMS *Titanic*.

The postmaster's wagon rumbled down the lane toward the small stone cottage. Séamus hadn't long returned from the graveside Mass and stood, absentmindedly, in the doorway, his cap in his hand and his shoes smeared with the freshly dug earth that the rain had quickly turned into rivers of flowing mud.

"Afternoon to ye," the postmaster shouted in an attempt to make himself heard over the howling wind as he pulled his dappled horse to a standstill on the rutted pathway. "By God it's a wild day to be sure. Never seen weather like it, I haven't, and I'm forty years living here." He jumped down from the wagon and stepped around the front. "You should be gettin' inside with a fire burnin', lad, never mind standing around in the doorway." Séamus didn't respond. "Anyway," the post-master continued, "here's a thing ye don't see every day—a message from the Marconi radio operator on the *Titanic*, no less!"

Séamus's attention was caught instantly. "From the *Titanic*? How?"

"The wonders of technology, eh? Sure, how would I know how it gets here from a ship in the middle of the ocean"—he laughed, rubbing away the drops of rain that had collected in his eyebrows—"but it has, and it's addressed to ye."

"To *me*?" Séamus reached out to take the small envelope, turning it over in his hand.

"That's what it says. Well, cheer up then. It's not every day a fella gets a message from the biggest ocean liner ever built!"

Séamus didn't reply, but stared blankly at the postmaster before walking inside the cottage and closing the door behind him.

"Well, there's manners for ye," the postmaster muttered to himself, climbing back into the sodden wagon and pulling sharply on the reins. His horse skittered to attention, shaking its mane, sending water flying into his face and a stream of curses gushing from his mouth.

With a clatter of hooves on the slippery stones, Séamus heard the postmaster ride off. Relieved to be on his own, he settled himself into the threadbare chair next to the empty fireplace, taking a second to survey his home. *His* home, as it was now; his walls, his possessions, sparse and tattered though they were. He was a nineteen-year-old man, and what he saw before him now was the sum total of his life so far. How he hoped that what he held in his hands would be a turning point, would be the answer he had been praying for every night since Maggie left.

Rubbing the edges of the thick cream card, he studied the various postal markings. He'd never seen a telegram before, let alone one from such a prestigious ship. He could only assume it was from Maggie, although how she had been able to send it he had no idea.

He thought again about the letters he had written to her. Was this her reply? Had she read them all, read his final question? His hands trembling with excitement at what she might say, he read the words:

```
                    W I R E L E S S
                                        Received

NO_____ CK_*_____              TIME RECEIVED_____


Marconi Wireless Telegraph Company of America
27 William Street (Lord's Court Building), New York
From Maggie Murphy Titanic to Séamus Doyle
Ballysheen Co Mayo Ireland


Dearest Séamus all is well Titanic is a fine ship I
hope your da is well Don't wait for me
```

Séamus sat motionless, reading the few words again and again. *Don't wait for me.* Had she given up on him, on their future? Had she read his letters? Was this a rejection of his proposal?

"No," he whispered. "No, Maggie. Not this. Please, not this."

Letting the piece of paper fall to his lap, he leaned his head back against the chair and gave in to the despair he'd suppressed since he watched the traps bearing Maggie and the others rumble off down the road. He gave in to the grief he'd denied himself since discovering his father's lifeless body in the bed after returning from his nighttime walk, his sleep having been disturbed by dreams of Maggie crying for help. An aching loneliness flooded his soul, a consuming emptiness he hadn't felt even when he watched his father's coffin being lowered into the ground.

As the wind continued to rampage across the landscape he so loved, tearing centuries-old trees from their roots and sending chimneys crashing down onto the roofs of the houses they had stood proudly upon for decades, Séamus sank to his knees and sobbed with despair, his cries exceeded only by the howling wind, his tears surpassed only by the heavy raindrops that streamed down the small windowpanes.

Sometime later, around dusk, he was roused by a knock at the door. Forgetting where he was momentarily, Séamus sat upright and looked around the room for his da, rubbing his swollen eyes. Then he remembered; his da was dead in the ground and his sweetheart had declined his offer of marriage.

He got up wearily and trudged to the door, barely able to face the prospect of speaking to anyone else that day.

"Who is it?" he sighed, rubbing his hands through his sandy hair, which had curled in the damp.

"Father Mullins" came the reply through the door.

"Right so, Father." Séamus smoothed his clothes, which were crumpled and misshapen, and opened the door. "Come inside, Father. Please excuse the mess—and myself," he added, looking self-consciously at the floor. "A drop of porter, Father?"

"No, Séamus, not for me, son."

The priest stepped inside, brushing the rain from his coat and hat, his cheeks flushed from the force of the wind, his eyes blazing with intensity, as they always did. He took a quick measure of his surroundings.

"You've no fire lit yet, Séamus—I hope you'll be seeing to that next. It won't do to be sitting about in this place all alone and cold, y'know." There was a stern, purposeful edge to his voice. It was a voice Séamus had been listening to at Sunday Mass for as long as he could remember, and he took notice when this man spoke. "Your da wouldn't like that at all now, would he?"

"No, Father, he wouldn't. He liked his warmth. Whatever little else we had, he would always see that there was turf burning in the grate. I'll see to it right away. I was just having a little nap, y'know, after the business of the burial an' all."

The priest nodded and stepped toward the small window. "He was a great man indeed. Hard worker—and very proud of his boys." He nodded at Séamus to impress this upon him before sitting down at the table in the center of the room. "I'm afraid I'm visiting many homes in the parish tonight, Séamus. I've received some rather unfortunate news."

Séamus noticed then, for the first time, the strain etched across Father Mullins's usually peaceful-looking face.

"Oh? What is it, Father?"

"I hate to bring this news to you tonight of all nights, with you having just buried your father, God rest his soul." The two men paused for a second then to cross themselves in respect to the dead man. "Inspector O'Brien was in contact with me earlier today," he continued. "He had himself been alerted by a Mr. Thomas Durcan in Castlebar. He's the local shipping agent for the White Star Line. I'm sorry to say, Séamus, that he reports *Titanic* has foundered in the Atlantic."

"Foundered! What d'ye mean, foundered?"

"It is understood that she struck an iceberg two days before she was due to arrive in New York, and according to the White Star Line office in Liverpool, she sank to the depths of the Atlantic Ocean."

Séamus couldn't believe what he was hearing.

"But it was such a big ship, Father—all the papers spoke of it being unsinkable and being made of triple screws, or something. I remember seein' it in the papers with my own eyes—the pictures an' all. It can't have *sunk*—surely to God it didn't sink."

"There are reports of around seven hundred survivors, mainly women and children, although we do not yet know whether those who left from this parish are among the fortunate ones." Father Mullins paused then, looking down at the floor, shuffling his feet as a pool of water gathered around them on the flagstones, the raindrops falling steadily from his overcoat. "It is a truly terrible business. A terrible business indeed. It was Peggy Madden's sister who suggested I come and speak to you. I understand you are friendly with Maggie Murphy, who was traveling with her aunt Kathleen Dolan."

"Yes, yes—I am. That's right." Séamus remembered then the telegram message that had been delivered to him just a few hours earlier. "But I just received a message from Maggie," he said, rushing over to the chair and picking up the telegram, showing it to the priest as if he wouldn't otherwise believe him. "Look. Here, see. It's from the RMS *Titanic*. It's franked and everything."

Father Mullins studied it for a moment before placing it carefully on the table and speaking in an almost whisper.

"Yes, Séamus, I see. A very unfortunate coincidence. You see it shows us here that the message was transmitted on the night of April fourteenth. That was the night, we believe, the incident occurred."

Unable to comprehend what he was being told, Séamus leaned against the table, pressing his palms hard to the cool, solid surface as if he were clinging to it for his life. He stayed like this for some time, his mind reeling, as Father Mullins relayed all the information he had himself been given. It was now a case of waiting for further confirmation and for news of any survivors. They were to prepare themselves for the worst, the priest warned before leading them both in prayer.

For seven days, Séamus and the other villagers of Ballysheen wandered around in a daze, unsure what to think or what to believe. Rumors skirted the town about reports in the local newspapers that all of the females had been saved. Others suggested that everyone had been lost. A farm laborer reported that he had seen Maggie Murphy's name among a list of survivors printed in the *Western People* that was being passed around at the market. It was impossible for Séamus to allow himself to believe anything until he heard from Maggie or saw her dead body.

There was a strange numbness about the village; people wouldn't look one another in the eye, afraid to suggest either hope or despair, not knowing which emotion to express from among the many they were feeling.

It was Thomas Durcan, the White Star Line agent, who finally arrived with the tragic news. Families watched anxiously, hidden in the dark interiors of their homes, as he walked with Father Mullins, knocking firmly on door after door to convey the news of what had become of their loved ones.

The two men walked, ashen faced, from home to home, the wailing and crying from within telling anyone passing what the fate of their family members was. Mothers were inconsolable, fathers wept for their lost sons and daughters. The grief and suffering were unbearable to behold.

Everywhere he went, Séamus overheard hushed conversations, secret, almost forbidden exchanges between neighbors about how individuals had reacted to the news.

"Poor Ellen Joyce's father was sellin' a cow at market when

he got the news. Trying to get back the money he'd paid for her passage, so he was," one woman whispered to another.

"Young Michael Kelly's grandmother can't sleep for nightmares, thinking that the sharks have his poor, dead body," another said.

It chilled Séamus's heart, and through it all he recalled his dream from the night his da died and reflected on Maggie's telegram.

Some families were left hoping, with names so similar to their loved ones' showing on the lists of survivors, only to be devastated when it was established that there had been confusion and, in fact, their relatives had been lost. So far it was known, or assumed, that all of the fourteen travelers had been lost except Peggy Madden, who had survived by clinging to a capsized lifeboat.

Séamus was at the lake throwing stones into the water when he felt Father Mullins's hand on his shoulder. He'd been dreading the moment the man would speak with him, and he squeezed his eyes shut tight, hoping to block out the reality of the news he was about to receive. He barely heard the priest when he spoke, the words seeming to flutter and drift around him like damselflies.

"She lives, Séamus," was all the man said. "Maggie survived. She is recovering in a New York hospital." He tightened his grip on Séamus's shoulder and then turned and walked away to allow Séamus to process this news in private.

He only nodded and let the tears fall as he continued to sit in silence. The girl he loved with all his heart was alive, had survived the most terrible tragedy. He wished he could feel joy, elation, but those elusive emotions were stifled by the overbearing knowledge that she did not want him to be in her life anymore. *Don't wait for me,* she'd said. *Don't wait for me.*

He sat watching the clouds gathering on the horizon, watched as each solitary one drifted lazily across the sun, casting everything into shade before moving off to let the warmth and brilliant light of the sun settle on him momentarily again. As the rhythms of nature moved constantly between light and shadow, so, it seemed, did the young man's heart.

The next few weeks were taken up with grieving and comforting those who had lost their loved ones. Séamus tried his best to help where he could, feeling a terrible guilt at receiving the news he had prayed for every night, while others had had their worst fears confirmed. With only a few hundred bodies of the fifteen hundred lost souls recovered, there were no funerals to be held, so it was without the bodies of their loved ones that the grieving families held their wakes.

For two days and two nights, wakes took place across the parish for those who were lost. Séamus visited each home, removing his cap to approach the bed where the poor soul had slept just a few weeks ago, a photograph placed carefully on the crisp white pillow while dozens of candles cast their soft light around the room. In home after home he visited, the same scene of unimaginable grief was played out, and he looked at the black-and-white faces staring at him from the photographs, unable to believe that these people, people he knew, were lost forever.

"It's the not knowing where she is that's so hard to accept," Maria Cusack's mother told him as she gripped his hands so tightly he thought she would never let go. "Not knowing where her body lies and what with her being so afeared of the dark and it will be so dark down there, won't it. I just cannot bear it, truly I cannot."

The rain fell steadily over the parish for those few weeks, as if the very sky was mourning along with those whose hearts lay broken in their chests in the simple homes below.

The last of the blossoms had fallen from the two remaining trees by the time the newspapers stopped reporting the news of *Titanic* and the findings of the inquiries and the aftermath.

Séamus took some small comfort by visiting the sixth cherry blossom tree every Wednesday. He would sit awhile under the dappled shade and remember. He wondered often how different things might have been if he had traveled with Maggie as she had so wanted him to. If his da had died a few weeks earlier, what then? Perhaps he *would* have gone with Maggie. Perhaps he would have drowned in the Atlantic Ocean too, and then what good would have come of it all?

When he felt stronger in his mind, he gave up remembering and sat under the cherry blossom tree planning. He would write to Maggie one last time. He would somehow find the address of the aunt she was traveling to stay with and he would write to tell her how his heart had sunk with despair to learn that she did not wish him to wait for her but had nevertheless leaped with joy when he heard she had survived the disaster. He would tell her he was so glad that she would be able to live her life, that he knew how much she would make of this chance God had given her and that he hoped hers would be a very happy and long life. He would tell her that with all his heart, he wished her the best life possible, even if he could not be the one to share it with her.

As the spring months gave way to summer and then the first leaves of autumn started to fall from the trees by the lakeside, Séamus resolved to sell his da's house and their small plot of land and travel to England with the money to work in the cotton mills. At least there he would have no reminders of the love he had known and lost. At least there he might stand a chance of putting Maggie Murphy and the horrors of *Titanic* from his mind. Fate had decided his path in life, and he now had to walk that path, wherever it might lead him.

WHITE STAR LINE

ROYAL AND UNITED STATES MAIL STEAMERS.

Mole Berth
Female Berth
Married Berth

ISMAY, IMRIE & CO.

WHITE STAR LINE

GENOA
NAPLES
BOSTON
NEW YORK
QUEBEC
MONTREAL

JAMES SCOTT & CO. Agents
QUEENSTOWN.

Agent at PARIS—
NICHOLAS MARTIN, 9, Rue Scribe.

OCEANIC STEAM NAVIGATION COMPANY, LIMITED, OF GREAT BRITAIN.

THIRD CLASS (Steerage) PASSENGER'S CONTRACT TICKET.
(NOT TRANSFERABLE.)

CHAPTER 33

New York,
April 19, 1912

Dearest Mammy,

It is with the deepest, deepest sadness that I write these words. I do not know if news of the awful event will have reached you yet in Ballysheen, but there was a terrible tragedy, Mammy, and the mighty Titanic is sunk in the Atlantic and there has been the greatest loss of life ever imaginable.

I have been at the White Star Line offices in New York waiting for news of our beloved Katie. The steamship Carpathia, which rescued the survivors, arrived in New York yesterday evening. I waited there for hours and hours until every last person was down the gangplank and the doors were closed again.

Katie did not come to me, Mammy.

She did not walk toward me and fall into my arms in the pouring rain. I did not scream her name in delight and relief as so many others did when they saw their loved ones emerge from that black night.

I have been to all the hospitals and anywhere I am told that victims have been taken—still I cannot find her, Mammy, and I sit here with the heaviest, heaviest heart as I find that it has fallen to me, your eldest child, to tell you the terrible news that little Katie did not survive the disaster—she did not manage to escape on one of the lifeboats that left Titanic.

With fifteen hundred others, Katie was lost to the ocean.

I think I have cried enough tears now to fill the depths of that ocean over and over and over again, because I cannot believe she is gone—cannot believe she didn't walk off that mighty ship to the sound of ragtime bands and the sight of ticker tape and flags and the joy of seeing my face in the waiting crowds.

I wish I could be there to comfort you all, Mammy, dearly I do. I will be making arrangements to travel home on the first ship I can secure passage on, but for now I am so sorry that these words are all I can send.

I have enclosed a pair of gloves that I had bought for Katie as a birthday and welcome gift. They were bought in Macy's department store—I think she would have loved them dearly and wish you to have them now to lay on her bed as you grieve for her.

I know there will be much mourning in Ballysheen, Mammy, with so many of our loved ones lost. I cannot imagine the sadness there must be there. The whole city of New York seems to be in mourning—nobody can believe such a thing could happen.

Please forgive me for writing this terrible news, and may God bless us and comfort us all at this terrible time.

Your loving, devoted daughter,
Frances

New York
April 24, 1912

My dearest Edgar,

Apologies for my recent lack of communication—as you will be aware from the many press interviews I have been giving recently, I was one of the many unfortunate victims of the Titanic disaster. Really, Edgar, it was the most frightful business altogether—the stuff of nightmares. Mother is overcome with grief at the tragic loss of darling Robert and the ruination of all the wedding plans. I am wracked with guilt about leaving him on the deck of the ship, but what was I to do with the officers insisting that the women and children fill the boats first—I had to go without him, he was quite insistent, and those poorly educated steerage people caused such an unnecessary panic and stampede it was almost impossible to hear oneself think, never mind pay any heed to one's own survival, let alone anyone else's.

So I found myself in the lifeboat with little Edmund, being lowered into the Atlantic before I really had much time to think about it.

Thank goodness for the first-class stewards encouraging us to dress warmly or I think I may have frozen to death in the lifeboat waiting for rescue. I actually gave one of my topcoats to a wretch of a girl who sat shivering in a thin cotton night-dress and light cotton coat that was drenched to the knee with seawater. I can only assume she was from steerage class—she was lucky, I don't think many of them survived. I suspect I will never see the coat again and I suspect it will be the nicest coat that she will ever own—it was from an exquisite little boutique in Rome. I quite liked it, but I suppose it was put to good use.

Well, Edgar, now that Robert is buried and I have had chance to grieve and rest and recover my spirits a little, I have considered your proposal to play a part in the studio's movie about the Titanic disaster. I agree that it would make for great drama, and I would, of course, be delighted to take a role, showing from firsthand knowledge what really happened that night. Perhaps Mr. Francis might make a suitable Captain Smith and Mr. Adolfi a crewman. With all the inquests and inquiries and haranguing of poor Mr. Ismay, I am sure such a movie would be welcomed by the *White Star Line* and might serve to put some of the more unpleasant rumors about the incident to rest.

In any event, I have arranged for the white silk evening gown I wore that night to be freshly laundered, as I thought it might be a nice touch to wear the very same gown in the reenactment—we could perhaps print the information about the gown on the studio posters.

I look forward to a prompt reply, and perhaps we could make arrangements to talk further over lunch. I am in desperate need of some stimulating conversation, and I think you may be the only person in this entire city who is capable of providing it!

Yours affectionately,
Vivienne Walker-Brown

WHITE STAR LINE
ROYAL AND UNITED STATES MAIL STEAMERS.

ISMAY, IMRIE & CO.,

WHITE STAR LINE

JAMES SCOTT & CO. Agents
QUEENSTOWN

Agent at PARIS
NICHOLAS MARTIN, 9, Rue Scribe.

OCEANIC STEAM NAVIGATION COMPANY, LIMITED, OF GREAT BRITAIN.
THIRD CLASS (Steerage) PASSENGER'S CONTRACT TICKET.
(NOT TRANSFERABLE.)

CHAPTER 34

Chicago
May 30, 1982

"Y ou must be Mr. Lockey," Grace said nervously, extending her hand. She wasn't used to making arrangements to meet total strangers in coffee shops, but there was something about the man's face that reassured her.

He was taller than she'd imagined, and his soft white hair had been left a little longer than that of most men of his age she had met. It made him look a little hippieish. While he was obviously in his sixties or possibly seventies, his face was youthful and there was a wonderful sparkle in his eyes. He was smartly dressed in a collared shirt and navy blazer, and a fresh scent of cologne added to the sense of good grooming. She immediately relaxed.

"Yes, indeed. And you must be the famous Grace Butler," he replied, shaking her hand warmly and smiling broadly. "I'm delighted to meet you—I so admired your article."

Grace felt herself blush a little, and she giggled as she spoke. "Well, hardly 'the famous Grace Butler,' but yeah, that's me."

They stood a little awkwardly for a few seconds, Grace twirling her long hair around her fingers as she was prone to when she wasn't quite sure what to do next, before Mr. Lockey gestured for them both to sit down at the table he had taken toward the back of the shop. It was a good choice, relatively quiet so they could have a conversation without the constant interruption of coffee orders shouted over their heads.

"So," he began, after ordering them each a coffee. "How very strange is this?"

"Um, very," Grace replied, laughing and reaching into her bag for her notepad and pen. "I wasn't even sure you'd turn up. My mom was convinced you would be one of those weirdos who lure young women away from home. She's sitting outside in the car, you know, waiting for me. How embarrassing!"

He chuckled. "Well, hopefully you're convinced I'm not a weirdo—I've been accused of worse over the years! Aha," he added, motioning toward her writing materials. "I see your journalistic instincts follow you everywhere."

"Oh, these? Yeah! Force of habit, I'm afraid. Don't worry, I'm not planning to record our conversation. I just like to have a pen and paper handy to jot things down."

There was another silence then, each wondering how to broach the subject of the letters. Grace didn't want to appear rude and demand to see them right away, but she felt as though she would burst if he didn't say something soon. Sensing her impatience, Mr. Lockey lifted a brown paper bag onto the table.

"Well, here they are," he said. "The coat and the packet of letters. Go ahead, take a look. I hope they're what you're looking for."

Grace carefully lifted the bag from the table, surprised at how much her hands were shaking, and placed it on her lap. She peered inside for a moment before lifting out a threadbare black overcoat and a relatively small packet of brown paper tied with a fraying piece of string. They were just as Maggie had described them to her. She could hardly believe what she was seeing.

"Oh, wow," she whispered, turning the fragile packet over and over in her hands and brushing the smooth cotton of the coat with her fingertips.

Mr. Lockey gave her a few moments to look over the items, smiling at her delight. "Is it them?" he ventured after a while.

"I really think it is, yes. They're just as my great-grandmother described them to me. It's amazing. They're so old. I can't believe they've survived all this time."

"Well, my uncle was a bit of a hoarder by all accounts. There's also this," he continued, passing Grace an envelope. "It's a letter he wrote to go with the items. It explains how he came to have them and what he wanted done with them."

Grace took the envelope from him.

"Go on, open it. I hope you don't mind, but I've read it—I had to, you see, to check whether there were any specific instructions. It's fascinating stuff."

Grace slipped the piece of paper out of the envelope and unfolded it. Delighted by the wonderfully old-fashioned script, she started to read.

April 28, 1912

This coat and packet of letters belong to a Miss Maggie Murphy. She is a seventeen-year-old girl who traveled with her aunt and several others from a town in Ireland. They boarded Titanic at Queenstown in County Cork, and I was their dining saloon steward. I got to know the girl Maggie, and some of the others she was traveling with, and had arranged for a Marconigram message to be sent from the ship, from Maggie, to her sweetheart back in Ireland.

When Titanic sank on the night of April 15 after hitting an iceberg, Maggie was rescued in lifeboat 16, which I was commanded to man by one of the ship's officers. We were rescued by the steamship Carpathia at dawn the following morning after eight hours drifting in the freezing cold. Maggie was suffering terribly and was lifted out of the lifeboat onto Carpathia barely conscious. I tried to find her on the Carpathia as we sailed on to New York, but nobody knew of a young girl called Maggie from Ireland, and her name was not on the survivor list. Everything was so chaotic on that boat it is a wonder anyone found anybody they were looking for.

I remembered that Maggie had been given the lend of a coat by one of the other passengers in the lifeboat; a Yank singer, Vivienne Walker-Brown, as Maggie had given her own coat to a young child. When the Carpathia arrived in New York, we first docked at the White Star Line pier to unload the lifeboats from Titanic, which had been hauled aboard the rescue ship, and I was asked to give the crewmen a hand. I know I probably shouldn't have, but I also planned to take the S.S. Titanic sign from the lifeboat I'd manned. I wanted to give it my father because he'd been too ill to see Titanic in Southampton docks. The lifeboats were all there was left—all he would ever see of her. As I was removing the sign, I saw a black coat in the bottom of the boat and grabbed it. Recognizing the name Maggie on the front of a packet that I found in the coat pocket, along with a set of rosary beads, I realized the coat must belong to the Irish girl.

In an attempt to get the coat and packet of letters back to her, I visited some of the hospitals in New York that I knew had taken in survivors. Being in reasonably good health myself, I was not admitted to hospital and was taken in by the Salvation Army until my employer, the White Star Line, could find accommodation for me in the city.

I was told at the St. Vincent's Hospital that a Maggie Murphy and a Peggy Madden (who I was so happy to hear had also survived) had been admitted, but had been discharged earlier that day. I had no idea where Maggie was traveling on to, although I did know that Peggy, whom I had become quite friendly with on the ship, was traveling on to St. Louis. I have a mind to try and track her down when we have all had a chance to recover from our ordeal.

Unable to find Maggie, I have kept her coat, which bears a set of rosary beads in one pocket and the packet of letters and some browned cherry blossom petals in the other. I assume the letters are very important to her, so I will keep them until such time as I might be able to find her.

I don't want to write about Titanic or what happened that night. I just want the haunting sounds and images to leave my mind, and I swear that I will never set foot on a ship again for as long as I live.

If, in time, this letter and the coat and letters belonging to Maggie are returned to her, please pass on my regards. She was a very brave young lady and I will never know how she must have felt stepping into that lifeboat, leaving those she was traveling with standing on the deck of the ship, which we then watched sink to the bottom of the ocean.

Whatever happens, I hope she goes on to live a very happy life and that she manages to return to her sweetheart in Ireland. From what little she told me about him, I think she must have loved him very, very much and I think he must have loved her equally.

I thank God that we are safe, and it would make me very happy indeed to see the letters reunited with their rightful owner.

Written by Harry Walsh (of sound mind),
New York
America

Grace folded the page up and placed it carefully on the table. For a while she couldn't speak.

"Incredible, isn't it," Mr. Lockey said. "You must keep the letter and give it to your great-grandmother. I hope she will be happy to know how Harry came to have her letters."

"What was he like, your uncle?" Grace asked, interested to hear more about this young man who had risked so much to save lives and whose integrity was such that, throughout his life, he had kept Maggie's possessions in the hope that he would one day find her.

"Ah, Uncle Harry!" Mr. Lockey chuckled. "*Lucky* Uncle Harry—the man with a permanent twinkle in his eye, a plan up his sleeve, and a spring in his step. He was like a second father to me, so I was extremely fond of him—where oh where do I start?"

For the next two hours Grace absorbed every detail of Harry's life—how he had been so traumatized by the events of that night and by the loss of so many of his colleagues from Southampton that he refused to ever set foot on a boat again and found employment with the Cunard line in the offices ("the safest place to work for a steamship company," he'd said), unable to bear the sight of the White Star Line swallowtail flag.

She heard how his mother was frantic, waiting for news of his fate, and how she and his sister had waited at the docks in Southampton, along with hundreds of other weeping mothers and wives, refusing to leave until they knew what had become of him. She listened as Mr. Lockey told her how Harry's parents and sister, Sally (Mr. Lockey's mother), had eventually traveled to New York to start a new life with him, how his father's health had improved and allowed him to work again at the docks, and how his mother had become a very influential figure at the Salvation Army, helping those less fortunate than herself.

She listened with amazement at how Harry had spent years trying to track down the girl, Peggy Madden, whom he was sweet on, only to eventually find her in St. Louis, married with two children. Apparently she had laughed when she saw him standing in the driveway and swore that if she didn't love her husband so much she would have run off with him there and then because he was the most persistent man she had ever met!

Sadly, she had lost contact with Maggie by the time Harry found her—something to do with several moves and lost address books—but she and Harry became firm friends, keeping in contact until he was an old man. Harry had never married, saying that he never met a woman his mother approved of and that he would rather be happy and alone than be with anyone other than the Irish girl who filled his dreams every night.

Grace found herself wiping away the tears by the time Mr. Lockey had finished telling her about his wonderful uncle.

"It's such a shame," she said. "If only he'd got to the hospital earlier he might have been able to form a relationship with Peggy or hand the coat and letters back to Maggie himself."

"Ah yes, but then we could also say 'If only *Titanic* hadn't sunk. If only that iceberg hadn't been on a direct collision course with the ship. If only the lookouts in the crow's nest had had a pair of binoculars.' Harry was a great believer in getting on with the hand life dealt you. He never once felt sorry for himself. He often said that someone had given him a second chance in life, and that while he sat in that lifeboat waiting for the rescue ship, he promised God, and himself, that he would make the most of that second chance. He believed he was the luckiest man alive after escaping from *Titanic*."

They fell silent for a moment then, each reflecting on everything they had shared and on the connection between them.

"Well, I guess I've taken up enough of your time, Mr. Lockey—I'd better head back to the car and free my mom! Thank you so, so much—for everything. You've no idea what this will mean to Maggie," Grace said, gathering her belongings. "So many strange things have happened since she told me about being on *Titanic*. It would almost make you think that the ship doesn't want to be forgotten—wherever it is."

Mr. Lockey scribbled down his phone number and address before they parted with a brief embrace. Grace thought for a moment about her father and how she missed the feeling of comfort and protection his hugs had given her.

As she walked back to her mom's car, she clutched the coat and packet of letters tight to her chest and wondered how Maggie would feel when she saw them again after all these years.

Cass County, Illinois
May 31, 1982

I met someone yesterday, Maggie," Grace ventured as she made tea in her great-grandmother's small kitchen. She waited for a response. There was none. Maggie was flicking through the TV channels. "Well," Grace continued, placing the teapot, cups, and a packet of cookies on a tray and carrying them into the small sitting room. "Don't you want to know who?"

"Of course I want to know who," Maggie replied, shifting herself to a more upright position in her chair, "but only after you've found a nice plate for those biscuits and set them out properly. Did I teach you nothing, girl?" She sighed, waving her hand dismissively across the poorly presented tea tray.

Grace laughed and went back to the kitchen. "What is it about you and cookies anyway, Maggie? We're never going to eat a whole plateful, are we?"

"That's not the point," the old woman chided. "If something's worth doing, then it's worth doing properly, even if it is only offering a biscuit with a cup of tea."

Grace did the necessary arranging on one of Maggie's "fancy plates," as she called them, and sat down opposite her.

"And," Maggie continued, "I saw them do it on *Titanic* and I promised myself that when I got to America, I would always serve my biscuits as nicely. So who did you see?"

Grace was almost afraid to tell Maggie about the letters, unsure of stirring up memories that her great-grandmother had clearly spent a lifetime trying to forget. She poured the tea.

"Well, I met a very, very nice gentleman named Edward Lockey."

"Do I know him?"

"Well, no. Not exactly. But he knows someone who *did* know you." Grace paused and looked into Maggie's eyes. She could tell her great-grandmother was interested. "He read my article in the newspaper and contacted me because he recognized the name Maggie Murphy."

"Oh? How? No one has called me Maggie Murphy for years and years."

"Well, you're not going to believe this, but his uncle was on *Titanic* too." At this Maggie raised her eyes again, her interest piqued. "His uncle was a third-class dining saloon steward," Grace continued. "His name was Harry Walsh."

CHAPTER 35

aggie's hands flew to her cheeks as she let out a tiny gasp. She sat forward in her chair.

"*The* Harry? Harry Walsh? Are you sure?"

"Yes! I know—it's unbelievable, isn't it? That Mr. Lockey happened to read the article about you and that he also had a relative on *Titanic* who, it turns out, you knew—out of all those thousands of people."

Maggie was lost in thought. "He saved my life, you know, Grace. I would never have got off that ship if it wasn't for him. He took us to the ladder, you see, and . . ."

Grace leaned forward and placed her hands on Maggie's. "I know, Maggie. I know." She wanted to try to calm her great-grandmother before she revealed the next bombshell. "But that's not all."

Maggie looked at her, wide-eyed. "What? What else?"

"Well, sadly, Harry isn't alive anymore."

She paused then, giving her great-grandmother a moment to register this fact.

"Really? Oh, that's sad. That's very sad. He was such a nice young man. I so hope he had a happy life."

"He did, Maggie. A very happy life. He lived to the grand old age of ninety—and he left something very important to his nephew in his will. That is why Mr. Lockey contacted me, because he wanted to return it to its rightful owner." She paused and reached for the coat and packet of letters in the bag beside her. "He wanted you to have these."

She handed over the items to Maggie, who recognized them instantly, her eyes widening in surprise.

"But this . . . this is my coat, and these . . ." She turned the packet over and over in her hands, lightly touching the brown paper and the fraying piece of string. "No," she whispered. "No. It can't be. That's impossible."

Grace explained as briefly as she could about Edward Lockey and how Harry came to have the letters. "They were in your coat pocket, Maggie. Harry found your coat when *Titanic*'s lifeboats were being lowered onto the White Star dock from the *Carpathia* when it reached New York. He was helping the crewmen and had gone back to your lifeboat to remove the S.S. *Titanic* sign to give to his father. He noticed the black coat in the bottom of the boat, found the packet of letters with the name Maggie on the front, and realized it must belong to you. He'd tried to find you on the *Carpathia*, but you hadn't given your name to any of the officials. He even looked for you in the hospitals in New York. He kept hold of the coat and letters all those years in the hope that he would someday find you. And now he has."

Grace wasn't sure whether Maggie had heard a word she'd said. She sat quietly, turning the packet of letters over and over in her hands and rubbing her fingers along the handwritten *Maggie* on the front.

"Shall I leave you to read them?" she asked, sensing that her great-grandmother would like some privacy.

"Yes," Maggie whispered, her voice barely audible above the sound of the breeze whipping around the trees in the garden outside. "Yes, please. I think I'd like to read them alone."

"Well, if you're sure you're not going to get too upset? Are you sure you don't want me to stay?"

Maggie smiled "I'll be fine. It will be nice to see the familiar handwriting again, and finally I'll see what was written all those years ago. Now go. I'll be perfectly fine."

Reluctantly Grace gathered her bag to leave. "Well, okay then, if you're sure. I'll stop by tomorrow morning. I haven't forgotten what day it is. Shall we visit the cemetery first and then go for afternoon tea?"

"Yes, dear. That would be lovely. I'll see you at ten as usual."

With that Grace kissed Maggie on the cheek and let herself out.

It wasn't until Maggie heard the car pulling out of the driveway that she untied the string and took the letters from the packet. The paper was yellowing and stained in places with what she assumed to be seawater, but overall the letters were in excellent condition considering what they had been through and how long ago they were written. Harry must have taken extremely good care of them, she thought, smiling at the memory of the handsome young steward and his strange southern English accent.

She read first through the letter from Harry that explained how he'd found the coat and letters. She felt as though she were back on the ship, back in that lifeboat.

Steeling herself for what she was about to read, she opened the first four letters, the ones she had read while sitting in her bunk bed in cabin 115 on *Titanic*. She had thought it the grandest cabin imaginable at the time. Seeing the letters again, she could almost feel the vibrations from the massive engines that gently rocked her to sleep each night. She studied the letters carefully, relishing the sight of Séamus's simple handwriting. Smiling at the memories his words evoked, she then started to read the letters she hadn't previously looked at. Her heart leaped and soared at the words they contained, just as it had that first night she had danced with Séamus at the Brennans' wedding. She read about the happy, carefree times they had spent together that summer until she reached the letters referring to the autumn, when her mother had fallen ill and Aunt Kathleen had arrived from America.

October 1911

It's autumn now, Maggie. I can hardly believe I've been lucky enough to spend the whole spring and summer with you. Sometimes I think I will wake up from a long dream! We've all been busy with the potato harvest these last few weeks, and with your mam falling sick we haven't had much time to see each other—but I've your face in my head all the time— I'm happy even to see a peek of those curls under your hat from across the market. I sometimes think I'd like to cut one from your hair and keep it for myself—that way I'll always remember how your hair shone in the autumn sun—but I think you look loveliest when they fall about your face, so I wouldn't want to take one from you. Some of the lads in the village tease me about you and ask me about being with a girl. I just tell them to get away out o' that and mind their own. I wish everyone could know how it feels to be with you, then they would know why I walk around like a drunken eejit all the time!

November 1911

Things are different now, Maggie, with your dear mammy dead and your aunt Kathleen arrived from America to take care of you. I know you take comfort from her being here, but I can't help but be worryin' that she'll want to be taking you back to America with her, come the spring. What with all her fancy notions of life there and all her talk of there being nothing to keep a young woman in Ireland, I'm afraid she'll take you away from me, Maggie. I'm sure Kathleen will be fillin' that pretty head of yours with tales of skyscrapers and fancy hats and shoes. She'll have you sailing away from me on a steamship before the new year is out, I just know it. I hope I'm wrong, Maggie. I don't know what would become of me if you left.

December 1911

Do you remember the snow, Maggie? The drifts against the fences and walls are as big as some of the houses. I haven't seen you for days and days what with the roads and tracks being blocked up. I've never seen snow like it in my life, and neither has Da. He says when it snows like this it means there'll be a change coming in the new year. I asked him what sort of a change. He just said "a change." I'm worried for his health. The cold air makes him cough something awful day and night. He coughs so hard sometimes I think his lungs will burst out of him altogether. I am miserable sitting in the cold cottage, listening to Da's retching and not seeing you. I can't imagine what life would be without you now, Maggie. You make me so happy I sometimes feel like the biggest fool the way I fuss and moon over you so. I hope I didn't embarrass you when I told you that I loved you. Because I do, you see. Very, very much, and I feel better for letting you know it.

Maggie's heart raced as she absorbed the words, remembering everything Séamus had written, everything he described of the times they had spent together in Ballysheen. She remembered it as clearly as if it were yesterday, not seventy years ago. She could almost sense him in the room now, could almost feel his weathered laborer's hands brushing against hers, could almost feel his breath on her neck. She shivered and continued reading.

January 1912

    You told me that you are leaving and my heart feels like it will break and I wish I could change your aunt Kathleen's mind on the matter. I know she doesn't mind me being around the house sometimes—I'm pleased to be of some use to her by fixing things or bringing supplies from the market when she can't travel herself. I like to try to impress her, you see, Maggie. I want her to know that I'm a good, reliable man who will always love you and protect you—that she doesn't have to take you away from me. Da's coughing is worse and worse with the hard winter we're having. The doctor says it's something called emfazeemer (I'm not sure if that's the right spelling at all) and that I should be praying for an early spring. The warmer weather will help him, he says. There's not much else that can be done for him now.

Maggie continued, reading on through the letters for February and March, barely able to make out the words through her tears.

Thinking she had read them all, she began to carefully fold

the letters to place them back into the packet. As she did, she noticed one more piece of paper. It was folded smaller than the others. Opening it out, she began to read.

April 1912

Maggie, you are leaving. My worst fears are come true and you are going off to America with all the others. I know you wish I could come with you, and I hope you know how quickly I'd jump on board that ship with you if I could, but Da is too sick to travel and too sick for me to leave him here. There's been some amount of crying in Ballysheen—sometimes it feels to me that ye have all died, what with the American wakes they are holding and all the drinking and praying and passing around of the holy water. It frightens me, Maggie, so it does—I'm not ashamed to tell ye. I sat by Da's bedside all day and night today—afraid to do anything else in case I saw you and hid you in our cottage until they've all gone off in the traps. I thought a terrible thing while I sat there. I wished my own da dead, so that I might come with you, Maggie. Isn't that the worst thing you ever did hear—a son wishing his own da dead so he can be free of the burden of looking after him and sail off with his sweetheart? I said twenty Hail Marys after thinking such a dark thought and am sure I could feel Ma frowning at me from up above, God rest her.

April 10, 1912

Today you leave. I don't know what to write anymore. I think I have used up all the words I will write in my lifetime and you have them all here to keep with you as you sail across the ocean to the New World. I'll never forget your beautiful face, Maggie, your eyes sparkling at me that night we danced at the Brennans' wedding, or the way your hair blows about your face in the wind. I will always wait for you under the cherry blossom tree on a Wednesday, and I'll keep doing that until you come back. I'll wait for you, Maggie—and I want you to come back home soon. I need you to come back to me, because I want to be with you all my life. I want to make a good husband for you, Maggie. I want you to be my wife. Will you marry me, Maggie Murphy? Please say yes.

Yours, always,
Séamus Doyle

Maggie folded the letters and placed them carefully in the packet. She rested her head against the back of the chair and let her eyes wander to the dark wood sideboard in the far corner of the room. She scanned the images in the picture frames: a lifetime of marriages, friendships, and births cataloged in the pictures displayed in the mismatched assortment of frames. She closed her eyes.

"Oh, Séamus," she whispered as the tears fell slowly down

her pale cheeks. "My darling Séamus, I miss you. I miss you so, so much."

She wasn't sure how long she'd slept or what had woken her. She'd dreamed that she was drowning and calling for Séamus to save her. He'd come running and dragged her to the shore. "I will always protect you, Maggie," he'd said. She'd reached out her hand to touch his face, and as she sat in the semidarkness of her sitting room now, she wasn't sure whether the hand that had touched hers was part of her dream or reality.

She heard a couple walking past outside laughing, a breeze rattling through the open upstairs window, the clock on the mantelpiece ticking its predictable, unchanging rhythm. She stood up slowly, grabbing the cane she used to steady herself, and walked through the house, turning on a few lights here and there until she reached her bedroom.

She knew what she was looking for.

Bending down slowly, she poked about under the bed with her cane, feeling for the small black suitcase. She wanted to look through her belongings. After a lifetime of forgetting, she now wanted to remember; wanted to remember everything, every last detail. She wanted to celebrate the lives of those she had loved and known so many years ago. She wanted absolution from the years of guilt and doubt she had harbored, from the crushing sense of remorse that she had survived amid so much death and destruction. She wanted to remember and then she wanted the whispers and echoes of that night to fall silently away so she could finally be at peace.

As she sat on the edge of her bed, lifting each precious memento from the small case, she knew what she had to do. Sharing her story with Grace, talking about *Titanic* and all those she'd loved and left in Ballysheen, reading the letters from Séamus—it all helped to heal a little of the pain of that terrible night. But Maggie knew that there was only one way she was ever going to be finally free from the burden of that ship. She had to go back to where it had all begun, back to Ireland, back to Ballysheen.

The following day was the tenth anniversary of Grace's great-grandfather James's death. She'd promised to take Maggie to the cemetery to place some fresh flowers in remembrance before they went for their usual Saturday morning cup of tea.

Grace knew that Maggie liked the cemetery because of the cherry blossom trees that stood just outside the boundary wall and cast a lovely pink hue over everything on a day like today.

It was a bright spring morning, and Maggie enjoyed the light breeze on her face as they walked through the cemetery gates. She noticed the single cloud in the blue sky and sensed the stillness about the place. It reminded her of the day she'd left Ireland. A distant memory flashed through her mind as she walked silently beside her great-granddaughter.

A young girl, dressed smartly in her best calico pinafore, staring out of the small cottage doorway, past the cherry blossom trees and across the vast expanse of fields and stone walls that divided up the land, the mighty mountain of Nephin Mór cast into shadow by a passing cloud, as if doffing its cap to the departing travelers. Her aunt's voice: "It is time." Stones crunching underfoot as she walked from home to home—her cousin Pat's white stone cottage first. Knocking on the door. "It's time," she called. The same at the Joyces' home, where she'd imagined Ellen's emotions torn between a deep worry for the sick mother she was leaving and excitement about seeing again her handsome fiancé, who would be awaiting her arrival in New York. More knocking on doors, stones crunching ominously under her black boots. Walking back toward her own home, her head bowed, her eyes fixed on her feet, her ears listening intently to the crunch, crunch, crunch of the stones. The thump in her heart as she saw him standing under the cherry blossom tree; come to say good-bye.

"Are you okay, Maggie? You seem very quiet today."

Grace's voice pulled Maggie from her thoughts.

"Oh, yes, dear. I'm perfectly fine. Just enjoying the peace and quiet. It's so beautiful here, isn't it? So still and calm. It reminds me of the morning I left home."

She looped her arm through Grace's and they strolled together again, her thoughts returning to her seventeen-year-old self.

There was something different about Ballysheen that spring morning, an eerie stillness after the flurry of activity and organization of the past weeks. Only the familiar crowing of the cockerel joined the sounds of tearful farewells and final exchanges as the travelers got into the traps that were gathered. She stood in silence, casting a final glance over the still snowcapped tops of the mountains in the far distance, the newborn lambs barely visible to the naked eye, the small white cottages and occasional farm buildings dotted about the landscape like dolls' houses scattered by a child. She had fond memories of running among those fields and mountains, temporarily free from the constraints of her domestic duties, at one with the landscape she so loved.

She watched Pat's weeping mammy lean up into the trap to pass him a sovereign as a good-luck token. One of the horses startled at a dog running around its feet, causing the trap to jolt slightly at the moment Pat reached to take the sovereign from her hands. She gasped as she watched the coin fall to the ground. This was a sign of bad luck, but the mammy picked it off the ground, rubbed it on her coat, and passed it to him again. Nobody spoke of it.

A strange silence surrounded them during the journey over the rugged terrain of the Windy Gap—the cart bumping and jostling her around in her seat, each turn of the wheels taking her farther away from home, from the man she loved, until they reached the train station. Still, they remained silent, standing on the chilly station platform, huddled beside piles of suitcases and trunks, as others around them exchanged tearful farewells. She felt a sense of foreboding and finality. It frightened her.

Hearts raced, hands shook, and adrenaline caused bodies to shiver as the gleaming green livery of the Midland Great Western Line train came into view, accompanied by the unmistakable screech of metal on metal and the muffled puff, puff of smoke rising from the funnel. How she'd gaped at the massive engine in front of her, the like of which she'd never seen before. How she'd stared up at the black funnel towering above the platform as the steady hiss of steam and the shouts exchanged between the driver and the stationmaster made her cover her ears. And then they were all bustled aboard, the guard blew his whistle, and with a great lurch the next stage of their journey began, weeping strangers left behind on the platform as they waved farewell to their loved ones through the misted-up windows.

"It's a dreadful sight, Maggie, it truly is," Peggy had said. "God love 'em. God love us all, every one."

The landscape rushed past at an incredible pace as the train clattered toward Claremorris station, beyond which she would be crossing new and unfamiliar territory. She felt for the packet of letters in her coat pocket, reassured by their presence. As long as she could feel his words in her hands, she sensed that Séamus would still be with her.

Maggie shivered at the memories and pulled her coat tighter around her as they approached the gravestone.

They stood for a while, heads bowed in respectful silence as each said a private prayer. Maggie took to fussing over the flowers then, removing all the dead and wilted ones and replacing them with the fresh ones she had brought.

"Freesias—your favorite," she whispered as she went about her work.

Grace watched her and smiled at her great-grandmother's undying love for the man she had spent most of her life with. She studied the inscription on the headstone. *Much-loved husband of Maggie and doting father to Harry, Kathleen, and Peggy. "To live in the hearts of those we love is never to die."*

"I remember him, you know." Grace spoke almost in a whisper. "He was a kind man, wasn't he? I remember the smell of the pipe he smoked. I remember him teasing me and pretending that he couldn't say the word *hippopotamus*. He would go on for ages and have me and Art in stitches. I always felt safe around him."

Maggie smiled fondly. "Yes, Grace. He was a very kind man. It's funny, I always felt safe around him too. He had that sort of—what do you call it . . . ?"

"Presence."

"That's right. A presence. You always knew when he was in the room—not in a fancy, showy way, like your brother. More in a quiet, gentle way." She paused for a moment and brushed a few fallen cherry blossom petals from the stone. "Yes, he was a very special man indeed."

The two fell silent then, remembering the man whose grave they stood at. It wasn't until Maggie muttered the word "Amen" that Grace knew she was ready to leave.

"Shall we go for that cup of tea then? The wind's getting a bit chilly. Come on."

As Maggie turned to leave, Grace was sure she heard her say, "Yes, I will." She looked around to see who her great-grandmother was talking to, but seeing nobody there, assumed she must have been mistaken and linked Maggie's arm through hers to support her as they made their way back to the car.

"By the way," she asked when they were settled in the warmth of the car. "Did you name your children after the people you traveled from Ireland with?"

"Yes, dear, I did. Kathleen, after my aunt, Peggy—your grandmother—after my friend, and Harry, after the steward. It seemed like a nice way to remember them."

"Did you keep in touch with Peggy? After the event?"

"I did, for a while. We'd exchanged our onward addresses at the hospital. I wouldn't have known where I was heading to at all if I hadn't kept that small black case. Aunt Kathleen had written a forwarding address label and attached it to the case, you see, so the nurses knew where I needed to get to. We didn't write immediately—both of us needed a bit of time to recover properly. But after a few months I wrote to her, and she wrote back and we continued to exchange letters for a couple of years."

She paused then.

"And . . . ?"

"Well, then we lost touch. I moved. I think Peggy must have moved too, because she was due to be married, and the years drifted by without my hearing anything from her."

"Oh, that's very sad."

"Yes, it is. She was the only living person I knew who had shared that terrible experience with me. I often wonder whether she's still living now."

"And you named your son Harry after the steward because he saved your life, I guess? Mr. Lockey mentioned that Harry had helped you to send a telegram from *Titanic*."

Maggie smiled ruefully. "Ah yes. Harry was friendly with the Marconi telegraph operators, and said he could get a message sent off the ship for me for free. I could never have afforded the price of a telegram, you see. You'd never believe it, though—that blessed message was only half sent. Wasn't the radio operator right in the middle of tapping out my little message when *Titanic* hit the iceberg? So the message got sent through to Ireland all right, but with some of the words missing. Quite an impact that half-delivered message had."

"Oh?"

"It all got sorted out in the end, though."

There was a silence then as Grace drove steadily along and Maggie gazed out of the window, the cherry blossom trees giving way to bare stone walls and fences, the car engine droning in the background, a million memories whirling around in Maggie's mind.

PART SIX

Geo E Foster Acting Premier Ottawa Ont.: Isadore
Strauss and wife not on board only Maid. Charles M
Hays also not on board only wife. Captain.

Marconigram message sent from the captain of
Carpathia to George E. Foster, acting premier of
Canada, Ottawa, Ontario, on April 18, 1912

CHAPTER 36

Cass County, Illinois
June 6, 1982

They'd arranged to meet by the shores of the lake. It had always been a favorite hangout of theirs during Jimmy's visits and seemed like the perfect location—not too public and not too isolated. There were always plenty of kids playing Frisbee, fathers pitching baseballs to their sons, or people falling off their Jet Skis. There would be enough distraction to mask their discomfort if the meeting didn't work out as Grace was hoping, and enough space for them to enjoy a good, long stroll if it did.

Their phone call had been brief and awkward, punctuated with uncomfortable pauses and hesitant exchanges, talking over each other inadvertently, causing the conversation to stop and start as each apologized and insisted the other one go on. It was nothing like the easy, relaxed chats they'd had for hours when they first got together. The use of the phone to call Jimmy had been the only real source of disagreement between Grace and her father, who frequently insisted she'd spoken for long enough. When she argued with him, he insisted that she would be paying the bill if she didn't hang up right away.

Grace played her brief conversation with Jimmy through in her mind all over again as she pulled into the parking lot. He'd told her he'd been well and had been amazed when he'd read her article in the paper. His voice had been receptive and not at all hostile—which had been her worst fear—and he hadn't allowed her to apologize for not writing to him, insisting that it would be better to meet in person and talk face-to-face. She hadn't been able to ask him outright if he had a girlfriend, but she guessed that if he was happy to meet up with her, he probably didn't. She hoped he didn't but had prepared herself for the possibility, just in case.

Checking her appearance in the rearview mirror, she was happy enough with how she looked but could already feel a nervous rash breaking out across her chest. She wrapped a silk scarf loosely around her neck, fluffed her hair, reapplied her lip gloss, and pushed her sunglasses up onto her head.

"Right," she said as she locked the car. "Let's do this."

They'd arranged to meet outside the Java Bean—a coffee shop they used to hang out at. Whoever got there first was to order two coffees to go and they would sit on the grass and talk. "Nothing else—no other expectations. Just talk and enjoy great coffee, huh? How 'bout it?" Jimmy's words buzzed around her head as she walked toward the rendezvous point.

Rounding the last curve in the sandy path, she saw him. Her heart pounding in her chest, she stood for a moment and stared, barely able to believe it was really him. After all this time, after all the pain and belief that she would never see him again, there he was, with a coffee cup in each hand, waiting for her.

She took in every detail of him. He looked taller than she remembered and had let his hair grow longer. It suited him. He was casually dressed, in a sweatshirt, pale denim jeans, and his trademark Converse sneakers. She watched as he shifted his weight restlessly from one foot to the other. He looked as nervous as she felt.

And then he turned.

Their eyes met.

Grace felt as though her heart would burst from her chest, it hammered so hard.

They stared silently for a few moments, and a steady smile grew across his lips as she walked toward him. It felt good. It felt okay.

"Grace Butler!" he said, standing tall in front of her. "Well, wow, would you look at you!"

"Look at *you*," she replied, smiling. "You look great!"

They laughed nervously, the spark of attraction they'd sensed during that first college lecture instantly there again, hanging in the air between them.

"I would hug you," he said, gesturing to the coffee cups in his hands, "but I'm kinda stuck here."

Laughing, Grace took one of the cups from him and they shared a long embrace, not saying anything, just remembering the touch of each other and inhaling the familiar scents of perfume and aftershave.

"Should we walk?" she suggested, eager to escape the prying eyes of the coffee shop customers and the continual flash of cyclists rushing past them.

"Yeah. Let's walk."

They strolled for a while, chatting easily, Grace catching up on news from Jimmy's college life and Jimmy asking about her family."

"So, that was some amazing story you pulled out of the bag!" Jimmy said as they settled on the grass beside the lake. "I bet

O'Shea nearly crapped himself when *that* manuscript landed on his desk. You did an awesome job, really; I loved it."

"Thanks. I was so nervous about it. You know how ruthless O'Shea can be. I couldn't believe it when Professor Andrews called me to say they were going to publish it!"

"And what about Maggie? Who would have known that quiet old lady had such a huge story to tell! How come she decided to talk to you about it after all these years?"

Grace told Jimmy all about Maggie sharing her story with her at her birthday party and about how she'd found the small suitcase in the attic with some of Maggie's *Titanic* possessions still inside.

"She seems to have just reached a point in her life where she felt that she wanted to talk about it again, wanted people to know," Grace explained, enjoying the light breeze that blew off the lake against her cheeks. "She told me she had missed being able to talk about it with my great-granddad—the only person in the family she ever really discussed it with. I think she just wanted to make sure that the story was left within the family before she . . . you know . . . dies."

"Well, if she's anything like I remember her, she won't be doing that anytime soon!" Jimmy laughed. "She's an amazing woman. I reckon she'll live to be at least a hundred."

"Oh, I dunno, Jimmy. There's something different about her these days. She looks older somehow. More fragile. She looks her age, I guess."

Grace told Jimmy about Edward Lockey then, and about Maggie's coat and letters and how Maggie had been able to piece together some of the missing events from that night and put to rest some of the things she had worried about over the years since.

"I don't think she's ever gotten over it, you know. After all these years, I really think she has never truly been able to come to terms with what happened—or the fact that she survived when she watched so many others die. It must have been so terrible. I just can't imagine. She once told me that she sometimes feels like she has never really gotten off that ship. That she walks those stairwells and decks every day, looking for her lost friends and family."

For a while, they avoided talking about their own relationship, neither one sure of how to broach the subject, anxious to avoid causing discomfort when they seemed to be getting along so well.

"Anyway, I just wanted to say thank you," Grace ventured when there was a pause in the conversation. "Thank you so much."

"For what?"

"For giving me a chance. For coming to see me. I really didn't think that after . . ."

He placed a finger delicately across her lips. "Don't," he said. "Let's not do that. Let's not do the whole postmortem thing. I don't want to go back there, back then. It's too painful for both of us. We both know what happened. We both have our whys and what-ifs and a need to explain ourselves, but I don't think it would help. We're here now, so let's talk about now. You seem so happy, Grace, and that was all I ever wanted, was for you to find happiness in your life again— whether with me or without me." Grace wanted to say something, wanted to tell him how much she wanted to be *with* him, but couldn't find the courage. She let him continue. "I could never fully understand what it felt like to be you—to lose your father like that and to give everything up to care for your mom. It wasn't my place to judge you for how you felt about us—about anything. I just hoped you and your mom and brother would find happiness again someday. I really hope you have, Grace. That's all."

Allowing the tears to fall then, tears of relief, tears for her father, tears for herself, Grace sank into Jimmy's arms and they sat together, talking and laughing until the sun started to set and he wrapped his jacket around her for warmth.

"So will you come with me then?" Jimmy asked as they strolled back to the parking lot, arm in arm.

Grace continued walking, trying to keep her voice as casual as possible.

"Come where? Where are you going?"

"Ireland. Well, Ireland and the rest of Europe. I'm traveling this summer after graduation. You always said you wanted to go there, to find your Irish roots—remember, we'd sort of planned it?"

Grace laughed, remembering the naïve, romantic, carefree conversations they'd had about traveling the world together. She also remembered how impulsive Jimmy could be.

"Seriously? You'd want me to come with you?"

He stopped and turned her to face him.

"Well, only if you want to. I figured it might be a good way for us to spend some time together, you know, get to know each other again. What do you think? Unless you've got other plans for the summer?"

She smiled, a beaming smile that seemed to spread through her entire body.

"It sounds like a great idea! Of course I want to go with you. I want to more than anything in the world!"

While her mother fussed over the dinner later that evening, Grace sat in the swing on the back porch, enjoying the relaxing, rhythmic sensation, thoughts of Jimmy and the wonderful words he had said dancing around her mind. Maggie sat on the bench opposite, smiling at her.

"What's got you all excited then?"

Grace sat up. "Excuse me?"

"What's got you so excited?" Maggie repeated. "Because something certainly has. You're practically fizzing."

Grace laughed at her great-grandmother's perceptiveness. "Good Lord, Maggie, nothing gets past you, does it? Are you sure you're nearly ninety years old?"

Maggie chuckled. "Sadly, yes, although some days I don't feel a day over seventeen, up here," she added, tapping her head. "So are you gonna tell me or am I gonna have to guess?"

Stepping down from the swing, Grace sidled over to sit beside her great-grandmother and clasped her hands in hers. "Oh, Maggie, it's just amazing. I just can't believe it. I met Jimmy today."

"Jimmy? *Your* Jimmy?"

"Yes!" Grace laughed. "*My* Jimmy!"

"Well, go on then. Tell me all about it. I can tell by the twinkle in your eye that you were definitely pleased to see him."

Grace had barely been able to believe everything that had happened since she'd spoken to Jimmy on the phone, but she was desperate to tell somebody, and she knew that Maggie would listen without judging her. So she told her all about the note she had written to Professor Andrews along with the newspaper article, and how Jimmy had called her and how they'd arranged to meet for coffee earlier that day and how it had been amazing, as if they'd never been apart. She hardly stopped for breath. Maggie listened patiently as she sipped her cup of tea.

"And you'll never guess what, Maggie."

"What?"

"He's going traveling around Europe this summer and he wants me to go with him. To Ireland! I've always wanted to go to Ireland."

"And are you going?" Maggie asked when Grace eventually stopped talking.

"Yeah. I think so. What do you think?"

Maggie put her cup and saucer down purposefully and stared Grace straight in the eyes. It was a look she gave people when she wanted their full attention; wanted them to sit up and take notice and not be distracted by anything else.

"You don't need to know what *I* think, Grace. It's what's in here that counts," she said, tapping her chest. "There are probably a hundred and one reasons for you not to go rushing off around Europe with a young man whose heart you've already broken once, but if there is just *one* reason why you should, then perhaps that's the reason you should listen to. You've been cooped up here in this sleepy town for two years longer than you'd ever planned to be. I think only you can truly know if now is the right time to move on, and if that includes traveling the world with Jimmy, then so be it."

She nodded after making this speech, as if to reinforce her words.

Grace sat and thought for a moment. "You're right," she sighed. "It may look crazy and rushed and foolish to people on the outside, but I've got a good feeling about this. I don't think I can go for the whole summer, though—I've got a lot of catching up to do before I go back to college in the fall. But he's planning on visiting Ireland first, so I thought maybe I'd just go there with him and then come back."

"Ireland, huh?" Maggie smiled. "D'you know, I never went back. I've never set foot on Irish soil since the day I stepped onto the tender that took us out to *Titanic* where she was moored offshore. I was too afraid, you see. I made a promise to myself while I sat in that lifeboat bobbing around on the great blackness of the Atlantic Ocean—I promised myself that I would never sail again. And it's a shame, because I often think that it would be nice to know what happened to that little cottage, to know whether anyone living in Ballysheen now knows about the fourteen of us who left that spring day." She sighed and laughed a little. "I wouldn't think the people living there now would have any notion of what happened to us all. They'll be too busy watching that awful MTV nonsense and doing that silly Rubik's Cube thing."

Grace chuckled. "Probably," she agreed. "Quite probably."

A silence fell across the porch then as the two sat in thought and watched the cat chase a bee among the camellia bushes.

G race's mother gave her absolute blessing for Grace to travel with Jimmy to Ireland. Grace had been putting off mentioning it to her, worried about her mom's reaction, wondering whether she would be okay with being in the house on her own.

"I think it's a wonderful idea, honey," her mother said. "And I'm delighted that you and Jimmy are finally patching things up. He's a good kid; I always liked him—and your father was fond of him too. Anyway, your aunt Martha's moving closer, so she can keep an eye on me. I'm gonna have to get used to being here without you when you go back to college in September. Imagine, all that laundry I *won't* have to do—whatever will I do with myself?"

Grace and Jimmy spoke every day on the phone, the love she felt for him growing stronger with every conversation. Within weeks the travel arrangements were made and the flights were booked.

t was over a cup of tea and a slice of apple pie in the Cherry Tree Café that Maggie made her surprising announcement.

"By the way, I was wondering if you kids wouldn't mind too much if I came to Ireland with you."

"What?" Grace exclaimed, bursting out laughing. "You're not serious?" She looked across the table at Maggie. She could tell immediately that she was deadly serious. "Are you?"

"Of course you can come with us," Jimmy interjected. "It would be our honor to escort you back there, wouldn't it, Grace?" he continued, kicking her under the table.

Grace was stunned. "Well, yes, of course, but . . . well, are you sure you'd be up to it, Maggie? It's a really long flight, and there'd be lots of traveling once we arrived in Ireland."

"Well, I figure I'd only have to sit in an airplane seat the same as I sit in that old chair of mine at home, and I don't reckon you'd be asking me to do any of the driving—so what's the difference, apart from a few hours here and there with the time of day?"

Jimmy and Grace stared at Maggie in shock.

"*Seriously,*" Grace asked one more time, "you *really* want to come?"

"I've never been more serious," Maggie replied. "I know, I'm nearly ninety years old and I don't really like to leave the house too much and I've never been on a plane before and all the other reasons why it sounds like absolute nonsense, but ever since you two got back together and decided to go to Ireland, I've been thinking about coming with you. I've tried to forget about Ireland all these years, but it won't leave me. I'm part of it, you know, and I think I'm ready to go back now, at long last. I doubt there'll be another chance, and I'll admit I would like to see the old place again, before it's too late. So, I figured, why not? Maybe it's time for me to finally go home."

"Well, I think that's fantastic, Maggie," Grace said. "Really fantastic, and we'd love to take you back. But are you absolutely sure? It won't be too upsetting, will it?"

"Hmm, probably. But I figure you don't get to be my age without being able to cope with a bit of upset now and then. I think it will do me good to see the old place again. I can travel back to Chicago with you, Grace, while Jimmy goes off exploring Europe. If an old lady won't cramp your style too much, I'd really like to come with you."

It was settled. Maggie would travel with them to Ireland, back to Ballysheen. The girl who had left all those years ago was coming home.

As the plane thundered down the runway and took off, Maggie closed her eyes, enjoying the sensation of speed and of being pushed back into her seat. She felt more alive than she had in years. She smiled as the land she had called home for most of her life faded beneath the clouds. She patted the pocket of her coat, which was carefully folded up on her lap. Yes, it was still there. The packet of letters was still there.

CHAPTER 37

Ballysheen, Ireland
July 2, 1982

The journey took a lot out of Maggie. She was exhausted by the time they landed at Shannon Airport, and was glad that Grace had insisted they stay overnight in a hotel before continuing their journey to County Mayo.

Sitting in the passenger seat of the rental car the next day, she watched, mesmerized, as the Irish countryside flashed past the window. Her mind wandered back to the train journey she had taken all those years ago from Castlebar, the great whistle of the engine startling her as they'd pulled out of the station with a groan and a jolt, slowly building up speed down the track toward Claremorris and from there to Limerick and then Cork. Eight or nine hours they'd traveled before they finally reached Queenstown. The salty sea air of that town had made her feel queasy—she remembered it now as if it were yesterday.

Jimmy drove through small town after small town, stopping here and there so they could have a cup of tea or a bowl of soup and some homemade soda bread. The vivid colors of the houses and shopfronts delighted them all; the smoke from the fires burning in the grates of the houses snaked skyward from narrow chimney pots, filling the air with the smell of turf. It was a smell Maggie recognized immediately and one that transported her right back to the small cottage she'd called home for seventeen years.

They drove out then into open countryside, past lush green fields, dry stone walls, and crops of wheat and barley. Maggie already felt oddly at home, at ease, at peace.

It was approaching noon as they reached the familiar landscape of County Mayo, and Maggie sat in silence as she surveyed the scenery around her. And then she saw it. The majestic, distinctive shape of Nephin Mór. It was still lightly snowcapped from the harsh winter.

A few fluffy clouds passed lazily across the sky as her gaze settled on the fields where she used to watch the men gather the potatoes at harvesttime. She recalled herself as a young girl staring at another failed harvest, the crops blighted. She remembered her mother telling her how there had been a time when those same fields were lush and green, all the food they could wish for ready to be gathered. It thrilled Maggie to see those same fields lush and green again, bursting with life and with food to feed the community ten times over.

Everything rushed back at her, memory after memory, season after season spent in this countryside; conversations, laughter, tears, heartache—it was all still here, all still hidden among these timeless stone walls and the enduring landscape. As they approached the village of Ballysheen, Maggie asked Jimmy to take her to the lake first.

It was exactly as she remembered it, as if she was looking at a snapshot taken seventy years ago. Nothing had changed since the morning when she and her thirteen fellow travelers had departed—it was as if time had stood still, as if these fields, mountains, and lakes had been waiting for her to return.

Jimmy and Grace watched from a short distance as Maggie picked her way steadily through the long grass, brushing the dandelion fluff from her skirt, using her cane for balance where the ground undulated beneath her. She stood at the edge of the lake, lost in a lifetime, breathing in the fresh, clean air, filling her lungs with the goodness and life contained within it. She watched the water as a breeze sent a flurry of ripples skidding across its surface. Snippets of past conversations skipped through her mind: Peggy and Katie laughing about life in America, Séamus asking her to dance, her aunt telling her in clipped, purposeful tones that she was taking her to a better life in America. She felt her own hesitancy and dread as she'd climbed up into the trap. She sensed his presence, felt him standing next to her, his arm slung protectively around her shoulders.

After a while, Grace and Jimmy joined her, and they sat for a time by the lakeside on the coats Jimmy had brought out of the car, listening to Maggie's memories, the young couple entranced by the silence and beauty of the place.

"For seventeen years I called these hills and fields home," Maggie told them, wistfully. "For seventy more I've called somewhere else home, but this is where I really belong. Now I am truly home."

A single cloud drifted momentarily across the sun, casting a shadow over the ground. As it passed, Maggie closed her eyes, enjoying the warmth flooding her body. She felt in her coat pocket for the small bundle of letters held together with a frayed piece of string and smiled.

"Are you ready to go into the village?" Grace asked, helping Maggie to her feet.

"As ready as I'll ever be," she replied. "Perhaps it would be nice to go to the church. St. Patrick's it's called, if I remember right."

Grace noticed Maggie wipe a tear from her cheek—she looked vulnerable. She could almost see the seventeen-year-old girl Maggie had been when she'd last set eyes on this place.

Jimmy parked the car, and they strolled together up the main street, the locals going about their business, laughing and chatting outside the post office and the butcher's, unaware of the significance of the old lady walking among them.

St. Patrick's church looked just as it had all those years ago, with its high, arched windows and soaring spire. The cool, hushed interior was a welcome relief from the bustle and noise outside. Maggie looked around, remembering the many times she had stood here at Mass, remembering the faces of those who had stood beside her: Peggy and her twinkling green eyes, Katie and her pretty smile, Aunt Kathleen and her look of steely determination.

She stepped forward to light a candle before saying a quiet prayer. Jimmy and Grace waited toward the back of the church, giving her some privacy.

"Hey, Grace, look at this," Jimmy whispered, pulling her toward a stone slab set into the wall by the door. The two of them stood and stared, amazed by what they saw.

Dedicated to the memory of all those who left this parish on 10th April 1912 to sail on the Titanic's maiden voyage to a new world and who perished when she sank in the Atlantic Ocean on 15th April 1912. We will never forget them. And to the only known survivors, Maggie Murphy and Peggy Madden, we welcome you home. Always.

"Oh my goodness," Grace whispered. "They remembered them. They remembered them all. This is what she always wondered. Whether they were known and remembered. She'll be so pleased."

When Maggie had finished praying, they took her to the inscription. She stood silently, reading all the names of those she had traveled with and loved, reaching out to feel the lettering etched into the cold stone, running her fingers across each name as if she were running her hand across the cheek of the person it belonged to.

Kathleen Dolan, 44 years
Ellen Joyce, 33 years
Katie Kenny, 24 years
Patrick Brogan, 22 years
Maura Brennan, 35 years
Jack Brennan, 37 years
Eileen Brennan, 32 years
Michael Kelly, 17 years
Mary Dunphy, 29 years
Bridget Moloney, 23 years
Maria Cusack, 22 years
Margaret O'Connor, 26 years

The priest, who had been watching their interest in the plaque for some time, wandered over to tell them something of its history. He explained that for several years *Titanic* and the loss of life from the area were not talked about, but that over time, descendants of the travelers had come to feel it right and proper to acknowledge the event and remember, every year, those who lost their lives on April 15, 1912. He pointed then to a grassy area to the right of the church, where there stood a bell that was rung once a minute for fourteen minutes, every April 15 at 2:20 A.M. to mark the moment when *Titanic* sank.

Maggie didn't tell him who she was, preferring to remain, as he imagined her to be, nothing more significant than a passing American tourist.

They walked then, through the village. Much had changed: the shops were new, the road was paved, and the cars and diesel farm machinery hummed past them, blowing out their choking exhaust fumes. Yet many things were reassuringly unchanged: the pub, the stone bridge, the old school building—albeit now converted into somebody's home. What struck Maggie most was that there were only two cherry blossom trees standing; park benches and flower beds now filled the space where the other trees once stood.

"But there used to be fourteen," she exclaimed. "Whyever would they have chopped them all down? They were so beautiful in the springtime."

She walked to one of the two trees still standing, the blossoms finished for the season, the vivid green foliage casting a pleasant shade on the pavement underneath.

"I'd just like to take a moment," she announced, touching the bark of the tree, circling it and glancing through the dappled shade to the branches above. She sighed. And then she noticed an inscription carved into the wood. *MM SD*. Saying nothing to Grace or Jimmy, she smiled as she recognized her and Séamus's initials.

"You romantic old fool," she said and chuckled quietly to herself.

She agreed to let Jimmy take a photo, as he'd promised to do for their entire trip, to capture the memories for her so that she need never forget or wonder again.

They strolled then to the edge of the town, to where the fields began. Grace and Jimmy hung back a little as Maggie walked purposefully toward a derelict stone cottage almost hidden from view by the long grass and weeds that grew rampant around the crumbling stones, creeping and twisting through the empty window frames.

"This was my home," Maggie told them as she pushed open a rickety wooden gate, which groaned and creaked against the thick grass that snaked around it. "This is where I once lived."

She stood at what remained of the doorway and imagined herself back there on that calm spring morning as she'd watched Peggy throw the petals onto Maura Brennan's head, laughing with excitement about the journey ahead of them. She remembered the swell beneath Maura's coat and closed her eyes against the memory of her standing on the deck of *Titanic*, one hand grasping her husband's, the other placed protectively over her belly. What a happy life they would have led had things worked out differently.

Standing in the ruined doorway, surrounded by rubble and gnarled, thorny branches, Maggie could almost feel her aunt Kathleen beside her: stiff, forthright, practical, confident Aunt Kathleen, standing with her hands on her hips as she watched Maggie go off to tell the others the traps were ready. Maggie recalled her face, the hint of a smile playing across her lips, so much to look forward to, so much to show her niece when they arrived in America. The image faded as a cloud passed overhead, momentarily casting Maggie, and the house, into a cold shadow.

"We never knew what happened to Aunt Kathleen that night, you know." Maggie said, speaking softly to Grace and Jimmy as she puttered around among the remnants of her home. "She made sure we were all aware of the danger and knew what we must do—and then we lost her. Gone, without a trace. All sorts of dark thoughts filled my mind while I watched that ship lurch and groan as she broke apart—maybe Kathleen was trapped somewhere; maybe hers was one of those desperate voices I could hear screaming in the waters around me."

"Don't, Maggie," Grace said, placing her arm gently around the old woman's frail shoulders. "Don't think that. She was a very good woman. She'll be at peace now."

"You'd never believe a lovely little home used to stand here, would you?" Maggie said. "But it did, and I can see it now if I shut my eyes, every last brick and stone. The kettle hanging over the fire, the smell of Mammy's oatcakes baking, the air musty and damp from the turf fire. Ah, it was a grand home. I was very sorry to leave it."

After giving her a moment to say a prayer among the stones and weeds, Grace and Jimmy walked with Maggie to the other homes that she wanted to visit. Most of them stood now as her own home did, blankets of weeds covering everything, obscuring the ancient windows and walls. And yet, in what appeared as just piles of rubble and weeds to others, Maggie saw memories. She saw familiar faces in every crumbled stone, saw smoke rising from the fallen chimneys; heard conversations through the broken doors, caught snippets of laughter through the open windows. Although they were all long gone from this place, something about the people who had lived in these broken homes endured.

For all the passing of time and the changes in how people

lived, there was a sense of history retained by the people of Ballysheen. Maggie had seen it with her very eyes on the engraved stone slab in the church and at the remembrance bell. It comforted her to know that she, her aunt, and all the others were not forgotten, not ignored, but remembered and commemorated for the lives they had led here and for the courage and fortitude they had shown in daring to leave it all behind in search of something better.

As the light of the afternoon sun began to fade, there was just one place left that Maggie wished to visit. It was a long walk, so she asked Jimmy if they could return to the car. From their parking spot at the church, she navigated from memory, down a side road that led in a slight incline toward the foot of the mountain. Halfway along the road, she asked Jimmy to stop.

"I won't be long," she said, getting slowly out of the car and walking through the gate that blocked the entrance to a field. She looked about her from right to left and waited for a moment before returning to the car, closing the gate behind her.

"Were you hoping to see something else, Maggie?" Grace asked tentatively.

"I was, dear, yes. This is where Séamus used to live with his father. It would seem that the house has disappeared without a trace. There's no sign of it, no trace at all. Well, never mind," she continued. "It cannot be undone now."

They returned to the lake to eat the provisions they had bought in the local shops. Maggie decided to stay in the car, letting the cool early evening breeze drift in through the open window while Grace and Jimmy stretched out easily on the coats spread on the grass. Maggie momentarily envied their youth and the ease with which they could move their bodies from sitting to lying to standing. Things you take for granted when you're in the flush of youth, she supposed, biting into the soda bread, savoring every mouthful.

She watched silently as the young couple strolled happily down to the lakeside, scouring the ground for the perfect skimming stone, laughing and joking as their various attempts succeeded or failed. It reminded Maggie very much of herself and Séamus and the many, many happy times they had spent at this very spot, doing exactly the same. From the back, Grace could almost be Maggie, except Grace's hair tumbled around her shoulders in a way that Maggie's never had. Maggie laughed at the memory of her obsession with her hair. And as for Jimmy, he could easily be mistaken for Séamus; the same broad shoulders, stocky build, and tousled sandy hair. *How easily those two people could be us, lost in time,* she thought. As she watched her great-granddaughter now with a man she clearly adored, Maggie was proud of the decisions she had made in her life, was proud of her family and how far she had come. But above all, as she looked at the stunning landscape around them, she was proud to be able to call this place home.

As dusk fell, they drove out of Ballysheen toward the nearby guesthouse they'd arranged to stay in. They were silent in the car, each taking in everything they had seen that day. Grace had been so moved watching Maggie walk around the ruins of her home and the homes of those she had known so well, and she had been touched by the way the parish remembered those who had sailed on *Titanic*. These were her relatives too. This was the land her ancestors had worked in their struggle for survival. She felt grounded by it, by being able to stand amid the bricks and stones where they had once baked their daily bread.

And yet she was still a little unsure whether it had been the right thing to do bringing Maggie back here, and was a little worried about her great-grandmother's silence since they'd left.

"So how do you feel having seen it all again, Maggie?" she asked, leaning forward from the backseat so she could be heard over the sound of the car engine.

Maggie considered the question for a moment.

"I've been thinking that myself, dear, and do you know something, I'm glad. I'm glad I came back to see for myself, and yes, it's very sad to see the homes all fallen about themselves, but what could I expect really after seventy years? It doesn't matter somehow. I can still feel the spirit of the place, and just by touching those fallen stones, I feel that I've reached out to everyone I knew, that I've touched them again in some way. It's as if they never left—as if they're still there among all the weeds and the rubble. How do I feel? Peaceful, I think. Yes, peaceful."

"I'm so sorry that Séamus's home wasn't there," Grace added. "I know you'd have liked to see it."

"Yes, it is a shame, but after all this time it's no surprise. The farmer who owns that land now wasn't to know that an old lady would come back one day looking for the home of a man who used to live there so many years ago."

"I think I would have liked Séamus," Grace mused as she looked out of the window at the passing countryside. "He sounds like such a lovely man. I'd like to have met him."

Maggie smiled to herself as she watched a rabbit darting back into its burrow, startled by the noise of the car.

"Well, dear, as it happens, you did. You did meet him."

"*What?*" Grace and Jimmy both reacted together.

"What do you mean?" Grace continued as Jimmy slowed the car and pulled off the road beside a gateway. "I never met him! How could I have met him when he lived in Ireland all his life?"

Maggie turned in her seat to face Grace.

"He was your great-grandfather, Grace. The man who used to tease you with his mixed-up words and smoke his pipe and tell you all those tall tales. That was Séamus Doyle—James Doyle, as you knew him, the English version of his name."

Grace's mind was reeling.

"*Séamus* was James? Great-Granddad James? But . . ." She burst into laughter. "I can't believe it. So you *married* Séamus? *The* Séamus. The Séamus who you loved and who wrote those letters. After everything you'd both been through, you *married* him!"

Now Maggie was laughing.

"Yes, dear. I married him! There was a big mix-up after my telegram from *Titanic* was delivered incomplete, and the poor lamb thought I didn't want to see him ever again, but luckily, after he'd learned of my survival, he got hold of my aunt's address in Chicago and wrote to me. I'll never forget the day that letter arrived. It was the first contact I'd had from home since the terrible disaster, and he said such kind things about hoping I would live a long and happy life and that with his da dead, he was selling his land and going to work in the English cotton mills.

"Of course, then that confused *me*, as my message had said for him to come to America as soon as he could. Oh, it was a dreadful time. You kids would be able to sort it all out now with a quick phone call or one of them fancy fax machines, but we didn't have anything like that back then and had to wait for letters to cross the ocean on steamships and chug down train tracks and trundle across dusty tracks in a horse and cart.

"Well, eventually we sorted it all out, and after he'd sold his father's bit of land he had enough money for a passage to America and he arrived in Chicago one day at Union Station, and as soon as he saw me he sank to his knees and wept and asked me to marry him, and I wept and said yes! He never mentioned that he'd already proposed to me in his lost letters. To his dying day, he wouldn't tell me what he'd written in those letters. He said it didn't matter now."

"Wow! So Séamus Doyle was my great-grandfather! But why did he change his name to James?"

"Well, he got so fed up with having to spell his name out for everyone. You see, the Americans didn't know how to pronounce Séamus properly—'Sea-mus' they used to say! Oh, how I used to giggle at him. So one day he announced that he was going to change his name to James, the English version, and that's how he was known for the rest of his life: James Doyle."

Grace couldn't take it in. She was so happy to know that Maggie had married Séamus after all—and that he was the same man as the great-grandfather she had been so very fond of. "It's amazing!" she said. "Oh, I'm so thrilled, Maggie. I'm so happy it was him—that I knew him. And you loved each other so much and, oh, it's just wonderful, Maggie. I can't believe I didn't make the connection."

"Well, why would you, I suppose—I always got so upset thinking about him since he died, I didn't really like to talk of him too much. And then all this started happening and that kind man found his letters and I was so wrapped up in all the memories. I guess I kind of assumed you knew it was the same man— it's so long since I've spoken about our life before *Titanic*, when I was Maggie Murphy and he was Séamus Doyle. We were different people for so many years afterward, it's almost like those two teenage kids were lost somewhere along the way."

They chatted for a while about the man Grace had known and how fate had conspired to keep Maggie and Séamus apart but they had found a way back to each other after all.

"Yes. He was a truly lovely man, and I was the luckiest woman in all of Chicago to marry him. I loved him very much. And, Grace," Maggie added, "he loved you, you know. He loved you very, very much. You were named after his own mother. He insisted on it."

CHAPTER 38

Cass County, Illinois
September 1982

T he leaves were already taking on all the wonderful hues of autumn when Grace left for college, the russet, gold, and copper shades glistening in the early morning sun, casting a warm glow over the lanes and fields that surrounded her home.

It wasn't easy leaving her mother, or the memories of her father that had surrounded and comforted her while she'd remained in the family home. But somehow, reconnecting with Jimmy, discovering the truth about her great-grandfather, and visiting the land of her heritage that summer had given her a renewed sense of purpose—a real sense of belonging, of security. It was a feeling she and her mother had been missing since the death of Grace's father, and it was the grasping hold of it again that meant it was all right to leave, to move on. Having seen the majesty of Nephin Mór, having walked on the land where her ancestors had worked, and having touched the stones of the walls of the humble homes where her family had originated, Grace was filled with a sense of existence and continuity that extended way beyond the boundaries of the white picket fence that surrounded her mother's neatly tended garden.

As she sat on her bed for a moment, taking in the memories and conversations that buzzed and flickered in the air around her, Grace recalled the time she had watched a calf being born, with her father beside her in the candlelit barn. "The continuity of life," he'd whispered as they sat on a hay bale and watched the wondrous event unfold in front of them. "The most primal of instincts. Whether it's a human baby, a calf, or a field of wheat being sown, we are all driven to continue—to carry on, to begin again. I hope you always remember this moment, Grace, and that you can always find a reason to begin again, whatever life has in store for you." Part terrified and part mesmerized, she'd been unable to tear her eyes away for a second as the young calf slipped onto the clean straw. She'd continued to watch as the cow licked the calf clean, and she'd clapped with joy as it stood on its shaky legs and took its first tentative steps.

Grace remembered all this as she glanced around her childhood bedroom. For so long, she'd been unable to find a reason to go on, to begin again. Sitting here now with the man she loved waiting for her in the car downstairs, her mother—who hadn't suffered any serious attacks for several months now—whistling contentedly as she puttered around with pots of paint and brushes ready to redecorate her daughter's room, Grace realized she had her whole future ahead of her. She felt a joy in her heart and a will to move on, to continue.

Before leaving for the interstate, Grace asked Jimmy to drive her over to Maggie's to say a final good-bye. She'd always loved this dear old lady but had grown so close to her in the last few months, knowing details of Maggie's life that even her own children had not been privy to. She felt privileged to have shared the most intimate thoughts, hopes, and fears of this incredible woman's mind—both as a seventeen-year-old girl and as an eighty-seven-year-old woman, who, as they'd flown home together from Ireland, had told her that finally, after all these years, the pain and fear from that dreadful night had for the most part faded away.

"It's like echoes, Grace, like I've been hearing the same echoes for seventy years—of the traps rumbling out of Bally-sheen, of the train thundering down the track to Cork, of the *uilleann* pipes as we sailed away from Ireland's shores, of the laughter in the general room the night we celebrated Katie's birthday, of those poor people thrashing about in the icy water, of that ship ripping apart, of the waves slapping against the lifeboat—all of it's been with me all my life. I don't hear it now, Grace. For the first time, I can't hear those echoes anymore."

After returning home to Illinois, Maggie had continued to be inundated with requests to appear on TV and radio to talk about her *Titanic* experiences. She didn't mind being a bit of a celebrity for a while, and made the most of the fancy lunches and bouquets of flowers. But there was one invitation to lunch that she treasured more than any of the lavish events. It had arrived in the form of a handwritten letter.

My dear, dear Maggie,

I can hardly believe I have found you again. After all these years! I open the newspaper over breakfast and there you are, a seventeen-year-old girl, smiling out at me, and your great-granddaughter is writing about your voyage on Titanic. I nearly passed out into my granola, I'll tell you!

I was so thrilled to know that you are still on God's good earth—and looking so well for your years. It cannot really be seventy years since that terrible night, can it? After we lost touch I didn't think I would find you again, Maggie—but here you are, living in Illinois, and here am I living in Chicago for the past thirty years—who could have believed it! It's a wonder we didn't turn out to be neighbors!

Well, I spoke to my granddaughter about you, and she insisted on ringing the paper and getting an address for you. Of course, they wouldn't give me your address, so I had to write to them and they have promised me they will pass the letter on to you. So help me God I'll cause some trouble for them if they don't. So, I hope this reaches you, Maggie, because it would mean so much to me to see you again. There is so much to tell you, so much I want to hear.

I wondered if we might be able to meet for lunch sometime.

I have enclosed my telephone number and address and would dearly love to hear from you.

With all my fondest wishes,
Peggy Kelly (Madden)

The two ladies had met on a sunny August afternoon. Grace had insisted that she drive Maggie, Maggie had insisted that they have tea and cake at the Cherry Tree Café, and Peggy had insisted that they all wear gloves and hats. There were many tears and much laughter as they recounted times past and shared intimate details of their lives. Nobody could have possibly

known from looking at them now what terror these two dignified, gentle ladies had experienced on that April night in 1912,
but *they* knew, and they held each other's hands and looked into
each other's faded, watery eyes as they nodded silently at the
memories they shared and the bond they would always share,
whatever amount of time or distance lay between them.

Well, Maggie, it's time," Grace announced as she embraced
her beloved great-nana on the front porch of her small
home. "I'm all packed, and Mom's already ripping the old wallpaper off my bedroom wall! I'm finally leaving."

Maggie held her for a little longer than she usually did.

"And about time too, young lady—you've a lot of life to
catch up on. You take good care of yourself and show those
newspaper folks what you're made of."

She pressed a small oval photo frame into Grace's hands then.

"What's this?" Grace turned the frame over and saw a faded
black-and-white photo of a handsome young man who looked a
lot like Jimmy.

"That's your great-grandfather, dear. That's Séamus just
after he arrived in America. Handsome devil, wasn't he? He
always took very good care of me, you know." Grace took a
moment to study the image, unable to find any words. "And
you make sure that young man of yours takes very good care
of you," Maggie added, smiling at Jimmy, who was standing
behind Grace on the steps.

"Oh, you needn't worry about that, Maggie. I'll be taking
very good care of Grace. I let her get away from me once. I'm
not gonna make that mistake again in a hurry."

"I'll write you and call as often as I can," Grace promised

as she gave Maggie a final, tearful embrace. "And thank you, Maggie—for everything."

The old woman understood and kissed her gently on the cheek.

"Go," she said. "Go—and be happy."

Maggie stood for a while on the doorstep after they'd gone, enjoying the warm fall sunshine on her face. As she watched the leaves swoop and swirl down to the ground, she felt a sudden urge to do something she hadn't done for years.

Walking carefully down the few steps, she stood patiently under the big maple tree at the bottom of her garden, waiting, waiting for a leaf to fall.

"If you catch one you can make a wish," she remembered Séamus telling her as they'd kicked through the piles of leaves the fall after they were married. "But you have to be quick."

She'd never managed to catch one, and he'd laughed at her leaping around and chasing them down the street as the wind blew them just out of her reach.

She stood now, watching, waiting, and very gently, one solitary, brilliantly golden leaf fluttered down and fell into her hand, effortlessly. She smiled, closed her eyes, and made a wish.

EPILOGUE

Cass County, Illinois
September 1, 1985

As Maggie sat quietly in her bed, reading again over the journal she had written from *Titanic* as a young girl, she didn't know that far away in the Atlantic Ocean, a group of scientists on board a research vessel were staring at a small TV screen, watching in disbelief as a blurred image of a ship's hull came into view. *Titanic*'s final resting place had been discovered.

Reading the words she had written that fateful year, she allowed the memories to wash over her—remembering in all its vivid detail the splendor of that magnificent ship. As she read her words, she was completely unaware of the images being beamed around the world as *Titanic* revealed itself once again: the proud bow of the ship, whose perfectly polished decks she had once stood on; the china coffee cups she had once drunk from; the spinning top of a young boy whom she had once watched playing happily; the *uilleann* pipes of a man whose melodies had once brought tears to her eyes.

Maggie didn't see any of these things, now embedded in the sandy sediment of the ocean floor, two miles below the surface. She didn't see the murky waters, enriched with the memories of everything they washed over: each tiny fragment of crystal glass, each discarded shoe, each piece of painstakingly hand-crafted furniture, each of the three thousand men and the three million rivets it had taken to build *Titanic*. Maggie didn't watch, didn't know that the memory of fifteen hundred lost souls was being stirred by the movement of the water while the camera panned slowly over the ocean floor.

Reaching the end of her journal, she lay back quietly against her pillow, a picture of James Doyle clutched in her hands, her small black suitcase at her side, and the bundle of love letters neatly tied up and placed carefully in her coat pocket, exactly as they were the morning she'd left Ballysheen. As she lay, she recalled something she'd whispered to herself while the lifeboat she sat in was lowered over the side of *Titanic* to the water below. She repeated the words now into the silent darkness.

"I'm coming home, Séamus. I'm coming home. I'm coming home. I'm coming home."

She closed her eyes then.

At peace.

Finally.

ACKNOWLEDGMENTS

They say it takes a village to raise a child, and I now know that it takes a family to write a book.

To my family in England and here in Ireland, I owe a huge, huge thanks. You have all written at least one chapter of *The Girl Who Came Home* with your amazing encouragement, advice, and babysitting services and will never fully know how much your support means to me. I am quite sure that I would have pursued my idea to write a terrible book about baking if it wasn't for your collective belief and honesty! Of course, I must especially mention the three men in my life, without whom there would, quite simply, be no book. Damien—thank you for giving me the space (and the attic!) to chase my dream. It may have taken four years to finally open, but I hope that bottle of champagne was worth it in the end. Max and Sam—your little notes, your little faces, your Lego people, biscuit wrappers, toy cars, and imaginary gladiatorial battles have been my constant writing companions, and I wouldn't have it any other way. Thank you both so much for being patient and letting Mummy do her writing.

I must also acknowledge my "extended" family—friends, neighbors, and fellow writers dotted around the globe who have all hoorahed, consoled, and cajoled at the appropriate times, usually over a much-needed glass of wine. You all rock in very large quantities.

I am also delighted to have a new family to thank—my American "family" in New York! My wonderful agent, Michelle Brower, who will never know how much her very first message meant to me. My fantastic editor, Lucia Macro, for saying the magic word "yes," for having such passion for my books, and for taking my writing on this new and exciting adventure. To Liate Stehlik, my publisher at William Morrow, and to the many other individuals who have worked on this book, I owe a huge thank-you: Mumtaz Mustafa for the beautiful, gasp-inducing cover art; Molly Birckhead and Jennifer Hart for their marketing brilliance; Laura Cherkas and the production and design team for their wonderful interior design and incredible eye for detail; the publicity team; and finally, Nicole Fischer for her tireless hard work and patience in answering my rookie questions. Your collective talents astound me and I am really quite humbled by you all.

With specific regard to *Titanic* research, I owe many thanks to Michael Molloy and Pauline Barrett of the Addergoole *Titanic* Society, who shared their parish's amazing stories with me through their website and through Pauline's wonderful parish book, *The Addergoole Titanic Story*—all of which inspired me to write this book. They patiently answered my questions and have been very supportive of my retelling of their parish's *Titanic* story.

Thanks also to Michael Martin of the Titanic Trail in Cobh (formerly Queenstown) for answering my many questions and to Walter Lord, whose fascinating book *A Night to Remember*, first published in 1956, led the way for everyone who has written about *Titanic* ever since.

And finally, thank you to you, the reader. It is for each and every one of you that this book was written.

About the author

2 Meet Hazel Gaynor

About the book

3 The Story Behind
The Girl Who Came Home

7 Glossary of Irish Terms

8 Reading Group Discussion
Questions

P.S.

Insights,
Interviews
& More . . .

Meet Hazel Gaynor

Deasy Photographic

HAZEL GAYNOR is an author and freelance writer. In March 2009, after a fifteen-year career in corporate training and development, Hazel swapped the boardroom table for the kitchen table, where she has been writing ever since. Originally from Yorkshire, England, she now lives in Ireland with her husband, two children, and an accident-prone cat. This is her first novel. Contact Hazel on Twitter @HazelGaynor or visit hazelgaynor.com. ॰

The Story Behind *The Girl Who Came Home*

WRITING A NOVEL about *Titanic* has been a long-held ambition of mine. There was always something about the era, the images of the ship, and the story of the tragic maiden voyage that I found timelessly powerful, tragic, and romantic. After I had talked myself out of tackling such an enormous story for years, the centenary year came along in 2012 and gave me the final push to write about *Titanic* and her powerful legacy.

The Girl Who Came Home was inspired by the true events surrounding a group of fourteen Irish emigrants who left their homes in County Mayo, Ireland, to travel on *Titanic* to relatives in America. The group is known locally as the Addergoole Fourteen. When *Titanic* sank, the loss of eleven passengers from the Addergoole group represented the largest proportional loss of life from one region. For the purposes of this novel, the names of all fourteen passengers have been changed. The town of Ballysheen, although based on Lahardane in County Mayo, is fictitious.

Maggie Murphy is based on two of the youngest girls in the Addergoole group (Annie Kate Kelly and Annie McGowan), and Kathleen Dolan is based on Catherine McGowan, the woman generally credited with organizing the Addergoole group's journey, although this has never been proven.

Annie Kate Kelly reported to the ▶

The Story Behind *The Girl Who Came Home* (*continued*)

Chicago Herald that she believed she was the last woman to leave *Titanic*, being helped into lifeboat 16 at 1:25 A.M. by a steward she had befriended. Of course, we now know that lifeboat 4 was the last to leave *Titanic*, at around 1:50 A.M., and was followed by the four collapsible lifeboats.

In her later life, Annie McGowan did indeed confess her *Titanic* story to her great-granddaughter.

Peggy Madden's character is based on Delia McDermott, who having gotten into a lifeboat, apparently returned to her cabin to fetch her precious new hat. Katie Kenny is also based on one of the girls from the Addergoole group, Nora Fleming, who was traveling to be reunited with her sister in New York and celebrated her twenty-fourth birthday on board *Titanic* on April 14, 1912.

The remaining characters in the Ballysheen group are loosely based on accounts of those who traveled in the party. With the exception of those noted below, the characters Maggie encounters on *Titanic* and all the events surrounding Grace and Maggie's family life in Illinois and Ireland are entirely fictitious.

The character of Vivienne Walker-Brown is loosely based on Dorothy Gibson, an actress who sailed on *Titanic* and went on to play herself in *Saved from the Titanic*, a silent movie made about the disaster shortly after the event. Dorothy Gibson did indeed wear the same dress in the movie that she had worn the night the ship sank. Edmund, Vivienne's dog, although fictitious, represents several dogs belonging to first-class passengers that were kept in the staterooms and were taken into the lifeboats. In total, three of the twelve dogs on board survived the sinking.

Some of the passengers whom members of the Irish group encounter aboard *Titanic* are based in fact. They include Father Browne, the Jesuit priest whose black-and-white images of *Titanic* are known worldwide; Father Byles, who led the Mass on the morning of April 14; Eugene Daly, the piper; the girl with the rash who was refused entry to the ship at Queenstown; young Douglas Spedden, the first-class boy playing with his spinning top; the Marconi radio boys, Harold Bride and Jack Phillips; and, of course, Captain Smith, Mr. Ismay, Mr. Andrews, Officer Lightoller, and Mr. McElroy. Thomas Durcan was the White Star Line agent in Castlebar.

The Marconigram messages at the start of each part of the novel are actual messages transmitted from *Titanic* and *Carpathia*. Any misspellings have been purposely included to remain authentic to the original messages.

The inquiries into the *Titanic* disaster, movies and books that followed, survivor accounts, newspaper reports, and continued media fascination with the event have all provided an immense amount of detail about the ship and her passengers. Details regarding *Titanic*'s ▶

The Story Behind *The Girl Who Came Home* (*continued*)

construction, her fixtures and fittings, even down to the handles on the dinner knives, provide a rich seam of source material for anyone interested in the event. Throughout the novel, I have made every attempt to draw on the available information and portray authentically what life was like for passengers and crew aboard the ill-fated ship.

After reading detailed survivor accounts, I hope to have accurately portrayed what the experience was like for the survivors who made it onto the rescue ship *Carpathia* and into the New York hospitals. I also hope to have sensitively portrayed the experience of family and friends, many of whom went for several days without accurate information regarding the fate of their loved ones. We can only imagine how difficult those days and nights of not knowing must have been. These aspects of *Titanic*'s tragedy are perhaps less well known and have been less well documented, and it was these—the survivors' experiences and the ordeal of family and friends back home—that I felt compelled to explore in writing this novel.

For further information on the Addergoole Fourteen, visit www.mayo-Titanic.com or visit Lahardane village in County Mayo, where you can walk Addergoole's *Titanic* trails, featuring the homesteads, many now derelict, from which the Addergoole Fourteen left for a better life in 1912. ᴖ

Glossary of Irish Terms

bodhrán (bow-ron): a shallow, one-sided Irish drum typically played using a short stick with knobbed ends

cailín (col-een): a girl or young woman; plural **cailíní**

céilí (cay-lee): an Irish/Gaelic gathering where traditional and folk music is played

craic (crack): enjoyable social activity, a good time

hooley: a wild or noisy party

jarvey: coachman; driver of a trap, cart, or jaunting car

melodeon: a small accordion, especially played by folk musicians

piseóga (pish-o-ga): superstitious practice

poitín (pot-cheen): a traditional Irish distilled alcoholic drink, made from potatoes or grain

Traveller: a tinker, gypsy, or other nomadic person

uilleann (ill-n): Irish bagpipes, played held on the knee using bellows worked by the elbow, and having three extra pipes on which chords can be played ∽

Definitions from the *Oxford English Dictionary* and from www.focal.ie, a dictionary of Irish terms.

Reading Group Discussion Questions

1. The *Titanic* disaster is one of the most documented historical events of the last century. By reading the book, what new information did you learn about *Titanic*? What most surprised you about the ship or the life of passengers on board?

2. We all know the fate of *Titanic*. What impact does this knowledge have on you as you read the book? How do you feel about the Ballysheen group as they leave their homes and as they board *Titanic* at Queenstown?

3. Kathleen Dolan is single-minded in her decision to take her niece back to America with her. Discuss Kathleen's role in Maggie's life and also her role in influencing the others in the Ballysheen group to travel to America.

4. There are several key relationships in the novel. Discuss your thoughts on the relationship between any of these: Grace and Maggie; Maggie and Séamus; Maggie and her aunt Kathleen; Frances Kenny and her sister, Katie; Maggie, Peggy, and Katie; Harry and Peggy.

5. Emigration was very common in Ireland in 1912, with many families separated by the belief and hope that there was a better standard of living to be found in America. The

"American wakes" were common occurrences across the country, marking the departure of loved ones. Have you experienced emigration in your own family? How would you feel if you had to make a decision similar to that made by the Irish emigrants who set sail on *Titanic*?

6. Grace makes a brave decision to drop out of college and stay at home with her mother after her father's death. Does Grace have a choice in this? How do her decision and the sacrifices she makes for her family contrast with the decisions forced upon Maggie in 1912?

7. What does Grace learn about herself through her interactions with Maggie and by reading Maggie's *Titanic* journal?

8. Who are you rooting for as the drama of the events of April 14–15 unfolds?

9. The passengers on *Titanic* are forced to make impossible decisions as the ship is sinking—wives leaving husbands, mothers leaving children in the care of their nannies. What do you think you would have done—or hope you would have done—under the circumstances?

10. The various warnings and predictions of disaster that the Ballysheen group experiences—the reading of the tea leaves, the warning from the stranger at Queenstown, the dropped "lucky" sovereign— ▶

are based on recorded facts. The near miss with the *New York* in the Southampton docks at the very start of *Titanic*'s journey also really happened. In addition, a novella, titled *Futility; or The Wreck of the Titan* was written in 1898 by Morgan Robertson and seems to predict much of the *Titanic* disaster: a large ocean liner sinks one April night in the North Atlantic after colliding with an iceberg and there are not enough lifeboats for all the passengers. Discuss the many aspects of superstition and myth that surround *Titanic*.

11. Maggie and the other survivors were in their lifeboat for eight hours before they were picked up, and they were then on board *Carpathia* for several days. Had you considered the experience of the survivors before reading this book? Discuss the extent of their ordeal after getting safely off *Titanic*.

12. Maggie discovers twenty-five dollars pinned to her clothing as compensation from the White Star Line and recalls signing a disclaimer for the company. This was actually recorded as happening to one of the survivors, Annie Kate Kelly. What is your reaction when reading this? Are you surprised that the shipping company would take advantage of survivors in that way?

13. Families and friends of passengers on *Titanic* were left confused and searching for answers about the fate of their loved ones, with early press reports stating that everyone had survived and later reports correctly reporting huge losses of life. Why do you think there was so much delay and confusion in confirming the facts and issuing survivor lists? Had you considered this aspect of the tragedy before reading this book?

14. Many *Titanic* survivors were reluctant to talk about their experiences. Are you surprised by Maggie's reluctance to talk about *Titanic* with her own family? What comments do you have about Maggie's experience of survivor guilt?

15. There have been many other shipping tragedies since *Titanic*. Cunard's passenger liner RMS *Lusitania* (traveling from New York to Liverpool) sank off the coast of Ireland in 1915 when the liner was struck by a torpedo fired from a German submarine. There were 1,198 civilian fatalities in the event. In the light of many tragedies with great loss of life since 1912, why do you think people continue to be so fascinated by *Titanic* a hundred years later? ▶

Reading Group Discussion Questions
(continued)

16. Australian businessman Clive Palmer is starting construction on a replica of *Titanic—Titanic II*—which is scheduled to re-create *Titanic*'s maiden voyage in 2016. There have been very mixed reactions to this project among relatives and descendants of *Titanic*'s passengers and *Titanic* enthusiasts. What are your thoughts on it? ∽

Don't miss the next book by your favorite author. Sign up now for AuthorTracker by visiting www.AuthorTracker.com.